Louise Penny is the num[...] [...]
author of the Inspector Gamache series, including [...],
which won the CWA John Creasey Dagger in 2006. Recipient
of virtually every existing award for crime fiction, Louise
was also granted the Order of Canada in 2014 and received
an honorary doctorate of literature from Carleton University
and the Ordre National du Québec in 2017. She lives in a
small village south of Montreal.

Praise for Louise Penny and the series:

'Louise Penny is one of the greatest crime
writers of our times' Denise Mina

'She makes most of her competitors
seem like wannabes' *The Times*

'A cracking storyteller, who can create fascinating characters,
a twisty plot and wonderful surprise endings' Ann Cleeves

'Outstanding . . . a constantly surprising series that
deepens and darkens as it evolves' *The New York Times*

'No one does atmospheric quite like Louise
Penny . . . a fantastic series' Elly Griffiths

'Louise Penny's writing is intricate, beautiful and
compelling. She is an original voice, a distillation
of both PD James and Barbara Vine at their peaks
and a worthy successor to both' Peter James

'[An] atmospheric, distinctive series' Kate Mosse

'Penny is an absolute joy' *Irish Times*

'The series is deep and grand and altogether
extraordinary . . . Miraculous' *Washington Post*

The Gamache series

LOUISE PENNY

The Madness of Crowds

HODDER

First published in the United States in 2021 by Minotaur,
a division of St Martin's Publishing Group
First published in Great Britain in 2021 by Hodder & Stoughton
An Hachette UK company

This paperback edition published in 2022

1

Excerpt from "Waiting" from *Morning in the Burned House: New Poems* by Margaret
Atwood. Copyright © 1995 by Margaret Atwood. Reprinted by permission
of Houghton Mifflin Harcourt Publishing Company. All rights reserved.

Excerpts from *Vapour Trails* by Marylyn Plessner (2000).
Used by permission of Stephen Jarislowsky.

Excerpt from "Suicide in the Trenches" from *The War Poems*
by Siegfried Sassoon. Copyright © Siegfried Sassoon. Used by
kind permission of the Estate of George Sassoon.

A CIP catalogue record for this title is available from the British Library

B format ISBN 978 1 529 37942 6
eBook ISBN 978 1 529 37940 2

Printed and bound in Great Britain by Clays Ltd, Elcograf S.p.A.

Hodder & Stoughton policy is to use papers that are natural, renewable
and recyclable products and made from wood grown in sustainable
forests. The logging and manufacturing processes are expected to
conform to the environmental regulations of the country of origin.

Hodder & Stoughton Ltd
Carmelite House
50 Victoria Embankment
London EC4Y 0DZ

www.hodder.co.uk

A Letter from Louise

When I was thirty-five, I thought the best was behind me.

I was lonely, and tired, and empty. Plodding through life. At thirty-five.

By the time I was forty-five, I was married to the love of my life, and my first book was about to be published.

And now I'm sixty. Living in a beautiful Quebec village, surrounded by friends, with thirteen books to my name. And counting.

This milestone birthday gives me a chance to look back in wonderment. And gratitude. And amazement. That I should be here, happy, joyous, and free.

No one quite appreciates, and recognises, the light like those who've lived in darkness. That awareness is what I try to bring to the books. The duality of our lives. The power of perception. The staggering weight of despair, and the amazement when it is lifted.

The gap between how we appear and how we really feel.

Those are foundations of the Gamache books.

Initially they were called the Three Pines books, which, of course, they are. Three Pines is the tiny hidden village in Québec. Not on any map, it is only ever found by those who are lost.

But, once found, never forgotten.

At their core, though, these books are about the profound decency of Armand Gamache, and the struggles he has to remain a good person. When 'good' is subjective, and 'decent' is a matter of judgement.

These books might appear, superficially, as traditional crime novels. But they are, I believe, more about life than death. About choices. About the price of freedom. About the struggle for peace.

Armand Gamache, of the Sûreté du Quebec, is inspired by my husband, Michael Whitehead. A doctor who treated children with cancer. Who spent his life searching for cures. Who saved countless young lives, boys and girls who now have children of their own.

Despite the dreadful deaths and broken hearts all around him, Michael was the happiest man alive. Because he understood the great gift that life is.

Michael gave that perception to Armand.

Michael died of dementia. And it broke my heart. But I still have Armand. And Clara, and Jean-Guy. Myrna and Gabri and Olivier. And crazy old Ruth.

At thirty-five, I thought the best was behind me.

As I celebrate my sixtieth birthday, I can hardly wait to see what happens next.

Ring the bells that still can ring
Forget your perfect offering
There's a crack in everything.
That's how the light gets in.

Welcome to the very cracked world of Armand Gamache and Three Pines. I am overjoyed to be able to share it with you.

Meet you in the bistro . . .

Louise Penny
March 2018

This book is dedicated to all those on the front line of the pandemic who have worked so hard, in often impossible conditions, to keep the rest of us safe. If ça va bien aller, it's thanks to you.
Louise Penny, 2021

The World of Three Pines

Rivière Bella Bella

Du Moulin

Old Stage Road

Du Moulin

CHAPTER 1

⁓

This doesn't feel right, *patron*." Isabelle Lacoste's voice in his ear-piece was anxious, verging on urgent.

Chief Inspector Gamache looked out over the roiling crowd, as the noise in the auditorium rose to a din.

A year ago a gathering of this sort would have not only been unthink-able, it would have been illegal. They'd have broken it up and gotten everyone tested. But thanks to the vaccines, they no longer had to worry about the spread of a deadly virus. They only had to worry about a riot.

Armand Gamache would never forget when the Premier of Qué-bec, a personal friend, had called him with the news that they had a vaccine. The man was in tears, barely able to get the words out.

As he'd hung up, Armand had felt light-headed. He could feel a sort of hysteria welling up. It was like nothing he'd ever felt before. Not on this scale. It wasn't just relief, it felt like a rebirth. Though not everyone, and not everything, would be resurrected.

When the pandemic was finally, officially, declared over, the little village of Three Pines where the Gamaches lived had gathered on the village green where the names of the dead had been read out. Loved ones had planted trees in the clearing above the chapel. It would be called, from that day on, the New Forest.

Then, to great ceremony, Myrna had unlocked her bookstore. And Sarah had opened the doors to her boulangerie. Monsieur Béliveau put the *Ouvert* sign in front of his general store, and a cheer rose up as Olivier and Gabri unlocked their bistro.

Banks of barbecues on the village green grilled burgers and hot dogs and steaks and a cedar-plank salmon. Sarah's cakes and pies and butter tarts were placed on a long table while Billy Williams helped Clara Morrow lug over buckets of her homemade lemonade.

There were games for the children and, later, a bonfire and dancing on the village green.

Friends and neighbors hugged, and even kissed. Though it felt strange, and even slightly naughty. Some still preferred to bump elbows. Others continued to carry their masks. Like a rosary, or rabbit's foot, or a St. Christopher medal, promising safe passage.

When Ruth coughed, everyone stepped away, though they probably would have anyway.

There were vestiges, of course. That dreadful time had a long tail.

And this event, in the former gymnasium at the University a few kilometers from Three Pines, was the sting in that tail.

Chief Inspector Gamache looked across the large space to the doors at the far end, where spectators were still streaming in.

"This should never have been allowed," said Lacoste.

He didn't disagree. In his opinion everything about this was madness. But it was happening. "Is everything under control?"

There was a pause before she replied. "Yes. But . . ."

But . . .

From the wing of the stage, he scanned the room and found Inspector Lacoste off to the side. She was in plain clothes, with her Sûreté du Québec ID clearly visible on her jacket.

She'd climbed onto a riser, where she could better monitor the swelling crowd and direct agents to any trouble spots.

Though only in her early thirties, Isabelle Lacoste was one of his most experienced officers. She'd been in riots, shoot-outs, hostage takings, and standoffs. She'd faced terrorists and murderers. Been badly wounded, almost killed.

Very little, at this point, worried Isabelle Lacoste. But it was clear she was worried now.

Spectators were jostling for position, trying to get a better view of the stage. Confrontations were flaring up around the large room. Some pushing and shoving was not unusual in a crowd with divided loyalties. They'd handled worse, and his agents were trained, and quick to calm things down.

But . . .

Even before Isabelle said it, he'd felt it himself. In his gut. In the tingle on his skin. In the pricking of his thumbs . . .

He could see that Isabelle was focused on an older man and a young woman in the middle of the hall. They were elbowing each other.

Nothing especially violent. Yet. And an agent was making his way through the crowd to calm them down.

So why was Lacoste so focused on these two especially?

Gamache continued to stare. And then he felt the hairs on the back of his neck rise.

The man and woman wore the same outsized button on their winter coats that declared, *All will be well.*

It was, he knew, a play on the word "well." Since the pandemic, that word had taken on several meanings. Not all of them, in Gamache's view, healthy.

He grew very still.

He'd been at many demonstrations and more than a few riots in his thirty-year career. He knew the flash points. The harbingers. And he knew how quickly things could spin way out of control.

But, but in all his years as a senior officer in the Sûreté du Québec he'd never seen this.

These two people, the man and woman, were on the same side. Those buttons declared their allegiance. And yet they'd turned their ire, normally reserved for the "other side," on each other. Anger had become free-floating. Falling on the nearest neck.

The atmosphere in the auditorium was stifling. Though dressing appropriately for the extreme cold outside, people were now inside and overdressed in parkas, heavy boots, scarves, and mitts. They were pulling off their woolen tuques and shoving them into pockets, leaving normally well-groomed people with their hair standing on end, as though they'd had either a great fright or a spectacularly good idea.

Standing cheek by jowl, the crowd was overheating physically as well as emotionally. Chief Inspector Gamache could almost smell the frayed nerve ends frying.

He looked in frustration at the tall windows behind Lacoste. They'd long since been painted shut, and there was no way to open them and bring in crisp fresh air. They'd tried.

The Chief Inspector's practiced eye continued to move over the crowd. Taking in things seen and unseen. It hadn't yet, he felt, reached the boiling point, the tipping point. His job, as the senior officer, was to make sure it didn't.

If it came close, he'd stop it. But he knew that also had its risks. Never mind the moral issue of stopping a gathering that had every legal right to be held, there was, foremost in his mind, the issue of public safety.

Having his agents move in and shut this event down could ignite the very violence he was trying to avoid.

Managing a crowd so it didn't turn into a mob wasn't science. Strategies could be taught; he himself had instructed recruits at the Sûreté Academy on managing large, potentially volatile, events. But finally it came down to judgment. And discipline.

Officers had to maintain control of the crowd, but also of themselves. Once, as a cadet, Gamache had seen trained officers at a demonstration panic, break ranks, and begin beating fellow citizens.

It was horrific. Sickening.

It had never happened under his command, but Gamache suspected that, given the right circumstances, it could. The madness of crowds was a terrible thing to see. The madness of police with clubs and guns was even worse.

Now, one by one, he asked his senior officers for their reports. His own voice calm and authoritative.

"Inspector Lacoste, what's your read?" he spoke into his headset.

There was a brief pause as she weighed her answer. "Our people are on top of things. I think at this point it's riskier to stop it than to let it go on."

"*Merci,*" said Gamache. "Inspector Beauvoir, how are things outside?"

He was always formal when speaking on an open frequency, preferring to use their ranks rather than just their names.

Despite his protests, Inspector Jean-Guy Beauvoir had been assigned, in his view banished, to the entrance.

4

In his late thirties, Beauvoir was slender, fit, though beginning to flesh out a bit. He shared second-in-command duties with Isabelle Lacoste, and also happened to be Gamache's son-in-law.

"We're going to exceed capacity, *patron*," he reported from on top of the overturned crate he was standing on.

Jean-Guy held his gloved hand up to his eyes to cut out the glare from the sun bouncing off the snow. Those still in line were stomping their feet, rubbing their mitts to keep the blood circulating, and staring at him, as though Beauvoir were personally responsible for winter.

"I'd say there are a hundred and fifty, maybe hundred and eighty still to go. They're getting pretty antsy. Some pushing, but no actual fights yet."

"How many are in now?" Gamache asked.

"We're at four hundred and seventy."

"You know the cutoff. What's likely to happen when you reach it?"

"Hard to tell. There're some kids here, families. Though why anyone would bring a child to this . . ."

"Agreed."

There were children in the auditorium now. Gamache had instructed his people to make them the priority, should the worst happen.

That was the nightmare, of course. People crushing the life out of others in a mad rush to get into, or out of, a place should anything happen. And the children were the most vulnerable.

"Any weapons?"

"No guns. No knives," Beauvoir reported. "A few bottles, and we've confiscated a whole lot of placards. People were pretty pissed about that. You'd have thought it was in the Charter of Rights to bring what amounts to a club into a crowded room." He looked down at the pile in the snow by the brick wall.

Most were homemade, in crayon, and stapled to sticks of wood. It was somehow worse when threats were in crayon. Some placards had even been made by children, with the phrase *Ça va bien aller*.

All will be well.

That alone was enough to make Beauvoir's blood boil. The demonstrators had co-opted a phrase that had, through the recent pandemic, meant comfort. And now they'd twisted it into a code, a subtle threat. Or, worse, made their children do it.

He looked out at the crowd and saw some pushing now, as spectators began to suspect they might not get in, and that their rival might.

"Things are getting more tense here," said Beauvoir. "I think we should shut it down, *patron*."

"*Merci*," said Gamache, and sighed.

While he'd certainly weigh what Beauvoir advised, and Jean-Guy might even be right, Gamache had to admit that in this rare instance, he didn't trust his second-in-command's judgment. It couldn't help but be colored by his personal feelings. Which was why, despite Beauvoir's protests, he'd been assigned the security outside, and not inside, the auditorium.

Gamache looked at his watch. Five minutes to four.

It was time for him to call it. To go ahead or not.

Glancing behind him once again, he saw two middle-aged women standing together in the darkness.

The one on the left, in black slacks and a gray turtleneck, held a clipboard and was looking anxious.

But it was the other one who held Gamache's attention.

Professor Abigail Robinson was nodding as the other woman talked. She laid a hand on her colleague's arm and smiled. She was calm. Focused.

She wore a light blue cashmere sweater and a camel knee-length skirt. Tailored. Simple, classic. Something, Gamache thought, that his wife, Reine-Marie, would wear.

It was not a comfortable thought.

The university lecturer in statistics was the reason these people had come out on a bitterly cold late December day.

They could be skiing or skating or sitting by the fire with a hot chocolate. But instead they were here, crowded together. Pushing and shoving. Hoping for a better view of this statistician.

Some came to cheer, some to jeer and protest. Some to hear, some to heckle.

And maybe some, maybe one, to do worse.

The Chief Inspector had yet to meet the woman who was about to take the stage, though her assistant, who'd introduced herself as Debbie Schneider, had approached him when they'd arrived and offered what had sounded like a favor, a rare personal audience.

He'd declined, explaining he had a job to do. And he had.

But he was honest enough with himself to admit that had it been anyone else, he'd have wanted to meet them. Would have asked to meet them, to go over the security arrangements. To lay down some rules. To look them in the eye and make that personal connection between protected and protector.

It was the first time in his career he'd declined, politely, to meet the person whose life was in his hands. Instead he'd gone through those arrangements with Madame Schneider, and left it at that.

He turned back to the auditorium. The sun was setting. It would be dark in twenty minutes.

"The event goes ahead," he said.

"Oui, patron."

CHAPTER 2

Gamache once again walked the backstage area, getting reports from the agents stationed there. Checking the doors and dark corners.

He asked the technician to turn the lights up.

"Who are these people?" the sound technician asked, cocking her head to indicate the crowd. "Who holds an event between Christmas and New Year's? Who comes out to one?"

It was a good question.

Gamache recognized a few faces in the crowd. They were, he knew, good, decent people. Some wore the buttons. Some did not.

Some of them were neighbors. Friends even. But most were strangers.

Québec was a society that felt things strongly and wasn't afraid to express them. Which was a very good thing. It meant they were doing something right. The goal of any healthy society was to keep people safe to express sometimes unpopular views.

But there was a limit to that expression, a line. And Armand Gamache knew he was standing on it.

If he'd had any thoughts that he might be overreacting, his doubts had been banished earlier in the day when he, along with Beauvoir and Lacoste, had arrived for the final walk-through.

As they'd pulled in, they were surprised to see cars already in the parking lot and people lined up at the door. They were shuffling from foot to foot, punching their arms, rubbing their mittened hands together in the bitter cold. Clouds of breath, like opaque thoughts, hung over them.

It was still hours until the event.

Taking off his own gloves, Gamache had pulled out his notebook and, ripping out pages, he'd given each a number depending on their place in line, with his initials.

"Go home. Get warm. When you come back, show that to the officers at the door. They'll let you in right away."

"Can't," said a woman at the front of the line as she took the paper. "We drove from Moncton."

"New Brunswick?" asked Beauvoir.

"Yes," said her husband. "Drove all night."

Others were now pressing forward, reaching for a number as though they were starving and this was food.

"The local café will be open," said Isabelle Lacoste. "Go there, have lunch, and come back when the doors open at three thirty."

Some did. But most elected to stay, taking turns sitting in warm cars.

As the Sûreté officers entered the building, Lacoste muttered, *"When were these seeds of anger sown / And on what ground."*

It was an apt quote, from a poem by their friend Ruth Zardo. Though the Sûreté officers knew perfectly well who'd sown the seeds that now had landed on the ground beneath their feet.

It wasn't joy, wasn't happiness, wasn't optimism that had propelled that couple almost a thousand kilometers from their home in a different province, through the night, along snowy and icy roads, to here.

It wasn't pleasure that had lifted others from their armchairs in front of their fires. Leaving behind their families. Their Christmas trees lit and cheery, the remnants of turkey dinner in the fridge. The preparations for New Year's Eve unfinished.

To stand in the biting cold.

It was the seeds of anger, sown by a genteel statistician and taking root.

The building caretaker, Éric Viau, was waiting for them in the old gymnasium. Gamache had met him two days before, when he'd first been given the unexpected assignment.

Armand had been on the outdoor rink in the middle of the village of Three Pines with Reine-Marie and two of their granddaughters. He had his own skates on and was kneeling down, lacing up eight-year-old Florence's skates, while Reine-Marie knelt in front of little Zora, doing up hers.

They were the girls' first pair. A Christmas gift from their grandparents.

Florence, her cheeks glowing red from the cold, was impatient to join the other children on the rink.

Her younger sister, Zora, was silent and leery. She seemed far from sure that strapping huge razors to her feet and stepping onto a frozen pond would be fun. Or a good idea.

"Dad," came a shout from the Gamache home.

"*Oui?*"

Daniel, tall, solid, stood on their front porch in his jeans and plaid flannel shirt. He was holding up a cell phone. "You have a call. Work."

"Can you take a message, *s'il te plaît?*"

"I tried, but apparently it's important."

Armand stood up, slipping slightly on his own skates. "Do they sound panicked?"

"*Non.*"

"Can you let them know I'm doing something important myself, and will get back to them in twenty minutes?"

"*D'accord.*" Daniel disappeared inside.

"Maybe Jean-Guy should take the call?" suggested Reine-Marie, also standing up and far steadier on her skates than her husband.

They looked up the hill that led out of the village. Their son-in-law, Jean-Guy Beauvoir, and his son were trudging back up to the top of the slope. Jean-Guy was pulling the new toboggan, a gift for Honoré from Père Noël.

On his very first sled run, the boy had clung to his father and screamed the whole way down. A shriek of delight, as Henri, the Gamaches' German shepherd, bounded after them.

They'd hurtled down the hill, past the New Forest, past St. Thomas's church, past the fieldstone and brick and clapboard homes. To tumble, laughing, into the soft snow on the village green.

"Some lungs your grandson has," said Clara Morrow. She and her best friend, Myrna Landers, were standing outside Myrna's bookstore, rum toddies warming their hands.

"Is it me, or was he actually screaming a word?" asked Myrna.

"*Non,*" said Reine-Marie quickly, not meeting her friends' eyes. "Just a scream."

Just then a piercing shout filled the air as Honoré and his father took off again.

"That's my boy," said the old poet Ruth, sitting on the bench between Florence and Zora, her duck Rosa muttering in her arms.

"What's Honoré saying, Papa?" asked Florence.

"He sounds like Rosa," said Zora. "What does 'fu—'"

"I'll tell you later," Armand said and glowered at Ruth, who chuckled, while Rosa muttered, "Fuck, fuck, fuck" and looked smug. But then ducks often did.

Rosa and Armand had a brief staring match, before Armand blinked.

For the next few minutes, he and Reine-Marie supported their granddaughters as they slid and stumbled on the ice. These were the first steps of what would become a lifetime of skating. And one day they'd teach their own granddaughters.

"Look, look!" Florence shouted. "Look at me. Fffu—"

"*Oui,*" her grandfather interrupted and saw Ruth on the bench not even trying to hide her delight.

It was midday, and they'd all been invited back to Clara's for a lunch of pea soup, bread warm from the oven, an assortment of Québec cheeses, and pie from Sarah's boulangerie.

"And hot chocolate," said Clara.

"That better be code for booze," said Ruth, as she hauled herself to her feet.

Armand carried their skates back home and, going into his study, he found the message Daniel had taken. It was from the Chief Superintendent of the Sûreté du Québec, calling from her ski chalet at Mont-Tremblant.

He returned the call and listened, surprised, as she told him what it was about.

"A lecture? From a statistician?" he'd said. Through the window he could see his family troop across the village green to Clara's small fieldstone cottage. "Can't campus police look after it?"

"Do you know this Abigail Robinson?" his superior asked.

Gamache had heard the name but couldn't quite place it. "Not really, *non*."

"You might want to look her up. *Voyons*, Armand, I really am sorry. The University's not far from you and the lecture will only last an hour. I wouldn't ask if I didn't think it would be easy. And, well, there is one other thing."

"*Oui?*"

"They asked for you specifically."

"They?"

"Well, someone at the University. I understand you have a friend there."

Some friend, thought Gamache, trying to think who it might be. He knew a number of professors.

He'd showered, changed, jotted a note for Reine-Marie, then driven the few kilometers over to meet with the building caretaker.

The venue had once been the gymnasium of the Université de l'Estrie, until a new sports complex had been built. They now hired it out for community events. Fundraising dances, reunions, rallies. Armand and Reine-Marie had been at a dinner there in late summer. It was the first indoor public gathering permitted since the pandemic had officially ended, held to raise money for Médecins Sans Frontières. One of the many organizations that had experienced a shortfall in donations during the crisis.

But that was months ago now.

Armand knocked the snow off his boots and introduced himself to the caretaker, Monsieur Viau. They stood in the middle of the large gym, the faded circle of center court just visible under their feet. The unmistakable musk of teen sweat still hung in the air, impossible to banish even though the teens who'd produced it were now probably parents themselves.

There was a stage at one end of the rectangular room, a wall of entrance doors at the other, and windows along one side.

"Do you know the capacity?" Gamache's voice echoed in the vast empty space.

"I don't. We haven't had to figure it out. It's never been close to full."

"The fire department hasn't told you the capacity?"

"You mean the volunteer fire department? No."

"Can you ask?"

"I can, but I know the answer. I'm the fire chief. Look, I can tell you that the building's up to code. The alarms, the extinguishers, the emergency exits all work."

Gamache smiled and put his hand on the man's arm. "I'm not criticizing. Sorry to be asking all these questions, and interrupting your holidays."

The man relaxed. "I imagine this isn't exactly what you want to be doing either."

There was truth in that. When he'd arrived at the old gym, Armand had sat in his car and checked messages. Reine-Marie had sent a photo from lunch at Clara's. It was of their daughter, Annie, and her baby, Idola, who was wearing reindeer antlers.

He'd smiled and touched Idola's face lightly with his finger. Then he'd put his phone away and gone into the building.

The sooner he got started, the sooner he could get home. There might even be some pie left.

"Why they agreed to this booking I don't know," the caretaker said as he showed the Chief Inspector around. "Two days before New Year's. And last-minute too. I got the email just last night, for Christ's sake. Fucking inconsiderate, excuse my English. Who is this person anyway? Never heard of her. Is she a singer? Will they need more than just a microphone? I haven't been told anything."

"She's a visiting lecturer. Her talk will be in English. A podium and mic should do it."

Monsieur Viau stopped and stared at him. "A lecture? In English? They pulled me away from a day skiing with my family because someone wants to give a talk?" His voice was rising with each word. "Are you kidding me?"

"Sadly, I am not."

"Jesus," said the caretaker, "were there no walk-in closets she could've rented? And why're you here? A Sûreté officer? What does she talk about?"

"Statistics."

"Oh, for God's sake, this place's going to be empty. What a waste of time."

Gamache climbed onto the stage and looked out at the room.

He agreed with the caretaker. If they got fifty people, he'd be surprised. But Armand Gamache was a careful man. Three decades of looking at the bodies of surprised people did that.

"I'll get the room dividers ready, Chief," said Monsieur Viau.

They left the stage and walked to the main entrance, where frost had encroached and encrusted the door handles.

"Do you happen to have blueprints of the building?"

"In my office."

Viau returned with scrolls, which he gave to Gamache. As the caretaker prepared to lock up and leave, he studied the cop.

He'd recognized the name, of course, when Gamache had called for the appointment. And he recognized the man himself when he'd arrived. It was strange to see someone in person who he'd seen so often on television, throughout the pandemic and before. While Monsieur Viau had heard that the head of homicide for the Sûreté lived in the region, they'd never actually met, until now.

What he saw was a large man. Slightly over six feet tall. Even with the parka, it was clear he wasn't fat, but he was substantial. Mid to late fifties, he guessed. Gray hair, curling slightly around his ears. And, of course, the unmistakable scar, deep at his temple.

The cop's face, the caretaker noticed, wasn't so much wrinkled as lined. And Viau could guess where those lines had come from.

They stepped outside, and though they were braced for it, the bitter cold still stole their breaths. It scraped the flesh of their faces and made their eyes water. Their feet crunched on the snow as the caretaker walked the Chief Inspector to his car.

"Why're you really here?" Viau asked.

Gamache squinted into the sun. So much light was bouncing off the drifts that his companion was almost lost in the glare.

"That's exactly what I asked my superior," he said with a smile. "To be honest with you, Monsieur Viau, I don't really know."

But then Armand Gamache hadn't yet done his research on the person who'd be standing at the podium. And what she, and her statistics, would be saying.

Now, with the event about to begin, Chief Inspector Gamache looked over the heads of the crowd and found Monsieur Viau standing at the far end, by the doors. In shock, as he leaned on his mop and watched the people pour in.

Gamache had used the plans he'd been given to work out that the official maximum standing capacity would be six hundred and fifty. He'd rounded it down to five hundred, believing that they wouldn't get close.

But as he'd done more research, Gamache became less and less sure.

He'd spent his evenings after everyone else had gone to bed watching videos of lectures given by Professor Robinson. Many of which had, in the past few weeks, gone viral.

What could have been a dry recital of statistics had become a near messianic message to a population hungry for, desperate for, hope.

Though the pandemic was now over, it had left behind a population worn down. People were tired of being self-disciplined, of self-isolating. Of social distancing and wearing masks. They were exhausted, shell-shocked, from months and endless months of worrying about their children, their parents, their grandparents. Themselves.

They were battered and bruised from losing relatives, losing friends. Losing jobs and favorite haunts. Tired of being isolated and driven near crazy with loneliness and despair.

They were tired of being afraid.

Professor Abigail Robinson, with her statistics, proved that better times were ahead. That the economy could recover, stronger than ever. The health care system could meet all their needs. That there would never be a shortage of beds, equipment, medicine again. Ever.

And instead of being asked to make a hundred sacrifices, the population would be asked to make just one.

It was in that "just one" that all the trouble lay.

Her report had been commissioned by the Canadian government

for its Royal Commission into the social and economic consequences of the pandemic. Into the choices and decisions made. Professor Robinson, a senior academic and head of the department of statistics at a western university, had been tasked with correlating the figures and making recommendations.

She had come up with just one.

But, having read the report, the members of the Royal Commission had refused to let her present it publicly.

And so, Professor Robinson had decided to do it herself. She'd held a small seminar for fellow statisticians. It was streamed online so others who couldn't get there could also see.

Armand had found it and watched as Abigail Robinson had stood in front of her charts and graphs. Her voice was warm, her eyes intelligent as she talked about fatalities and survival and resources.

Others had also found it. Not just academics, but members of the public. It had been shared and reshared. Professor Robinson had been invited to do other talks. Larger talks. And larger still.

Her message boiled down to four words, now emblazoned on T-shirts and caps and big round buttons.

All will be well.

What had started as a dry research project, destined for a government file cabinet, had slipped its moorings. Gone public. Gone viral. A fringe movement had taken off. Not yet mainstream, but Gamache could see it was just a matter of time. Like the pandemic itself, Robinson's message was spreading quickly. Finding people vulnerable to just this curious mix of hope for the future, and fear of what might happen if they didn't do what Robinson was suggesting.

All shall be well. And all shall be well. And all manner of thing shall be well.

It was a quote from one of Gamache's favorite writers, the Christian mystic Julian of Norwich. Who'd offered hope in a time of great suffering.

But, unlike Julian of Norwich, Professor Robinson's brand had a dark core. When Robinson said *All will be well*, she did not, in fact, mean everything. Or everyone.

Other buttons were beginning to appear at her events, sold to raise money for what had gone from a study to a cause to, Gamache could see as he sat in his quiet study with the Christmas tree lit in the living room, a crusade.

The new buttons supporters were wearing had a more dire quote. One he also recognized. It was a line from a nutty, though brilliant, old poet. With a demented duck.

Or will it be, as always was, TOO LATE? The "TOO LATE" was in caps, bold. Like a shout. A shriek. A warning and an accusation.

In a few short months a research project had become a movement. An obscure academician had become a prophet.

And hope had turned to outrage, as two clear sides solidified and clashed. There were those who saw what Professor Robinson was proposing as the only way forward. As a merciful and practical solution. And those who saw it as an outrage. A shameful violation of all they held sacred.

As the din in the auditorium rose, Armand Gamache looked behind him at the middle-aged woman waiting to go on, and wondered if the prophet was about to become a messiah. Or a martyr.

CHAPTER 3

—

The night before the event, when the children had been bathed and put to bed, when the home had fallen silent, Jean-Guy Beauvoir had joined his father-in-law in his study.

He'd actually been on his way to the kitchen for the last mince tart when he spotted the light under the study door.

Hesitating for just a moment, Jean-Guy made up his mind, and knocked.

"Entrez."

Jean-Guy's dark hair had some gray now, and a few lines had appeared on his handsome face. His complexion was rosy after a day in the bright sun and gusty wind. Though he'd made it clear he preferred "rugged" to "rosy."

Now he looked down at the plate he was holding. A dollop of hard sauce was melting on top of the fragrant mince tart, which Jean-Guy had warmed in the microwave.

He swallowed some saliva, then put the plate down in front of his father-in-law.

"Here. Myrna dropped it over this afternoon when we were building the snow fort and you were napping."

Jean-Guy smiled. He knew perfectly well his father-in-law had been out working. He'd offered to go along, but in this rare instance, Armand had said he should enjoy his vacation. And in this rare instance, Beauvoir had not insisted.

Jean-Guy and his family had moved back to Montréal from Paris, and he'd recently rejoined the Sûreté, sharing second-in-command duties with Isabelle Lacoste.

After the rigors, the horrors, of the pandemic, this Christmas vacation in Three Pines was a welcome respite. A relief.

Once home, the children had gotten into warm dry clothes and sat on the sofa with a hot chocolate while the dogs, Henri and old Fred, slept by the hearth along with little Gracie. Who might, or might not, be a dog. Or a ferret.

The smart money among the villagers was on the tiny creature being a chipmunk. Though Stephen Horowitz, Armand's godfather, who now lived with them, took pleasure in insisting Gracie was a rat.

"They're very intelligent, you know," the ninety-three-year-old told the children when they crawled onto the sofa beside the former financier.

"How do you know?" Zora, the serious one, asked.

"Because I used to be one."

"You were a rat?" Florence asked.

"Yes. A big fat one, with a long, long silky tail."

Their eyes widened as he regaled them with tales of his adventures as a rat on Wall Street and Bay Street. On rue Saint-Jacques in Montréal and at the Bourse in Paris.

That was in the afternoon. They were all in bed now. Asleep.

Though one was still stirring.

Armand hit pause on his screen and looked up. He heard the familiar creaks and cracks as the temperature dropped and frost settled into the bones of the old home. There was something profoundly peaceful about knowing his family was safe in their beds.

"*Merci.*" Armand nodded toward the tart and smiled his thanks to Jean-Guy.

Then he took off his glasses and rubbed his eyes.

"This the person you're protecting?" Jean-Guy asked, taking a seat and gesturing toward the computer.

"*Oui.*"

Armand's answers were unusually curt, and now Jean-Guy paid more attention to the image on the screen.

It showed a middle-aged woman at a podium, smiling. It was a pleasant smile. Not a sneer. There was no malice, no guile. It was neither smug nor maniacal. She looked nice.

"Something wrong?"

Jean-Guy looked at his father-in-law and what he saw was a man deeply unsettled.

Armand tossed his glasses onto the desk and nodded toward the screen. "This's a recording made at Abigail Robinson's last event just before Christmas. After I watched it this afternoon, I called the President of the University to ask that the event tomorrow be called off."

"Really? What did he say?"

"That I was overreacting."

Armand had wanted to believe the President. He wanted to roll up the blueprints, close his notebook, put on his parka and join his family.

He wanted to sit with his grandchildren, a heavy rug covering their legs, and watch Gloria's swaying tail as the horse pulled the big red sleigh up the north road out of the village.

Instead he'd gotten in his car and driven over to North Hatley to see the Chancellor.

CHAPTER 4

————

C hief Inspector Gamache took off his parka and boots and followed the Chancellor into her living room.

"*S'il vous plaît,* Armand." She indicated a comfortable armchair by the fireplace.

The room was lined with books, and above the mantel there hung an A. Y. Jackson. Gamache glanced at it but kept walking to the French doors at the end of the gracious room. Standing in front of them, his hands clasped behind his back, he looked out over Lac Massawippi. The large lake, surrounded by thick forest, was frozen over. A great field of sparkling white. Except. Right in front of the house, just offshore, a rectangle had been cleared, and flooded, and frozen again so that it formed an ice rink.

A hockey match was under way, though how they could tell who was on which team he didn't know. They all wore Montreal Canadiens, Habs, sweaters.

"Family?" he asked as she joined him.

"And some neighboring kids, but yes, mostly grandchildren. You and Reine-Marie have a couple now too."

"Four."

"Four? Not quite enough for a hockey team, but close."

"They've just started skating," he said, returning to the armchairs. "If only hockey could be played on hands and knees."

The room was warm, inviting. It reflected the Chancellor perfectly.

Colette Roberge had held the mainly ceremonial post at the University for two years. Before that she'd retired as Dean of the mathematics department and been made a Professor Emeritus.

He considered her a friend, though not a close one.

"Coffee?" she asked.

"Non, merci."

"Tea?"

"Nothing for me, thank you, Colette." He smiled and waited for her to sit before taking his own seat. "How's Jean-Paul? I'd like to say hello."

"He's at the lake, refereeing the game. Your family? All got through the pandemic?"

"Yes, thriving, thank you."

"And Stephen? After what happened in Paris?"

"His old self."

"That can't be good," she said with a smile.

In her mid-seventies now, Chancellor Roberge was a tireless champion for the University, and an accomplished academic. And now, in the midst of her own holidays with her family, she'd made time for him, greeting him as though he'd been expected.

And maybe, he thought, he had been.

"What can I do for you, Armand?"

"It's about Abigail Robinson."

The shaped brows rose very slightly. Her manicured hands folded one on top of the other, and he noticed a slight squeeze. But her expression remained pleasant.

The Chancellor was smart enough not to feign ignorance.

"Yes? What about her?"

"You know she's speaking tomorrow afternoon at the University."

"I'd seen that, yes."

"And you approve?"

"It's not for me to approve or disapprove." A very slight chill had crept into her voice. An early warning. "Nor is it for you."

He crossed his legs, a subtle indication that he was just settling in and wouldn't be intimidated.

Seeing that, the Chancellor rose and threw another log on the fire, sending giddy sparks up the chimney. And with it, her own message.

She had all day.

"I'll come right to the point," he said. "I think the event should never have been booked, but since it has, I think it should be canceled."

"And you come to me with this? There's nothing I can do even if I wanted to. My position is honorary, as you know. I have no real power."

"I did ask the President."

"Really? And what did he say?" There was, Gamache could hear, some amusement in her voice.

The President of the University, while a titan in his field, was far from that as a leader and policy maker.

"He declined."

"Let me guess." She shut her eyes. "The purpose of a university is to give safe harbor for dissenting voices." Opening them, she saw her guest smiling.

"He's not wrong," said Gamache.

"No."

"But this isn't just a dissenting voice." He leaned toward her. "You have influence, Colette. You could contact the Board of Governors. They respect you. Convene a conference call."

"And what would I say?"

"That this sort of lecture wrapped in academic garb is not just non-sense, it's dangerous. That in hosting her, the University risks giving her views legitimacy."

She studied him for one beat. Two. Appearing to consider, though Armand would have been surprised if she hadn't anticipated this con-versation. And prepared her answer.

They had that in common. Anticipating events. Preparing. He'd done the same thing while driving over. He didn't always win the ar-gument, didn't expect to. Some battles were unwinnable. But some-times just showing up was enough.

And he had to try.

"If you think it's dangerous, then stop it yourself," she said. "You have the authority, as a senior Sûreté officer. That is, if you think Abigail's breaking the law. Do you?"

"*Non.* If I did, I wouldn't need to be here, as pleasant as this is."

She smiled at that. "So, Armand, you want me to do your dirty work? You don't want to be seen to abuse your power, but you want me to abuse mine?"

Though he could see the thin sheet of ice creeping toward him, he was nevertheless surprised by what she said next.

"You'd hide behind a seventy-three-year-old woman? Are you that much of a coward?"

He cocked his head to one side, quickly reassessing the situation. It was a direct, even coarse, personal attack. It didn't hurt. He knew he wasn't a coward. And, what's more, she did too.

He'd been accused of many things in his career, but even his enemies hadn't dared throw that in his face.

So why would the Chancellor? It was unworthy of the woman he knew and respected.

Far from allowing himself to be goaded, he grew even calmer. His focus and attention sharpened, even as his breathing steadied. As it always did when preparing for a confrontation, either physical or intellectual.

He'd known, as he drove over, that this might be a tense conversation, but he had not expected this reaction from the Chancellor.

"Well, I am afraid," he said, his voice reasonable. "If that's what you mean. Not just that it will turn violent—every public gathering has that potential and this more than most. But I am afraid that hosting this event will not just sully the University but help spread her message. It has the potential to infect the whole province. And beyond."

"You consider free speech an infection? Ideas a virus? I thought you believed in the Charter of Rights and Freedoms, or is that just for public consumption? Are your situational ethics showing? Free speech is fine, as long as it doesn't bump into your personal beliefs, your ideology?"

"I have no ideology—"

Colette Roberge laughed. "Don't kid yourself. Everyone has beliefs, values."

"Those I have, yes. But that's different. You didn't let me finish. I have no ideology beyond finding and defending that spot between freedom and safety."

She was quiet for a moment. "And you think the talk violates that?"

"Do you know what she's saying? What she advocates?"

"In broad strokes, yes."

"And you're okay with it?"

"Again, it's not for me to approve or disapprove. If we only ever allow lectures on topics we're 'okay' with, the University wouldn't be much of a place of learning, now would it? We'd never explore new ideas. Radical ideas. Even what might be considered dangerous ideas. We'd just keep going around and around saying and hearing the same old thing. The echo chamber. No, this university is open to new ideas."

"This isn't a new idea." He stared at her. "It sounds like you agree with Professor Robinson."

"I agree with the importance of dissenting voices, of unpopular stands, of even dangerous thoughts as long as they don't cross a line."

"And what's the line?"

"That's for you to decide, Chief Inspector."

"You're abdicating your moral responsibility to the University and giving it to the police?"

Their voices were rising, not quite shouting at each other, but intense. They were, Armand knew, on the verge of crossing a line themselves.

Indeed, Colette had crossed it when she'd called him a coward. And he might have just crossed it too when he accused her of abdicating her responsibility. But there was a reason he'd said it.

"You're advocating an abuse of power," she said. "Stifling free speech. And that's called tyranny. Watch yourself, Chief Inspector. You're on very thin ice. I thought you would assure that this event would go on safely. But now you're sounding like a fascist."

Gamache paused before he spoke. "You're the reason I was given this assignment?"

The Chancellor realized she'd been provoked into saying too much. And, looking at the man across from her, she realized he'd almost certainly done it on purpose. Goaded, pushed. Prodded. Until she'd lashed out. Lost sight of the line she'd set for herself.

But she suspected she was already off balance before he'd arrived. Unsure of the stand she was taking, of the ground she stood on. Unsure she'd done the right thing. In fact, very much afraid she had not.

But it was too late. Still, he didn't know everything.

Now she inclined her head, raising it again in acknowledgment.

"Was I wrong to ask for you?" she said. "I thought you'd be fair and professional. But maybe that's asking too much. Given your personal circumstances, maybe you'll find it difficult to protect Professor Robinson, if it comes to that."

Now she really had crossed a line, but this time she'd done it on purpose. To shift the focus. She could see the shock on his face, quickly replaced by anger.

"I'm sorry," she said, almost immediately, though her sincerity was in doubt. "I shouldn't have said that. But it's a fair question."

"It is not, Madame Chancellor, and you know it. You just dragged my family into it. You accused me of tyranny. Even allowing a person to be hurt, maybe killed, because I don't happen to agree with their ideology."

"No. I accused you of being human. Of defending your family. And while we're at it, you accused me of allowing thousands of young men and women to be compromised because I don't want to get involved."

They stared at each other. Seething. Each had lost their hard-won composure.

My God, thought Gamache, pulling back from the edge. *This's how it starts. This's what Abigail Robinson does, even from a distance. Just discussing her can sow the seeds of anger. And, with it, fear.*

And yes. He was afraid. That her statistics and graphs would take root. That people would come to believe, to support, the insupportable.

He took a deep breath. "I'm sorry, Colette. What I said went too far."

She was quiet. Not yet ready, it seemed, to offer her own apology.

"Why did the University agree to this booking?" he asked.

"You're asking me? I don't okay events." Still snippy.

"And why did Professor Robinson choose to come here?"

"Why not?"

"Don't you find it curious that while all her other lectures were out west, when she does come east, it's not to the University of Toronto. Not to McGill or the Université de Montréal. Not to a big venue in a major city, but to a small university in a small town."

"The Université de l'Estrie has a very good reputation," said the Chancellor.

"*C'est vrai,*" he said, nodding. "It's true. But it's still surprising."

His voice, though, had grown detached as he followed a train of thought. One that hadn't occurred to him until now. He'd been so distracted by the moral, legal, logistical issues that he hadn't paused to wonder why the Université de l'Estrie.

"Maybe the other places refused her," he said, thinking out loud.

"It doesn't matter," she said.

He sighed. "I've struggled with this, Colette. Gone back and forth in my mind, until last night. That's when I watched her most recent lecture and the aftermath. How the spectators turned on each other. Is she breaking the law? Is it hate speech?" He ran his hands through his hair. "No. But it's already led to some very, very ugly confrontations."

"Which is why I asked for you. I know it would be beyond campus security to protect Abigail."

"Abigail?"

"Yes, that's her name, isn't it? Abigail Robinson."

"*Oui.* But you used the familiar. Not 'Professor Robinson.'" He uncrossed his legs and leaned toward her. "Do you know her? Personally?"

And now something else occurred to him.

"Is that why she chose the Université de l'Estrie? Did you invite her?"

"Are you kidding?"

"*Non.*"

The Chancellor stared at him. Then relented.

"You're right, I did know her. Years ago. But I didn't invite her here."

"How do you know her?"

"I don't see how it matters, but since you ask, I knew her father. We did some studies together. He was a statistician too. A friend. He asked me to look after Abigail when I was a guest lecturer in Oxford. She went there to read Maths."

"What was she like?"

"Does it matter?"

"It helps to know the personality of the one I'm protecting. Are they aggressive? Fearful? Compliant? Will they listen to instructions or argue?"

Chancellor Roberge gazed over his shoulder and into the past.

Seeing the bright young men and women, barely more than boys and girls, ranged in front of her. They were just beginning to realize a hard truth. While they'd easily outpaced the other students in their schools back home, here at Oxford they'd struggle just to keep up. They'd gone, in the blink of an eye, from exceptional to average.

Many did not thrive, couldn't adapt. But Abigail had managed to adjust quite quickly.

"Unlike most of her cohort, who could be maladroit, she was easy to like," said Colette. "She didn't come from an affluent background. It was a home that valued intellectual achievement. She was focused, likable."

"Ambitious?"

"No more than you," said Colette with a smile.

"And her work?"

"Was exceptional." Now that they were talking about academics, Chancellor Roberge relaxed. "I'm not sure if you realize that mathematics isn't linear. It's a curve. And in the brightest, most nimble minds, it arcs around to meet philosophy, music, art." She laced her fingers together. "They're intertwined. If you listen to Bach, it's as much a work of math as music."

Gamache had heard this before. Had listened as Clara Morrow, their friend and neighbor and a gifted painter, had mused on just such a convergence. Perspective. Proportion. Spatial reasoning. Logic and problem solving. And portraiture.

"A friend of ours quotes Robert Frost," he said. "*A poem begins as a lump in the throat.* The artists I know feel the same way. Do mathematicians?"

This was, the Chancellor knew, more than a casual question. It was a hand grenade. An interesting one, but potentially explosive nevertheless.

"I wouldn't say that. I think for mathematicians, statisticians, the lump in the throat comes at the end. When we see where our work has taken us."

"And how it can be perverted?" When Colette didn't answer, he said, "Do you think Professor Robinson has a lump in her throat when she looks at her graphs?"

"You'll have to ask her. Look, I'm not defending her."

"It sounds like you are. Letting this lecture go on is wrong," he said. "I've gone over and over the laws on censorship. On what constitutes hate speech. If I could cancel it on those grounds, I would. And it's possible that tomorrow, at the lecture, I'll be able to cancel it on public safety grounds, but for now, I don't have cause."

His words hung in the warm air between them, as the fire muttered and shouts of joy drifted up from the rink on the frozen lake.

A goal had been scored, but for which side?

And then the room settled back to silence.

"I'm asking you," said Armand, his voice low. "Begging you, Colette, to call it off. Use any excuse. The building's heat is off. The workers need their holidays. A bureaucratic mistake was made in taking the booking. Please. This is not going to go well, for anyone."

The Chancellor studied the man in front of her. She'd known him for decades. Seen his rise through the ranks. Seen his great fall.

And seen him put himself together again and go back to doing a job that was far more than a job for him.

It was written on his face. The lines and creases. Not age. Not all, anyway. They were a map of his life. Of his beliefs. Of the stands he'd taken and the blows he'd suffered.

She could see it in the deep scar at his temple.

No, this man was no coward, but he was, as he admitted, afraid.

But then so was she.

Rising to her feet, Colette Roberge said, "I will not cancel the event, Armand."

Chief Inspector Gamache had known, before he'd even left his study, that this was a battle he almost certainly would not win. Still, while he didn't leave this home with a concession, he did take away more information than he'd arrived with. Including that the Chancellor had known Abigail Robinson. Well enough to still call her by her first name.

He wondered if one of the Christmas cards on the bookshelves and along the mantelpiece was signed *Abigail*.

He couldn't see how it mattered, but then no information was wasted.

"Thank you, Madame Chancellor, for hearing me out."

"I'm sorry to have dragged you into this. I can see it's causing you discomfort."

"It goes with the territory."

"When you have a grandchild with Down syndrome," she said.

He paused at the door as he put on his gloves and looked at her. She obviously knew more than she let on.

"*Non.* Idola is the solace, the balm. The pain is making decisions like this."

"I won't ask where the pain is."

He laughed. "Will you be there?"

"*Moi? Non.* I'll be hiding under the covers and not taking any calls. Listen, Armand, you and I both know this is moot. Professor Robinson will give her talk tomorrow, but it'll be to an empty auditorium. And that'll be the end of it."

She leaned forward and kissed him on both cheeks.

"*Joyeux Noël. Bonne année.* Give my love to Reine-Marie."

"And to you, Colette, and Jean-Paul."

As he walked back down the path to the car, Armand turned and noticed the pages still plastered in the front window of the Chancellor's home. On the paper were rainbows, probably drawn by the grandchildren during the pandemic, with the words in crayon, *Ça va bien aller.*

He turned away, his face grave. *All will be well.* It depended, he knew, on what "well" meant. And he had a sinking feeling he and the Chancellor had two different ideas on that.

Colette Roberge pulled her cardigan tighter and watched as the Chief Inspector drove away.

Just then she heard young voices raised in shouts and heated arguments as her grandchildren returned with their friends.

Doors banged, cold air blew in. Thuds were heard as winter boots were kicked off and skates tossed into corners.

"Hot chocolate?" she asked.

"Yes, please, Granny."

Even those not related to her called her Granny. In fact, Colette knew that some of her colleagues and even the Premier Ministre du Québec called her *Grand-mère*.

It was, she'd decided, both a term of endearment and an advantage. They were far less likely to be guarded around their grandmother.

She stirred the pot of cocoa and watched her husband in the corner, where he'd been all morning, lost in his jigsaw. While life swirled, unnoticed, around him.

That night, as he sat in his study with Jean-Guy, Armand leaned forward and clicked play on his laptop. They watched as Abigail Robinson, the nice woman on the screen, began talking.

Twelve minutes later Jean-Guy reached over and hit pause.

"Is she saying what I think she is?"

Armand nodded.

"Fuck," whispered Jean-Guy. His eyes shifted from the computer to his father-in-law. "And you're going to protect her?"

"Someone has to."

"Did you know what she was saying when you agreed?"

"*Non.*"

"Did you know what she was saying when you told me you didn't need me there?"

"*Non.*"

They held each other's eyes. Jean-Guy's complexion had gone from a rosy glow to a flush. The seeds of anger sown.

"I'm going upstairs," said Jean-Guy.

"I'll come with you."

Armand turned off the Christmas tree. In the darkness he could see the three great pine trees anchoring the village green. Their multi-colored Christmas lights glowed red, blue, and green under the weight of snow on their boughs.

Henri and Fred slowly followed them up the stairs. Gracie was already asleep in Stephen's room.

Armand kissed Florence and Zora good night, then went next door, where Jean-Guy was staring down at his daughter. A cold wind puffed out the curtains, dropping the temperature in the room. As though something nasty were approaching.

Armand lowered the window until it was open just a crack, then pulled the blankets up over Honoré. Somehow he'd managed to sneak his new toboggan into the bed. Kissing the child, Armand then joined his son-in-law.

Little Idola was sleeping peacefully, unaware of the forces gathering around her.

Jean-Guy raised his eyes. "I know you've brought Isabelle in to help with tomorrow's event, and others from the department. I want to be there too."

"It's not a good idea, and you know it."

"If I'm not there on your team, I'll be there as a spectator. Either way, I'm going."

Armand saw that the seeds had taken root. "I'll let you know in the morning."

Later that night, Jean-Guy went down to the living room and sat in the armchair by the fire, now just embers. He found the video Armand had shown him and this time watched it all the way through.

He now understood why Armand had gone to the Chancellor and asked her, probably pleaded with her, to stop the event.

And he knew why his father-in-law did not want him anywhere close to this woman.

CHAPTER 5

—

"Professor Robinson? I'm Chief Inspector Gamache of the Sûreté." He couldn't avoid speaking with her any longer. "Are you ready to go on?"

Abigail Robinson looked at the man who'd just approached her.

Though they hadn't yet met, Debbie had pointed him out as the officer in charge. Though she needn't have. His authority was obvious.

He wasn't in uniform, instead he wore a jacket and tie. Good material, well cut.

While not classically handsome, there was something compelling about him. Perhaps it was his calm. But what was most noticeable, now that he was standing right in front of her, were his eyes.

They were deep brown and clear. Alert, as she'd expect. He was assigned to security, he should be alert.

There was intelligence there, but it went beyond that. His gaze was thoughtful.

Here was someone who would consider before he acted. It was rare, she knew, to have some space between thought and action. Most people didn't. They thought they did, but most acted on impulse, even instinct, then justified it.

Professor Robinson knew that that gap, that pause, meant the person had control over their actions. Had choices. And with those choices came power.

This man had choices, and power. And right now, he was choosing to be civil. He tried to hide his dislike for her behind a naturally gracious manner, but she could see it in his thoughtful eyes. He thought very little of her.

"Professor?" he repeated. "It's just after four. The auditorium is full. It's best if you start as soon as possible."

She could hear a rumble behind the thick curtains. It sounded like a large freight train bearing down. The place had begun to shudder slightly, from excitement, impatience, and anticipation. It was the sound of hundreds of people. Waiting. For her.

He held his arm out, trying to shepherd her forward. But her assistant stepped between them.

"Do you have everything you need, Abby?" She looked around. "Is there water on the podium? You have your notes?"

"I have everything, Debbie, thank you."

Gamache could see that, beyond being employer and employee, they were also friends.

Professor Robinson turned back to him. Had he not known better, had he not seen the videos of previous events, he'd think by the look in her eyes that she was a nice person.

But he did know better. And what he knew was that her eyes did not reflect what was going on in her mind or what was about to come out of her mouth.

Though there was another possibility.

That Abigail Robinson believed that what she was advocating was reasonable, even noble. Not an act of obscene cruelty, but kindness.

"Is something wrong?" Isabelle Lacoste asked into his earpiece, her voice slightly higher than usual. "Is she going to start?"

He could hear the noise beyond the curtain getting louder.

"*Oui*," he said, then turned to Robinson. "If you don't mind, it would be best if you went on. Does someone introduce you?"

He looked around. There was no one else backstage except Madame Schneider and the sound person. In a moment of panic, Gamache thought it would fall to him.

And maybe, just to get her out and settle the now raucous crowd, he'd actually do it.

Professor Robinson glanced toward the door, then said, "No. I'll go out alone. No need for an introduction. These people know who I am." She smiled. "For better or worse."

She's waiting for someone, thought Gamache. *That's why she'd been stalling. Hoping someone shows up.*

Someone who might, at that moment, be hiding under the covers, not answering her phone.

"Good luck. You'll do great, Abby Maria," said Debbie, and beamed at her friend.

Though it was obviously meant as support, it seemed to annoy the professor. Perhaps, thought Gamache, she was of the belief that saying "good luck" would jinx it.

Most of the scientists he'd met were profoundly superstitious. As were cops, for that matter.

"Come with me, please," he said and walked her toward the opening in the heavy curtains. "I've seen the footage from your last event. We will not have a repeat here. If it looks like the audience is getting out of control, you will tell them to calm down. If that doesn't work, I'll come out onstage and repeat the request and warn people if they don't behave with civility, I'll end the lecture."

"I understand, Chief Inspector. Believe me, I don't want a repeat either."

"Is that true?"

"Yes. If you didn't just watch but listened to what I said, you'd know I don't advocate violence. Just the opposite. This is about healing. Unfortunately, some people twist my words and meaning."

Her statement was so appalling, so inaccurate, that he just stared at her for a moment. With all his heart, Armand Gamache wanted to challenge what she'd just said. But this wasn't the place, the time, or his job.

For now, his job was to get everyone out of there in the same condition in which they'd arrived. Though he feared that could never be totally achieved. Many would leave with some terrible idea planted. Like a weed in a crack, weakening the foundation.

"Inspector Beauvoir, how's the door?"

"There was some pushing when we announced no one else could get in," reported Beauvoir. "But it's quiet now."

"*Bon, merci*. We're about to begin."

Beauvoir clicked off his microphone and looked at the closed door. He knew, in his bones, in his marrow, that he shouldn't do this thing. But he also knew he would.

Turning to the Sûreté officer next to him, he said, "You're in charge out here."

"Sir?"

"I'm going inside."

Chief Inspector Gamache watched as Abigail Robinson took a deep breath, composing herself.

It was the same thing he'd seen Olympic divers do, as their heels hung over the edge of the platform, their arms in the air, their backs to the pool.

That instant before the impossible plunge. The irrevocable.

It was exactly what he himself did when standing at the closed door. His hand, in a fist, lifted. He paused, giving the family inside that last moment of peace. Before the plunge.

And then his knuckles rapped the wood.

I'm sorry to inform you . . .

Abigail Robinson took a deep breath and stepped onto the stage.

Armand Gamache took a deep breath and let her.

CHAPTER 6

⁓

The reaction was immediate and so overwhelming that it almost knocked Gamache back a step.

He'd heard roars, uproars, before. From the stands during hockey playoffs when the Habs scored. Or Grey Cup finals. At concerts, when the group finally took the stage.

But this was a whole other creature.

He looked out.

Perhaps it was the density of the crowd, though he'd been careful to underestimate capacity. Perhaps it was the acoustics in the old gymnasium, but the noise was far more than five hundred people should have been able to produce.

And he quickly realized what was causing it.

There was cheering, shouts of support, chanting. But there were equal parts booing. Cries of "Shame!" Howls of derision.

And there were shrieks. It was impossible to tell if they were cries of support, of contempt, or just from people overwhelmed with emotion and needing to blow it off.

It all came together in an acoustic body blow.

He stepped farther out from behind the curtain, to get a better look. He expected to see Professor Robinson stopped in her tracks, or even turning back, backing up. Momentarily staggered, even paralyzed, by this assault.

Instead she kept walking. Slowly. Calmly. As though she were alone in the room.

Armand Gamache watched her measured progress through the cacophony, and recognized courage when he saw it. But this was not what he'd call valor.

It was the courage that came with conviction, with absolute certainty. When all doubt was banished. It was the courage of the zealot.

And then came the stomping, heavy winter boots hitting the old wooden floor. The place was heaving. Gamache spared a thought for the caretaker, who must have been in despair right about then.

At the back of the auditorium, Jean-Guy Beauvoir stood on tiptoes to see.

Everyone in front of him was doing the same thing, and he needed to sway back and forth to catch glimpses of the woman walking, almost strolling, across the stage.

Apparently oblivious to the sensation she was causing.

He'd watched the video of her event ten days earlier. That had been raucous. But nothing like this.

From her vantage point on a riser halfway down the room, Isabelle Lacoste took in the movement of the crowd. People were swaying back and forth, side to side. Like some great churning ocean. Had she suffered from seasickness she'd have been green.

Her sharp eyes scanned for trouble spots. For eddies and surges. This was one of the danger points. When the crowd first sees the focus of their adoration, and rage.

She looked at the agents she'd installed at various points around the walls and in the crowd itself. Some in uniform. Some in plain clothes.

Inspector Lacoste then turned to the stage. Not to the single person on it, almost at the podium, but to the Sûreté agents lined up in front of it.

And then, from the middle of the crowd like some tribal call to war, the stomping began.

"Chief," she said. "This's about to explode."

"Hold on," Gamache said, opening the channels so all officers could hear him. "Steady. Steady. This will pass."

He was within twenty feet of the agents lined up in front of the stage. If there was a rush, they'd be the first to get it.

He looked at their faces. Mostly young. Strong. Determined. Eyes forward. He saw the officer in charge of that section say something, and they, as one, stepped their right legs back. A subtle move to brace themselves, while not threatening the men and women facing them.

None of his agents had a gun. It was far too easy, in an unpredictable and potentially violent crowd, to have someone take the weapon off them in the mêlée. And use it. He'd seen it happen, with tragic results.

So Gamache had ordered their firearms be left in the detachment. But they did have truncheons.

Before the doors had been opened to admit the spectators, he'd briefed the agents on the worst-case scenario. And he made it clear that the worst case was when the cops, there to restore order and protect people, escalated the violence.

"This"—he held up the bat-like truncheon—"is a tool, not a weapon. Understood?"

"*Oui, patron*," they said. Many were still annoyed at having to leave their guns behind.

As Gamache gave them a quick refresher course, Monsieur Viau, the caretaker, watched, gripping the handle of his mop as though it were a club.

"These are your neighbors, your friends," said Gamache. "Think of them as your mother and father, your brothers and sisters. These are not bad people. They're not your enemy. Do not hit them except as a very last resort."

He'd looked into their eyes, drilling home his point. They nodded.

Then the Chief Inspector demonstrated how to use the club defensively, to pry people apart if they were fighting. To restrain, while using restraint.

He could see by their faces that they really had no idea what they'd be facing. Many were feigning boredom, implying experience they did not actually have. Because those who'd been in a riot were paying close attention. Mostly the senior officers. Lacoste, Beauvoir, and a few others.

They knew what could happen. How ugly it could get, and how quickly.

When this event was first assigned to him, two days earlier, Chief Inspector Gamache had asked that a single local agent, already on duty, be loaned to him. Just for the hour.

Then, as he'd learned more about the professor, his contingent had grown to fifteen agents, brought in from regions nearby. He'd placed the calls himself, asking junior agents and senior commanders if they'd be willing to join him that one day.

None had refused.

And now there were thirty-five Sûreté agents watching, as he went over, quickly, expertly, how to drop their grandmothers to the floor. If necessary.

Abigail Robinson had reached the podium. She bent the microphone closer to her and spoke her first words.

"Hello? *Bonjour?* Can you hear me?" Her voice was calm, cheerful, almost matter-of-fact.

It was not what Gamache had expected, nor was it what the crowd had expected.

The surge stopped. The stomping petered out. The crowd grew still, and quiet, except for a few random shouts.

And Gamache immediately saw the genius of it.

Instead of launching into her talk, she'd greeted them in the most polite, most familiar fashion. And since these were, for the most part, good, decent people, they responded. In the most polite fashion.

Gamache wasn't fooled. This disarming start hadn't miraculously

40

eased all the emotions. It was a respite that allowed Professor Robinson to begin, to be heard.

Yes, it was brilliant. And calculated.

She smiled. "Oh, good. I'm always afraid when I make what feels like such an endless walk from way over there"—she pointed to the wings—"to here, that once I arrive, the microphone won't work. Can you imagine?"

Now her shoulders rose and she chortled. There was no other word for it. A cross between a laugh and a giggle. It was charming, self-deprecating. And, once again, calculated.

The place grew even quieter. A few laughs could be heard.

The friends and neighbors, mothers and fathers, sisters and brothers were listening. Drawn in. Far from the frothing maniac the protesters had expected, what they saw was their sister, their aunt, the woman next door. Standing alone on the gym stage, smiling.

She wished them a merry Christmas, a *joyeux Noël*. A happy new year and a *bonne année*.

There was scattered applause for her Anglo-accented French.

And then she went into a dissertation. Citing figures. Dates. Data. Facts compiled by various sectors both before and during the pandemic.

She cited projections.

As she talked, Gamache realized it wasn't just words. There was a rhythm, a cadence, to what she was saying.

There was a musicality in her voice, a beat not unlike Bach, as she went through the litany of disasters. Of crises facing not just the health sector but also education. Infrastructure. The environment. Pensions. Jobs. The monstrous national debt that would eat the children's futures.

What was clear was that there were too many calls on dwindling resources. It was a crisis heightened but not created by the pandemic.

The place had grown quiet as she methodically built her case.

Her voice never wavered, never rose above a drone. It was calming, mesmerizing, and somehow made what she was saying sound reasonable.

The Chief Inspector knew, from years of interrogating murderers, that if you yelled at someone, they clammed up. Walls rose. Minds and mouths closed.

But if you spoke softly, their defenses might drop. At least you had a better chance of it.

That's what she was doing. With a melodic voice, Abigail Robinson was crawling into people's heads. Mining their bleakest thoughts, drawing forth their buried fears.

As he listened, Armand Gamache realized that the Chancellor had been right.

This lecture on statistics, on mathematics, was also music. And it was art. Albeit a dark art. Not at all the sort Clara Morrow created, with her luminous portraits.

Professor Robinson was, before their very eyes, turning thoughts into words, and words into action. Facts into fear. Angst into anger. It was artful.

Abigail Robinson was not simply an academic, she was an alchemist.

This was the moment, Gamache knew from watching her previous talks, when she'd reached the turning point.

Having painted a bleak picture of a society on the verge of collapse, she would now offer hope. *All will be well.* Professor Robinson would tell them what they needed to do to move forward into a bright new world.

She would give them her simple solution. One revealed, ironically, by the pandemic itself.

Abigail Robinson paused now and looked at the gathering.

As did Gamache.

What he saw in their upturned faces was desperation. They'd just been through hell. They might've lost family members, friends. Many had lost jobs.

But he also saw hope.

Still, he wondered how many who'd followed her this far would be willing to take this next step. And he wondered how many who'd come to protest had changed their minds after listening to her rhythmic litany of disaster.

He could even see some of the agents, especially the younger ones lined up in front of the stage, turning to grab quick glances at her.

Their senior officer obviously said something because the faces snapped back forward. But still . . .

A child was hoisted up on a man's shoulders. Then another one.

"Inspector Lacoste—" he began.

"I see them, *patron*," she said. "I have eyes on twelve children in the auditorium. Agents are ready to grab them if things turn."

"*Bon*. Inspector Beauvoir, how many children came into the hall?"

There was silence.

"Inspector?"

"Sir," came an unfamiliar female voice. "He's not here, but Inspector Beauvoir did make note. There are fifteen children."

"*Merci*. Inspector Lacoste, did you hear that."

"I did. I'm on it."

Gamache could see that the press forward had begun. Professor Robinson had come to the *moment juste*.

The noise in the auditorium rose, as demonstrators awoke from their daze.

"Shame!" they shouted.

"Too late!" the others screamed back.

It became a primal call and response. The beating of drums before battle.

"Where did Inspector Beauvoir go?" Gamache asked the agent at the door.

"But there is a solution," he heard Professor Robinson break her silence, as his sharp eyes scanned the now pulsing crowd. "It takes courage, but I think you have that."

"He's inside," the agent said.

"Inside?" said Gamache. "Are you sure?"

If it was true, Jean-Guy Beauvoir had disobeyed orders, abandoned his post, and, worst of all, brought the gun in with him. There was now a loaded weapon in this crowd.

It was not only shocking, it was unforgivable.

"Yessir."

"Shame, shame," half the crowd chanted.

"Too late," came the angry response.

"—money and time and expertise are being spent on what is futile. Hopeless. Even cruel. Do you want your parents, your grandparents, to suffer, as too many already have?"

"No!" came the cry from the crowd.

"Do you want your children to suffer?"

"No!"

"Because they will. They are. But we can change that."

Gamache stepped out onto the stage, quickly assessing the situation. He saw that, while the situation was volatile, his officers had it under control.

Still, he could . . . No one would blame him . . .

But he did not stop it. Instead he gave a brief, reassuring nod to the nearest agent on the front line. A young man who reminded him of another impossibly young agent from a lifetime ago.

The man nodded back and turned forward, to face the crowd.

"But it's not too late. I've done the numbers and the solution is clear, if not easy," Abigail Robinson was saying. "If the pandemic taught us anything, it's that not everyone can be saved. Choices must be made. Sacrifices must be made."

Gamache kept his eyes forward.

"It's called—"

From the middle of the auditorium there came a rapid series of explosions.

Bang. Bang. Bang.

Gamache flinched but recovered almost immediately. Running to the center of the stage, he pointed into the crowd. "Lacoste!"

"On it."

He saw her leap off the riser and head toward the smoke rising from the middle of the hall. Saw the line of Sûreté officers brace.

Saw the crowd ducking down as it reacted to the explosions. Heard the screams. Saw the beginning of a panicked surge for the doors.

Holding up his arms, he shouted, "*Arrêtez!* Stop. They're firecrackers. Stop."

He knew they weren't shots. He'd heard too many of those to be fooled. But the fathers and mothers, sons and daughters, husbands and wives squeezed together in the hot gym had not.

It sounded to them like automatic weapons fire. *Rat-ta-ta-ta-tat.* And they did what any reasonable person would do.

They ducked, then turned toward the exits, in the natural instinct to get out.

"Stop," he shouted. "There's no danger."

No one was listening. No one heard.

He pushed Professor Robinson aside and grabbed the microphone off the podium.

"Stop!" he commanded. "Those are firecrackers. Stop where you are. Now."

He repeated it quickly, in French and English. In a clear, authoritative voice, until slowly, slowly the panic eased. The surge ebbed, stopping just sort of a crush.

Isabelle Lacoste found the string of firecrackers, black and smoldering, and held it up.

The room began to settle. There was even some nervous laughter as foes a moment earlier smiled at each other in relief.

And then there was another loud bang and the wood of the podium beside Gamache splintered.

This was no firecracker.

Gamache knocked Professor Robinson to the floor as another shot hit the stage inches from them.

He covered Robinson's body with his own, squeezing his eyes shut, and waited for the next shot.

He'd had to do this once before, when there'd been an attempt on the Premier's life. They'd been out for dinner together at the bistro Leméac in Montréal and were walking along rue Laurier one summer's evening. The Sûreté du Québec security detail was just ahead and just behind the leader of the province as Armand strolled beside him, the two deep in conversation when the shots were fired.

Fortunately, the would-be assassin was a terrible shot and the Chief Inspector was quick to react, knocking the Premier to the ground and covering him.

When it was over and they were safe, the Premier, who was openly gay, joked that that would be the photo on social media within minutes. The Premier and the head of homicide frolicking together on the grass.

"You could do worse, *mon ami*," said Gamache.

"As could you."

Still, neither man would forget the look on the other's face in those split seconds, as they hit the ground and the bullets struck around them. As each waited for the sharp shock, as one found its mark.

Now Gamache covered Abigail Robinson with his body. To die for the Premier was one thing, but for her?

"Got him," came Lacoste's crisp voice in his earphone. "We've got the shooter. Chief, are you all right?"

"*Oui.*" He got quickly to his feet and saw that Lacoste and two others had wrestled a man to the floor.

But he also saw a terrible sight. Bodies everywhere. Hundreds of people sprawled on the floor. He knew, in his rational mind, that they were not hurt. That the only bullets fired had come in his direction.

But still, he felt a wave of horror.

And then they stirred.

Mere seconds had passed since the first shot. He knew this was the gap, the gasp, before shock turned to real panic. It was that moment of grace when a riot might be avoided.

He found the microphone among the debris of the podium and, grabbing it, he called for calm.

Keeping his voice steady, standing visible and reassuring on the stage, apparently unperturbed, Gamache repeated over and over, in French and English, that they were safe.

He almost said, "*Ça va bien aller.*" *All will be well.* But stopped himself.

The problem was, Gamache had no idea if there was another shooter still out there. Or even a bomb.

They needed to evacuate the place as quickly as possible. And he saw his agents doing exactly that. Monsieur Viau, the caretaker, was also guiding people to the exits. Using his mop to push them along.

"Abby!" Debbie Schneider ran across the stage to where Professor Robinson was sitting up.

He turned briefly, saw she was unhurt, and told them to get off the stage.

As he directed the operations, as the place emptied out, as Lacoste contained the gunman, Inspector Beauvoir appeared.

"*Patron*—" he began, but was cut off.

"I'll deal with you later," Gamache snapped. "Go outside. Help the injured."

He could see through the open doors the flashing lights of emergency vehicles. In another act most had considered a vast overreaction, Gamache had asked that two ambulances and a team of first responders be at the ready.

"We've secured the gunman," said Lacoste.

"Search the building," he commanded. "Block the roads into and out of the University. Search every person and go over every vehicle."

The auditorium was almost empty now. The place littered with boots and tuques and mittens. Buttons and papers. A few handbags and knapsacks and phones were on the floor. But no people. No bodies, Gamache saw with relief.

The officers not searching the building were outside, along with the paramedics, tending to the shocked and frightened people. Checking for injuries. Checking IDs. Checking for weapons, in case a second attacker had slipped out with the crowd.

The gunman, head down and cuffed, was being led out the back way.

Monsieur Viau stood at the far end, by the big doors, gripping the long handle of his mop. A warrior-king surveying his land after a battle.

Through the open door, through the darkness, Gamache could see the outline of men and women moving in front of the flashing lights of emergency vehicles.

People were sitting in snowbanks, while others knelt to help. All animosity forgotten. For now.

Monsieur Viau lifted his mop in acknowledgment, as Gamache lifted his hand. In thanks. Then the caretaker left, and Gamache was alone.

He looked at the room and thanked God and his lucky stars that no one, as far as he knew, had been killed. Though the shock, the psychic damage, would be with each person for a long time to come.

"Could've been worse," came the voice behind him.

Gamache didn't turn. Couldn't turn. Could not stand to look at her. "Please leave."

"You saved my life," said Professor Robinson. "Thank you."

He continued to stare straight ahead until he heard her footsteps recede and the place again fell into silence.

He closed his eyes, and in that silence Chief Inspector Gamache again heard the shots. The shouts and screams. The wails of the children.

And he heard the last word Professor Abigail Robinson had uttered. "Mercy—"

The solution is called mercy—

And then the firecrackers had gone off, and the shots were fired. But Gamache could finish her sentence. The word she didn't get a chance to say.

Killing. But it wasn't mercy killing she was proposing. It was, he knew, just plain old killing.

CHAPTER 7

Late that night, when the family was asleep and they were finally alone at home, Jean-Guy approached Armand.

He stood in the doorway of the study.

Armand knew Jean-Guy was there but needed to finish this last report and send it out. His fingers dashed along the keyboard. Part of him knew he was really too tired to write this message, but he needed to get it off.

Then he could crawl into bed with Reine-Marie. Could curl his body around hers and know that he could rest for a little while.

Finally he hit send. Then, taking off his glasses, he turned toward the door.

"Yes?"

"Can we talk?"

It was the last thing Armand wanted to do. He was drained after what had happened and the aftermath.

Taking care of the injured. The search of the building, and the people, and the vehicles.

Interviewing witnesses, none of whom saw anything, though that was probably shock. Someone saw something, they just needed time to come back to their senses.

They had the gunman, a local man named Édouard Tardif. Aged fifty-three. He worked cutting trees in the forest, for firewood.

Tardif had been questioned but refused to say anything. Including whether he had an accomplice.

"What news on the weapon?" Gamache had asked, on leaving the interview room.

"A handgun," said Beauvoir, almost running to keep up with the striding Gamache. "Registered to him. He belongs to the local gun club and keeps it locked up there, of course. The manager says he's a very good shot. Tardif visited the place yesterday, fired a few rounds, then left. I'm getting the security video."

"Right. We need to interview his family and friends. Employers. Anyone who might've shared his view about Professor Robinson. And we need to track down those fireworks."

Tardif's wife and family were shocked. Could not believe he'd do that. The only one they couldn't contact was his brother, who was on a snowmobile trip six hundred kilometers north, in the Abitibi.

He'd left that afternoon.

"Find him," said Gamache. "Those fireworks and the gun got into the gym somehow. Presumably not with Tardif through the front door."

He'd glared at Beauvoir, who colored and stammered, "No. I mean yes. No, I mean no."

The media had descended on the University by then.

Chief Inspector Gamache had stood outside the gym, in the cold and the glare of camera lights, and issued a statement, reassuring the population that the gunman had been arrested.

Then he answered reporters' questions.

"What's his name?"

"We won't be releasing that just yet."

"Is he local?"

"I can't tell you yet. The investigation is ongoing."

"What investigation? If you have him? Was there anyone else involved?"

"We're looking into that. We have to cover all possibilities."

"How did he get a weapon into the event?"

"That we don't know. We had officers at the door, making sure no one entered with a weapon. We confiscated some bottles, some placards. But no knives or guns. I don't think anyone could have gotten through with a handgun."

"And yet they did."

"Yes. They did. And we'll find out how." He looked into the cameras and asked that anyone who might have information come forward. And that anyone who'd been at the event and recorded it send the video to the Sûreté.

The email address and phone number would appear on screen when the news was broadcast.

He answered a few more questions, made a couple more statements, before turning away to rejoin the investigation.

"Why was Professor Robinson even allowed to speak?" one of the reporters called out. "Given what she's advocating, shouldn't you have stopped it?"

Gamache stopped and turned back. Pausing for a moment, he looked into the glaring lights.

"I'll be honest with you, it was something we struggled with. There are, in any free society, competing and sometimes contradictory needs. The need for freedom of expression, even those, especially those views we might not agree with. And the need for safety. A judgment was made that Professor Robinson's thesis, though controversial, did not break any laws and therefore should proceed."

"She's advocating mass murder," yelled someone who might, or might not, have been a member of the press. "Are you saying you agree?"

Gamache heaved a sigh, stronger than he'd expected, before saying, "I'm saying that my job is to defend the law. And the law, in this case, was clear. Therefore, the role of the Sûreté was to protect the people inside the auditorium. I need to get back to work. When there's more to report, I promise to let you know. For now, everyone needs to know this was a targeted, isolated event, and they are safe."

"You thought that about the lecture," a voice called after him, as he stepped away from the microphone and the harsh lights. "And look what happened."

Gamache returned to the gym, setting up a temporary office backstage, to oversee the million details that went into an investigation of this sort. The witnesses to interview, the evidence to collect. The reports to write. The phone calls to make and take. There were a hundred things his investigators needed to do, and a hundred things only the Chief Inspector could do.

Édouard Tardif had no record. There was no history of violence. It seemed he'd woken up that morning, picked up a gun, and decided to murder someone. In a crowded auditorium.

Of course, one of the big questions remained, how did the gun get inside? Did they miss it at the door, or was there indeed an accomplice? Someone who hid it beforehand?

Gamache knew, as did the other senior officers, that they had to assume there had been someone else. And they suspected that someone had fled to the Abitibi, knowing his brother would be caught immediately.

Finally, Armand had arrived home. Jean-Guy had stayed behind, supposedly to coordinate with the Sûreté in the Abitibi and organize the other units who would work through the night.

But they both knew the real reason.

He did not want to drive back with his Chief. Even less, with his father-in-law. He did not want to be alone with the man who could barely look him in the eyes.

By the time Armand returned to Three Pines, the older children were fed, bathed, and already in bed.

Reine-Marie met him at the door and, embracing him, she whispered, "We heard."

After decades as the spouse of a senior cop, she knew not to ask if he was all right. Clearly he was not. Instead she just held him tight.

"Jean-Guy?" asked Annie, standing at the door and shielding baby Idola from the gust of winter that came in with her father.

"He'll be home soon." Armand closed the door, took off his parka, then reached for his granddaughter.

With Annie's permission, he took Idola upstairs and, rolling up his sleeves, he bathed her, careful to keep her upright. The scent of the baby soap so soothing.

He put on her diaper, his hands expertly folding and fastening and testing.

Not too tight. Not too loose. "Just right," he whispered.

He chatted with her the whole time. Singing a little. Resting his large hand on her back and neck and head as she smiled up at him.

Such a cheerful child.

He thought of Abigail Robinson and tried to suppress his rage. And the fleeting thought of what would have happened had he not reacted quite so quickly.

When he'd put Idola in her crib, Armand kissed Honoré, who was once again sleeping with his toboggan. Then he went next door to his granddaughters.

Florence had made a tent of her bedding and was under it with a flashlight, reading *The Little Prince*.

She looked guilty when her papa interrupted, but he gave her a wintergreen mint and reassured her he wouldn't tell.

Once downstairs, he found Daniel at the door with the dogs.

"Walk?" Daniel asked.

"Me or the dogs?"

"Both. If you promise not to run away, I won't put you on a leash."

Armand laughed. The first one in what seemed a very long time. Father and son strolled around the deserted village green, heads bowed, bobbing slightly and in unison with each step. They chatted. They paused, to find Orion's Belt and the Big Dipper in the Northern Hemisphere sky. They threw snowballs for Henri to catch, while old Fred and little Gracie looked on and seemed to say, *Silly dog*.

Daniel finally asked, "Can you talk about it, Dad?"

In the dark, Armand nodded. "It's probably good to talk."

And so he did. And when he finished, Daniel had questions, which Armand answered fully. More fully than he'd answered the reporters. He knew Daniel would keep this private.

Though there was one thing Armand didn't tell him.

Jean-Guy had returned by then and was sitting with everyone else in the living room. When Daniel and Armand returned, they found the television on.

"We were going to watch the news. Do you mind, Armand?" Reine-Marie asked.

"*Non*. I need to see how it's reported." He poured a weak scotch and joined them.

Watching all this with shrewd eyes, Annie knew something was wrong. Her father hadn't spoken to her husband. Could barely look at him. And vice versa.

"What's wrong? What happened?" she whispered to Jean-Guy as they sat together on the sofa.

But he just shook his head.

The events at the Université de l'Estrie led the news.

"Are you kidding," whispered Stephen, as the reporter described Professor Robinson's thesis, her growing popularity, and the increasingly violent confrontations.

There was footage, taken from phones in the hall. It was, of course, shaky, but it gave the sense of what had happened.

The firecrackers going off.

Then the screams, the shouts. The beginning of panic. They could hear Armand's voice, calling for calm. And then the shots.

Reine-Marie inhaled sharply, a sort of gasp. The others looked at Armand. Except Jean-Guy, who was staring straight ahead.

Abigail Robinson was interviewed. She refused to discuss the contents of her lecture, saying what mattered now was that everyone was safe.

It was, Gamache thought as he held Reine-Marie's hand, typically masterful. She came across as caring, thoughtful. Deeply distressed and profoundly empathetic.

It could have been worse.

She didn't say it now. She was far too sophisticated for that. But she'd said it to him.

And she was right. But it could also have been better.

That was, Armand realized, the professor in brief. Stating a truth, but leaving out a greater truth.

He appeared in the report, answering questions about public safety and reassuring the population that this was a targeted crime. They were safe.

On the television, Armand praised the audience members for their extraordinary restraint in not panicking. In helping each other get out, and once out, comforting those who needed help. He talked about their caring for, and about, each other. And what a difference that made.

He praised the building caretaker and the Sûreté officers who'd done their duty under extremely trying conditions.

Annie saw her husband drop his eyes and stare at the rug between his slippered feet.

"Jean-Guy?" she whispered.

He turned and looked at her, managing a smile.

She smiled back. Warm. Loving. Supportive. He wondered how long that would last, if she learned the truth. No, he thought. Not if, but when. He knew he'd tell her what he did, and what he did not do.

But first, he had to talk with Armand.

After the news, they said *bonne nuit* and went to bed. Though Armand still had work to do.

He sat at his laptop, reading updates and writing reports.

Around him the house settled into familiar sounds. Water running. Footsteps on creaky floorboards overhead. Muffled conversations that became hushed, then fell to silence.

The slight groans and cracks as the temperature dropped still further and frost crept once again into the bricks and beams of the old home.

Armand could sense Jean-Guy's presence before he actually saw him. He could always tell when the younger man was close.

After finishing the last email of the evening, a detailed report to the Premier of Québec, he turned.

"Yes?"

"Can we talk?"

Armand reached over and turned off the lamp on his desk, then got up.

Using his reading glasses, he pointed into the empty living room and the fire dying in the grate. As he left his study, he glanced at the stairs, which would take him up to bed. To Reine-Marie.

He could decline to talk with Jean-Guy, explaining that he was tired. It would wait until morning. He could climb the stairs, shower, then pull up the comforter and feel it warming up around his body. Feel her, warm in his arms.

But he knew this really would not wait. They needed to talk. This was another injury done that day. Best not to let it fester.

"Actually," said Jean-Guy, "I was hoping we could get out of the house."

"The dogs have already been walked." Armand had decided to call Gracie a dog, for simplicity's sake. And for his own peace of mind. Who needed a chipmunk in the house?

Though Stephen had now taken to telling the children that, after careful scientific study, he'd concluded that Gracie was almost certainly a ratmunk. A fantastical cross between a chipmunk and a rat.

"With, just possibly," he'd explained as they bent toward him, "a bit of duck. We'll have to wait until Gracie gets older, to see if she can fly."

"Fly?" sighed Zora.

It was hard to tell if the children actually believed him, but they at least humored the elderly man.

"I was thinking the bistro," said Jean-Guy.

Armand glanced at his watch, then out the window. It felt like three in the morning but was, in reality, just before midnight. He could see the bistro's cheerful lights and was pretty sure he recognized Myrna's distinctive silhouette as she passed from the bar to the sofa by the large stone hearth.

Before arriving in Three Pines, Myrna Landers had been a prominent psychologist in Montréal, specializing in especially difficult cases. Part of her work was in the SHU, the Special Handling Unit, reserved for the worst, the most troubled offenders. The insane.

Dr. Landers decided there were better ways, better places, happier people to spend her life with. So she'd submitted her resignation, cleared her case files, sold her home, packed her car, and one spring morning she'd turned south.

Her goal was to keep driving until she finally, Ulysses-like, found a community where the people did not know what an ice scraper was. But, losing her way after only an hour of driving, she crested a hill and found a tiny village in a valley. It wasn't on her map. In fact, her GPS was warning her she was in the middle of a meadow, in the middle of nowhere.

But it was wrong. She was somewhere.

From the top of the hill she could see fieldstone homes, clapboard cottages, and brick shops surrounding a village green. Perennial gardens were in their first blush. There were peonies and huge purple lilac bushes. Banks of lupins grew wild down the slope.

Three massive pine trees stood in the center of the village.

She drove down and parked in front of the shops. Getting out, she took a deep breath of fresh air and fresh baking. Going into the bistro to ask for directions, Myrna Landers sat down, ordered a café au lait and a fresh, crispy, warm amandine. And pretty much never left.

She rented the shop next door, opened a new and used bookstore, and moved into the loft above.

Armand suspected the other glass of red wine he could see Myrna carrying was for her best friend, the artist Clara Morrow.

"*D'accord*," he said to Jean-Guy. "The bistro it is."

As he put on his parka and boots, he wondered why Jean-Guy wanted to leave when the home was warm, and private. But as they walked across to the bistro, he understood.

Home was home. A safe, almost sacred place.

Jean-Guy did not want to sully it with what was about to be said. And once again Armand was reminded of how much he admired and respected Jean-Guy Beauvoir.

Which made what was about to happen all the worse.

CHAPTER 8

———

Clara looked up as the door opened and a gust of cold air blew in, bringing with it Armand and Jean-Guy.

A pretzel she'd absently stuck in her hair, thinking it was a pencil, fell to the old pine floor. Stooping to pick it up, she popped it in her mouth and wondered just how many pencils she might have eaten, mistaking them for pretzels. Since it didn't bear thinking of, she stopped.

"Huh," said Myrna, also turning to look. "Didn't expect to see them."

She began to rock her large body out of the deep sofa. But stopped when she saw Armand's face.

Beside her on the sofa Rosa the duck muttered, "Fuck, fuck, fuck," and also looked surprised. But then ducks often did.

"Who's that?" asked the woman in the armchair closest to the fire. Unused to winter, she wore layers of itchy wool under her flowing fuchsia caftan. A wool scarf around her neck met the hijab covering her head, framing her lined face.

Though only in her early twenties, Haniya Daoud looked much older.

Her lips were thin in displeasure. Her eyes narrowed in suspicion.

"Cops," said Ruth Zardo. "Sûreté du Québec. Brutal. Especially to people of color, as Myrna knows. Probably heard you were here." She looked around. "Too late to run."

"For chrissake, Ruth," snapped Myrna. She turned to Haniya. "It's not true."

But it was too late. The newcomer was gripping Ruth's thin arm. "Save me. I know what police do to people like me. You have to help me." Her voice had risen in panic. "Please. I'm begging you."

Ruth, seeing what she'd created, was desperately trying to walk it back. "No. No, no, no" was all she could get out.

Haniya started to wail and rock back and forth. Rosa let out a mighty "Fuuuuuuck."

Only when Myrna started to laugh did Ruth get it. Her eyes narrowed, and she looked at Haniya. "Are you messing with me?"

"And why would I do that?" the young woman said, perfectly composed now and smiling.

But there was a sharp glint in her eye, which Myrna the psychologist and Clara the artist both recognized. It wasn't amusement, it was malice.

Armand and Jean-Guy had taken off their coats and were making their way across the bistro, with its wooden beams and wide-plank floor. Huge fieldstone fireplaces on either end were lit and throwing warmth.

Neither man acknowledged their friends and neighbors. They kept their eyes forward and kept walking.

A hush had descended. Everyone in the bistro knew what had happened at the University that afternoon. Ruth gave them her usual greeting, but they ignored the raised finger.

Jean-Guy in particular looked grim.

Armand passed any number of places before choosing a small round table far from everyone else.

He pointed, indicating Jean-Guy should sit at the far seat. The one in the corner. Jean-Guy wondered if that was on purpose. Like a naughty child.

Very little of what the Chief Inspector did was without purpose.

As he squeezed in, Jean-Guy glanced at the group by the fireplace. How he wished they were headed there. To sit by the fire and talk about a day that had been uneventful. To hear how many books Ruth had stolen from Myrna, claiming to believe her bookstore was a library. To hear about Clara's latest painting and watch crumbs drop from her hair as she moved her expressive hands through it.

To exchange insults with the crazy old poet, and pretend not to hear the mutterings of that odd duck. To be joined by Olivier and Gabri, at the end of their day running the bistro, and pretend not to be interested in gossip about who'd be at the New Year's Eve party the next night, up at the big house on the hill.

As they'd walked over to their table, he'd noticed there was someone else sitting by the fire. Someone he didn't recognize. An older woman in a hijab.

And it came to Jean-Guy who this must be. Myrna had said she'd be picking her up in Montréal that evening. There was much excitement in the village about the arrival of Haniya Daoud. A woman who'd endured so much. Survived so much. Spoken at the UN. Led a movement for social justice. Led so many others to freedom. Was nominated for the Nobel Peace Prize.

Myrna Landers, with the support of others in Three Pines, had been among the first to answer Haniya Daoud's call for help. A human rights campaign was launched, in a corner of the world few seemed to know about and fewer still seemed to care about.

Madame Daoud was in Canada to thank Myrna and others for their support.

Now Jean-Guy wondered, in passing, if she'd be at the New Year's Eve party. Did people like that go to parties, or was it too frivolous?

He also wondered if he'd be going, or still be stuck in the corner.

All this flashed through his mind as he sucked in his stomach, whose size was beginning to surprise him, and maneuvered into the seat.

"What will you have?" Armand asked.

"I'll get it," said Jean-Guy, struggling to stand up again.

"Sit. I will. What do you want?"

As Armand spoke, Olivier was making his way across the room to their table.

The bistro owner was smiling. Not fully, but warmly. Like everyone else, he'd heard what had happened. Seen the reports on the internet and television.

"Armand," he said, and put a hand on his arm. "All right?"

Armand smiled thinly and nodded. "Fine."

"I believe it. You?" he asked Jean-Guy.

"Okay."

Olivier studied them for a moment, and while wanting to say something that would help, he could see that whatever was wrong, it was beyond his ability to fashion comfort into words.

So he offered what he could. "We have some lemon meringue pie going begging."

"Just a sparkling water for me, *patron*," said Armand. "*Merci.*"

"I'll have a Diet Coke. Thanks." *Don't leave, don't leave, don't leave.*

Olivier left, offering a glance of support to Jean-Guy. While he could not fathom what was up, he knew a world of trouble when he saw it.

As he made his way back to the bar, he headed off Gabri. His partner had been on his way over to greet Armand and Jean-Guy and commiserate.

"Don't."

They waited to talk until their drinks were put in front of them.

A slice of lemon bobbed in Armand's sparkling water. Though he hadn't asked for it, it was, Olivier knew, how he liked it. And a twist of lime in Jean-Guy's drink. As he liked his.

Gabri had insisted on being the one to take them their orders. Large and naturally voluble, he didn't say a word as he placed a wedge of lemon meringue pie between them.

"*Merci,*" said Armand, while Jean-Guy stared at it as though at a holy relic.

The toe of St. Jude, of lost causes. The knucklebone of Ste. Marguerite, the patron saint of people rejected by religious orders, which made her Jean-Guy's favorite saint.

And now the holy tarte of St. Gabri. Though Jean-Guy knew even this offering could not work miracles. Unless Gabri could also bake a time machine, there'd be no answer to his prayers.

When Gabri left, a crushing silence descended.

The red, blue, and green Christmas lights on the huge pines on the village green played on Armand's face. The cheery lights at stark contrast to the look in his eyes as Armand waited for his second-in-command to say something.

"Would you like my resignation?" asked Jean-Guy, quietly.

"I'd like an explanation first, then I'll decide."

"I'm sorry."

Chief Inspector Gamache remained silent. Waiting for more. But his hands, clasped together on the table, tightened, until the knuckles were white and the intertwined fingers almost purple, suffused with trapped blood.

"I wanted to hear her for myself," said Jean-Guy. "I wanted to see what it was about. To get a sense of how much support she really has. How convincing she could be. How dangerous she really is."

Jean-Guy waited for his father-in-law to say something. But in the prolonged silence he realized that would not happen.

His father-in-law was not there.

Jean-Guy was sitting across from his boss. The head of homicide for the Sûreté du Québec. A man who'd once led the entire provincial police and who'd turned down the offer to head the national Royal Canadian Mounted Police.

Instead Armand Gamache had returned to homicide. To hunt killers.

Sitting across from Jean-Guy was the man who'd found him years ago, banished to some remote Sûreté outpost. Stuck in the basement evidence locker because none of the other agents could stand working with him.

Chief Inspector Gamache, there to investigate a murder, had gone down to the locker, taken one look at Agent Beauvoir, and requested he be assigned to the case. The station commander was all too happy to do it, no doubt in hopes Agent Beauvoir would get himself killed. Or disgraced and fired. Either would work for the commander.

As they'd driven through the woods, to the side of the lake where the body had washed up, Chief Inspector Gamache had talked. In a quiet voice he'd instructed the young agent on what to do, and what not to do.

Once parked, Gamache had stopped Beauvoir from getting out of the car. He'd looked him square in the face, holding him there.

"There's something else you need to know."

"Yes, I've got it. Don't disturb the evidence. Don't touch the body. You've told me all that, and it's pretty obvious."

"There are," said the Chief, unbothered and undeterred by what he'd just heard, "four sentences that lead to wisdom. Do with them as you will."

No one had ever spoken to Beauvoir in that way.

Do with them as you will. Who talks like that?

But, more than that oddly formal phrase, no one in Beauvoir's experience had ever strung together three words without saying "fuck," or "*calice*," or "*merde*." Including, especially, his father. And his mother, for that matter. And they sure had never mentioned wisdom in his presence.

He stared at this older man, who spoke so softly. And Jean-Guy Beauvoir found himself actually listening.

"'I'm sorry.' 'I was wrong.' 'I don't know.'" As he listed them, Chief Inspector Gamache raised a finger, until his palm was open. "'I need help.'"

Beauvoir looked into Gamache's eyes and in them he saw something else that was new. It was kindness.

It had so shocked him that he blushed. And blustered. And practically fell out of the car in his hurry to get away from something he didn't understand, and that terrified him.

But he'd never forgotten. That moment. When he'd met kindness for the first time. And been shown the path to wisdom in four simple, though not easy, sentences.

Jean-Guy had often wondered exactly what the storied head of homicide had seen in the fucked-up, insecure, neurotic, and egotistical agent. Probably the same thing Gamache saw in his other recruits.

The homicide department was made up of the dregs, the refuse. The lost and the broken. But each had been found by the man sitting across from Beauvoir now.

The night before, over Idola's crib, he'd begged Armand to let him be part of the team.

That morning, Armand had agreed. And assigned him the duty of securing the outside of the auditorium.

After the briefing and just before they'd opened the doors, the Chief Inspector had taken Lacoste and Beauvoir aside. Gamache had reached behind him and taken his own handgun off his belt, and given it to Jean-Guy.

"You said no—" Beauvoir began.

"I know what I said, but we need at least one officer with a weapon, in case. And it needs to be you, the senior officer outside the building. If there's trouble—"

"I'll be there, *patron*," said Beauvoir, taking the weapon in its worn holster and attaching it to his belt.

But he hadn't been.

He'd abandoned his post. Disregarded orders. Left a junior agent in charge outside. Not because some crisis had arisen inside, but because he wanted to see Robinson for himself.

The cheery light from the Christmas trees in the Chief Inspector's eyes could not hide the outrage there. In fact, they somehow made it worse. Like the angry placards in crayon.

"I've never believed in the temporary insanity defense," said Jean-Guy, finding his voice. "I thought it was bullshit. Now I believe it. It was a moment of insanity."

"That's your explanation? Temporary insanity?"

"I don't know." Beauvoir dropped his gaze to the table, then he looked back up into those eyes. "I don't really know why I did it. It was wrong, and I'm sorry."

"I think you do know." Gamache's voice was strained, his anger barely contained.

"I don't. I've asked myself over and over. I can't explain it."

"Of course you can," said the Chief. "You're just too afraid to look that deep."

Jean-Guy felt a flush as his own anger rushed up his neck to his face, burning his cheeks.

"I need more than 'I don't know.'" Gamache's eyes bored into Beauvoir's. "You abandoned your post. You essentially left the entrance unsupervised. You took a weapon into an incendiary situation, the very thing I'd said must not be done. You endangered lives. Do you realize how close it came to a tragedy? Not the professor or me getting shot, but hundreds of people trampling each other to death? The children—"

Gamache stopped, unable to go on. Overcome with the nightmare vision of what might have been.

The lines down his face became crevices. There was a noise in his throat, as he gagged on his own words, his own rage. It was almost the rattle they'd heard too often, in those about to die. And this felt to Beauvoir like a sort of death. The end of something precious and, as it turned out, fragile.

Trust.

Jean-Guy watched in dismay, knowing if trust had died, he'd murdered it.

Gamache composed himself and finally got the words out. "You made it worse."

The words were like a slap across Beauvoir's face. And with it he seemed to wake up. To come to. And he saw with clarity why he'd done it. It might not be enough to satisfy the Chief Inspector, but it might satisfy his father-in-law.

"Idola—" Jean-Guy began, but only got the one word out.

"Don't you dare blame your daughter. This isn't about her and you know it."

And that was it. Jean-Guy exploded.

"What I know . . . sir, is that I'm her father. You're only her grandfather." All bonds had broken and he was again free from all constraint. "You're nothing. You'll be long dead and buried, and she'll still be living with us. Forever. And then, one day, she'll be Honoré's burden. So don't you ever, ever fucking tell me what is or is not about my daughter. Because everything is."

By the time he finished, his snarl had turned into a shout. His hands gripped the table, and in his anger, his sudden madness, he jerked it and the lemon meringue pie bounced off and crashed to the floor.

The bistro had grown quiet as patrons stared, then looked away. As though Jean-Guy had unexpectedly stripped down to his underwear. To what normally never showed.

And then, with that one word, that too fell. Until he was as naked as the day he was born.

Burden. Burden.

Another silence enveloped them, punctured only by Jean-Guy's small gasping cries as he struggled for breath, and fought off the tears that were taking him under.

He shoved his chair back, or tried to. Tried to get up. To get away. But he was too tightly wedged in.

And still Gamache said nothing.

About to yell at him again, to scream at Gamache to let him go, Jean-Guy looked directly at the Chief. And saw tears in his father-in-law's eyes.

"What's wrong with them?" asked Haniya Daoud.

She alone had continued to stare.

"Nothing," said Clara. "They've had a hard day."

"Yes." Haniya recognized the larger, older cop, from the news reports. "Why don't you like them? What've they done to you?"

"Nothing," said Ruth.

"Well, they must've done something. When they came in, you did this." Haniya held up her middle finger. "I believe it means 'go fuck yourself.'"

Myrna's brows shot up in surprise.

"It's also a term of endearment," said Ruth. "If you win the Nobel Peace Prize, you might start with that."

Haniya Daoud smiled, but her eyes were hard as she stared at the elderly woman. Then over to the two Sûreté officers.

"They're angry. Unstable. And no doubt armed." She looked around. "I don't think I like it here."

CHAPTER 9

⁓

Jean-Guy dropped his head and covered his face, his hands muffling the sobs.

Armand remained quiet, though the laugh lines at the corners of his eyes were filled with tears.

He brought out a clean handkerchief and pushed it across the table, then used a napkin on his own face.

Finally, after wiping his face and blowing his nose, Idola's father looked at her grandfather.

But before Jean-Guy could speak, Armand said, "I'm sorry. You're right. Everything in your life now is about Idola and Honoré. I should have known that. Forgive me. I should never have put you in that position. It was wrong of me."

What was it about this situation, about Abigail Robinson, that brought out the worst in people? Though Gamache now faced his own uncomfortable truth.

Professor Robinson was revealing, not creating, the anger. The fear. And yes, perhaps even the cowardice they kept hidden away. She was like some genetic mutation awakening illnesses that would have normally lain dormant.

She was the catalyst. But the potential, the sickness, was already there.

And now Abigail Robinson was moving across the country, around the world on the internet, triggering, with her dry statistics, people's deepest fears and resentments. Their desperation and hopes.

Jean-Guy had dropped his gaze to the floor and was staring as though comatose at the wreckage of lemon meringue pie.

"What is it?" whispered Armand, sensing there was more. "You can tell me."

"Burden. I called my own daughter a burden." He raised his gaze to Armand's bloodshot eyes. "And . . ."

Armand waited.

". . . and I meant it." Each word had dropped in volume until the last one was barely more than mouthed.

His eyes held a plea now. A watery cry for help. Armand reached across the table and grasped Jean-Guy's arm.

"It's okay," he said softly. "Go on."

Jean-Guy, his mouth open, his breathing rapid, said nothing.

Armand waited. Keeping his hand on Jean-Guy's sweater.

"I . . ." Jean-Guy began and paused to gather himself. "I'm afraid that part of me agrees with her. About aborting . . . I hate her."

It came out in a rush, and he looked up to see how that was greeted. The eyes that met his were thoughtful. And sad.

"Go on," said Armand, quietly.

"She's saying what I've felt. Feel. There're times I wish someone, a doctor, had told us we had to abort. That we had no choice. So that Annie and I wouldn't feel guilty about doing it. So that we wouldn't have . . . her. So that life could be . . . normal. Oh, God." Jean-Guy lifted his hands to his face again. "Help me."

Only when Jean-Guy lowered his hands did Armand speak.

"Why didn't you?"

"What?"

"Abort. You found out the fetus had Down syndrome early enough in the pregnancy. You could have."

Far from being afraid of this question, this conversation, Jean-Guy felt nearly overwhelming relief. The dark thing curled around his heart was exposed. And far from reeling away from him in disgust, Armand was behaving as though all this was painful but perfectly natural.

And maybe, Jean-Guy began to think, it was.

"Annie and I talked about it. Were going to. We had the appointment. But just couldn't. It wasn't religious. You know we don't belong to any church or religion. It just didn't feel right. We decided that if the fetus developed normally in every other way, we'd—"

What, thought Jean-Guy, keep her? It made their daughter sound like a puppy.

But that had been the decision, and the wording they'd used.

"—keep her." Jean-Guy hesitated. "I'm so afraid."

"Of what?"

"That I won't love her enough, that I won't be a good father. That I'm not up to this."

Armand took a deep, long breath, but remained quiet. Letting Jean-Guy get it all out.

"I look at her, Armand, and I don't see Annie, or me. Or you, or Reine-Marie. My parents. I can't see anyone in the family. There're times I think I can't live without her, and there are times she feels like a stranger."

Armand nodded. "She fell far from the tree."

It took Jean-Guy a moment to understand the reference, and then he smiled a little and looked out the frosted window. At the village green. At the three huge pines.

"But maybe not so far," he said quietly, and felt lighter than he had in a long time. Perhaps, he thought, the burden wasn't Idola. It was the shame.

"You know, don't you," Armand said, "that almost every parent feels like you do at some stage. Wishes they could go back to a carefree life. I can't tell you how often Reine-Marie and I looked at Daniel and Annie throwing tantrums and wished they were someone else's children. How many times we preferred the dogs to the kids."

For some reason, hearing that made Jean-Guy want to weep. With relief.

"There's a difference between what you just said about struggling to decide whether to keep Idola," said Armand, his voice steady, certain, "and the mandatory abortion of any fetus that isn't perfect. That's what Professor Robinson is moving toward, what she's now hinting at. It's couched in different language, but it's still a form of eugenics. Can you imagine the people we'd lose?"

Armand could feel his rage threatening to become outrage.

And what Abigail Robinson was advocating went far beyond that.

After studying the statistics on who died in the pandemic, and doing the cost-benefit analysis, she'd concluded there was a way to kill two birds with one stone. And Abigail Robinson was, in her pleasant way, happy to throw that stone.

What if those in unimaginable and uncontrollable pain, the dying, those left bedridden and vegetative by strokes, the frail and sick, what if they could be helped? Their suffering eased? With an injection. They'd be spared suffering, and society would be spared the expense. The burden.

Though that word was never actually used, it was understood. That was the code.

If what had happened by mistake in the pandemic, the wholesale deaths of hundreds of thousands of elderly men and women, were to become policy, wouldn't that be a mercy? A kindness? Humane even?

After all, don't they put down suffering animals? Wasn't that considered an act of love? What could be the difference?

The Royal Commission, when given Robinson's report, had refused to hear it. To legitimize any such suggestion.

But . . .

But then she'd gone on tour, put up her graphs and shown in her calm, measured way the surprisingly clear correlation between money saved and money needed for rebuilding after the economic ruin of the coronavirus.

If they did what her findings suggested, all would be well.

And wasn't assisted suicide already legal in Canada? This was just one step further.

Of course, if Professor Robinson's findings were implemented, it meant the right to die became the obligation to die, but sacrifices needed to be made. In a free society.

And recently, emboldened by growing support, Professor Robinson was delicately turning her attention to the other end of life. Babies. With birth defects.

And how their suffering might be relieved.

It felt now to Gamache as though they were locked in a sort of passion play, the outcome of which would decide their direction for generations to come.

Though there was one way to stop it. If the person leading, legitimizing, the campaign were to . . .

"I've written my report about the events this afternoon," said Gamache, interrupting his own thoughts. "There'll be an inquiry, of course."

"I'll—" Jean-Guy was about to say, . . . *have my letter of resignation to you in the morning.* But was interrupted.

"How?" Gamache asked, leaning forward, his arms on the table, his hands clasped lightly together. "How did the firecrackers get in? And the gun? How did it get into the shooter's hands? Tell me honestly, at what stage did you leave the front door?"

"Not until everyone was in, and the doors had been closed. No one came in behind me, *patron*. And everyone who did get in was thoroughly searched. I know that."

Gamache believed him. "Then someone must've planted it there. Someone who had access to the building beforehand."

"Tardif's brother."

"Yes. Probably. But we need to look further afield. To someone who knew early on that the event was going to happen and could get into the old gym."

"The caretaker?"

"Possibly." Gamache didn't want to think that Éric Viau could be involved, but knew it was a legitimate question.

Unfortunately, security cameras had never been installed in the old gym. Too expensive for a building rarely used and not particularly valuable. But Beauvoir had a thought.

"The video we were watching from her talk a few weeks ago. It was too clear, too professional to be some random audience member with a phone. I bet she hires someone to record her events."

"You might be right. Though the camera would be trained on the stage, not the audience. But you never know. Any luck with the videos taken by spectators?"

"Not yet. Like you said, the phones were aimed at the stage. Then, when the firecrackers went off, everything goes nuts. Too shaky to see anything. You think the two are related? The firecrackers were set off to cause panic and cover the shots? Make sure no one noticed the shooter in the stampede?"

As he replayed it in his mind, Gamache slowly shook his head. "I don't know. It seems a stretch that it could be a coincidence, but if it was planned, it didn't work. The shots were fired thirty-two seconds after the firecrackers went off. By then people had begun to calm down. You'd have thought they were meant to happen together."

"Maybe it was a coincidence, and when Tardif heard the firecrackers, he saw his chance and scrambled to get a shot off. But in his hurry he missed Robinson."

"Could be." Gamache paused in thought. "The manager of the gun club said Tardif is an excellent shot, didn't he? And yet he missed. Twice."

"The stress of battle. We've all missed. With the panic around him, his arm might've been jostled. And he didn't miss by much, *patron*."

"That is true." He was still picking bits of the podium out of his jacket. "If the point was to not just kill Robinson, but cause complete mayhem, then maybe it was executed perfectly. First the firecrackers to shatter nerves, then the shots to guarantee a riot."

To guarantee a stampede for the doors. And the subsequent crush. The injuries and deaths of men, women, and children. What sort of monster, Beauvoir wondered, was this Tardif?

"So even if Professor Robinson survived," he said, "the deaths in the crowd would forever be associated with her campaign. It would kill her movement, if not her."

"But would it?" Gamache asked. "Think about it. A riot with tens, maybe hundreds of injuries and deaths, would be news worldwide. She'd get publicity no amount of money could create. She wouldn't be blamed. In fact, she'd be a victim, narrowly escaping assassination. It's already happening. In the news tonight she had her reaction pretty perfect. Almost as though she'd prepared."

"Wait a minute." Jean-Guy held up his hand, trying to catch up to the Chief's rapid train of thought. "You think she's behind it?"

"Tardif's an expert shot who missed," said Gamache. "Twice."

"Barely," Beauvoir repeated. He also knew, but didn't say, that had he been Tardif, he'd have taken the shot and not missed.

He brought out his notebook and made a note to see if there could have been any contact between Tardif and Professor Robinson or her assistant.

Then he stopped and looked at Gamache.

"You're not fired," said the Chief, understanding the look. "In the reports I sent off tonight, I didn't mention you."

"You lied?"

"The sin of omission. I couldn't see the benefit to the Sûreté, or the public, if an exceptional officer was fired for a one-off event that did not actually hurt anyone."

"If it comes out, you'll be fired," Beauvoir said.

"I've been fired before," said Gamache. "I suspect by now they're tired of changing the name on the door. Look, Jean-Guy, the fault was mine. While I was protecting a stranger, you were protecting your daughter. You said it last night. You warned me. And you were right. She needs protecting. That's your life's work. The one that matters."

"I disobeyed orders," Beauvoir pointed out.

"I know that. Look, do you want to be fired?" When Beauvoir shook his head, Gamache said, "*Bon*, then stop arguing. Just accept."

"*Merci.*" Then something occurred to Jean-Guy. "Is Serious Crime going to take over? It's not a homicide. Not our department."

"*Non.* I've asked to be given the investigation. They've agreed."

Jean-Guy began to ask why Gamache wanted this dog's breakfast of an investigation but stopped himself. He knew why.

If Serious Crime took over, they'd dig into what exactly had happened. And they'd discover Beauvoir's dereliction of duty.

Gamache was doing it to protect him. But Jean-Guy suspected it went further than that.

Armand Gamache wanted to know more about this Abigail Robinson. Knowledge was power, and he needed as much power as he could get, to protect his granddaughter and others like her. And unlike her.

Jean-Guy glanced toward the hearth and Haniya Daoud, the extraordinary woman sitting there. Who'd, at great peril to herself, led so many to safety. Especially children. Leaving her own behind.

He tilted his head toward the fireplace.

Armand, understanding what he meant, stood up and pulled the table from the corner, releasing his prisoner.

As Jean-Guy slipped by, Armand laid a hand on his arm.

"You don't look anything like me," he said. "But you're still my son."

Olivier and Gabri had joined the women, and now all got up to greet Armand and Jean-Guy. Even Ruth.

As he embraced her, Jean-Guy could feel the birdlike bones beneath the moth-eaten sweater, and marveled that maybe the mad old poet was Rosa's mother after all.

"We made a mess, *patron*," Armand said to Olivier, pointing to the pile of pie on the floor. "We can clean it up."

"No worries. I can do that. I have a disposal system." He looked over at Ruth.

The only one who'd remained seated was the guest, in her bright fuchsia-and-gold caftan and hijab.

"I'd like to introduce you to Haniya Daoud," said Myrna. "Haniya, these are our friends Armand Gamache and Jean-Guy Beauvoir."

Now that he was closer, Jean-Guy could see that she was actually quite young. The scarring on her face and her large, worn eyes had made her look much older.

Haniya Daoud stared at them. "You're police."

"Yes. And neighbors," said Armand. "It's an honor to meet you, Madame."

He bowed slightly, not offering a hand he knew she would refuse.

"I don't like police," she said after staring at him for a moment.

"I don't blame you. I wouldn't either if I'd been through what you have."

She smiled at him. "I've met people, men, like you. Dignified. Thoughtful. Powerful. A natural leader, no?" She looked around, and the others nodded. She dropped her voice and leaned forward, so that he had to bend further to hear her. "I also know what you do with that power, and what you'd do to hold on to it. You don't fool me."

"I'm not trying to," he whispered back. "You don't know me,

Madame Daoud. I hope that might change in the next few days." He straightened up. "It's late and we're all tired. I hope you have a good night's rest. Perhaps this will all look different in the morning."

"Will the snow be gone? Will there be flowers and grass?" She glanced toward the window. "I've never seen a bleaker landscape."

"No," said Armand. "The outside won't change, but the inside might. We can but hope."

"We can do more than that, Chief Inspector, if we choose. Hope on its own is rarely enough."

Her smile only deepened the scars, the slashes down her face.

"So you do know who I am," said Gamache. "You called me Chief Inspector."

"I know your rank, and yes, after watching the news reports I think I have a pretty good idea who you are. And what you are."

Haniya Daoud muttered something into the hearth.

"Excusez-moi?" said Gamache.

"Was my French not good? I said"—she raised her voice for all to hear—*"faible."*

She looked into the surprised faces of the friends and neighbors. "Am I pronouncing it right?"

"Oui," said Gabri, and got sharp elbows in both sides from Olivier and Clara.

"Good. I'm just learning. Beautiful language, French. I think '*faible*' sounds better, softer, than the English word. And is more nuanced."

She was speaking directly, and exclusively, to Gamache now, having disappeared the others.

"It's what came to mind when I watched you on the news tonight, Chief Inspector. It means weak. Small. Feeble. Am I right?"

"That is the translation," he agreed, more curious than insulted. Why would Haniya Daoud bother to insult him? To what purpose?

Haniya pushed herself up from the depths of her chair, and said, "I'm going to bed." She looked at Clara. "I believe I'm staying with you. There's a luxury Inn and Spa, just up the hill."

"The Auberge, yes," said Clara.

"Good. I will move there tomorrow. And now I give the smug-faced crowd the traditional gesture of endearment and wish you all a *bonne nuit*."

She raised her middle finger.

As Gamache stepped back to let her pass, she stopped dead in front of him.

"You want to know why I call you weak."

"To be honest, I don't really care."

"I wonder if that's true. I think you care about a lot of things, including how you're perceived. You know what that woman is preaching."

"Abigail Robinson?" said Gamache. "*Oui.*"

"Mass murder. I watched the report, several times. I recognized the look in your eyes when you were watching her. It was loathing, wasn't it."

When he didn't disagree, she continued.

"And yet you not only failed to stop her event, you actually saved her life. You made it look like heroics, but I know better. I know you, Chief Inspector. Met thousands of you. You'll give money. I imagine you even donated to my cause. You'll serve food to the needy and collect coats for the homeless. You'll give impassioned speeches, but you won't actually lift a finger to stop a tyrant. You want others to do it. You want me to do it. You're small. Feeble. A hypocrite. I think . . ." She looked at him more closely. Her eyes running over his face, pausing at his own scar, at his temple. "Yes, I think you're probably a good man, at least you like to think so. Decent. But you're also *faible*. I, on the other hand, am not. I'm neither decent nor weak." When Armand didn't reply, she lowered her voice. "Best to get out of my way."

"They're thinking of giving her the Nobel Peace Prize?" said Ruth, watching her leave. "Who else is on the list? Kim Jong-un? Putin?"

Myrna turned to Armand. "You okay? Looks like she hit a nerve."

Armand gave a short laugh. "My fault for leaving it exposed."

The nerve she'd hit, either by a good guess or some strange insight, was his own earlier thought. Of what would have happened had he moved just a little bit slower . . .

And part of him, part of him, wished he had. And part of him wondered if maybe Haniya Daoud, the Hero of the Sudan, was right. He lacked courage.

It was the second time in as many days he'd been accused of cow-ardice. All to do with Abigail Robinson.

As he and Jean-Guy walked home, Armand thought of the scars on Haniya's young face and wondered what she'd been like as a child. Before. What she would have been like had she been born and raised here.

If her cheeks had been brushed by winter winds and not sliced by machete blades. He wondered what he, what Reine-Marie, what Annie and Daniel would have been like had they been born and raised in her village.

Armand paused at the path to their home and looked up. Into the clear night sky and the stars above. Jean-Guy stopped and also looked up.

While angered by what that woman had said, Jean-Guy mostly felt relief. The weight he'd carried for so long had been at least partially lifted.

It helped that he remembered there were butter tarts in the cookie tin in the kitchen.

Armand spoke, his words directed at the Big Dipper, the huge ves-sel in the sky.

Jean-Guy lowered his gaze. "*Pardon?*"

"I said, *Sneak home and pray you'll never know / the hell where youth and laughter go.*"

"Nice." *Don't tell me it's a poem*, thought Jean-Guy.

"It's a poem," said Armand.

Please, don't make it a long one.

Armand met his eyes and smiled. "She called us a 'smug-faced crowd.'"

"*Oui.*" *Butter tarts. Butter tarts.* "So?"

"I wondered if she was referring to a line from that Sassoon poem, from the Great War."

"Not everything comes from a poem. And how could she know it?"

"She knows far more than I think we realize, *mon ami.*"

Including the hell where youth and laughter go.

But then, he thought, *so do I.*

CHAPTER 10

Y ou'll never believe it."
Annie came bounding down the stairs the next morning. They could hear her heavy tread—*thump, thump, thumpity thump*—and looked toward the door as she practically danced into the kitchen.

Her face flushed, her eyes bright with excitement, she looked at them around the large pine table enjoying their breakfast of pancakes and bacon.

"Haniya Daoud is here."

"What?" said Roslyn, looking up from trying to dab maple syrup off Florence's sweater. "Here? In Three Pines? I thought she wasn't coming until tomorrow."

"Well, she's here now. Jean-Guy and Dad met her last night in the bistro," said Annie. "Didn't Dad tell you, Mama?"

"No," said Reine-Marie. "I was asleep by the time he came in and got up before he did. He's showering now."

It was just after seven on New Year's Eve and still dark outside.

When Reine-Marie had dressed and gone downstairs, she found the lights on and Daniel already in the kitchen. He'd started the fire in the woodstove and put the coffee on.

She also found Honoré sprawled by the front door. He'd gotten himself into his snowsuit, and was struggling to put his boots on the wrong feet.

His trusty toboggan lay at his side, and Henri and Fred were circling and nudging him, anxious to go out. Little Gracie, the ratmunk, was still in Stephen's room, both fast asleep.

Reine-Marie and Honoré had taken the dogs for a walk around the village green. Henri and Fred played in the snow while Honoré dragged his toboggan on a rope behind him and asked his grandmother questions.

What's a year? Why do we need a new year? Is the old one broken? How many pancakes can I have?

He showed her the Big Dipper, which was really just a random star still visible in the early-morning sky, and they went inside.

By the time they got to the kitchen, others were already up, coffee was poured, the maple-smoked bacon was sizzling in the huge cast-iron pan.

Reine-Marie cooked up the first batch of blueberry pancakes.

Armand had come down and gone, unnoticed, to his study. Standing at the window, he'd watched Reine-Marie and Honoré on their walk.

It was going to be a brilliant, bitterly cold day. A day where it felt like the air itself was crystalizing.

Then he sat at his laptop and read the messages that had come in overnight.

Sûreté patrols were out on snowmobiles, looking for Édouard Tardif's brother. Without luck so far. It was a huge area, with many trails and cabins in the forests.

The videos sent in by spectators so far revealed nothing useful. No indication yet who might be an accomplice. Who might have set off the fireworks, if not Tardif himself.

And Tardif was refusing to talk. Gamache would go in and interrogate him later that day.

He heard Reine-Marie and Honoré return and his granddaughters race downstairs on their way to breakfast.

After reviewing all his messages and making notes on the day ahead, he joined the others in the kitchen.

When she'd woken up that morning, Annie had known, instinctively, that she was alone in the bed. Drowsily sneaking her hand over, to confirm, she felt the bedding cool. Not cold. He hadn't been gone long.

Throwing on a dressing gown, she went to the room next door and found Jean-Guy at Idola's crib, looking down at her.

"Where's Honoré?" she asked, sleepily.

Jean-Guy nodded toward the window.

"On the roof?" she asked as she strolled over. "Brilliant."

There was just enough light for Annie to make out the two figures. She smiled as she watched little Honoré walking beside his grandmother. The two deep in conversation. And she remembered doing the same thing with her mother. Walking hand in hand through the park near their apartment in Montréal. Telling her mother how the world worked.

It wasn't until she was in her twenties, and at the Université de Montréal law school, that she'd begun to listen.

"I know it's your turn to get her up," said Jean-Guy, "but do you mind if I do it this morning?"

"Are you kidding," said Annie, turning back to him. "I'd pay you. But"—she looked at him more closely—"are you okay?"

"Why do you ask?"

"I was just wondering if you're getting a cold. Is your nose blocked?"

Since the pandemic, even though they'd all had the vaccine, even though there hadn't been a new case in months, they still worried every time someone coughed.

"Why do you ask? Oh, God, don't tell me. Is it that bad?" He bent over Idola and inhaled. "I don't smell anything."

"Not even bacon?"

"It smells like bacon?"

Now that would be a miracle, he thought before he realized what Annie was saying.

She was smiling at him. "If anyone could have a child whose *merde* smelled of smoked meat, it would be you, but no. It comes from downstairs. Normally when you smell bacon, it's all I can do to get you decent before you head down."

She watched as he finished what he was doing and picked their daughter up, protecting her floppy head as the doctors had shown them. It now came naturally.

Holding Idola secure in his arms, he looked at Annie, who was staring at him with those thoughtful eyes, so like her father's.

"Everything okay?" she asked again.

"There's something I need to tell you."

"About Idola?" asked Annie, her voice rising in timber.

"*Non.* Not really." He sat on the side of Honoré's bed.

Annie joined him. "What is it? Is it bad? Did something happen yesterday? You seemed so distracted."

Jean-Guy brought Idola closer to him. Smelling her hair. Feeling her tiny fingers grasping his collar.

"Last night, in the bistro," he said, not looking at her. "Your father and I talked."

"Yes . . . ?"

This was it. He'd tell her about disobeying orders and abandoning his post. He'd tell her how he felt, sometimes, about their daughter. About their decision.

He'd tell Annie everything.

And that's when he told her.

About Haniya Daoud.

"News?" Jean-Guy asked when he arrived in the kitchen with Idola.

He'd put her into a pretty little onesie, a Christmas gift from Stephen. It was covered in cavorting pink mice, each holding what looked like a wedge of cheese, or lemon meringue pie.

"*Non.* Nothing," said Armand, kissing Idola's head. "She smells nice. New powder?"

"It's the bacon, Dad," said Annie, and turned to Roslyn. "Men."

"I know. For years Daniel thought our children smelled of croissants."

"They don't?" asked Daniel, and looked cross-eyed at Zora, who laughed.

"I've spoken to Isabelle," said Jean-Guy, pouring himself a coffee.

"We're set to interrogate Tardif later this morning. His lawyer will be there, of course."

"Of course."

Idola sat on Armand's knee as he listened to Zora, Florence, and Honoré describe the day ahead.

Just then there was a flurry of dings, pings as texts arrived for Annie, Roslyn, and Reine-Marie. All with the same message from Clara, inviting them over for breakfast with Haniya Daoud. It seemed slightly more than an invitation, Reine-Marie noticed. More like a plea.

Roslyn composed an excited reply.

Yes, plenty. So exited. Can I binge the girds? Mercury.

Not her best composition, but Clara understood and immediately sent back a text saying, *best not to bring the grills.*

"I wonder why not," said Roslyn.

"Too scary," said Jean-Guy, catching Armand's eye.

"You're right," said Annie. "We don't want to overwhelm Haniya. She must be a little fragile."

Reine-Marie, who'd declined the invitation with regret, saying she had work to do, walked over to her husband.

"I saw that look. What's up?"

"I'll tell you later," he whispered.

The breakfast dishes were cleared away so that Annie and Roslyn could go and have their second breakfast with the honored visitor.

Stephen was up by then and dressed as always in a crisp shirt, sweater, and gray flannels. Ready for a board meeting, should one arise.

"Still finding monkeys?" he asked Reine-Marie, after getting a mug of coffee.

She was now sitting by the woodstove at the far end of the kitchen and bending over a large cardboard box. *"Oui."*

"What's the count?" he asked, joining her.

"Fifty-seven, so far."

"What a weird person, collecting monkeys," said Stephen, cradling Gracie, his ratmunk.

"Wish I could say it's the strangest thing I've found going through people's things."

Having risen to chief archivist in Québec, Reine-Marie had recently decided to retire and take on consulting work.

This was a commission from a local family to go through their mother's things. The matriarch had recently died, leaving them far less wealth than expected, a rambling old house, and boxes and boxes of clothes, papers, knickknacks, and a completely unexpected collection of monkey dolls, monkey postcards, stuffed, painted, and illustrated monkeys. All in boxes in the attic.

Though by far the largest collection of monkeys were hand-drawn on all sorts of documents.

It was a puzzle, and one Reine-Marie hoped to solve.

"Any of them valuable?" asked the old financier.

"Not that I know of," she said, holding a moth-eaten monkey doll by an ear.

Armand had joined them, carrying a dossier.

"All right," said Reine-Marie. "Before you lose yourself in work, what did that look between you and Jean-Guy mean, when we were talking about Haniya Daoud?"

"It's just that if Annie and Roslyn are expecting a saint, they're going to be disappointed."

"Why? What's she like?"

When he didn't answer, her eyes grew serious and she understood.

"It's a miracle she survived at all," said Reine-Marie, "and that she turned her own pain into doing so much good. Not surprising she'd be . . ." What was the right word? "Difficult."

"*Oui,*" said Armand. "And then some. Certainly wounded, maybe even unbalanced, in that she sees quite clearly what's wrong with the world but can't seem to see what's right."

Though Haniya Daoud had certainly seen into him. If not his head, then she'd seen through the cracks, into his broken heart.

And now here is my secret, a very simple secret. It is only with the heart that one can see rightly; what is essential is invisible to the eye.

Armand wondered if Florence understood that line from *The Little Prince.*

He hadn't, as a child. It was only as he got older that he knew it to be true. And now he thought about Haniya Daoud, and what she had seen. With her own broken heart.

"An Asshole Saint," said Stephen. "Not the first. I think most were, weren't they? In fact, she wouldn't even be the first around here."

"You're not talking about yourself, are you, Stephen?" asked Reine-Marie. "Because, at least according to Ruth, only one of those words applies to you."

"Really? You'd take the word of a madwoman who carries around a duck? Treats that thing like it's her child, isn't that right, Gracie?" He kissed the ratmunk on her whiskered nose.

But both Reine-Marie and Armand knew who Stephen meant. Their resident Asshole Saint lived in a cabin in the woods, preferring his own company to that of anyone else on earth.

Everyone else on earth felt the same way.

They'd grown so used to calling him that, and he even introduced himself as the Asshole Saint, that the villagers had almost forgotten who he really was.

"I haven't met him yet," said Stephen. "So what makes him an asshole?"

"If he's there tonight, you'll probably see," said Reine-Marie. "The saint part is a little more hidden."

Armand smiled. That was true. But it didn't mean it wasn't there. The man had actually devoted much of his life to improving conditions for the vulnerable. For the forgotten and dismissed. Though whether he actually liked those people was a matter of debate.

"Well, now I'm really curious," said Stephen. "Do you think he'll be at the party tonight?"

"Probably," said Reine-Marie. "It's at his son's place."

"The Auberge," said Stephen. "Will you be going?"

The question was directed at Armand.

"I hope to. Have to see."

Actually, he hoped not to. Not that he didn't want to be there. But he hoped he'd be arresting and interrogating a suspect. The accomplice. And closing this case.

"Isabelle just called," said Jean-Guy, leaning against the doorway into the kitchen. "She'll be at the University auditorium in twenty minutes."

"Bon." Gamache got up and looked at the clock. "I'll come with you. The President and Chancellor have asked to meet with me."

"In the principal's office, Armand?" asked Stephen.

"Feels a bit like that."

CHAPTER 11

———

"Explain yourself," said Haniya Daoud, staring at Roslyn, whose eyes were wide and getting wider. "You spend your days designing clothing for rich people?"

"Explain yourself," said the President of the Université de l'Estrie, staring at Gamache.

Otto Pascal sat behind his large desk while Colette Roberge, the Chancellor, was in a high-back chair that looked uncomfortable. The President had not invited Gamache to sit.

"*Oui*. How could this happen?" the Chancellor asked.

Gamache turned to stare at her.

"Let me explain," said Éric Viau, the building superintendent, as he stood in the old gym with Inspectors Beauvoir and Lacoste. "All the doors are kept locked and are attached to alarms that sound in my home"—he waved toward the road and the small house by the entrance to the University—"and at campus security. They also give off a god-awful siren."

"The alarms didn't go off in the last week?" asked Isabelle Lacoste.

"No. Nothing."

"And there were no other events here over Christmas?" Beauvoir asked, looking around at the hats and mitts, the bags and boots that lay where they'd fallen.

They were standing where the firecrackers had gone off. The floor there was charred.

"Nothing. It's not exactly anyone's first choice for a venue. We only use this place if all the other venues are booked. But not recently, *non*. Not over the holidays."

"So why was it booked for the event yesterday?" asked Lacoste. "And at short notice? Was every other place already taken?"

Monsieur Viau looked at her in surprise. "You're asking me? I just try to keep the old place standing. I have no idea why someone would choose it."

"Wait a minute, Armand," said the Chancellor, getting up from her chair by the President's desk. "Are you saying this all might've been planned and carried out by Professor Robinson herself? For publicity?"

"What I'm saying is that it's a possibility, one of many we're looking into." He'd gone through the various theories they were pursuing. It interested him that the Chancellor had landed on that one.

President Pascal had also gotten to his feet. He came around his desk and stood beside and slightly in front of the Chancellor as they confronted the Chief Inspector.

Otto Pascal was looking more and more agitated. This was far beyond his understanding, which stopped sometime around 600 BC and the Sack of Thebes.

The twenty-first century was a cipher to the Egyptologist. He studied the Sûreté officer's face, as though hoping he'd found the Rosetta Stone.

"You've arrested the man who took the shots. So why keep digging?"

"Why do you?" asked Gamache. "In case there's something you missed. In case there's something else to be found. Like you, we need to be thorough."

Dr. Pascal was pale and looked like he wanted to sit back down. He also looked like he'd spent most of his life sitting down. Which he had.

As an authority on hieroglyphic literature, when he hadn't been sitting for the last forty years, he'd been bending over. Some would say backward. Trying to first see, then convince the rest of the world, that such a thing as hieroglyphic literature existed.

Which is to say Dr. Pascal, now President Pascal, believed that some of what had been presumed to be nonfiction accounts of ancient Egyptian lives and events, etched carefully into stone, were actually the ancient equivalent of novels. Mostly thrillers.

Which is to say he'd spent his career, pinned his career, on the ability to turn truth into fiction. Which he seemed desperate to do in this meeting.

"Well, I," stammered Roslyn. "Yes, I suppose that's . . . I also design children's—"

"Clothes for children?" asked Haniya. "Presumably children of the privileged. And what do they cost?"

Roslyn mumbled.

"Sorry, what?" said Haniya.

"Well . . ." Roslyn looked to Clara for help, but her friend and host had been through the wringer herself, several times that morning, and was already deflated.

She'd gotten out of bed partly reluctantly, partly excitedly.

Haniya Daoud, the toast of the Free World, was asleep in the next room.

Except she was not. Clara found her in her studio, going through the oil paintings propped against the wall.

"They're from an earlier show," Clara said from the doorway. "I haven't gotten around to hanging them."

Haniya, now in a splendid deep green silk caftan, turned to Clara and said, "I can see why not."

It was then, as her scalp went cold but her cheeks burned, that Clara had composed the text to Myrna, Reine-Marie, Annie, and Roslyn. The SOS. To save her soul from the Asshole Saint.

Now she dropped her eyes to the phone in her lap and sent off a quick message to Myrna.

Where are you?

Sorry. Can't come.

Can't or won't?

Yes.

Bitch, Clara typed and got a smiley face back.

"That's a beautiful sari you're wearing," Annie said.

Roslyn turned a grateful face to her sister-in-law, who'd just distracted the ogre. But Clara suspected there was more to it than that.

It was a subtle rapier thrust, pointing out to Haniya the hypocrisy of criticizing Roslyn while enjoying the fruits of similar labor.

That sari must've cost a pretty penny, was probably a gift from a wealthy benefactor, and might even have been made by child laborers in some hellhole sweatshop in India.

"It's called an abaya," said Haniya. "It comes from a network of women's co-ops I formed in Nigeria. It's funded by a banking system I set up which is also run by . . ."

Clara thought she might throw up, and Annie looked light-headed.

Roslyn, on the other hand, was leaning forward, taking in every word.

"Did you see anyone hanging around the building in the last week or so?" asked Isabelle.

"I thought you caught the gunman," said Monsieur Viau.

"We have," said Jean-Guy. "We just need to make sure no one else was involved."

As he said that he watched Monsieur Viau for any reaction. A slight change in skin tone, in breathing. A sprint for the door.

But the caretaker was just listening.

"Did anyone set up an appointment to see the place in the last couple of weeks?" Beauvoir asked. "Were there any workers? Repairs?"

"Not a worker, but some fellow came by. Wanted to hold a fundraising dance and had heard this place was cheap."

"Did you ever leave him alone?" Lacoste asked.

"No."

"Did you take him anywhere else in the building?"

"No. Just here."

"Could he have hidden anything without you seeing?" asked Beauvoir.

Monsieur Viau considered, then shook his head. "No. I was with him the whole time. I'd have noticed that."

"Is this the man?"

Isabelle showed him their photo of Édouard Tardif.

As Monsieur Viau studied it, the blood drained from his face. "*Oui.*" He looked up at them. "I let the gunman in?"

"You couldn't have known," said Isabelle. "Did he rent the place?"

"You'll have to ask someone in Administration about that."

"The Chief's over there now," said Beauvoir, taking out his phone. "Meeting with the President and Chancellor."

"Lucky man," said Viau.

"I'll see if he can get the information." As he sent off the text, Lacoste turned back to the caretaker.

"Just to be clear, this man you met here was alone?"

"*Oui.*"

"You're sure?"

Now Viau hesitated. "Well, I didn't see anyone else, but I suppose someone could have been with him. Waiting outside."

"You unlocked the door when this man arrived," said Isabelle. "Could someone else have come in after him, without you seeing?"

Viau considered, then nodded. "Yes, I guess so."

Lacoste and Beauvoir looked at each other.

"Do most people who rent this place see it first?" Beauvoir asked.

"I'd say almost all."

"Then who from Professor Robinson's group toured it? And when?"

Viau's brows drew together. "They didn't. At least not as far as I know."

"How did they know about this place?" asked Beauvoir. "And who rented it for her?"

Gamache could see the old gymnasium building from the President's office.

He returned his gaze from the window back to President Pascal and Chancellor Roberge.

He'd gone through what had happened the day before. Step by step. A report. Facts.

"What's the most likely scenario?" President Pascal asked.

"At this stage, I can't say."

"Can't or won't?" asked the Chancellor.

Gamache remained silent.

"Basically, Chief Inspector, you're saying you're considering every option," said the President.

"Except space aliens, yes."

"Including that Professor Robinson herself orchestrated it," said Pascal.

"That's one scenario, *oui*."

"That sounds like one small step up from space aliens," said the Chancellor, with a weary smile. This had not been her, or anyone's, favorite twenty-four hours. "Sounds to me like a spurious correlation. Connecting things that don't actually go together."

"We need to look at everything, no matter how unlikely," Gamache reiterated. Though the more he thought about it, the more Professor Robinson orchestrating an attempt on her own life seemed unlikely. Too many variables. Too many things could go wrong.

As a statistician, she would know that. Would she take the risk?

He doubted it.

"How did the gun get into the place?" asked the President. "I'm assuming he didn't walk in with it."

"No. It must've been hidden there before the event." He decided not to tell them that they believed Tardif had an accomplice.

Gamache looked at the President with some sympathy.

Otto Pascal led a small, even sleepy university, and had woken up this morning to chaos. The campus was overrun with police, with journalists from around Québec, soon from around the country and even the world.

The Administration must, by now, be fielding awkward questions from frightened parents. Wondering if their children should return. And not just because of the shooting.

All the journalists, and many of the parents, would be asking how any academic institution could possibly allow a talk by Abigail Robinson, a person many, most, considered a lunatic.

President Pascal looked longingly at his desk, where the latest photos from a find in the Valley of the Kings was awaiting his interpretation.

Otto Pascal had come up with his theory on hieroglyphic fiction in his postdoc work, only because no one else had thought of it. Then he'd spent the last four decades slowly realizing why that was.

Still, it had gotten him some notice. Granted, not as much as his roommate, who had, as a joke and, given this conversation, somewhat ironically, decided to declare that the hieroglyphs, and the pyramids themselves, were the work of ancient aliens.

It pissed Pascal off. Why hadn't he thought of that? Now he was stuck with the dumb literature theory.

"Mr. President?"

"What?"

The senior Sûreté officer was nodding toward the window.

Through it, President Pascal could see the offending gymnasium. A carbuncle of a building if there ever was one.

"You have a good view of the site," said Gamache. "I don't suppose you saw anything in the last week?"

"Me? No. I haven't been in."

Gamache noticed Pascal's quick glance at his desk and took a step over. On it were printouts dated two days earlier.

Pascal noticed him noticing. "Well, only to get those. I took them home, then brought them back here when I realized I'd have to spend most of today putting out fires."

He looked at Gamache as though he'd personally put a match to the University.

Gamache fought the impulse to point out he'd asked, begged, both the President and the Chancellor to cancel the event.

His phone vibrated and he glanced at the message from Beauvoir.

"We need to know," he said, replacing his phone in his pocket, "who rented the auditorium for Professor Robinson."

"The Administration offices are closed for the holidays," said President Pascal.

Gamache raised his brows. "I think maybe whoever's in charge can come in, don't you? It shouldn't take long. I'd hate to have to get a warrant."

"No need for that," said the President. "I'll make sure you get the information you need within the hour."

"Bon, merci," said Gamache. "If there are no further questions . . ."

"I just wish you'd canceled the event, Armand, after we spoke," said President Pascal as they walked him to the door. "Still, I'm grateful to you for what you and your people did."

Gamache caught Colette Roberge's smile of sympathy.

"I think I can get you the information you need," she said. "My office is in the Administration Building. I have the key."

CHAPTER 12

Gamache looked around the room, then at Colette Roberge. "This's your office?"

"*Oui*. I'd ask you to sit, but—"

There was nowhere to sit except at the very old, stained swivel chair behind the desk that looked like it had been salvaged from a dumpster.

Gamache had seen holding cells larger and more inviting.

"They didn't expect the Chancellor to actually do much work," she said, leaning against the desk strewn with papers.

"They obviously didn't know what they were getting when they appointed you." His expression grew serious. "Why're we here, Colette?"

"To get you the event booking form you asked for."

"That could be scanned to me. By someone other than the Chancellor."

"True."

He waited.

"I think you can guess."

"I think I don't want to."

She nodded, then reached for a drawer in her desk. "I can give you the booking request and receipt of payment for the gym right now. I don't have to look it up."

She brought a slip of paper from the drawer but didn't yet hand it to him.

"Abby called just before Christmas."

"You didn't tell me this before."

"No. But I'm telling you now. It wasn't unusual. Like most people who don't know each other well but want to stay in touch, we connected at Christmas. She'd sent me the paper she'd prepared for the Royal Commission and I'd been following the controversy. She said she'd like to come visit."

"But they're not staying with you. They're at the Manoir Bellechasse, aren't they? I have agents there in case there's more trouble."

"My place was already packed with houseguests, as you saw, so we couldn't put them up. But . . ."

"Yes?"

"We spoke on the phone last night. She and Debbie were so shaken I invited them to come to us today. The kids can sleep on the sofas in the basement."

Gamache's mind moved quickly. This was probably a good thing. Easier to protect a private home than a hotel.

"When she called and said she wanted to visit, did she say why?"

Now Colette smiled. "I'd assumed she wanted my wisdom, my advice. But seems not. She hasn't asked for it."

"Did she mention doing an event while she was here?"

"No. None was planned."

"So how did it come about?"

Now the Chancellor looked decidedly uncomfortable. "That was my doing, I'm afraid. I mentioned in passing, more as a joke than anything, that if she needed to write the trip off, she should give a lecture. Two days later she called back—"

"She called? None of this was done by email or text?"

"No. All calls."

Armand took that in. It meant no paper trail. No way to confirm anything except that the calls happened. But not what was discussed.

"She asked if there was an arena or something she could book. I thought it was her turn to joke. An arena. But then I watched her last talk and saw the crowd."

"So you booked the gym for her?"

The slip of paper in her hand had been a pretty good indication that the Chancellor was responsible, but it was still an unpleasant shock to have it confirmed.

"What was I supposed to do? It was my idea."

"Say nothing was available. Decline. Refuse. Lie." He was staring at her, trying to understand how a person he'd always thought of as intelligent could do something so stupid.

And then a thought occurred. "You didn't want to turn her down. In fact, you made the suggestion knowing she'd jump at it. You wanted to make sure she came. Why?"

Chancellor Roberge pressed her lips together and placed the requisition slip on the messy desk.

"She was brilliant, such a dazzling intellect, like her father. But she'd gone so far off the rails, coming to conclusions that seemed not just abhorrent but actually wrong. Yes, I wanted her to come. It was the least I owed her father. I wanted to figure out what had happened. To try to get her back on course."

"So you arranged for her to give a lecture?" he asked.

"I know, I know," she said. "Look, I didn't think anyone would actually come out. A last-minute talk on statistics, in English, in rural Québec, the week between Christmas and New Year's? It had failure written all over it. Until it happened, I still didn't believe anyone would show."

"Okay, it's done. Let's set that aside for now. But Colette, if the purpose of her trip wasn't the lecture, and it wasn't to see you, then why was she coming here?"

"I've wondered that myself. She's never been before, so why now? I think there must be someone she wants to meet, someone she thinks can help her."

"She didn't say who?"

"No, and I didn't ask."

"Is that true?"

It seemed incredible that this academic, in the same field, wouldn't be more than a little curious about who it was. Perhaps even jealous. Who was more prominent and better placed than the Chancellor?

Gamache was more than a little curious.

"Yes, it's true," said the Chancellor. "It's none of my business."

"It was exactly your business, Colette."

"Not anymore. I've long since retired from the thrilling field of statistics."

Her attempt at self-mockery was lost on Gamache. He continued to stare as the silence stretched painfully on.

And then the Chancellor spoke, her voice serious now. "Abigail is a unique person, Armand. It's hard not to get swept into her universe. You must've seen it yesterday."

He had. Not many could grip an audience made up mostly of people who probably hated math with a lecture on statistics. Chancellor Roberge was right. Her former student was riveting. And Abigail Robinson did it not with histrionics, but with a voice so quiet people had to almost strain to hear. It was a kindly crayon voice that carried conviction because it apparently didn't try.

"Are you saying you were mesmerized by her?" he asked.

"I'm saying there are just people you want to please. Abby is one."

"Professor Robinson arrived two days ago, a day before the lecture," said Armand. "Did you see her?"

"No."

Gamache was well schooled in picking up when someone was hiding something. He wasn't sure if she'd just lied, or if this was simply an evasion. That there was something he wasn't asking.

Then he remembered a moment, just before the lecture began, when he'd asked Professor Robinson if someone was going to introduce her. She'd said no but had glanced at the door.

He'd had the impression the professor was stalling. Waiting until the very last minute, and beyond, to go on. Waiting for someone.

"Were you supposed to be there? Did Professor Robinson ask you to introduce her?"

"No."

The denial was quick. Absolute.

And he didn't believe it.

"Why didn't you tell me all this when I went to your house?"

"I didn't think it was pertinent." At a look from him, she amended her answer. "I didn't want anyone to know my involvement. I regretted making the booking almost immediately, but it was too late—"

"It wasn't too late," he snapped. "I came to you, practically begging you to cancel, and you refused. Did you regret it or not? Your words say one thing, but your actions say something completely different."

"As I told you," she snapped back, "I didn't think anyone would show. I thought you were overreacting, and that canceling would draw more attention to it than if it just went on and died a natural death."

They were words she immediately regretted. She was gripping the edge of her desk and leaning toward him, and now she dropped her head. When she raised it, she looked him square in the face.

"I'm sorry. I was obviously wrong. You wanted this." She handed him the booking slip.

"Your name isn't on it. It says Tyler Vigen. Who's he?"

"Nobody. I didn't want to use a real name, so I made one up."

He folded the paper, put it into his pocket, then studied her.

"Are you involved in this?" he asked quietly.

"The shooting?"

"Don't sound so shocked. It's a natural conclusion. You'd read her paper, you invited her here. You booked the auditorium and had access to it."

"But you've arrested the gunman."

"True, but he might've had help."

"If he did, it wasn't from me." Then her eyes sharpened. "You think that's how the gun got into the gym. Someone else put it there."

"We think it's a possibility, yes. And if that's the case, the person's still out there. Are you sure you want to take Professor Robinson and Madame Schneider into your home? With your grandchildren?"

Chancellor Roberge stared at him, her mind clearly working. Then she nodded.

"Thank you for telling me. We'll be extra careful and make sure the alarms are set."

Armand stared at her, waiting for more. When none came, he said, "And the children?"

"They're staying until the weekend. They have ski passes."

"You're inviting a person who's already had one attempt on her life into your home, with a possible second killer out there. Don't you think the children at least should leave?"

She considered and gave a sigh. "You're right. I was just so stuck on having them there. They'll be disappointed."

"But they'll be alive. I'll assign agents to guard your home. I'll be by later this afternoon to speak to the professor."

He put on his tuque, then stopped at the door. "You said Abigail Robinson was, is, brilliant."

"She is. A genius in the field."

"If she's such a genius, how did she get the pandemic data and conclusions so wrong?"

"She didn't."

"Pardon?"

"I've been over her research, her statistics. Even sent her preliminary study to a close friend whose opinion I value. He came to the same conclusion. She's not wrong."

"But you said she'd gone off the rails, that they're—"

"Morally abhorrent, but factually correct."

"Jesus, don't you guys smell it?" asked Isabelle.

"Smell what?" asked Jean-Guy, and looked at Armand, who shook his head, apparently perplexed.

Gamache had walked over to the gym and joined them in the basement, where the Incident Room was being set up. It had been the boys' locker room.

Technicians were putting in lines, computers, desks, chairs, boards. It wasn't quite chaos, but it was close kin.

"It smells like someone put Oka cheese in a sweaty sock, wrapped it in an old banana peel, then sat on it," she said. "For ten years."

"Oh," said Gamache. "That."

"I like it," said Jean-Guy.

Armand laughed.

"Maybe there's a less smelly place," said Isabelle, looking around. "The bathroom for instance."

Monsieur Viau had returned with a slip of paper on which he'd written the name and number of the man he'd met a week earlier.

"*Merci*," said Lacoste. She glanced at it, then showed it to Gamache and Beauvoir.

Their faces betrayed nothing.

Édouard Tardif.

Their only surprise was that Tardif hadn't even tried to hide his identity.

Gamache looked around. "Is there someplace quieter we can go?"

"I can put a table and chairs on the stage upstairs, if you like," said the caretaker.

While Viau did that, the officers stepped outside into the fresh air. Isabelle took a long, long, deep breath.

Gamache squinted into the sun and pointed. "That's where President Pascal has his office."

It was a very old, very attractive fieldstone building with a bright red metal roof that had the ski-jump swoop particular to homes of the *patrimoine québécois*. It had been built centuries earlier and was almost certainly original to the property. It stood in stark contrast to the brutal gymnasium, built in the early sixties.

"He has a good view of the place," said Lacoste.

"True, but he says he was only in his office briefly a few days ago. And he didn't see anything."

"Says?" asked Beauvoir. "You don't believe him?"

"The President has a particular bent toward the make-believe, but"—Gamache considered—"I think he's telling the truth."

"He would have access to the gym, though," said Beauvoir.

Gamache tried to imagine Otto Pascal sneaking over, letting himself in, and hiding a gun. But his imagination didn't stretch that far.

The door behind them opened and Monsieur Viau said, "Ready when you are."

Before going up onstage, Gamache ducked under the police tape and walked to the center of the room where charring marked where the firecrackers had been set off. And where the shots had come from.

He stood pretty much where Tardif had been. Why so far back? Why not right up at the stage, to guarantee a kill?

Was it possible he really didn't want to hit her? And maybe, by standing there, Tardif thought he had a better chance of escaping.

Gamache looked at the exits. Yes. It would be a good vantage point from which to escape. Though not to succeed, if the plan really was to kill Professor Robinson.

He glanced at the floor. At the items that had been dropped in the rush to get out.

There, lying almost on top of the burned wood, was a Habs tuque. The unmistakable red knit cap with the large *C*, for the Montreal Canadiens hockey team, known affectionately as Les Habitants. The Habs.

It was an exceptionally popular hat. Almost everyone in Québec had one. He was pretty sure he had one, somewhere among their winter things.

Still . . .

He called over a technician and asked to have the tuque bagged and analyzed.

Once on the stage he walked to the edge and looked out, his hands clasped behind his back, like a ship's captain, searching the horizon for land. Or an iceberg. Jean-Guy and Isabelle joined him, standing on either side.

"What're you thinking, *patron*?" asked Isabelle.

"I'm thinking that Monsieur Tardif was standing farther away than he had to be."

She turned to him in surprise. Surprise that she hadn't seen that herself.

"That's true. Why wouldn't he come right up here?" asked Beauvoir. "He couldn't miss then."

"Maybe that's why," said Gamache, who then walked to the table in the middle of the stage. "Another question to ask him."

The caretaker returned with a plate of shortbread cookies decorated as Christmas trees and snowmen, with those silver balls that looked like buckshot, and were just as edible.

He also put down three mugs of strong hot tea.

They thanked him and put their hands around the mugs. Winter had seeped into the large, empty room, and the warmth felt good.

At a nod from the Chief Inspector, Lacoste and Beauvoir reported on their conversation with Viau.

"It looks like the purpose of the visit was for Édouard Tardif to distract the caretaker while someone else hid the firecrackers and gun," said Isabelle.

"Possibly his brother," said Beauvoir. "Cops in Abitibi are still trying to find him, but he might not be there at all. We've circulated his picture and information."

Gamache took a sip of tea and looked at the Canadiens hat, still slumped on the floor.

"Suppose the accomplice wasn't the brother," he said. Trying to see it. "Suppose the accomplice was here too? He'd hidden the things a few days earlier, so he'd know where they were." As he spoke, the images, like a film, played before his eyes. A man, in a Habs tuque, coming in with the crowd. Sneaking away. Maybe to the bathroom. Finding the gun and firecrackers where he'd hidden them. Slipping the gun to Tardif.

"Maybe his job was to set off the firecrackers, set off the panic," said Isabelle. "While Tardif concentrated on firing the shots."

"Maybe, in the rush for the door after the firecrackers, he planned to run to the front and shoot her then," said Beauvoir. "Taking advantage of the chaos."

"But why not just position himself there to begin with?" asked Gamache.

"Maybe he meant to but saw you and the line of agents there and realized he'd never get off a shot," said Beauvoir. "He had a better chance from farther back."

"Okay. We have to keep looking for Tardif's brother, but explore the possibility that someone other than him was involved," said Gamache. "What about the lighting and sound technicians?"

"They're both students," said Beauvoir. "It's possible Tardif paid them to take something in, not knowing what it was."

"Wouldn't they have come forward?" asked Lacoste.

"You've never had teenagers," said Gamache. "It's like living with a ferret."

Which, in thinking of Gracie, they might well be doing.

"I'll interview them," said Beauvoir. "I have a way with kids."

"Since when?" asked Isabelle.

"Since I was issued a gun. There's also the caretaker."

"*Oui*," agreed Gamache. It was true, but it gave him no pleasure to think Monsieur Viau had a hand in this.

This was a premeditated attempt on the professor's life. And while there'd been very little advance notice of the event, the person who'd had the most warning, and the most time to plan, and the most familiarity with the layout of the venue, was its caretaker.

Though there was, Gamache thought, as he looked out the huge windows, across campus, toward the Administration Building, one other person with even more opportunity.

CHAPTER 13

‾‾‾

They listened as Chief Inspector Gamache reported on his meeting with the President of the University and the Chancellor.

"Not much there," he admitted when he'd finished. "Mostly I answered their questions."

Then he told them about his private conversation with Chancellor Roberge and watched as both Jean-Guy's and Isabelle's expressions went from interested to astonished.

"She booked the gym?" said Beauvoir. "And didn't tell you that before?"

"*Non.*"

"It's more than booking the gym," said Isabelle. "The event itself was her idea. What else isn't she saying?"

Beauvoir picked up the receipt Gamache had placed on the table and studied it.

"She used a false name. Who's he?"

"A name she made up. Go on, say it."

"I know she's a friend, *patron*," said Jean-Guy, "but really, it's looking more and more like the Chancellor's in it up to her neck."

"I agree. That's how it looks. But isn't that always our problem? Things that seem fairly reasonable, though perhaps a little odd, in normal life suddenly look a lot worse when a crime is committed. It's easy to overinterpret."

"She lied to you," said Isabelle. "And put a false name on this paper. It would be hard to overinterpret that."

"I have no desire to defend Colette Roberge. But do I think she's behind the attempt on Abigail Robinson's life? No. I think at worst she didn't want it to come out that she was helping Professor Robinson, so she lied and covered her tracks."

"Do you think she supports Robinson?" asked Jean-Guy.

Armand took a deep breath. "I don't really know."

"But she's letting Robinson and her assistant stay at her home," said Isabelle. "That's gotta say something."

"It says she's a good friend," said Gamache. "It does not say she agrees with the professor. In fact, she said it was more for the sake of her friendship with Robinson's father that she was doing it."

"We need to speak to him," said Isabelle.

"Can't," said Gamache. "He died years ago."

"So she's doing all this for a dead man?" asked Jean-Guy. "That's some relationship."

The wooden chair squeaked as Gamache slowly leaned back. After a few beats he said, "Isabelle, if there was an attempt on the life of someone you knew but not well, would you take them into your home?"

She considered. "Yes, I would."

"With your family there?"

"No, of course not. I'd get the family out."

Gamache nodded and looked at Jean-Guy, who said, "Same."

"And yet, when I told Colette about the accomplice and that there could very well be a second attempt, she didn't say that the children would leave. I had to convince her."

She thought for a beat. "The only way you'd invite the target of a possible attack into a home with children is if you knew, knew for sure, there wouldn't be another one."

Gamache was nodding. That was exactly what he was thinking.

Beauvoir put his elbows on the table and leaned toward them. "And the only way Chancellor Roberge would know that is if she was involved in the first one. If she was the accomplice."

"Or knows who is," said Gamache. "I'm beginning to think I was wrong earlier. Chancellor Roberge might be more deeply involved."

"And she's just invited Robinson into her home," said Beauvoir. "Should we stop it?"

Gamache thought for a moment, then shook his head. "If she is involved, and that's a big 'if,' there's no way she'd allow another attack in her own home. No, I think this's just about the safest place for Professor Robinson."

Beauvoir met Lacoste's eyes. They knew famous last words when they heard them.

"Is she gone?" Myrna asked, standing just inside the door of Clara's cottage and craning her neck to see beyond the mudroom and into the kitchen. "I can still smell sulfur."

"That's probably Ruth." Clara shut the door firmly against the cold, then turned to Myrna. "And yes, she's moved up to the Inn and Spa. You're a shitty friend, by the way."

"Gâteau?"

Clara took the chocolate cake, but made it clear this didn't mean they were even.

"I begged you to come over and you didn't. She's your guest, and you left me alone with her. All night. Do you know she ordered French toast for breakfast? I've never even made it for myself. But I figured it out, then she decided it was, in her word, 'disgusting,' and refused to eat it."

"Did you?"

"Eat it? Yes. But that's not the point."

"You offered to put her up."

"When I thought she was a remarkable person, yes."

"She's still that." Myrna removed her boots and put on the slippers she kept at Clara's.

"And a shit."

"Well, yes. Things they don't mention in the Nobel Prize citation."

They cut the cake into five equal pieces and took them into the living room, where Reine-Marie, Annie, and Ruth were gathered around the fire.

"Where were you?" Annie demanded. "You coward."

"Cake?"

Annie took it and seemed at least somewhat mollified. Or at least distracted. As a diversion, few things were as effective as chocolate cake.

"I wanted to come," said Myrna, plopping onto the sofa and sending Ruth and Rosa, at the other end, bouncing into the air. "But I had urgent business."

"A used-book emergency?" asked Clara. Though, with her mouth filled with cake and creamy icing, it came out as "Uh oozed ook emerenthy?"

"This's all your doing," said Ruth. "Bringing that woman here. What were you thinking?"

"I was thinking that she's a brave woman who should be supported and celebrated."

"From a distance," said Annie. "Of say a continent or two."

"May the Lord bless her, and keep her," said Clara, "far away from us."

"*Fiddler on the Roof*?" asked Annie. "Isn't Gabri hoping to do that for this year's production?"

"Yes. He's trying to convince your father to play Tevye."

"He won't do it?" asked Myrna.

"Have you ever heard Armand sing?" Reine-Marie asked.

"And where were you?" Clara turned to her. "You could've come over."

"I'm actually sorry I didn't. I'd like to have met her. I suspect now I won't. Madame Daoud will be gone soon, right?"

"One way or another," said Ruth.

"Now, Ruth," said Annie. "Remember what we talked about."

"I'm not allowed to kill anyone."

"Good. Remember that."

"I think what we all need to remember," said Reine-Marie, as she looked at the semicircle of friends, "is what Haniya Daoud has been through in her life. She's younger than you," she said to Annie. "She lost her own children, but has saved thousands of others. She's been sold into slavery. Raped and tortured. Imagine, try to imagine the horrors she's been through. And out of that she's started a movement that has saved and empowered women around the world. And we expect her to make small talk? To be polite? And when she isn't, when she's impatient and angry, we joke about killing her?" Her eyes, her voice, her expression had turned hard. "Killing her?"

There was silence.

Clara sighed. "You're right. I think she moved to the Auberge because she could tell that I didn't want her here."

"After all she's gone through, how could we expect her to be like us?" asked Annie.

"No," said Ruth. "Not like us. Better than us. We really were expecting a saint."

"Not flesh and blood with feelings of her own," said Myrna. "She might've been unpleasant, but we were mean. Cruel even. Letting her know she wasn't wanted."

Myrna Landers knew there were few things worse than being excluded, shunned. It was seen in some communities as a punishment worse than death.

"Why didn't you come over?" Clara asked Reine-Marie.

But Reine-Marie wasn't listening. She was thinking of her conversation with Armand, about Haniya Daoud. How he'd described her. There was respect, compassion, but there was also concern. An awareness of the damage damaged people could do.

"Maman?" Annie interrupted her thoughts.

"Oh, sorry." Reine-Marie turned to Clara. "Work got in the way, I'm afraid."

"More monkeys?" asked Myrna.

"*Oui.*"

"My favorite was always Davy Jones," said Clara.

"You really are a daydream believer," said Myrna.

"What's the count now?" asked Ruth.

"Sixty-three. What could they mean?" Reine-Marie asked Myrna, their resident psychologist. "Why would someone spend more than half a century secretly collecting monkeys?"

"The question isn't why monkeys," said Ruth. "The question is why a secret?"

"She's right," said Myrna, turning astonished eyes on the mad poet at the other end of the sofa.

"She was bound to be right eventually," said Clara. "Law of averages."

"Is there such a thing?" asked Annie. "Can't math, numbers, be interpreted, massaged to mean just about anything? To predict any outcome?"

They all knew what Annie was really thinking.

It wasn't about Ruth's chances of finally being right. Nor was it about the chances Haniya Daoud, a distinguished but disappointing stranger, and her insults would finally hit a nerve.

Annie Gamache was thinking about statistics. About graphs. About a law of averages that seemed to have predicted that a lunatic theory would take hold. Eventually.

And that probability grew by the day, by the click-through, by the event.

It grew every time Professor Abigail Robinson opened her mouth.

CHAPTER 14

—

"A rmand," said Colette Roberge, and surprised the Chief Inspector by kissing him on both cheeks as though he were just a friend dropping in for a visit, and not the head of homicide for the Sûreté du Québec, in her home to investigate an attempted murder.

"Madame Chancellor," said Gamache, stepping back and introducing Isabelle Lacoste.

Despite Jean-Guy's assurances that he could be civil, Gamache had thought it better if he didn't accompany them, but instead interview the lighting and sound techs.

"We're in here," said Colette as she led them through the house and to the kitchen.

It was a comfortable room, with open shelving displaying blue-and-white china. Tins lined up on the counter said *Farine. Sucre. Café. Thé. And Biscuits.*

The ceiling had whitewashed beams, and French doors at the far end opened onto a large garden, now buried in snow.

In the corner by the door, bathed in sunshine, was a card table with a child's jigsaw puzzle. A remnant of the grandkids.

Two women stood by the fireplace and turned anxious faces to the newcomers. It was clear neither had slept much. They looked disheveled, exhausted.

"Has the gunman said why he did it?" asked Debbie Schneider, stepping forward.

"No," said Isabelle. "He's not saying anything. We're not releasing his name or any details yet, but I can tell you that he's not a professional. In fact, he has no prior record at all."

"Just a local crazy," said Madame Schneider.

"There's no indication he's that either," said Lacoste, her voice cool.

Debbie Schneider opened her mouth to argue the point, but Abigail Robinson interrupted.

"Thank you again, Chief Inspector," she said, offering her hand. "I watched the videos last night. I think I must've been in shock. It's clear that if you hadn't acted I probably wouldn't be here."

"You're welcome," he said, taking her hand.

Isabelle Lacoste considered the two women as they all took seats in front of the warm woodstove. She'd only seen Professor Robinson at a distance, onstage.

There she'd been calm, assured. There'd been a warmth about her that Lacoste had found disconcerting.

But this was a different woman.

She was tense. Haggard. It was a perfectly normal reaction to what had happened.

The other woman, Debbie Schneider, was new to Isabelle.

She and the professor must be about the same age, but there was about Madame Schneider the sense of harder roads. Steeper climbs. A life not longer in days, but longer in other ways.

"We have a photograph of the gunman," said Isabelle. "I'd like to know if you've seen him before."

As the women leaned in to look, Lacoste turned her attention to Chancellor Roberge. She was short and stout, elegantly dressed even mid-morning on New Year's Eve.

Her eyes were clear blue like the winter sky and held an almost fierce intelligence.

Gamache was also observing Colette Roberge.

It had occurred to him that, in their conversation earlier that morning, the Chancellor hadn't actually asked anything about the gunman. Neither had the President of the University, but then his curiosity ended with Cleopatra.

"He looks . . . ," said Abigail, studying the photograph and searching for the word.

"Normal?" asked Debbie Schneider.

"Nice," said Abigail.

Armand was tempted to say that she did too, but of course, he did not.

"The people who were hurt?" said Abigail. "How are they?"

"Recovering. They're keeping one in hospital to do more tests on his heart."

"Can I send a card?" she asked.

"If you give them to me, I'll make sure they're delivered."

"Debbie, can you . . . ?"

While Debbie made a note, Professor Robinson said to Lacoste, "I imagine you'd much rather be with your family than figuring out why some nice man took a potshot at someone you probably think deserved it."

"Abby!" said Debbie.

It was such an extraordinary thing to say that Lacoste was momentarily at a loss.

Extraordinary because it was partly true.

"I'm very glad he didn't hit his target, Professor."

Abigail smiled. "Thank you for that."

Her smile wasn't a beam. It was much more intimate than that. It was gentle and warm. Understanding and inviting. Isabelle Lacoste was being invited in from the cold. Into the world of Abby Robinson, where all would be well.

While Isabelle was far from taken in, she was very much taken by this effect the professor had on her. Abigail Robinson had discovered, within moments of their meeting, a crack in her well-fortified wall. One she herself didn't even know was there.

Isabelle Lacoste, second-in-command in homicide for the Sûreté du Québec, also yearned for all to be well.

Who didn't?

She knew then that the professor was dangerous not simply because of her views, but also because she was so very compelling. So very attractive. And, most dangerous of all, so very normal.

This was no charismatic maniac. This was the woman next door who you trusted with your dog when you went away. If she said something was true, you believed her.

"You've known each other long?" Isabelle asked, trying to recover her equilibrium. Trying to paper over the cracks.

"All our lives, it seems," said Debbie Schneider. "Abby Maria and I lived next door to each other as kids. Grew up together."

She looked at Abigail, who gave her a smile, though it seemed to Gamache, who was following this closely, that it was strained. That there was some warning in her eyes. One that brought blood to Debbie's cheeks.

"And where was that?"

"Nanaimo," said Abigail. "British Columbia."

"Beautiful area. Do you still live there?"

Yes.

Lacoste's questions continued.

While neither had children, and both were single, Debbie was divorced and Abby had never married. They'd eventually drifted apart, their lives taking them in different directions.

"You know she went to Oxford?" said Debbie. "While the rest of us were mooning over boys, she was reading about the curriculum, years before she was old enough to even go." Debbie turned to the Chancellor. "That's how you two met, right?"

The Chancellor nodded. She, like Gamache, had been sitting back. Observing.

"I knew Abigail's father, Paul. He was a good friend and a great mathematician. Almost as gifted as his daughter."

Abigail smiled. "*Merci.*"

"He died in Abby's first year," said Debbie. "We reconnected at the funeral."

"I wonder what he'd make of what's happening now," said Abigail.

"I think we know," said Debbie. "After all he did for you, he'd be very proud with what you've done with your life. And he'd be proud of your study. He felt strongly that the truth, no matter how awful, must come out. And sometimes, it's pretty awful."

Abigail stared at her friend and colored. She gave a curt nod and turned to the fire.

"I agree," said the Chancellor. "He'd be proud of you for having the courage to speak up. He was a kind man, a brave man. A believer in mercy, in all its forms."

Gamache tipped his head back so that he was looking at the support beams above his head. Giving himself that gap between thought and action. So that he didn't speak his mind.

Merciful. Had Colette really just equated what Abigail Robinson was promoting with an act of mercy?

But he did have an answer to one of his questions. He lowered his head and looked at the Chancellor, who seemed to agree with Abigail Robinson after all.

"You two work together now," Lacoste was saying to Debbie and Abigail.

"That's a nice way of putting it," said Debbie. "I work for Abby, yes. Though it doesn't actually feel like work."

"What do you do?"

"Everything," said Abigail. "Debbie does everything."

"Except the research, the writing, the meetings, the lectures. But yes," Debbie said with a smile, "besides that, I do everything."

"She finds the flights," said Abigail, "books hotels, pays the bills, fixes the laptops, finds the chimney sweep, organizes the winter tires, the lawn mowing, the—"

"Social media?" asked Gamache.

"Yes."

"You post videos of the events?" he asked.

"Yes," said Debbie. "You wouldn't believe how popular they've become."

Gamache, who'd been watching the likes tick up, would.

"The videos seem to be getting better," said Lacoste. "More professional."

"They are. At first the footage was from what people sent in," Debbie explained, "but we needed something easier to watch, so now I hire local videographers."

"And yesterday? Was the event recorded?"

"If it had been, Inspector, we'd have given you the tape," said Debbie. "It was too last-minute to find anyone."

"I saw the recording of your event before Christmas," said Gamache, his voice casual.

"Yes, well, most of that was taken by people in the audience," said Debbie. "We decided not to put up the one we had."

"Because of the violence?"

There was silence.

"It seems you pick and choose which truth you're going to tell," said the Chief Inspector.

"Don't we all?" asked Professor Robinson. "I can't imagine you're telling us everything you know. For instance, how did that man get into the gym with a gun? I saw your people at the door. They were checking everyone as they went in."

Gamache looked at the Chancellor, to see if she'd told them about the suspected accomplice, but it seemed Abigail Robinson had figured this out on her own.

"We're looking into it. There is a chance he wasn't alone."

The only sound was the crackling of the fire.

"So someone's still out there?" said Debbie, her wide eyes going to the French doors and the garden beyond.

"We have Sûreté agents watching this house," said Gamache. "And we're doing all we can to find the accomplice. If there is one."

"You don't even know that? How can you find someone you're not even sure exists?" demanded Debbie, her voice rising.

"It's all right," said Colette. "They're very good at their jobs."

"Like they were yesterday, when a gunman got in?" demanded Debbie.

Abigail placed a hand over her friend's. Debbie took a deep, calming breath and squeezed Abigail's hand.

One thing was becoming clear to Gamache. Abigail Robinson and Debbie Schneider were a couple, as surely as any lovers. Perhaps even more than most. Having sex did not define an intimate relationship, any more than not having sex prevented one.

"Can you think of anyone who might want to hurt you?" Lacoste asked. "Colleagues? Former partners, anyone who might hold some grudge?"

"Well, there's half of Canada, it seems," said Abigail.

"I mean personally."

"I can't think I hurt anyone so badly they'd want to kill me. Can you?" she asked Debbie, who also shook her head.

"You work at the University of Western Canada, is that right?" Lacoste asked.

"UWC, that's right. I actually took over my father's old job."

Isabelle considered all the dynamics that suggested. It felt Shakespearean. Greek even. But was it a tragedy, or kindly Fate bestowing a gift on a gifted child?

"He must've been relatively young when he died," said Lacoste.

"He was. Stroke."

"And you were in Oxford when it happened?"

"She was," said the Chancellor. "I got the call and had to tell her."

"The hospital called you?" said Gamache.

"*Oui*. Paul put me down as the person to be notified. If anything happened, he didn't want Abigail to hear any news like that on her own."

"He sounds like a careful man," said Gamache.

"He was a loving father," said Colette. "Preparing for the unpredictable."

"Practicing probability theory?" asked Gamache.

"You'd know, Chief Inspector," said Abigail. "Don't you generate theories, based on probability, and then eliminate them as facts come in? Isn't that how you find killers?"

"Very true. But we also have to consider emotions. How we feel about things influences how we see them."

"Bit of a wild card," said Colette.

"Oh, you'd be surprised how clearly the heart can see. What I do know is that how we feel drives what we think, and that determines what we do. Our actions leave behind evidence, those facts you mention. But it all starts with an emotion."

"Fortunately, numbers don't have feelings," said Abigail.

"No, but the mathematician, the statistician, does. Can't help but. As do homicide investigators. We can make mistakes. Overinterpret evidence. Even manipulate some facts to suit a convenient theory. We try not to, but we're human and it's tempting. Fortunately, if we do misinterpret facts and arrest the wrong person, the case is dismissed."

"But not always," said Chancellor Roberge. "Innocent people are sometimes convicted. And the guilty are freed."

"My point exactly," said the Chief Inspector. "The same set of facts can lead us to different conclusions. Our interpretation of facts can depend on our experiences. Even our upbringing. On what we want the facts to say."

"Lies, damned lies, and statistics?" asked Abigail.

He raised his brows, acknowledging the famous quote. But said nothing.

"You think that's what I've done?" She didn't seem defensive, merely curious. Almost amused. "You're not the first person to say that. Can statistics be manipulated? Absolutely. We've all seen it. Politicians, pollsters, ad execs. Anyone with an agenda can spin statistics. But I can tell you, and I suspect Chancellor Roberge will agree, that few academics would do that, if only because we'd soon be found out in peer review. We'd lose all credibility, lose the respect of colleagues, and risk censure by our university."

"As you have."

There was a pause as that dug in.

"True," she finally said. "But it's not because I'm wrong. In fact, it's because they know I'm right and it makes them uncomfortable."

And Gamache remembered what the Chancellor had said, as he'd left her office. That while shocking, even abhorrent, Professor Robinson's figures were actually correct.

But correct and right were two different things. As were facts and truth.

He leaned forward. "Why are you here?"

"The Chancellor thought it would be more comfortable," said Abigail.

"No, I mean why come to Québec? This area? At this time of year? It wasn't to do an event. That wasn't organized until after the decision had been made. What brought you here?"

"We wanted to see Colette," said Abigail. "It'd been a difficult few months since the Royal Commission turned down my report. I wanted a change of scene and I wanted her advice."

"And yet you didn't exactly rush over to see her."

Abigail glanced at the Chancellor, who'd dropped her eyes.

"Okay, you want the truth?"

"Please."

"The main reason we came now is simple. I've sold my house, and the place is filled with boxes."

"It's a complete mess," agreed Debbie.

"So you flew across the continent to get away from boxes?" asked Lacoste.

"It's hard to explain," said Abigail with a sigh. "After my father died I'd just stuck all the boxes from his place in the attic and forgot about them. But now I have to go through it all and decide what to keep. It was"—she thought for a moment—"emotional. I felt overwhelmed. Colette had always said how beautiful it is here, especially at this time of year. How peaceful." She looked at Gamache. "I wonder if you understand. All I wanted was peace."

"So you held a rally?" asked Lacoste.

"One hour out of my holiday," said Professor Robinson. "Who could have seen what would happen?"

Gamache took a breath and chose not to pursue that again.

"Still, some good has come of it," said Debbie.

"And what's that?" asked Gamache.

"We had a call this morning. Haven't had a chance to tell you yet, Colette."

"From?" said the Chancellor.

"The Premier of Québec," said Debbie. "He saw the news reports. I guess he realized there's growing support. He wants to meet to discuss Abigail's findings. You might have to enforce a whole new law."

What had been political suicide two days earlier had suddenly become viable.

Gamache didn't react except to grow even more still. While beside him, Isabelle Lacoste imagined forcing the elderly and sick to accept a lethal injection.

Gamache glanced at the Chancellor and said, softly, "I wonder if that was predictable."

But she was paying no attention. Colette was looking out the window at her husband walking hand in hand with one of the grandchildren.

"They're still here?" Gamache asked. "The children?"

"Leaving after lunch," said Colette.

"We've also had calls from most of the major news organizations. I've lined up interviews for Abby all afternoon," said Debbie. "In fact, we have a live one with CNN in a few minutes, then the BBC after that. We've already done the Canadian shows. Our followers on social media have doubled since last night."

Gamache knew this. He'd been tracking the surge since the shooting.

"May I have a word?" Gamache asked Chancellor Roberge, who nodded and rose.

CHAPTER 15

⁓

They left the warm kitchen and walked through the living room and into a small study. It was crammed with memorabilia. Photographs. Awards. Degrees. The Chancellor's Order of Canada and Ordre National du Québec.

And books, books, and more books.

She turned. "What can I do for you, Armand?"

"I'd like to see any emails between you and either Professor Robinson or Madame Schneider."

"You don't believe her?" At a look from him she smiled. "Or me."

"Let's just say I too am thorough."

She sat at her desk, just as a distant door burst open. Gamache turned quickly toward the sudden bang, but relaxed when he saw a gang of kids pour into the mudroom down the hall. Their cheeks were rosy, their hair askew from tuques. They'd obviously spent the morning on the slopes and were arguing over skiing versus snowboarding.

The Chancellor, glasses on, looked at him. "They're leaving. I promise."

From the kitchen, where he'd left Lacoste, he heard Debbie try to quiet the kids, explaining that an interview was about to begin.

"There they are, Armand," said Colette, pushing back from the desk. "Not many. Would you like me to print them out?"

"Yes, please."

"Old school," she smiled, and hitting a key, she walked over to the printer.

"Just old." He pulled his chair up in front of the screen, and brought out his reading glasses.

He could hear Professor Robinson from the kitchen, beginning the interview. Creating a split screen, he put CNN Live on one side, the emails on the other.

The host started off politely enough, asking after her well-being. Then they showed clips from the event. It was footage the Sûreté, as far as he knew, had not been given.

From what he could see, there was nothing new in it. The camera was focused on the stage, of course, not the audience.

It showed the pandemonium. The restoration of a fragile calm. And then the shots.

When the video ended, the host started in on Professor Robinson.

"You make it sound like what you're proposing is some sort of kindness, but aren't you actually saying, 'God help you if you get sick, 'cause society sure won't.' We all saw what happened in care homes during the pandemic, and now you want to make that government policy?"

"First of all, I'm not saying anything. The statistics speak for themselves. And what we learned in the pandemic is that that tragedy must never, ever be repeated. No one should die like that. This would prevent—"

Gamache turned it off, and Colette noticed that his right hand was trembling just slightly.

"She's very good, isn't she?" said the Chancellor.

"She knows how to handle herself in an interview, yes." Which was, he knew, far different from being good. "How well did you know Abigail's father?"

"What do you mean?"

"You seem to have had an intimate relationship."

She smiled and sat down next to him. "I guess we did. But not in the way you might mean. He was older than me. A combination of mentor and older brother. It was more a meeting of the minds than the hearts."

"And his wife, Abigail's mother? How did she feel about your relationship?"

"I never met her. She'd died. Why're you interested? It was decades ago. Maybe you want to concentrate on the living."

He smiled. "I've chased ghosts before, but no, I just like to get a full picture. With both her mother and father dead, Abigail must've grown close to you."

"No, not really. After Oxford she went back to BC, and Jean-Paul and I returned to Québec."

"And there was no one else? No brother or sister?"

"She had Debbie. That seemed to be enough." She smiled. "What's that suspicious mind of yours conjuring?"

Creases appeared at the corners of his eyes and ran deep down his face as he too smiled. "Nothing. An occupational hazard. Seeing specters where none exist."

"And accomplices?"

"Oh, I'm pretty sure they exist."

He got up and, walking over to the bookcase, pulled out a volume he'd noticed as he'd entered the study.

He looked at the cover, then turned it around to show her. The Chancellor laughed.

"That was a gift from my husband when we got engaged." She took it and looked down at it as though at a beloved face.

The book was called *How to Lie with Statistics*.

From the kitchen he could hear the kids making noise again, and knew the interview must be over. Bringing out his phone, Armand checked Abigail Robinson's social media account and saw the numbers clicking, churning, sweeping upward. As fast, he thought, as the American national debt meter he'd seen in New York City. And now he watched with the same alarm as Professor Robinson's numbers flew up. A barometer of a moral deficit.

Armand pocketed his phone and walked to the door of the study. Down the hall he could see Inspector Lacoste standing with Abigail and Debbie. He caught her eye and nodded.

They were leaving.

He turned to the Chancellor. "Please don't let them go off the property. Not until we catch the accomplice."

"Suppose you never do?"

"You have a big house . . ."

She laughed. "I'll do my best. *Bonne année*, Armand. Let's hope the new year starts better than the old year has ended."

"Inshallah. *Bonne année*, Colette."

As Lacoste turned the car out of the driveway, she asked, "What do you make of the Chancellor? Do you think she's involved?"

"Oh, she's involved. I just don't know how."

Jean-Guy stood on the threshold and rang the bell. This was where the sound tech lived.

He'd already interviewed the lighting tech, who'd said he spent the event dozing off in a booth at the back of the auditorium.

He spoke no English and had been out drinking with buddies the night before. The English lecture on statistics held absolutely no interest for him.

The young man was a theater major at the University and did the lighting part-time, to make money.

Since the old cop had told them to keep the lights up the whole time, there wasn't much to do, he told Beauvoir. So he slept. Only waking up when the firecrackers went off.

No, he didn't see who did it. By the time he was fully awake, they'd stopped and the crowd was beginning to panic. Then there were the shots.

"Scared the shit outta me. *Ostie*."

"Did you record any of it?"

"I do lighting, not audio."

"I realize that," Beauvoir said, his voice and patience strained. "But you can see everything from that booth. It's right at the back of the auditorium and up high. If someone wanted to record an event, that would be the perfect spot. Right?"

"I guess. But why would I want a recording?"

"You wouldn't, but someone else might." He gave the kid a shrewd look. "Did someone ask you to record it? Maybe even pay you?"

"To record an event? Without signed permission of the principals? That's against the law."

"*Merci,*" said Beauvoir. "Now, I'll ask you again, because I like you and I don't want you to get into even bigger trouble by obstructing justice in an attempted murder inquiry. Are you sure you didn't record the event?"

"Look, the job's easy and pay's decent, so I'm not gonna fuck it up by illegally recording something. I'm asked all the time, especially by kids who want to bootleg a concert. Like you said, I have a great view of the stage. But I don't do it. Anyone watching the video would know where it was shot from and I'd be in shit."

"Have you been to the building in the last week?"

"No, why would I?"

"Did anyone give you anything to bring in?"

"Like firecrackers?" When the Inspector didn't say anything, the boy's eyes widened. "You mean the gun? I wish."

The Chief's wrong, thought Beauvoir, as he got back into his car. That kid's not a ferret. He's a wolverine.

Next was the sound tech. He parked in the driveway of her home, where a huge Père Noël on the roof waved at him. From the car, Jean-Guy considered the herd of reindeer on the front lawn, all with blinking red noses. It was ridiculous.

He kinda liked it.

A text came in from Isabelle saying they were on their way to the local detachment to interview the gunman, Édouard Tardif.

Join you soon, he replied, then walked up the front steps and rang the bell.

"What've you found out?" Gamache asked, half an hour later.

The head of detachment had given them his office. It was a space they knew well from previous investigations.

"I spoke to the sound and lighting techs," said Beauvoir. "Both are theater students at the University."

He didn't bring out his notes. Didn't have to. There wasn't much to remember.

"Lighting guy says he slept through until the firecrackers went off.

He says he didn't record the lecture for anyone, but he's a bit of a shit. I doubt he follows rules."

Gamache suppressed a smile. It was almost word for word what the station chief had said about Agent Beauvoir when they'd first met.

"The student doing sound?" asked Isabelle. "Did she see anything?"

"No. She only got the call that morning to go in. She showed up an hour before Robinson went on and hadn't been to the auditorium since the Christmas break. She stayed backstage the whole time. She's still pretty shaken. I've set up an appointment for her with our psychologist."

Gamache nodded. This was the Jean-Guy he'd met years ago. A kind man in shit's clothing.

There was a knock on the door and an agent put his head in.

"The lawyer's here, Chief Inspector."

"*Merci.* Can you show her into the interview room, please? Then wait ten minutes and bring Monsieur Tardif."

"*Entendu.*"

"Fine way to spend New Year's Eve, Armand," said Maître Lacombe as she placed a notepad and her phone on the metal table. She nodded to Beauvoir and Lacoste. "The holy trinity? That's a lot of firepower for a case that's over."

"Is it?" asked Gamache, taking a seat.

"Over? I think so. My client had no priors. He's cooperating. Didn't resist arrest and it was clearly not a serious attempt."

"Well, that's quite a list of lies and half-truths," said Isabelle. "My people had to wrestle the gun from him, he took shots in a crowded enclosed place almost causing a riot, and it was only because the Chief Inspector shoved Professor Robinson aside that she wasn't killed."

"Perception, Inspector." She leaned forward. "Listen, Édouard Tardif's a decent, if deluded, man. He's gotten it into his head that what Professor Robinson is saying is somehow a threat. He's been wound up by a hostile media. By fake news. He took a wild shot—"

"Two," said Beauvoir. "That barely missed."

"But they did miss. And who's to say he didn't intend to miss all along? He's an expert shot. Had he wanted to kill her, he would have."

At a nod from Gamache, Édouard Tardif was brought in.

It was the first time Gamache had met him, beyond a brief exchange at the gym.

Here was a fifty-three-year-old man. Large, powerfully built.

"You can take them off," Gamache said to the agent, pointing to the cuffs around Tardif's thick wrists. After introducing themselves, Gamache said, "We have some questions for you, sir."

"Before we start," said Tardif, "how're the people taken to hospital?"

His voice was as he looked. Gruff, rough. A kind of growl. But not, Gamache thought, vicious.

"Mostly scrapes and bruises," said Isabelle. "Shock. One man is still in hospital for observation. A suspected heart attack."

"I hope he's all right."

"If he dies, you'll be charged with murder," said Isabelle.

"Manslaughter at most," said Maître Lacombe.

"Shall we begin?" asked Gamache. "We hope you can clear up some things."

He looked at Lacoste, who began.

She asked deceptively simple, easy questions to begin with, to get him relaxed. Where he lived, his age, his workplace.

"The forest," said Monsieur Tardif, in answer to that question.

It was the simple truth, said without sarcasm. Édouard Tardif cut and hauled trees for firewood out of the forest. He did it with his horse, because the woods were too thick for a tractor.

He felled the trees, then together they dragged them out, one by one.

"Ones," he explained, "that were about to die anyway."

"You do this alone?" asked Gamache.

"Sometimes with my brother but mostly alone."

"Dangerous work to do by yourself," said Lacoste. "Deep in the woods."

"Well, young people today don't want to work hard. And I like it by myself. No one to bother me."

"Or save you."

Now Tardif looked at Jean-Guy, who'd just spoken. "There're worse places to die than in the forest. Worse ways."

"Like being shot or crushed in a crowded auditorium?" asked Beauvoir.

Tardif's lower teeth gripped his upper lip, drawing it in.

"Monsieur Tardif did not mean to hurt Professor Robinson," said his lawyer. "It was meant to scare, that's all."

"We're not interviewing you, Maître Lacombe," said Gamache. "Please let your client answer." He turned back to Tardif. "I suspect you can speak for yourself. I also think what happened yesterday wasn't some sudden flight of fancy. What did you intend?"

"I advise you not to answer that," said Maître Lacombe.

Tardif looked at her, then at the three Sûreté officers. "I learned my trade from an old woodsman named Tony. I was a kid, and only knew maples. And chestnuts. And pines, of course. He taught me that there're different types of maples, of pines, of oaks and cherry. The weed trees, the hardwoods. The evergreens. The ones that were dying and the ones that could be saved. I learned to listen to people who know more than I do. Why would I have a lawyer and not listen to her? I'll pass on that question."

His answer, so well reasoned, so succinctly put into context, surprised even Maître Lacombe.

"What you do in the woods," said Jean-Guy, "choosing which trees will die soon anyway and cutting them down, that's gotta be good for the health of the whole forest. The other trees benefit."

"Sure."

"So why do you have such trouble with what Professor Robinson is saying? Isn't it the same thing? The ill, the terminal, sacrificed for the greater good?"

"I guess I have trouble with it because there's a difference between a tree and a person."

Maître Lacombe laughed. *"Touché."*

"You're a member of the gun club, an expert shot," said Isabelle. "You know what guns, what bullets can do. And yet you chose to fire one off, twice, in a crowded hall. You almost caused a riot. Hundreds could've been killed, including children."

"I didn't think of that."

"Bullshit," said Beauvoir. "You're clever. You want us to know you're clever. And now you're saying you didn't think of the obvious? You just didn't care. You didn't care about those kids. Those elderly men and women. Who'd be killed in the riot? Probably not the young, healthy ones. It would be the vulnerable, the sick, the slower, the weaker. You're no better than Robinson."

Beauvoir was all but shouting at the man.

Gamache let it happen, curious to see what Tardif would do.

"I care," exploded Tardif. "Why do you think I did it."

"Why?" demanded Beauvoir.

"Don't answer that," snapped Tardif's lawyer, laying a hand on his large arm.

"To save others. To stop her."

Maître Lacombe moaned and sat back. "There we go."

"Why?" demanded Beauvoir.

"Wouldn't you? Do you want her to go killing old people? Kids? What sort of person wouldn't want to stop her? I knew I'd be caught, and it was worth it. Someone had to do it. Someone had to try." Now the woodsman glared at Gamache. "But you saved her."

Those few words contained all the disgust nature had placed in this man. He all but spat at Gamache.

"I did. No one has the right to take another life without permission." Only a slight flush gave away Gamache's feelings. "Not Professor Robinson, not the government. And not you, Monsieur Tardif."

Now it was Tardif's turn to redden.

"Why were you so far back in the room?" Lacoste asked, her voice matter-of-fact.

"I didn't expect so many cops. My plan was to be at the front and shoot from there."

"From there you couldn't miss," said Lacoste.

"Don't," warned his lawyer.

"But when I saw so many cops, I backed off. I thought if I stood in the middle I could get away."

"So you did want to get away," said Beauvoir.

"If I could, yes. I didn't want to get caught. But I expected to."

"Who set off the firecrackers?"

"I did."

There was silence. Until Gamache spoke.

"That's not true, is it."

"It is."

"What was the purpose of the firecrackers?"

"To distract."

"Really? And yet they had the opposite effect. Everyone was now looking in your direction. Who was your accomplice?" Lacoste asked.

"No one."

"Someone hid the gun and firecrackers three days before the event," said Lacoste. It was the first time Tardif looked surprised. Off balance. "While you distracted the caretaker. Who was it?"

Tardif's face hardened.

"Was it your brother, Alphonse?"

Tardif stared at her, stone-faced.

"He left for the Abitibi the day of the attack. It's impossible to see that as a mere coincidence."

"He had nothing to do with what happened. I acted alone."

"We know that isn't true." Her voice grew cold and hard. "Listen, despite what happened, no one was actually killed. If you cooperate, we can move forward and end this. We'll find out soon enough. You must know that. We're having your brother picked up. It would be better for you, for him, if you just tell us."

Édouard Tardif crossed his huge, muscled arms over his chest. Isabelle Lacoste pushed some more, but it was obvious that the interview was over.

"The arraignment's scheduled for tomorrow," said Gamache as he walked Maître Lacombe to the front door of the detachment.

"*Merci*, Armand. I'll be there."

"Tell your client to cooperate," he said. "If there's a co-conspirator out there, we don't want him harming Abigail Robinson, or anyone else. If he succeeds, Monsieur Tardif will be charged with murder. And that charge will hold. You know that."

Maître Lacombe slipped on her gloves and nodded. "I'll talk to him."

"*Bon.*"

At the door, Gamache said, "It sounds as though you agree with Professor Robinson."

She paused and looked at him. "Don't you? What sort of society allows its people to suffer when there's no hope? It would be a kindness."

"It would be a cull."

"Culls happen for the health of the community. They're unfortunate, but necessary. *Bonne année*, Armand."

CHAPTER 16

—

The party was in full swing when Armand and Reine-Marie walked into the Auberge just before ten o'clock that evening.

A huge spruce, fragrant and festooned with sparkling glass ornaments, candy canes and strings of popcorn, dominated one corner of the living room.

Pine boughs with bright red bows rested on the mantelpiece along with tall columns of flickering candles. Beneath the mantel, a fire crackled in the grate.

Marc Gilbert had hung a sprig of mistletoe on the chandelier in the entrance, and people were hugged and kissed as they arrived.

Armand smiled as he looked around. And felt a wave of relief.

A year ago . . . a year ago . . . this had seemed impossible. Gone forever. As the second wave hit and the virus spread, taking with it more shops, more jobs, more freedoms, more lives.

But just as things had fallen apart so quickly, so too did they recover once the vaccine was discovered and shared among nations.

Like a forest after a fire, he thought, as he took their coats to a back room where a bed was heaped high with them. There was loss, but vivid new life had also emerged from the ash.

Stores had reopened. Hotels and restaurants were packed. Employment was higher than ever. It was as though people were awakening after a long nightmare and wanting to make up for lost time. To enjoy a freedom they no longer took for granted.

Returning to the foyer and looking through the living room windows at the far end, he spotted Florence, Zora, and Honoré. They were out-side with the other children, roasting marshmallows by the bonfire, supervised by Monsieur Béliveau the grocer.

He then scanned the room and found Reine-Marie chatting with Clara and Ruth. He caught Clara's eye and recognized the look.

Even though it had been years since Marc and Dominique Gilbert had taken over, Clara couldn't yet call the place the Auberge, or the Inn and Spa. It would always be the Old Hadley House to her. And to him.

It would always be the horror on the hill, overlooking their pretty little village. The Old Hadley House watched as they went about their lives. Their happiness, their contentment, only seemed to make its shadow longer, darker. Elongating toward them even as the paint peeled, the roof lost shingles, the wood rotted. The happier they were, the fouler it had become.

It was a menace. The villagers held a meeting, and it was decided that they should tear it down. But then one lone voice made another suggestion.

They'd turned in their seats in St. Thomas's church and stared in astonishment as Ruth Zardo suggested maybe it could be saved.

A vote was taken and the decision reached to give the place another chance. And so, it was rebuilt, refurbed, repainted by the villagers. Cleaned and even cleansed in a ritual led by Myrna, using sage and sweetgrass and holy water.

Then, when they'd done all they could, the Old Hadley House was sold at cost to the young couple and became the Inn and Spa.

Now, when they looked at it, the villagers saw not a horror but a second chance.

And yet Clara could never step into the place without feeling the cold breath of dread. Without seeing it as it had been. And still was, she suspected. Beneath the coat of fresh paint.

Even now the scent of rot seemed to ooze from the walls. The artist in Clara knew that paint didn't change anything. It just covered what was, and always would be, there.

And she could see that Armand felt exactly the same way. Felt the same thing.

It was unfair, Armand knew, as he ladled punch into glasses. But he still saw, beneath the new plaster, the bones of the place. The snakes in the basement, the rat skeletons curled in corners. The thick spiderwebs waiting to catch and consume some living creature.

He could smell the decomposition beneath the fresh pine and ginger and cinnamon of the season.

"Drink?" he said, handing Clara one of the glasses of spiked punch. *"Merci."*

He gave the other to Reine-Marie.

"What about me?" demanded Ruth.

He looked at the vat of scotch the old poet was gripping. He recognized it. It was actually a flower vase. From their home.

Kids came in from outside and grabbed treats off the long table filled with tourtières and boeuf bourguignon. Assorted cheeses and sliced baguettes. A whole poached and decorated salmon had been provided by Gabri and Olivier, while a separate table was filled with mince tarts and butter tarts, with cookies and cakes, jars of licorice allsorts and jelly beans and chocolate-covered cherries.

A huge gingerbread house, a replica of the Inn and Spa, sat in the middle of the table.

Clara bent down and looked through the gumdrop-encrusted door.

"What're you looking for?" asked Ruth.

"Your lost youth," said Clara, straightening up.

"You won't find it there." Ruth raised her vat.

Outside, Daniel was comforting Florence, who was staring dejected at the charred and smoldering marshmallow sagging off her stick.

Honoré, following the lead of the older boys, plunged his stick, marshmallow and all, into the heart of the fire, as though slaying a dragon. Embers burst forth and drifted into the night sky.

Zora stood way back. Neither she nor her marshmallow was in danger of getting singed. But neither would they get toasty warm. As Armand watched, Daniel moved over to his youngest daughter and knelt beside her in the snow, whispering, reassuring, coaxing, but not pushing her forward.

Zora took one tentative step. Then a second.

Brave girl, her grandfather thought. Armand knew the terror of that first step. He also knew that the key to a full life was taking it. The trick wasn't necessarily having less fear, it was finding more courage. Zora had that. She also had a father who knew the difference between carrying and supporting.

"Where's numbnuts?" asked Ruth.

"At home. He and Idola will be by soon," said Armand.

They'd long since accepted that that was Ruth's name for Jean-Guy. And Jean-Guy himself accepted it, or at least had grown numb to it.

"I haven't seen Idola in two days," said Ruth. "Is she talking yet?"

"Not yet," said Reine-Marie. "And for God's sake, we don't want a repeat of the Honoré fiasco."

Ruth chuckled and looked anything but contrite. She'd taught the boy his first, and still his favorite, word.

"Wasn't me." Ruth glanced accusingly at the duck in her arms.

"Fuck, fuck, fuck," said Rosa in an ineffective defense.

"And Stephen?" Ruth asked, casually. "Is he coming?"

"Are you blushing?" said Reine-Marie.

"She can't," said Gabri. "To blush you need blood in your veins." He nodded toward the scotch. "If ever embarrassed, she'll turn golden."

"I think that's called jaundice," said Clara.

"Did I hear my name?" Stephen walked slowly across the crowded room, using his cane to clear the way. Just as Ruth had shown him.

"Hello, Jaundice," said Ruth.

"Hello, Liver Failure," said Stephen, kissing her on both cheeks. "And fuck, fuck, fuck to you," he said to Rosa, who looked at him with something close to adoration. Which ducks very rarely did.

As people chatted around him, Armand glanced outside again at the glowing faces and bright eyes staring into the bonfire. It felt like it could be the dawn of time.

Primal and ancient. A new year, a new day dawning.

Armand often went to the little chapel on the hill. More for the silence than the sermons. And he almost always found Ruth already there. Sitting alone and scribbling in her customary seat, and sometimes on it. She sat under the stained-glass window of three of the village boys who'd gone to the Great War and never returned.

On the wall was the polished plaque with the unforgivably long list with names like Tommy and Bobby and Jacques. And below the names was engraved: *They Were Our Children.*

Then shall forgiven and forgiving meet again. Armand thought of Ruth's seminal poem as he watched the children around the fire.

Our children, he knew, had much to forgive.

Or will it be, as always was, too late?

"What're you thinking?" Reine-Marie asked, seeing the faraway look in his eyes.

"Actually, I was thinking about your poem about forgiveness," he said to Ruth. "Have you ever met Abigail Robinson?"

"The madwoman?" asked Ruth. She turned to Stephen. "If she has her way, we'd both be put down."

"Maybe not so crazy," Gabri said to Olivier.

"My God," said someone in the crowd. "I don't believe it."

Armand turned to see what they didn't believe.

The whole room had grown quiet. Even the kids stopped running and shouting and slowed to a halt, gingerbread men halfway to their mouths. They too were staring toward the wide stairway that swept up from the foyer.

Haniya stopped, halfway down the stairs. And stood there. Perfectly still. Until every eye in the room was on her.

"Is that?"

"Can't be."

"But what's she doing here?"

"My God, she's magnificent," Reine-Marie whispered.

And she was. Haniya Daoud, the Hero of the Sudan, was standing on the sweeping stairway, head high, chin up, body enfolded in a rich rose-and-gold abaya and hijab.

She was luminous.

It was Reine-Marie's first glimpse of Haniya Daoud. After her conversation with Armand and her friends, and their less-than-flattering descriptions of the woman, Reine-Marie had expected someone gloomier. Certainly dimmer.

What she saw was a woman who seemed ageless, timeless. A powerful woman who commanded the room before she'd even entered it.

If this was broken, Reine-Marie thought, what must whole be like?

"I'm going to have to go over there soon," said Myrna a few minutes later, looking across the room at Haniya, who was holding court next to the Christmas tree.

"Why?" asked Jean-Guy. He and Idola had joined them. She was in a chipmunk onesie, with little ears and a tail.

Olivier took and cradled her, turning away from Gabri's outstretched arms as he reached for the child. "Mine."

Parents were shoving their children forward, toward Madame Daoud. So that one day they could tell their own children they'd met a saint.

Photos were taken, while Haniya stared stone-faced into the cameras.

As a little girl walked away, they heard her ask her mother, "Do all saints have scars?"

"I can answer that," said an older man who'd just joined their group.

"Hello, Vincent," said Reine-Marie, smiling as they kissed on both cheeks, then turning to Stephen.

"I don't think you've met. This's Dr. Vincent Gilbert," she said. "And this is Stephen Horowitz."

"Ahhh," said Stephen with a smile. "The Asshole Saint."

"That's me," agreed Gilbert, as the two older men shook hands. "And you're the failed billionaire."

"Please, I'm now living off my godson and his family. Can't call that a failure."

Gilbert laughed. "Nice crowd." His eyes scanned the room, looking, Armand thought, for someone.

Myrna took a swig of punch and said, "I think I'll do the deed now before her mood completely sours. Such a shame she doesn't drink."

"What deed?" Vincent Gilbert asked.

"An apology." She turned to Reine-Marie. "I'll introduce you. Clara?"

"What?"

"Come on, you know what."

"Oh, all right." Clara drained her glass and gave it to Annie. "If we don't come back, know that I loved you all."

"Can I have your painting of Ruth?" asked Gabri.

"No, I want that," said Ruth. "It's the only one that isn't crap."

"So much for love," said Myrna as they headed across the room.

"That's the famous Hero of the Sudan," said Dr. Gilbert, taking Reine-Marie's place beside Armand. "I heard she might be here."

The Asshole Saint was staring at Haniya with curiosity and unconcealed resentment.

Having lived for years not only in the forest, but in his spacious ego, Dr. Vincent Gilbert had grown to expect he'd be the center of wonderment and awe at any gathering.

"She's younger than I thought."

"She's twenty-three," said Armand. "Madame Daoud was kidnapped and sold into slavery when she was eleven."

"*Oui.* Terrible story."

Gamache was reminded why this man was known as the Asshole Saint. He was certainly part saint, but it wasn't lost on anyone who met him that while his medical research had improved the human condition, he himself did not actually like humans.

"I didn't expect to see the Hero of the Sudan in the dark hole of Québec," said Gilbert. "What's she doing here?"

"She's visiting Myrna."

"That doesn't really answer my question, does it?"

"I thought it did."

Vincent Gilbert was in his mid-seventies and looked every minute of that age, and then some. Slight, sinewy, his skin lined and leathery from his latter life as a recluse, living in a log cabin in the middle of the forest.

"You're not normally this vague, Armand. I wonder if that event yesterday took something out of you."

Despite the words, Vincent Gilbert's tone was gentle. Inviting Armand to talk about it, if he wanted to. Every now and then, Armand thought, the saint part showed a bit of ankle.

But then something occurred to him. Maybe Vincent Gilbert didn't want to listen, maybe he wanted to talk about the events at the University.

"Vincent, do you know Abigail Robinson?"

"Only by reputation. I've read her study."

"And?"

"And nothing. I'm a doctor, not a statistician."

"Then why did you read it?"

"I got tired of reading articles on compost. Interestingly, I did find that her recent research makes good fertilizer. *Excusez-moi*, Armand. Marc!"

Reine-Marie fought it, but finally had to admit that she found Haniya Daoud difficult.

She tried to look sympathetic as Haniya listened, stone-faced, to Clara's apology. It didn't help that Myrna's apology had been met with silence. And now, into that abyss, Clara poured words that sounded, and probably were, less and less sincere.

As Reine-Marie watched Haniya, and saw the curling lip, all she could think of was the line from Ruth's poem.

Who hurt you once, so far beyond repair?

Though they knew who'd hurt her. Not just her torturers. They all had, by their silence and inaction.

It was five past eleven. Almost time for the play.

Patting his pockets, Armand realized he'd left his phone in his parka and he wanted to take pictures. Coming out of the cloakroom with his phone, Armand heard one of their hosts, Dominique, talking to some late arrivals.

"You can put your coats in the room, just throw them on the bed, and then make yourselves at home." But a slight flattening of Dominique's normally cheerful voice made Armand look down the hall at the newcomers.

As he did, his smile faded.

Facing him, also stopped and staring, was Colette Roberge. And behind her were Abigail Robinson and Debbie Schneider.

CHAPTER 17

———

Bonjour," said Armand, not bothering to smile. "I didn't realize you'd be here."

"I invited Chancellor Roberge," said Dominique, sensing the tension and trying to plaster over it. "She called this afternoon and asked if we were holding our annual New Year's Eve party. I said we were and she was welcome to come."

They threw their coats onto the bed, then returned with Armand back down the hall.

"I asked if I could bring some guests," Colette explained.

"I thought you meant your husband," said Dominique.

"We seem fated to run into each other, Chief Inspector," said Abigail Robinson when they'd stopped in the foyer.

"*Excusez-moi.*" He took Chancellor Roberge aside and dropped his voice. "I thought I asked you to keep Professor Robinson at your place. To not leave the property."

"You did, but—"

"But we aren't under arrest," said Abigail, joining what was clearly meant to be a private conversation. "Are we? Being here isn't breaking any law, is it?"

Armand took a deep breath. "*Non.* But for your own safety and the safety of others—"

"No one knew we were coming," the Chancellor pointed out. "Not even our host."

Now it was Colette's turn to take Armand's arm and lead him farther from the group.

"I didn't expect to see you here, Armand. How do you know the Gilberts?"

"They're neighbors. We live in this village. Why are you here, Colette?"

"Abby insisted. Remember I told you there was someone she wanted to meet?"

"They're here?"

"Maybe."

"Maybe?"

"Look, all I know is that she asked me to call around and find out if there were any parties happening here."

"Here? In this village?"

"Yes. She knew about Three Pines. So I called Dominique and she invited us."

"She invited you and Jean-Paul, not—" He nodded toward Abigail, then looked out at the gathering.

So far no one had noticed who'd just arrived. Most were still stealing glances at Haniya Daoud, though few were approaching anymore. She was beginning to look like a fortress, with a moat widening around her.

Even Reine-Marie had moved away.

"Who has Abigail come to see?" asked Armand. "You must've asked."

"I did, but she wouldn't tell me."

"Why not?"

Colette sighed. "I don't know."

He stared at her. "You could've refused, you know. You didn't have to bring her here. What're you playing at, Colette?"

"Nothing. Just trying to help the daughter of a friend."

"Why?"

"*Pardon?*"

"Why? Why go through all this? What do you owe him? Or her? Why're you doing all this for her? You know how this looks."

"How?" The Chancellor was also getting annoyed. "How exactly does this look?"

"You set up her talk. You have her staying with you. You bring her to this party. It looks like you support her campaign."

"I support her right—"

"Oh, please. Save it for the Board of Governors. We both know you're making some very"—he paused for the right word—"dangerous choices."

"Dangerous?" She almost laughed. "Are you feeling threatened, Armand? A strong, smart woman is putting forward compelling arguments that fly in the face of your beliefs. And you don't like it."

"I'm the head of homicide for the Sûreté du Québec, Colette, not some student who can be lectured, frightened, or bullied into falling in line. The threat against Professor Robinson is real and proven, and you've taken her out of a safe place and back into the public. Possibly endangering not just her, but everyone here. Including my family. That's the dangerous choice you've made. It's not against the law, but it sure flies in the face of good judgment."

Some of the other guests had begun to recognize Abigail Robinson.

Phones were swinging from Haniya Daoud to the newcomer. Photos taken.

He turned back to Chancellor Roberge. "I'm not trying to stop her. I'm actually trying to keep her alive. Are you?"

"What's that supposed to mean?"

He gestured toward the phones pointed at Abigail. A buzz had gone through the room.

"It'll be all over social media in moments. If you have an ounce of reason left, you'll tell her to meet whoever she came to see tomorrow. At your place. Privately." He stared at her. "Go home, Colette."

As he spoke, he noticed that Abigail Robinson was looking at someone in the crowd.

Haniya Daoud.

The Nobel nominee's arms were folded tight across her body. And she was staring back.

Surely not her, thought Armand.

But . . .

Vincent Gilbert had asked why Madame Daoud was there. Maybe

it wasn't to visit Myrna. Maybe that was just the excuse. And this was the reason.

Was Professor Robinson here to meet Madame Daoud? And Haniya Daoud here to meet Abigail Robinson? But if so, to what end? What could the Hero of the Sudan and a woman proposing mass and targeted killing have to talk about?

Unless it wasn't to talk.

Get out of my way, Haniya had said just last night.

Would I, this time? Step aside?

Armand felt a cold draft on the back of his neck and glanced at the front door, but it was closed.

"Is that Haniya Daoud?" Debbie Schneider asked. "Why would she be here?" There was a pause before she said, "My God, Abby. I think it is her. If we could get her endorsement . . ."

But Abigail's eyes had moved on. She was no longer looking at Haniya. She was staring at the Asshole Saint. Vincent Gilbert.

Armand was behind her and couldn't see her expression. He could, however, see Dr. Gilbert's. He was staring beyond Abigail Robinson. At the Chancellor.

A silence had fallen like concrete over the crowd, slowly crushing the gaiety out of the New Year's Eve celebrations. All eyes, even Gilbert's, were now on Abigail Robinson.

Armand heard Dominique say to her husband, "Worst party ever."

"It gets worse," whispered Marc. "Dad's here and Ruth's found the booze."

Armand saw Annie take Idola from Olivier, while Jean-Guy put his arm around them both. Reine-Marie joined her daughter and granddaughter.

One by one Daniel, Stephen, Clara, Olivier, Ruth, Myrna surrounded Idola. As though Professor Robinson's very thoughts could harm the little girl. And, Armand knew, they could.

"Maybe we should leave," said Chancellor Roberge, unsettled by the mood in the room.

"Maybe . . . ," Debbie muttered to Abby.

"No. We've come too far."

Raising her arms slightly in what looked like surrender, Abby stepped forward and broke the silence.

"I know most of you recognize me, and that this isn't necessarily a welcome surprise. I want you to know that our hosts didn't invite me."

She smiled. Just as at the event, her voice was soft, reasonable. Personable. Armand could feel the tension lower.

This wasn't the monster they'd expected. The lunatic with the crazy ideas. This was someone just like them. Nice.

"So," said Abigail. "No need to shoot them. Just me."

At that there was some nervous laughter.

Armand had rarely seen a crowd turned so quickly. It didn't mean anyone there was suddenly going to join the professor's crusade, but he could see their own defenses dropping.

They liked her, if not her goals.

Though there was one other person in the room who'd managed to turn the crowd equally quickly, just in the opposite direction. Haniya Daoud had managed to turn almost everyone away.

From down the hallway there came a commotion, young voices raised in excitement.

It was 11:25. The rehearsal was over. The main event was about to begin.

"What is this?" Haniya asked Roslyn as the village kids excitedly shoved the adults off the raised foyer and took their places on what had become a stage.

"It's a Québécois tradition," Roslyn explained. She was watching her daughters take their places. "I did it when I was a child."

Roslyn hadn't noticed that Haniya was staring at Abigail Robinson when she'd asked, *What is this?*

Now Haniya Daoud refocused on Roslyn. "Did what?"

"*Les Fables de La Fontaine*. Each New Year's Eve the children choose one of his stories and act it out."

"God," said Haniya. "More torture."

Clara caught Haniya's eye and, just before Haniya turned away, Clara saw a smile. She'd, unexpectedly, made a joke. For just that moment

Clara saw the young woman behind the scars. Whose wounds had momentarily healed at the sight of children in homemade costumes, pushing and shoving each other on the "stage."

And then the moment passed, and the scars reappeared, deeper than ever.

Clara shifted her gaze to see what Haniya was now looking at.

Who she was looking at.

Abigail Robinson was making her way through the crowd, which parted as though the professor wore a tattered cloak and carried a scythe.

"Oh, this's one of my favorites," said Myrna, elbowing Clara. "'Les Animaux Malades de la Peste.'"

"'The Animals Sick of the Plague,'" Roslyn translated for Haniya.

Not with the plague, Haniya noted as she followed Abigail's progress across the room, but of it.

She too was sick of it.

"Vincent Gilbert, is it not?" said Abigail Robinson, smiling.

He inclined his head but did not offer his hand. "Professor."

"This's my assistant, Deborah Schneider, and Colette Roberge—"

"The Chancellor of the University," said Gilbert. "We've met."

A commotion onstage caught their attention, and they turned toward it.

It generally took at least two minutes for the annual Fable de La Fontaine to descend into debacle, but this one had got there in record time.

The little girl playing the donkey was in tears. Despite Gabri's reassurance that it was just an act, still the child took the dialogue personally as the other animals blamed her, or rather the donkey, for the outbreak of plague.

She was howling, "It's not my fault."

They paused while Gabri and the girl's parents sorted it out.

In the unexpected intermission, Chancellor Roberge said, "I'm not sure if you know that Dr. Gilbert did landmark studies on the mind-body connection."

"I know who he is," said Abigail. "And I know about his research."

"And I know about yours," he said. "You're making quite a splash in the scientific community. Maybe we can talk about it sometime."

"Are you interested in endorsing my findings, Dr. Gilbert? We seem to have a lot in common."

"How so?"

"I've often thought you didn't get the proper recognition, especially for your early work. I'd be happy to try to get you what you deserve."

Armand had positioned himself close to Professor Robinson. His back was to them, and while he listened closely to the conversation, his eyes remained on the stage, watching his grandchildren.

Honoré, in his first Fable, was wearing huge bunny ears and had dragged his toboggan onstage with him. Florence and Zora were both dressed as piglets and were trying to comfort the donkey. Saying the plague wasn't her fault. They were just pretending.

"I'm retired now," said Gilbert. "It doesn't matter anymore."

"The truth always matters," said Professor Robinson.

"Truth?" Gilbert's tone was amused. "No real scientist talks about the truth."

There was a pause. "Are you saying I'm not a real scientist?"

The chilly undercurrent had reached the surface.

"But then," Abigail was saying, "I understand why you wouldn't be a fan of the truth."

"Actually," said Gilbert, "I am. Now I have more time on my hands, I'm finding the truth far more interesting than facts. The truth is, no serious scientist is taking your conclusions seriously. The Royal Commission won't even let you present them. And for good reason. It might not be intellectual madness, but it is moral insanity."

There was a pause as a pit opened in the conversation.

Abigail filled it with a single hoot of laughter. "Moral insanity? You, of all people, would say that?"

Listening to this, Armand was trying to work out what exactly was happening. What was really being said. What was really going on. Because something was.

"You need help," said Gilbert. "Look at those faces. Half the people here, given a chance and a gun, would pull the trigger."

Professor Robinson looked at the crowd, then back to him.

"And the other half, Doctor? They know that what I'm saying is rational and realistic. What scares people like you is that I'm just voicing what most are thinking."

"Most?" said Gilbert. "I don't think so."

"You're right. Not yet. But give it time. The Royal Commission might not listen to me, but others will. Others are. I have an appointment with the Premier next week. Now, you know my calculations are right. If you'd like to endorse what I am saying—"

"Your statistics might be right—"

"They are."

"—but your conclusions are wrong. Don't you care about that?"

"Right? Wrong? Suddenly you're the arbiter? Such hypocrisy, Dr. Gilbert. After all, there were some pretty controversial studies out of your own university, I believe. Didn't Ewen Cameron work at McGill?"

Now Armand did turn around and saw the surprise on Vincent Gilbert's face.

"He was a monster," said Gilbert.

"True. But monstrosities live a long time. And monsters beget other monsters." She looked again at the other guests, including Jean-Guy and Annie, who were watching them. "All that's missing are pitchforks and torches. But maybe I'm not the one they should be coming for."

Now Armand was confused. Had she just called Vincent Gilbert a monster?

"What's that supposed to mean?" demanded Gilbert.

Up onstage the play had resumed. A lion was reciting, *"By history we find it noted / That lives have been just so devoted. / Then let us all turn eyes within, / and ferret out the hidden sin."*

"Abby Maria, maybe we should—" Debbie began but was interrupted by Gilbert's laugh.

"Abby Maria? As in Ave Maria?" he said.

"I'm sorry," Debbie began but was ignored.

"You call yourself Abby Maria?" Gilbert sneered. "You are out of control."

"Come on," said Debbie. "No one cares what he thinks."

Though Armand thought that wasn't true. He thought Abigail Robinson cared. She cared so much that she'd traveled thousands of miles to meet him.

He looked over at Colette, who'd been silent through all this. Was silence agreement? And if so, who did the Chancellor agree with?

"You have no moral authority to judge me." Abigail Robinson's voice was low, and it dropped further as she said, "Don't think I don't know."

Up on stage, the Fable de La Fontaine was wrapping up, with all the animals turning to the audience and reciting the final lines.

> Thus human courts acquit the strong,
> And doom the weak, as therefore wrong.

CHAPTER 18

You can stop pretending you're not listening, Armand," said Gilbert.

Colette and Debbie were heading down the corridor toward their coats. Preparing to leave.

But Professor Robinson was taking a different tack. She was heading straight for Annie and Jean-Guy.

Surely the professor could see she was sailing into a storm. But maybe, after that confrontation with Gilbert, that's what she wanted, thought Armand. Needing to blow off steam and spoiling for a fight, she'd chosen the people most likely to give her one.

"You two were really going at it," he said to Vincent. "What did she mean just now when she said she knows. What does she know?"

"Nothing. She's a sociopath."

Armand continued to watch Abigail Robinson. They all did, it seemed. Everyone in the room was riveted on her. While the Hero of the Sudan had all but disappeared.

It was twenty minutes to midnight.

"And what about Helen Keller?" said Annie, a few minutes later. "You can't tell me she was a burden to society."

"That's a good point. A valid point," said Abigail. She saw Debbie and Colette in their coats, standing by the front door, giving her the high sign. It was time to leave.

Abigail put up her hand in the "five minutes" signal, then turned back to the group.

"Yeah," said Debbie. "There's no way she's leaving in five minutes. Now what? I'm getting hot."

"Let's get some fresh air," said Colette.

"I'll text to let her know we're outside." Debbie put Abigail's coat down on the chair by reception, sent the text, then left with Chancellor Roberge.

Abigail refocused her attention, but her heart wasn't really in these arguments anymore. She had other things on her mind.

Abby Maria. It was the last straw. Gilbert had repeated the name as though vomiting the words up.

Abby Maria. *Full of grace.*

She just wanted this to be over.

Pray for us sinners.

Abigail realized they were waiting for her to say something. To defend herself. She sighed.

"What I'm saying is that resources are limited. That's just a fact. We need to save those who can be saved, and give the rest a dignified, merciful, and, yes, swift end."

She noticed the child in the young woman's arms.

"Oooh, a baby." Abigail leaned forward. "May I?"

Across the room, Ruth and Stephen had joined the Asshole Saint and Armand.

The gathering had returned to a party atmosphere. The play, and the happy children leaping off the "stage" to wild applause, had helped. And now there was the thrum of pleasant conversation, outbursts of laughter, and anticipation as the clock counted down the final minutes of a year both trying and triumphant.

The teenagers in the group were getting a little rowdy, and Armand knew why. If they were anything like he was at that age, and Daniel and Annie for that matter, they'd stashed some beer or cider in the woods, and were enjoying their first drunk.

Tomorrow morning, he also knew from experience, would be a lot less enjoyable.

"Is Reine-Marie still finding monkeys?" asked Ruth.

"*Oui,*" said Armand. He'd been glancing over to see how his family was coping with Abigail Robinson.

Judging by Jean-Guy's face, not well.

"Monkeys?" asked Vincent Gilbert. "Have I missed something?"

"It's what Reine-Marie does now," said Ruth.

"Looks for monkeys? And she finds them? Here?"

"No, you idiot," said Ruth. "They're not real monkeys."

"She's finding imaginary ones?" Dr. Gilbert turned to Armand. "That can't be good."

"A family has asked Reine-Marie to go through their mother's things," Armand explained. "The woman died a few months ago, and in cleaning out the house, they've come across boxes in the attic filled with letters, documents—"

"And monkeys," said Stephen.

"How many so far?" Ruth asked.

"Eighty-six at last count," said Armand.

"Monkeys?" repeated the Asshole Saint.

"Not real ones," snapped Ruth. "And not imaginary."

Now Vincent Gilbert was genuinely interested. "Then what are they?"

"Drawings mostly," said Stephen. "Poor one must've lost her mind."

"A lot of that going around," said Gilbert, glancing over at Abigail Robinson.

Armand gave a small hum. In his experience there was almost always a reason for what people did. And often a rational one, if they could just find it.

"I wonder if there'll be a hundred monkeys," said Gilbert. "That would be interesting."

"And eighty-six isn't?" asked Ruth.

Jean-Guy moved to step between Abigail and Idola. But Annie put a hand on his arm and whispered, *"Ça va bien aller."*

It'll be okay.

He held her gaze, then stepped aside.

"Why do you say a hundred monkeys would be interesting?" Stephen asked.

Seeing Abigail Robinson reach out to move the blanket around Idola, Ruth started forward, clutching her cane and her duck. Rosa was looking very determined. A battle duck.

But Armand put out his hand. *"Non.* Let them."

"Idola—" Ruth began.

"Is safe." Though he didn't take his eyes off them. He wasn't sure what he was afraid of. He knew Abigail Robinson wasn't going to harm his granddaughter. Not there. Not then.

They watched Robinson lean in. They watched her straighten up. They watched as she said something to Annie and Jean-Guy. And Annie responded.

Armand saw Reine-Marie smile. Only then did he return his attention to Gilbert.

"The hundredth monkey theory?" Vincent Gilbert was saying. "Never heard of it?"

"Should we have?" Stephen asked.

Gilbert laughed. "I guess not. Living on my own gives me time to read obscure articles. This one's on human nature and crowd mentality."

"Wait a minute," said Stephen. "Is it the study from those anthropologists in Japan?"

"Yes. I'm not even sure it was a real study," said Dr. Gilbert. "It seems like bullshit, and yet . . ."

"Maybe not." Stephen turned to the others with enthusiasm. "It was passed around in the investment community years ago. It's pretty odd, but some think it explains why certain stocks, certain industries or products, like bitcoins, suddenly get hot. Why some ideas take hold, no matter how crazy, while other, even better ideas, just die."

"Like Betamax," said Ruth. It was her answer to everything that should have succeeded but didn't. That and the Avro Arrow.

"What is this study?" Armand asked. Anything to do with human nature interested him.

"Back in the nineteen fifties, I think it was," said Gilbert, "sweet potatoes were dropped on a Japanese island for the monkeys that lived there. The monkeys liked the taste but hated the sand that covered the food. Anthropologists studying the monkeys noticed that one day a young female washed a sweet potato in the ocean. A few others eventually did it too, but most just watched and continued to eat the sandy potatoes. Have I got that right?"

"That's what I remember," said Stephen.

"Not much of a story," said Ruth. "Have I ever told you about the Avro Arrow?"

"She's a friend of yours?" Gilbert asked Stephen.

"Not her. It's the duck who's the friend."

"Down syndrome?" asked Abigail.

"Idola," said Annie.

Reine-Marie looked over to Armand, who would be, she knew, watching. And smiled.

Then she turned back to Abigail. "I'd like to show you something."

The others followed as Reine-Marie led her across to the window and pointed to a pane. "There are others at different windows at the Inn and Spa. In fact, every home and business in Three Pines—"

"Probably Québec," said Gabri.

"—has one."

Taped to the windowpane was a child's drawing of a rainbow, and beneath it the words *Ça va bien aller.*

"Yes. I've seen one at Colette's home," said Abigail. But she didn't seem to be looking at the drawing, but beyond it, to the bonfire.

"It's the French translation of the Julian of Norwich quote," said Myrna. "One I believe you know. *All will be well*."

"Children drew rainbows," said Clara, "as I think they did around the world. But here they also wrote that phrase. They gave them away during the first wave."

Within weeks of the lockdown every home and shuttered business in Three Pines had one in their window.

Ça va bien aller became not just a comfort, but a battle cry. A call for calm and reason. A call for resistance to despair. To panic. To loneliness. To denial and even idiocy.

It had given the villagers hope that they'd one day return to Myrna's bookshop and sit by her woodstove. That they'd meet in the bistro for drinks. That they'd be invited to each other's homes for a meal.

That they'd once again hug. And kiss. Or just touch.

Ça va bien aller.

One day.

There was no overstating the importance, the power, of that phrase. And now this academic, this professor, had co-opted it. She was using it to attack the very people it was meant to hearten.

"This one was done by our granddaughter Florence," said Reine-Marie. She recognized the slapdash nature of it. Though perhaps "exuberant" was a better, if less accurate, word.

Daniel, Annie, and the grandchildren had joined them in Three Pines before the travel ban was put in place. Before the bubble closed around them.

But Armand hadn't made it in, and neither had Jean-Guy. Their absence was felt every moment of every day. And night.

Reine-Marie remembered the day the bistro closed. Then the bookstore. The bakery. Monsieur Béliveau had stayed open, and had quickly run out of toilet paper. And yeast.

The grocer had run himself ragged, and to the brink of bankruptcy, helping others. As had Sarah the baker. As had Olivier and Gabri, making meals for the elderly, for families who'd been thrown out of work. For children whose school food program was no longer an option.

Myrna left books on doorsteps, of friends and strangers, practically emptying her store.

Donning masks and slathering on disinfectant, villagers had delivered meals and medicine. Books and puzzles.

Standing outside, often in the bitter cold, they'd talked to frightened and lonely elderly men and women, through closed windows. Trying to reassure them. And themselves.

All would be well.

They returned home each evening. Exhausted. Bewildered by the speed at which all they'd known was crumbling. And not knowing how bad it would get.

So fragile was life that they could be killed by a cough.

And they were among the lucky ones.

Armand and Jean-Guy were not.

They, along with all those on the front lines, were working sixteen-hour days, coming into contact every hour with people who were desperately sick and needed help.

At the end of their days, Armand and Jean-Guy couldn't even go home to their families. They had to isolate in Montréal, for fear of spreading the virus.

Every morning Reine-Marie would send Armand her favorite short video. Of the bells in Banff. The clapping in London. The singing in Italy. The retrievers Olive and Mabel. The funny. The profane. The moving and inspirational. And the just plain silly. So that he'd go back into the day with a smile.

And every night, often well past midnight, Armand would place the video call. She could see, in the window behind him, the cheerful posters Florence and Zora and Honoré had made for their grandfather.

As the days and weeks and months went on, he looked increasingly haggard. As did she, she suspected.

And then came that night. He'd called later than usual. And he looked like hell. He looked like death.

"Are you sick?" she'd asked, her voice rising. "Do you need to go to the hospital?"

He shook his head but couldn't yet answer. He'd looked at her, pleading for something. For help?

"What can I do? What's happened?" She reached out, but instead of his warm, familiar face, her hand touched the cold screen.

As she watched, he lowered his head and, covering his face with his hands, he sobbed. Finally, he raised his head and lowered his hands and told her.

About getting the call to go to a nursing home. When he'd arrived, he found the daughter of a resident standing in snow that had drifted across what should have been a shoveled path to the front door. But it hadn't been cleared in days.

Her eyes were wide in shock. He put her in his warm car, then called for help.

On the windows he could see the signs of what had happened inside. Not happy hopeful rainbows, but something else smeared on the glass.

Putting on personal protective equipment, he'd gone inside alone.

As he opened the door to the building, he recognized the smell even through his mask.

He didn't describe to Reine-Marie in detail what he'd found. But he'd told her enough, and she'd seen the subsequent news reports to know that all had been as far from well as it was possible to get.

The most vulnerable. The weak. The infirm. Those who could not care for themselves had been abandoned. Left to die. And die they had.

Armand had been the first in and last out. Staying with each man and woman, each body, until all had been removed.

He'd immediately sent teams to other nursing homes, until all of them had been checked. And all the horrors uncovered.

It was a shame he'd carry all his life. Not that he himself had abandoned these people, but that Québec had. Quebeckers had. And he, as a senior police officer, hadn't realized sooner that this could happen in a pandemic. That this could ever happen. Here. Here.

Not given to conspiracy theories, Armand had, nonetheless, formed and harbored a suspicion that while authorities hadn't actively hastened the deaths, hadn't intentionally turned their backs, neither had they chosen to look in that direction. No one had been in a hurry to use precious and increasingly rare resources on those who would die soon anyway.

> Then let us all turn eyes within,
> And ferret out the hidden sin.

Reine-Marie knew that Armand had started a private file, investigating those responsible.

It might take months, years, but he would ferret out the hidden sin.

And now, to hear the phrase *All shall be well* used to justify ending the lives of the frail and most vulnerable appalled her.

Yes, she thought, looking at Abigail Robinson, they were sick of the plague. And here, among them, was the new carrier.

"The numbers of monkeys washing the potatoes slowly crept up over a period of months—"

"Oh, God," said Ruth. "Are we still talking about monkeys? Let's just agree that Peter Tork was the best and move on."

"Then," Gilbert continued, "one morning the hundredth monkey, by the scientists' count, picked up a sweet potato and washed it. And that did it. Something broke. By nightfall all the monkeys on the island were washing their potatoes."

"Are we sure that's not a euphemism?" asked Ruth. "They are monkeys after all."

"Why?" asked Armand, ignoring her, but unable to suppress a smile. "Was that monkey an alpha? A leader?"

"No, nothing special at all about her," said Gilbert. "Interesting, isn't it? Why it should suddenly take off like that. What difference that one monkey, the hundredth, made. What's even more interesting is that they then discovered monkeys on other islands doing the same thing. None of them had washed their sweet potatoes before, but now they all were."

"Oh, come on," said Ruth. "That's not possible. Are you saying the monkeys had ESP? They communicated by, what? Brain waves?"

Rosa snorted.

"I'm not saying it," said Gilbert. "The anthropologists just reported it. They were as baffled as anyone else. It's become known as the hundredth monkey effect. Whether it was a hundred monkeys or not, the point was that when a tipping point is reached, when a certain number of monkeys—"

"—or people," said Stephen.

"—start doing the same thing—"

"—or believing the same thing," said Stephen.

"Exactly," said Vincent. "The idea explodes."

"It takes on a life of its own," said Armand, glancing at Abigail.

He wondered if, thanks to the event at the gym and the errant gunshots, that hundredth monkey had been reached. He also wondered if that had been the purpose of the shots.

He was deep in thought when Honoré, still wearing his bunny ears and dragging his toboggan, came up to him.

"Papa—" he began, but that was as far as he got.

Bang! Bang! Bang! Explosions filled the room.

Armand pulled Honoré to him, swiftly turning his back on the shots, bending over and enveloping the boy with his body.

Across the room, Jean-Guy grabbed Annie and Idola while Haniya Daoud dropped to her knees, bending over, covering her head with her hands. Making herself as small as possible.

Seconds later the shots stopped and, keeping Honoré behind him, Armand swung round. His sharp eyes scanned the room. Body tense, prepared to act, even as his mind said—

"They're firecrackers, Armand." Stephen was looking with concern at his godson. Reaching out a bony hand, he placed it on Armand's chest. "It's all right."

Honoré was looking at his grandfather in shock. His bunny ears askew. His lower lip trembling.

"Oh, no." Armand dropped to his knee, to be at eye level with the child. "No, no. It's all right. I just . . ." Just what?

Just thought it was gunfire. But he didn't say that.

The day before, at the event, he'd immediately recognized the firecrackers, but then he'd been alert and prepared for something to happen. Here, now, he'd been taken by surprise.

He held out his arms, and Honoré walked into them.

Across the room, he saw Jean-Guy looking shaken. Then his gaze went to Haniya Daoud being helped to her feet by Roslyn and Clara, and shaking off their hands.

No one else had reacted to the noise. Just them. Everyone else heard firecrackers. While they'd heard gunshots.

As he held his grandson, Armand Gamache wondered how deep their wounds really went. How much damage had been done.

And if they'd ever really heal.

CHAPTER 19

*D*ésolé," Félix called as Jean-Guy and Armand stepped outside.
"The little shit's not sorry at all," said Jean-Guy.

It was clear now that the firecrackers had been thrown onto the bonfire by Monsieur Béliveau's eleven-year-old assistant.

"You can't tell me you wouldn't have done the same thing, Jean-Guy, when you were his age. Fireworks? A bonfire? You'd have thrown the whole damn box into the flames."

Jean-Guy grinned. It was true. Pinwheels. Roman candles. Those whistling rockets. All would have gone up in one glorious demonstration of his impotence.

Monsieur Béliveau joined them, his boots crunching on the hard-packed snow. "*Désolé*. I'll handle this. My fireworks. My fault."

Monsieur Béliveau looked across the flames at Félix, who was inching toward the big open box of fireworks.

"*Eh, garçon. Non.*" His voice was firm, but when he turned back to Armand and Jean-Guy, he was amused. "Kids."

Though dour and childless himself, the grocer was unfailingly kind and patient with children. As though instead of having none, he had them all.

While Monsieur Béliveau went to speak to Félix, Armand and Jean-Guy warmed themselves by the bonfire, holding their bare hands to the flames. It was a crisp, clear winter night, though the wind was picking up.

"Weather's closing in," said Jean-Guy, looking up at the stars. Instinctively finding the Big Dipper.

Just in sweaters, they got as close to the fire as they dared.

There was a familiar scratching as ice crystals, picked up by a gust, slid across the surface of the snow. The same gust caught smoke and embers from the bonfire and blew it toward them.

Armand and Jean-Guy closed their eyes and turned away. When it had passed, Armand asked, "Everything okay?"

Jean-Guy smiled. "It's smoke. I think I'll survive."

"I meant Professor Robinson."

"She saw Idola," said Jean-Guy. Armand was silent, staring into the crackling bonfire, knowing there was more. "I tried to stop her, Armand. I think Annie thought it was because I wanted to protect Idola, and it was mostly that. But . . ."

Armand waited.

". . . but a small part of me didn't want her to see."

In the wavering light of the flames Armand saw, for the first time, lines on Jean-Guy's face. Had so many years really passed, Armand thought, since they first met? So many lines produced.

And now he noticed too the beginning of gray in Jean-Guy's dark hair.

"But you let her," Armand said.

"Only because of Annie. She said it would be all right."

"And is it? All right?"

Jean-Guy gave a short laugh, and Armand saw that the deepest lines actually ran from the corners of his son-in-law's eyes. Laugh lines. "It's getting there."

Beauvoir glanced into the room behind them. A television had been positioned by the fireplace and tuned to the annual Radio Canada year-end special, *Bye Bye*.

Chairs were being pulled forward and guests were wandering over, plates and drinks in hand.

"Come in," Reine-Marie called from the door. "It's almost time."

"Wind's picking up," said Monsieur Béliveau. "I'll stay outside and watch the fire." He turned to Félix. "You go in too. Get a hot chocolate and get warm."

"No," said the boy. "I want to stay with you. Fire needs watching."

"Come along," Armand said to Jean-Guy. "We'll see this year out together."

"You're not going to kiss me at midnight, are you? By the way, you're on fire."

Armand looked down. Sure enough, embers had landed on his sweater.

Jean-Guy pulled the sleeves of his own sweater over his hands and batted the embers out.

Once inside they got two hot chocolates and took them out to the grocer and his apprentice, then joined the others around the television.

Reine-Marie put her arm through Armand's and leaned into him. "You're smoking."

"Smoking hot?" he asked with a grin.

"No, no, just smoking."

He looked down. Seemed Jean-Guy hadn't quite got all the embers.

Reine-Marie patted him down. "This sweater was a Christmas gift, monsieur. You've had it a week."

"Mrs. Claus is going to be disappointed."

"Mrs. Claus understands that sometimes men set themselves on fire, for no particular reason."

He laughed. "Thank you for saving my life."

"I saved the sweater. You happen to be in it." She hugged him tighter, smelling the wood smoke and singed wool mingling with sandalwood and rose. It was earthy and strangely pleasant.

"Shhhhh," Ruth hissed. "It's almost midnight."

They leaned forward, toward the unblemished new year, as numbers appeared on the screen.

". . . *sept, six, cinq* . . . ," they counted down. ". . . *trois, deux, un! Bonne année!*" they shouted, laughing and hugging.

Reine-Marie and Armand embraced and kissed, as did other couples. Stephen tilted his head at Ruth, who closed her eyes and leaned toward him before Rosa popped up between them and he ended up kissing the duck.

A Roman candle lit the sky above the Inn and Spa. Monsieur Béliveau had also found silent fireworks, so as not to upset the animals. Which somehow made the display all the more magical.

Armand sought out Daniel, and gave him a hug. "I'm so glad you're home."

"*Moi aussi,*" said Daniel. Together they went outside to watch the fireworks.

The cold was forgotten as ooohs and aaahs filled the air. The crowd pointed and exclaimed. Pinwheels spun and skyrockets twisted and dragon's eggs appeared overhead, lighting up their faces and the village of Three Pines below.

Sparklers were handed out to the kids. Félix showed Honoré how to dip the tip into the bonfire until a fountain of tiny stars burst from the end. Then he showed him how to write his name in the night. Soon all the kids were doing it.

"Little monkeys," said Vincent Gilbert, coming up beside Armand and Reine-Marie, just as the display was ending. Gilbert was the only one smart enough to have put on a coat.

When all the fireworks were exhausted, they ran back inside to the fireplace, shivering and laughing.

Another year done. Another begun.

Billy Williams, left outside to tamp down the fire, smiled as he shoveled snow onto the flames and relived those moments to midnight. He'd positioned himself next to Myrna.

"... *deux, un! Bonne année!!*"

He'd turned to her and asked above the cheers and laughter, "May I?"

When she'd nodded, he'd leaned in and kissed her, lightly, briefly. On the lips.

He'd felt her hand on his arm. Not to stop him, but to keep him there. And he'd kissed her again. Kissed her longer.

Now he paused, leaning on the shovel. Reliving that moment, so long longed for. Then a glow caught his eye as the bonfire leaped to life.

Another gust had revived it, he thought, as he thrust the shovel into a drift.

A few minutes later, just as he was about to go back inside, Billy noticed a commotion. He looked off to his right, into the darkness.

One of the teens had stumbled out of the woods and was calling to his friends.

They'd be sixteen, seventeen years old, Billy guessed. He knew them all. Seen them grow up. Not yet of drinking age, he knew, but that didn't stop them. Just as it hadn't stopped him when he'd been their age. He still couldn't smell cider without feeling sick.

Smiling, he threw one last load of snow onto the fire and heard the dying embers hiss at him. Now there were more shouts. Something in the tone made Billy pause. He stepped further into the darkness.

Then, out of the woods, first one, then another and another stumbled. Their eyes, caught in the light from the living room windows, were wide, wild.

Billy Williams dropped the shovel and moved forward.

Tired and happy, Armand and Reine-Marie were just about to head down the hallway to their coats when Armand stopped.

Turned.

And looked back.

CHAPTER 20

———

Armand slid to a halt and dropped to his knees beside the body face-down in the snow.

He was about to grab the coat and turn them over, when he drew back.

Jean-Guy fell to his knees on the other side of the body and also reached out.

"Don't."

With his bare hand Gamache carefully burrowed under the person's scarf, to feel for a pulse he knew he wouldn't find. Then he looked up, and across the body, at Beauvoir.

When the alarm had gone up, Armand's heart had recoiled. Hearing the terror in the cries, he'd immediately thought some teenager had been found passed out drunk and frozen to death in some snow-drift.

He'd rushed out so quickly he'd left his coat and boots behind. Others had also started for the doors, but Jean-Guy had headed them off with a curt "We'll let you know."

The temperature had plummeted, and the wind was picking up, moaning through the trees, lifting the top layer of snow and swirling it about.

Armand tapped Jean-Guy's arm and pointed. "Be careful."

Beauvoir looked at the ground beside him and saw dark marks in the white snow, by the dead woman's head.

It was a woman. And she was dead. That much was obvious. As was one more thing.

The dark marks were blood. Her head had been bludgeoned. This was no case of hypothermia. No sad accident.

Bringing out his phone, Beauvoir switched on the light and the video, recording, capturing the scene. It went beyond standard procedure. The weather was closing in. Even now, fingers of snow were drifting across the body, as though some great hand had reached up out of the earth and was trying to drag her down.

With every passing moment evidence was being lost. Even now, the bloodstains were being buried.

"Go back inside," Gamache shouted, having to raise his voice over the now howling wind. "Parents will be worried. Just say there's been an accident, and we're tending to it. They need to stay in the Auberge. No one leaves."

"Right." Jean-Guy was on his feet, running for the Inn.

"And bring our coats," Gamache shouted after him.

Drawing his shoulders in, and praying Beauvoir had heard, Gamache hunched over, trying to protect his core. He knew it didn't take long for frostbite, then hypothermia, to take hold. Bringing out his phone, and pressing video, he continued to record while placing two calls. First to the coroner, then the officer on duty at Sûreté headquarters. In homicide. Through chattering teeth, he told him to send the Scene of Crime unit.

As he spoke, he moved so that he acted as a windbreak, protecting the body. Protecting whatever evidence he could before the elements swallowed it all up.

The body was that of a grown woman, not a teen. That much was clear, though her face was completely buried. Her neck was cold, near frozen, to the touch. She felt like marble, as though a statue had toppled off the path.

Her arms were at her sides. She'd made no attempt to break her fall.

Unconscious as she fell, he thought as he leaned closer to the wound on the back of her head, or already dead. Even with his flashlight, he couldn't see much except the dark stain on her dark tuque. And the drops of blood still visible on the snow.

Gamache looked at his watch. It was seventeen minutes past twelve. She'd been dead, he figured, at least twenty minutes.

A gust hit him, then moved on, taking his breath and much of his body heat with it.

His face was growing numb, and his bare hands shook as he slowly, slowly moved his camera over the scene, recording and describing what he saw. Though he suspected the words were next to unintelligible as his lips and cheeks froze. A shiver, more a shudder, passed through him just as he heard a crunch on the snow behind him.

"*Patron.*"

He felt the parka being draped over his shoulders and strong arms lifting him to his feet. He was trembling now. As Beauvoir helped him into the thick coat, he could feel the relief immediately. The wind and cold had stopped ripping into his flesh. Winter was being chased out of his bones.

He made a noise he thought would be a slight moan of relief but came out sounding more like a squeal. It would, almost certainly, be played in open court one day. But he was beyond caring.

Beauvoir shoved a knitted tuque down over Armand's ears, then said, "Here. Give me your hands."

Gamache did as he was told. Beauvoir put insulated gloves on each hand, already warmed by pocket heaters. "Better?"

Gamache nodded as Beauvoir knelt to help him on with his boots.

"*Non, non*, I can do that," protested Armand, but Jean-Guy was already doing it, providing his shoulder for Gamache to lean on.

Within a minute the world had gone from bitter, biting, ferocious cold to blessed warmth.

"*Merci,*" he mumbled, through still numb lips.

Together, they looked down at the woman at their feet. Though they hadn't said anything, neither investigator was in much doubt who this was.

All his instincts, all his humanity, screamed at Gamache to turn Abigail Robinson over. There was something grotesque about leaving her facedown like that in the deep snow. But she was beyond saving or caring. And the best they could do for her now was to find out who'd done this to her.

"The Scene of Crime team and coroner are on the way," he told Beauvoir.

It had begun to snow. Not big, gentle flakes of a flurry. These were tiny, vicious barbs. Searching for flesh. Invading any opening in their clothing.

The area around the body had been trampled. Not by them. They'd been careful, though they couldn't, of course, avoid making some prints.

The young men and women who'd rushed to the body when it was discovered had, unintentionally, obscured any prints that could be evidence.

They were a hundred yards into the forest along a trail normally used for cross-country skiing. Gamache could easily make out the crisp parallel lines of the skis. Though closer to the body, they'd been trampled. And even those boot prints were being quickly filled in by the blowing snow.

The light from their phones created a world of strange, ghastly shapes in the woods that shifted as their beams moved.

"No weapon," said Beauvoir. "How long ago did this happen?" He'd barely touched the body, so he didn't know.

"Dead just before midnight, I'd say," said Gamache.

"While we were distracted by the countdown?" He heard Gamache hum agreement.

Beauvoir looked behind him. The attack had occurred within sight of the Auberge. He could see the Christmas tree, bright and cheerful, through the living room windows. He could see Annie and the others sitting quietly around the fireplace.

The party was over.

Dr. Harris stood up and indicated to the head of the unit that they could turn the body over.

They were in the Scene of Crime tent, erected around the body to protect evidence and privacy.

Sharon Harris stepped back and stood between Chief Inspector Gamache and Inspector Beauvoir, two Sûreté officers she knew well from previous investigations.

She'd arrived still dressed, under her long winter coat, in her party clothes.

"*Bonne année,*" she'd mumbled to Gamache as he greeted her.

Industrial lights had been installed as the homicide unit swung into their routine.

Thermoses of coffee were stuck upright in the snow for the agents unfortunate enough to be on call when the call was made.

Wind and snow beat against the sides of the tent, and the agents had to raise their voices to be heard above the buffeting. There was little talking anyway, beyond what needed to be said. Gamache had instilled in each of them that the site of every murder was to be treated as near sacred.

He understood perfectly well that joking was a way to deal with the trauma and stress. But there were better, more effective tools for coping.

To help them deal with the horrors of their job, Chief Inspector Gamache had brought a counselor into the homicide department and made it clear that he himself went to those private sessions once a month, sometimes more.

And slowly, slowly, most of the other officers did too.

Now he watched as the stiff body of Abigail Robinson was turned over.

He stared. Then looked at Jean-Guy. Who was also staring.

"Just a moment, please." Gamache stepped forward and bent over the body, then looked up at Jean-Guy Beauvoir. Both men were surprised.

But not, perhaps, as surprised as Debbie Schneider.

Dr. Harris completed her initial examination of the body, then Beauvoir pointed toward the entrance of the tent.

"Must we?" asked Dr. Harris.

Still, she followed them outside, steeling herself against the elements.

Though they were ready for it, the wind and snow still yanked their breath away. The cold roared down their throats, burning their lungs.

For a moment they couldn't breathe, then all three coughed as their bodies fought back, trying to expel the icy air.

"*Merde*, Armand," Dr. Harris gasped. "You sure know how to pick 'em."

"Not my choice," he rasped.

They were huddled together, as snow devils, tornados of flakes, swirled around them.

"What can you tell us?" Gamache's words turned to vapor, which froze to the stubble on his face.

They were beginning to look like members of Scott's Antarctic expedition. And that hadn't ended well.

"Can we go inside?" Dr. Harris called above the wind. "It's too cold out here to talk."

Beauvoir motioned one of the agents over. "Come with us. You'll need to take notes."

"Inside, sir?" she said. It was, at that moment, better than winning Loto-Québec.

"Yes, inside," said Inspector Beauvoir, and if he could have smiled, he would have.

Standing on what had, just hours earlier, been a stage for the Fable de La Fontaine, Gamache, Beauvoir, and Dr. Harris looked at the anxious faces.

Everyone, except the sleeping children, had stood up and turned to them.

Armand felt the trickle as snow melted down his burning cheeks and the back of his neck. Beside him, Dr. Harris took in the crowd, noting the children, many in animal costumes, asleep on sofas, chairs, and the carpet in front of the fire. It looked like a tableau vivant. Until one woman moved.

Abigail Robinson stepped forward, turning for a brief moment toward the door. Expecting one more person to walk through it. Hoping . . .

"What's happened? Where's Debbie?"

Colette Roberge whispered, "Abby."

But Abigail wasn't listening. She crossed the room, and grabbed Armand's arm.

"Where is she?"

"I want to speak to you," he said, gently. "First, though, I need to say a few words to everyone here. Then we can talk. Privately."

"No, now. I need to know." Her voice was rising.

He placed his hand over hers. "In a moment. Please."

He nodded to Colette, who came forward and led Abigail a few steps away. Beauvoir had a quiet word with Dominique and Marc, then indicated to Colette that they should follow Dominique down the hall.

Abigail now looked disoriented. Uncertain what to do. She looked around. For guidance. For Debbie.

"Go with them," Beauvoir said quietly to an agent. "Record anything they say and do."

Abigail allowed herself to be led down the hall, past the eyes of parents hugging their children, protecting them from the sight of such intense sorrow.

Ruth held Rosa's head gently in the hollow of her shoulder, shaped especially, it seemed, for a sensitive duck.

Once they'd left, Armand stood beside the fireplace. At eye level with his friends, neighbors, family. Intensely aware of the children, including his own grandchildren, now awake and watching. Listening.

Armand Gamache was also very aware that he might be in the company of the person who'd done this. He scanned the faces, looking into the eyes of Haniya Daoud. Vincent Gilbert.

Stephen.

Not that long ago his godfather had joked that elderly people made perfect murderers.

"Life in prison isn't much of a threat, or deterrent." Stephen had laughed. But Armand knew him well enough to know he also meant it.

To protect Idola, and all the Idolas unborn, would this elderly man kill?

And Armand knew the answer. Stephen Horowitz might very well be the most dangerous person in the room. Kind, generous, brilliant. Ruthless, determined, and skilled. And with nothing to lose.

But kill Debbie Schneider? A woman, as far as Armand knew, he'd never met. Why?

Why would any of them kill her?

The answer was clear. They hadn't. The murderer had killed Abigail Robinson, or thought they had.

He cleared his throat, still raw from the icy cold, and described in words that would not scare children, but that adults would understand, that someone had died and they needed to find out why.

"I'm sorry, but you won't be allowed to go home just yet. We'll need to speak with each of you. We'll start with parents of the youngest children and work our way up. I hope it won't take too long."

He thanked them for their understanding. Before he could leave, Reine-Marie approached him.

"Do you mind if I take Ruth and Stephen home? Then I'll come back."

Armand looked over at them. Both looked worn, drained. He nodded. "Good idea. I'll speak with them tomorrow."

Beauvoir had had a word with Annie, and then joined Gamache and Dr. Harris in the foyer. "I was just outside. The agents assigned to protect Professor Robinson followed them here and stayed in the car. They didn't see anyone approach or leave the Inn."

"Professor Robinson?" Gamache asked.

"In the library with Chancellor Roberge."

"*Bon.*" Gamache drew them further aside and turned to the coroner. "Tell us what you found."

"Barring any surprises during the autopsy, I can tell you that death was due to blunt force trauma. I'd say one catastrophic blow to the back of her head, driving skull shards into her brain. It looks like death was immediate. There wasn't much bleeding. Two more blows were struck after she'd fallen, pushing her face deeper into the snow. I'm assuming you haven't found the weapon."

"Not yet," Beauvoir confirmed. "Any ideas?"

"I'd look for a log," said the coroner. "There were traces of bark and dirt on the tuque, and the shape of the wound corresponds to firewood."

She made a wedge with her hands.

"Oh," said Gamache. It came out as a sort of grunt.

He was afraid of that.

"What?" asked Dr. Harris.

But Jean-Guy knew. He'd immediately thought the same thing. Both men looked through the living room and past the French doors.

"There was a bonfire," said Gamache. "I think our murder weapon's gone up in smoke."

"Time of death?" Beauvoir asked the coroner.

"In this cold, it's hard to say, but I'd guess an hour and a half, two hours."

They checked the time. It was three minutes after two in the morning.

"So around midnight?" asked Beauvoir.

"Roughly, yes. Armand, the woman who was so upset, that was Abigail Robinson, wasn't it? She's the professor who was shot at yesterday. I saw her in the news."

"Yes. The dead woman was her best friend."

"Tough few days for her."

Gamache considered the coroner for a moment. "Sharon, how would doctors feel about mandatory euthanasia? And terminating all pregnancies with defects?"

"You mean the things Professor Robinson's promoting?"

Dr. Harris considered. This surprised Gamache. He'd expected an immediate condemnation.

"'Appalled' is the word. But then many were initially appalled with physician-assisted suicide. But once it became law, we got used to it. We can even see the virtue in it, to ease suffering."

They were walking toward the front door as they spoke.

"It's the mandatory aspect that's troubling," she said. "To say the least. It seems inconceivable that any government would allow what she's suggesting."

"We've seen a lot of the inconceivable lately. *Merci*," he said, shaking her hand.

"I won't wish you happy new year," she said.

"Ahh, it's always worth wishing. *Bonne année*, Sharon."

Dr. Harris watched them walk grim-faced down the corridor, to do the very worst part of a job rife with terrible deeds. Then she walked into the night, the new year biting at her flesh.

CHAPTER 21

Not surprisingly, the library was lined with bookshelves. A worn oriental rug was on the floor, and the room was furnished with old leather chairs and a deep green velvet sofa.

Gamache nodded toward the French doors, and Beauvoir crossed the room.

"Locked," he reported.

Despite the fact the fire had been reduced to ash and a few embers, the room was pleasantly warm.

Abigail got to her feet when they entered. Chancellor Roberge stood beside her, a hand on her arm.

Gamache knew there was no gentle way to put this and trying would only prolong the agony. It was best to be quick, clear, though not, if possible, brutal.

He was also aware that he was simply confirming what Abigail Robinson already knew. But that did not diminish the pain of what he was about to say.

"A body has been found in the woods." He paused a beat and dropped his voice. "I'm sorry. It's Deborah Schneider. She's dead."

Abigail tensed and lowered her head, turning it away slightly. She squeezed her eyes shut, as though hit by a particularly bitter gust.

Then she lifted them to Gamache. "Are you sure?"

"Yes."

Abigail compressed her lips and steadied herself, lifting her chin slightly.

"Thank you. I know this must be difficult for you . . ." Her voice trailed off, but her eyes remained fixed on Gamache.

Beauvoir, who loathed what this woman stood for, quickly searched his feelings for any sign of pleasure at her pain, and found none.

"Please," he said, indicating the sofa. "Sit."

The Sûreté officers dragged up chairs, so they were within feet of them.

"Did Madame Schneider have family?" Beauvoir asked. "Someone who should be notified?"

"Oh, God. Her parents. And a brother. They're all out west. Should I . . . ?"

"We'll arrange for them to be told," Beauvoir said, and saw her relief. "But we will need their address and phone number if you have them. With social media, these things get out."

"Of course," said Abigail and fumbled for her phone. She gave them the information.

"Can you tell me how?"

"Not yet." Jean-Guy hesitated a moment before saying the next part. "Only that it was no accident."

Both he and Gamache watched closely for a reaction. It wasn't hard to see.

Now both Abigail's and Colette's mouths dropped open. But nothing came out. Not even, it seemed, breath.

"Meaning?" Colette Roberge finally managed.

"Meaning Debbie Schneider was killed," said Gamache.

"Killed?" whispered Colette. "Murdered?"

"*Oui.*"

At that moment there was a tap on the door and Dominique carried in a tray with a teapot, coffeepot, milk and sugar and mugs.

"*Pardon.*" Without looking into anyone's eyes, she put the tray down and left. Fled, really. Never to forget the look in Abigail Robinson's eyes.

Hands plastered to her face, she was staring at Gamache. In horror. As though he'd done it. As though he'd killed Debbie.

And then the dam burst.

She began to cry. Sob. She was choking. Sputtering. Gasping for breath as the grief heaved out of her.

Colette rubbed Abigail's back and made soothing sounds, as a mother might to a child. Until the sobbing slowed to gasps and hiccups.

"I'm sorry. I'm sorry."

Having already found a box of Kleenex, Gamache handed her tissues.

Off in the corner, the young agent was staring. Terrified by what she was seeing. A grief so great it threatened to swallow them all. She glanced at the Chief and saw sympathy. But she also saw that he was completely focused, his eyes shrewd.

She double-checked that her phone was recording and leaned forward.

Abigail balled the Kleenex in her hand and looked around. For her friend. Who would take the damp tissues from her. Who would always take any unpleasantness away.

Then her hand dropped to her lap and her eyes came to rest on Gamache. "How?"

"We can't tell you that," said Gamache.

"Can't," said Colette Roberge, "or won't?"

"Won't. But we believe death was quick."

He nodded toward Beauvoir, who took over the questioning.

"When was the last time you saw Madame Schneider?"

Pausing for a moment to gather her thoughts, Abigail turned to Colette. "Before midnight. You went out for a walk. I saw you both by the bonfire."

"When was this?" Beauvoir asked the Chancellor.

"After the, umm, the discussion with Dr. Gilbert," said Colette. "Debbie and I got the coats. We were going to go home. We waited for you"—she looked at Abigail—"outside."

"In the cold?" asked Beauvoir.

"It seemed more hospitable than the party. Besides, we were getting hot in our coats."

"Did you join them?" Beauvoir asked Abigail.

"No. I'd wandered over to a group and got caught up in a conversation about my work and the pandemic." She focused on Beauvoir, as though seeing him for the first time. "You were there."

"Yes."

"You're a police officer?"

"He's my second-in-command at homicide," said Gamache. "And my son-in-law."

Abigail's mind, mired in shock, tried to work that out. "So, the young woman's your daughter?"

"Yes," said Gamache.

"And the older woman I was talking to about the rainbow drawings? Your wife? That would make the child your granddaughter."

"Yes."

"I see," said Abigail, nodding. "I understand."

"Understand?"

"Your objections to my findings."

"Abby . . ." Colette warned.

But Gamache wouldn't be drawn. If anything, he was curious. It crossed his mind that Abigail Robinson had instinctively, or perhaps intentionally, moved the conversation away from the murder of her friend and into a territory she understood. Had, in fact, mastered. The endless debate about her work.

Beside him, he could feel Jean-Guy stiffen.

Up until that moment Jean-Guy had managed to separate Abigail Robinson, the grieving friend of a murder victim, from Professor Robinson.

But now the two collided.

"Idola isn't an objection," Armand said before Jean-Guy could respond. His tone was calm, reasonable. Firm. "She's my granddaughter and has no place in this conversation. Let's move on."

"Are you so sure?" asked Colette Roberge.

"What do you mean?" demanded Beauvoir. There was a warning there no one in that room could miss.

"Do you think the attack on Debbie was random?" the Chancellor asked Beauvoir.

"Of course it was," Abigail interrupted. "What else could it be?"

She glared at Colette. Hating her in that instant for putting what they were all thinking, the unthinkable, into words.

"You know," said Colette, quietly, then turned to Gamache. "So do you. Why would anyone kill Debbie? It makes no sense. But something else does."

"No," snapped Abigail. "It was a random attack, maybe even an accident. A drunk kid, fooling around. There were lots of them. And somehow Debbie got in the way. Or she slipped and fell. Or . . . or . . ."

"Or you were the intended victim," said Beauvoir. Getting his swipe in. He was honest enough with himself to admit it felt good.

"No." Abigail shook her head decisively. "Not possible."

"Why not?" he asked, feeling his emotions, so well controlled up until Idola had been mentioned, spinning out of control.

"It was dark," he continued. "She was in a big coat, with a hat. No one could tell."

"No." Abigail folded her arms, viselike, across her body.

"Yes," snapped Beauvoir. "That should've been you out there."

"Inspector!" Gamache's voice acted as a slap, and Beauvoir's cheeks reddened, but he continued to glare at her, before turning blazing eyes on Gamache.

He took a deep breath and managed, *"Désolé."*

Gamache took over the questioning. Turning to Chancellor Roberge, he asked, "When did you last see Debbie Schneider?"

"As I said, we were outside waiting for Abby, but we could see through the window that she was deep in conversation, and we both knew that could take a while, so we decided to take a walk."

"Where did you go?"

"Just around the house. We stopped at the bonfire, then looked at the stables. It was getting colder. I wanted to go back in, but Debbie said she'd wait for you." She looked at Abigail. "She was sure you'd come outside and she didn't want to miss you."

Abigail was staring at her hands gripping each other in her lap. "I forgot."

They all imagined Debbie Schneider, alone in the dark and cold. Waiting for a friend who'd forgotten her.

"Was there anyone else out there?" Gamache asked.

"Just some older kids. I think they were drinking in the woods."

"What did you do then?"

"I came inside."

"What time was that?"

"I think it was a few minutes before midnight. The TV was on and tuned to *Bye Bye*."

"I didn't see you," said Gamache.

"No. You two were out at the bonfire by then. I decided it was so close to midnight, I might as well stay. I went outside briefly to see the fireworks, then came in here. I always find the company of books soothing."

"Why did you need to be soothed?" Gamache asked.

"Couldn't you feel the tension, the animosity in that room? And it wasn't just aimed at Abigail. Debbie and I also felt it. Guilt by association. I just wanted to relax for a few minutes before going out to find Abigail and Debbie and heading home."

"When did you leave the room?" Gamache asked.

"When I heard the commotion. I guess about ten past midnight."

"Not before?"

"No. I was only here for a few minutes."

Gamache noted the pile of split logs by the hearth. "Was a fire lit?"

"Yes. I was cold, so I put another couple of logs on."

"What were you reading?"

She smiled. "Does it matter?"

"It might."

"It's over there." She looked toward a table beside the wing chair closest to the fireplace.

Gamache got to his feet and walked over. Picking up the book, he raised his brows.

It was one he knew. He'd found the same obscure old volume among his parents' collection. It was now in his bookcase at home, though he'd never read it.

He turned to her and she answered his unasked question.

"*Extraordinary Popular Delusions*," she said, holding his eyes, "*and the Madness of Crowds*. You see, Chief Inspector, I was here."

He brought the book back with him, crossing his legs and balancing it on his knee. "Did you see Madame Schneider at the fireworks?"

"No. But I wasn't really looking. I was watching the display."

"Did you see Professor Robinson?" He nodded toward Abigail, who'd lapsed into silence.

"No, but again, I was looking up into the sky. A beautiful display. Then we all came back inside and I came in here."

"Professor Robinson, where were you during the countdown to midnight?"

"I was with all of you, around the television."

Gamache nodded slowly. "And what was on the television?"

Now she smiled, a little. "You don't believe me?"

He met her smile and waited.

"It was some French show with skits."

That was close enough. "What happened at midnight?"

"What happened? What do you mean?"

"What did people do?"

"What they always do. Everyone yelled 'Happy new year,' and hugged."

Beauvoir shifted in his seat but said nothing. He'd noted she'd used the English phrase, where actually everyone, even the Anglos, had yelled, *"Bonne année."*

"What did you do?"

"I looked for Debbie."

"Why?"

"To hug her. Wish her a happy new year." She closed her eyes, a moment of privacy, to gather herself before continuing on. "But I couldn't find her. I thought she was still outside, so I put on my coat and went out. The fireworks had started by then. I looked around, and when I couldn't see her I waited by the bonfire with everyone else, thinking she'd show up. I saw you there," she said to Gamache and Beauvoir, then turned to Colette. "But I didn't see you."

"And I didn't see you."

Throughout this interview Gamache had the impression that these two were nudging each other toward him. To get him to focus on the other. It reminded him of a *Far Side* cartoon that Jean-Guy had cut out and left on his desk. It showed two bears in the crosshairs of a hunting rifle. One bear was grinning and pointing to the other.

While there was no grinning here, there seemed a lot of pointing.

"Then what did you do?" Gamache asked.

"After the fireworks?" Abigail asked. "I came back inside. I was tired and wanted to go back to Colette's place, so I looked around for Debbie and you." She turned to the Chancellor. "But didn't see you. I guess you were in here. And then the kids started yelling, and you ran outside."

"We met up in the living room," said Colette, "and looked around for Debbie. We didn't think anything had really happened. Not to Debbie anyway. But when we couldn't find her, and then we were all told not to leave, and time went on . . ."

"Is there anything else you can tell us about tonight?" Gamache asked. "Anything you saw or heard?"

Both shook their heads. Then Abigail paused. "There is one thing, but you'll think I'm just being vindictive."

"Don't worry about what we think," said Gamache. "Just tell us."

"There was someone else I didn't see by the television or inside after. Vincent Gilbert."

Gamache cast his mind back and realized he hadn't seen Gilbert there either. He turned to Chancellor Roberge, and she shook her head.

There was just one more thing to ask.

He leaned toward Abigail Robinson. "Why did you come here? To the party?"

"If you must know, I came to meet someone."

So she did come to see, maybe even confront, Vincent Gilbert, thought Gamache.

"Ruth Zardo," said Abigail. "To thank her for the use of her poem. She's been very supportive."

CHAPTER 22

They got through the next interviews fairly quickly.

The parents of young children didn't see much, beyond trying to corral overtired and sugar-hyped kids.

Annie, Daniel, and Roslyn were interviewed, and when they admitted they too had seen nothing, they left, carrying the children down the hill to bed.

At the door, Jean-Guy kissed Annie and the children. "I'll be home when I can."

By then Professor Robinson and Chancellor Roberge, with a Sûreté escort, had left for home.

The Scene of Crime unit was still at work. The body of Debbie Schneider was still in the tent and would be taken to the morgue once they were done.

It was close to three a.m. when they got to the teenagers and their parents.

The kids seemed to have taken a solemn oath of silence that lasted until Beauvoir's first question. Then it came out. They'd stolen beer and cider and Tia Maria from parents and stashed it in a snowbank in the woods.

Beauvoir felt some sympathy for the Tia Maria boy, who looked especially green. He remembered his own first drunk. He and his friends had poured whiskey, beer, wine, and Drambuie together in what they decided was a cocktail.

The rest he couldn't remember, except waking up facedown in the grass in his own vomit.

The last teen they spoke to was Jacques Brodeur. He was the one who'd found the body.

Athletic, handsome, he seemed the leader of the group. But Beauvoir quickly discovered a frightened boy beneath the bravado. Jacques's parents sat on either side of him, as he told the story.

"We put the bottles in the snowbank. We'd heard warm alcohol makes you sick."

"It's not the temperature that'll make you sick," said Beauvoir. His tone had softened. Recognizing the boy wanted to talk. Needed to talk. "You're not in trouble. At least not from us. Just tell us what happened."

Jacques looked at his parents, who nodded.

"We were all pretty pissed by midnight. I had to pee, so I went into the woods. The fireworks lit up the ski trail, so I just followed it until I thought no one could see, and I let loose against a tree."

Just the memory of that relief made the boy sigh.

There was a sharp inhale of disapproval from his father, while his mother compressed her lips in what might have been anger, or amusement.

"But then the fireworks stopped and it got real dark. I put on my phone flashlight and looked around. That's when I saw it."

"Now, be careful here," said Beauvoir. "What did you see?"

The boy paused before speaking. "A dark patch on the snow, like a big branch had fallen. It hadn't been there before."

"Before? You'd been there before?"

"Well, yes."

"To urinate?"

"Yes. And throw up."

Now Jacques's father actually moaned.

"For God's sake, Geoff," his wife said, leaning around their son to look at him. "I met you at fifteen, at a St. Jean Baptiste party, when you were leaning against a tree throwing up. Give the boy a break."

This almost derailed, for a moment, the inquiry, as Beauvoir was sorely tempted to ask some questions about that. Like how she could possibly have been attracted . . .

But he resisted.

"What time were you last there, before you found the body?" Beauvoir asked.

"I dunno."

"Try. Was it before the firecrackers?"

"The ones that scared you?"

"Yes," said Beauvoir. "Those."

"I guess it was a little later. About ten to twelve. I went inside and watched *Bye Bye*."

"Did you see anyone else going into the woods last night?"

"My friends."

"Yes, but anyone else? Any adults?"

He thought, then shook his head. Then stopped. "Well, yes. Two women. At least I think they were women. They were by the fire, then walked away. I watched them because I was afraid they'd find the booze, but they just kept walking. I'm not sure they went into the woods."

"Did you see them come back?"

"No."

"Let's get back to the body," said Beauvoir. "When you saw it on the ground, what did you do?"

"I thought someone had dumped a bunch of clothes. I called my friends over."

Which was, the homicide investigators knew, natural but unfortunate.

"And?" said Beauvoir.

"And we looked more closely."

"Did you touch the body?"

"No," he said. "But . . ."

"Yes."

"I poked it."

"Sorry?"

"I picked up a stick and poked it."

"Jacques!" his father said.

"What? I didn't know. That's when I realized . . ." His chin dimpled and his lips compressed. His father laid a hand over his, and gently squeezed. "That was," he gasped, "when we"—he wiped his eyes with his sleeve—"all started to shout for help."

Beauvoir reached out and tapped his knee. "It's okay. I see this sort of thing all the time and it still upsets me. It would be pretty terrible if it didn't. If you think of anything else, you'll let us know?"

Jacques nodded.

"I have a question," said Gamache.

The boy turned to him. He was more than a little in awe of the Chief Inspector, having seen him many times on the news.

But Gamache was looking at Madame Brodeur. "What were you doing this evening?"

"Me?"

"Yes."

They looked at each other for a moment before Madame Brodeur smiled slightly and relented. "I was watching over them."

"Maman! You were spying on me?"

She turned to her son. "No one loves you more, but no one knows better what a numbskull you can be. Honestly. You once went skinny-dipping in Lac Brume, then forgot where you left your clothes—"

"Mom!"

"It's okay, you come from numbskull stock." She looked beyond Jacques, to his father, who was grimacing agreement. "I knew you and your friends would probably be drinking, so I just kept an eye on you. It's dangerous, isn't it? Drinking outside in the winter."

Gamache nodded. "What did you see tonight, Madame?"

"Unfortunately, nothing that Jacques hasn't already described."

"Is that true?" Gamache pressed.

"Yes. The idea wasn't to spy on him, just to make sure he and his friends were safe. So I looked for him, but didn't follow him."

"And once they came inside?"

"He was safe. I was off duty and could enjoy myself. Sort of. It sure felt strange. Not the best party atmosphere. Between Madame Daoud being so unpleasant and then that professor who's going around saying sick people should be put down, well . . ."

Well. Well, thought Gamache. How succinctly she'd just put it. He turned to the young man. "What did you do with the stick?"

"The one I touched her with?"

"Yes."

"I threw it into the fire. Was that wrong?"

"*Non*, I don't think it would've helped." Then he thought of something. "The fire was still burning when you threw it in?"

"Yes."

"Now listen closely." Gamache leaned toward the boy. "Was it just embers, or were there flames?"

Taken aback by the cop's intensity, Jacques thought before he answered. "Definitely flames."

Gamache leaned back and nodded. *"Merci."*

So the last time one of them went for beer or to pee, before Jacques found the body, was about ten minutes to midnight. And there was no body.

And at quarter past midnight, the alarm had been raised.

That meant the window for the murder had become a single pane. There were roughly twenty-five minutes between no body and the body.

After a few more interviews, they looked up to see Haniya Daoud standing at the door.

"I'm next."

Gamache and Beauvoir suspected that might not be true, but chose the better part of valor. Jean-Guy indicated the sofa, and when she sat down, Gamache asked, "Are you all right?"

"Sorry?"

"This is upsetting for everyone, but you've been through more than most. A murder can trigger all sorts of things. I just want to know how you are."

She stared at him as though he'd said something not just nonsensical but idiotic.

"Of course I'm all right. This's nothing. A quiet evening in Darfur."

But he didn't believe it.

When those first fireworks had gone off, the three of them had all flinched. Ducking into a world no one else knew existed. One where it was reasonable to mistake a car backfire, a large book falling to the floor. Firecrackers. For gunshots.

Their nerves had been both shattered and strengthened by their experiences.

"Things are strongest where they're broken," he said to her.

And while the words seemed to come out of nowhere, he could see she understood.

He could also see that the scars on her face went far deeper than her skin.

She smiled. "I'm not quite as broken as you seem to think." She studied him. "You're trying to work out if I killed that woman, thinking she was Professor Robinson. Let me save you some time. I did not."

"But you would have liked to," said Gamache. "You told me as much the other night in the bistro."

"I'm hardly alone. Millions feel as I do."

"True, millions are appalled. But a growing number, it seems, are beginning to agree with her. Including people in a position to implement her suggestions. Unless, of course, she doesn't make the meeting."

"So you're saying I decided to stop her from getting to meetings I knew nothing about?"

"You could have heard about her upcoming meeting with the Premier. It wasn't a secret. That could have been the impetus."

"A lot of could-haves, Chief Inspector. That's a pretty shaky house you're building. It'll never stand the monsoons."

"Then let's move on to solid facts. Not only did you make it clear that you thought I should have let her be gunned down, you said, 'Best to get out of my way.'"

"Now, while I think you're a moral coward, I did believe, until now, that you were at least intelligent. Do you really think, if I had plans to kill Professor Robinson, that I'd challenge you to watch? And, as though that wasn't stupid enough, I chose to do it at a party with fifty people present, then kill the wrong person?"

"Mistakes happen," said Gamache. "It was dark, cold, the killer must have been in a hurry—"

"I don't make mistakes," she said. "Not when human lives are at stake. It's true, I would have little trouble killing Professor Robinson, but I wouldn't make such a shit show of it. That is the expression, no? Shit show, shit storm. You seem to like your *merde* around here."

She leaned forward, and Gamache was reminded, yet again, how very young she was. Only in her early twenties. In which case, unlike Stephen, the threat of life in prison was very real.

But he suspected she was already in prison. Those scars her bars.

"I didn't kill Madame Sch—whatever. On purpose or by mistake."

"Schneider. And forgive me if I don't take your word for it. I can't remember seeing you at midnight. Nor did I see you at the fireworks."

"You didn't see me because you didn't look."

The words, said so plainly, held a plain truth.

No one, including himself, had turned to the Hero of the Sudan, the possible next recipient of the Nobel Peace Prize, to wish her *bonne année*. To wish her health and happiness and long life.

No one reached out to embrace her. And he suspected she hadn't reached out to anyone.

"That doesn't mean you were there," said Gamache.

"And it doesn't mean I was off killing the wrong person."

"What were you doing in the minutes on either side of midnight?"

"I was watching that stupid show on the television. Then I went outside and watched the fireworks." She paused. "I'd never seen them before. Not in person. They were . . ." As she searched for the word, Gamache waited for the insult. ". . . very beautiful. Almost sweet. The way they lit up the village below. Not pyrotechnics, but just an old man and boy setting them off in a backyard."

She seemed tired, but also calm. "It's good to be reminded now and then that such things exist."

"What things?"

"Beauty. Peace." She held his eyes. "Goodness. But they're fragile and can so easily disappear, unless people are willing to do what's necessary to defend them."

"I'm not sure that goodness is all that fragile," said Gamache.

Off in the corner the young agent looked from one to the other of them, not sure she was following this conversation in English. Were they, the Chief Inspector and a suspect, debating goodness?

"If not fragile, it's mercurial," said Haniya. "Good. Evil. Cruelty and kindness. Guilt and innocence. An act can be all those things at once, depending on your perspective. It's so easy to delude ourselves, wouldn't you say, Chief Inspector?"

"Into believing killing one person to save millions is an act of moral courage?"

"I don't think that's a delusion."

"And if you kill the wrong person?"

"If I?" She smiled again. "Once again, and please pay attention this time, I did not kill that poor woman. And who knows, it might not have been a mistake."

"Why do you say that?"

"Just a possibility. Maybe she knew something, or saw something. Or maybe there's a maniac around. I'd start with the old woman with the duck. Personally, I think the duck is the more dangerous. Did you know people actually have attack geese? Very mean."

Beauvoir, who'd been chased out of several farmyards by geese, and at least one malicious rabbit, nodded. He too suspected Rosa might not be all there.

"Most helpful," said Gamache, getting to his feet. "You're staying here tonight?"

"Yes. That artist woman invited me back to her home, but I could see it was more out of guilt than sincerity."

"She's a good person," said Gamache. "A good friend. I think she was sincere."

"You also think I committed murder tonight. You'll forgive me if I don't take your opinions seriously."

"It was a question, not an opinion," said Gamache as he walked her to the door.

But before reaching it, Haniya stopped and turned to face him. "You've told me why you think I'd want to kill Professor Robinson. Now, let me tell you why I would not."

"I'm listening."

"Because, as satisfying as killing her might be, I know that murdering a person doesn't kill the idea. In fact, just the opposite. If you want an idea to flourish, the best fertilizer is the body of a martyr. I don't want her ideas to flourish, but someone else might. Something to think about, Chief Inspector."

"*Merci*," said Gamache, who'd already considered exactly that, certainly when it came to the shooting in the gym. And maybe the attack that night.

He was impressed, though, that Madame Daoud had gotten there so quickly.

"I spent a lot of the evening watching Professor Robinson, and you want to know what I saw? I saw the fox."

Gamache raised his brows.

"You're surprised? How do you think I stayed alive when so many around me were killed? I watched, carefully. Through the rapes and beatings, mine and others, I watched and listened and learned how things worked. How human nature works. It's why I don't much like humans. Or nature, for that matter."

"Doesn't leave a lot else," said Beauvoir.

"True."

"But there are always fireworks," said Gamache, and saw her smile.

"Want to know what I see when I look at you?" Haniya asked.

"Not really."

"I see the lion."

CHAPTER 23

Before the next guest arrived to be interviewed, Beauvoir asked, "Fox?"

"The Fable de La Fontaine, I think," said Gamache. "'Les Animaux Malades de la Peste.'"

The Animals Sick of the Plague.

"Oh, right. I was really only watching Honoré. He was a terrific rabbit."

"One of the greats," agreed Armand.

"So who was the fox?"

"The cunning one who convinces the others that someone innocent is actually guilty. Blaming the victim."

"That does sound like the professor. At least Madame Daoud saw you as the lion."

Gamache wasn't so sure it was the compliment Beauvoir believed.

The lion, while nominally in charge, had actually been taken in by the fox.

He wondered who Haniya Daoud would be, in that fable.

She'd asked how he thought she'd survived the rapes and torture. He honestly didn't know, but he did wonder if two things in particular compelled her to survive. A burning desire for revenge that incinerated despair, and her ability, her willingness, to be as brutal, when the time came, as her captors.

It was a life hard to shake once back in polite society, as many warriors knew. As the fox would know.

"Well, there is one piece of good news," said Jean-Guy, holding up his phone. A message had just come in from the detachment in Abitibi. "They picked up Tardif's brother, at a hunting cabin outside Val-d'Or. They're bringing him down tomorrow morning."

Vincent Gilbert arrived just then. He looked more than usually disheveled, with bags under his eyes, gray hair sticking out, and patchy white stubble around his chin.

Beauvoir rubbed his hand over his own face and felt the scratch. And saw his father-in-law's salt-and-pepper growth of beard.

Then he looked at the young agent. As fresh as the moment she'd arrived at work, sixteen hours earlier. She looked over at them, bright-eyed, at 3:35 in the morning.

"Thank you for staying up," said Gamache.

"Are you telling me I had a choice?" Gilbert sat down with a tired groan. "This's a terrible thing to happen."

"Yes, very sad," said Gamache.

"Can't be good for business," said Dr. Gilbert, clearly not thinking of the same tragedy as Gamache. "There's already the persistent rumor that the place is haunted. Bullshit, of course. There's no such thing. But try to convince the great unwashed."

Armand suddenly felt the need to shower.

At a glance from Gamache, Beauvoir took the lead and asked Dr. Gilbert about his movements just prior to, and just after, midnight.

He was a little vague. He'd been in the living room for a while. He'd been outside for a while. He'd even been in the library. For a while.

"Hiding, I'm not ashamed to say. I hate parties. Only come to this to support Marc and Dominique. People expect me here."

He made it sound like his legion of fans expected him. It was true, though, that people knew this was just about the only time they were guaranteed to see the Asshole Saint.

Gamache wondered if Abigail knew that. She'd said Ruth Zardo was who she'd come to see, but he doubted that. She hadn't approached the elderly poet. But she had made a beeline for Vincent Gilbert.

"When did you leave here?"

"The library? When the fireworks started to go off."

"You weren't in the room for the countdown to midnight?" asked Beauvoir.

"So that people could hug me?" He grimaced. "No."

Though Gamache had the fleeting thought that maybe the Asshole Saint had come in here so that he didn't have to face no one hugging him.

"You were vague earlier this evening," said Gamache, "when I asked how you'd read Professor Robinson's study. Now I'll ask you again. How did you come to read it?"

"God, it was months ago. I can't remember. Once I've memorized the Cheerios box, I get desperate. The winters are long, and I don't have many visitors." He looked at Gamache. "But you're one, Armand. You bring me books."

Gamache nodded. Whenever he approached the log cabin, he was reminded of Thoreau, who'd said of his own cabin on Walden Pond, "I had three chairs in my house; one for solitude, two for friendship, three for society."

Vincent Gilbert had two chairs. He did not like society, and society did not like him.

"Someone sent you Professor Robinson's research?" asked Beauvoir.

"Must have because I read it."

"Who?"

"I can't remember. I get all sorts of junk."

"Was it Professor Robinson herself?"

"No."

"Then who? You know we can find out," said Beauvoir, though at the moment he couldn't think how.

Not used to having his statements questioned, Vincent Gilbert bridled and dug his heels in, like an obstinate ass, thought Gamache. Then he remembered the poor donkey in the fable. Blameless, but blamed.

And he remembered something else.

"Chancellor Roberge told me she'd checked Professor Robinson's findings herself, then sent them to someone she trusted, to get their opinion. Like a good scientist, she wanted corroboration. Were you that second opinion?"

Vincent Gilbert held Gamache in a stare that had had generations of interns quaking. But Gamache just stared back.

"Good guess."

"Was it Colette Roberge?" Gamache pressed. He needed confirmation, not word games.

"Yes."

"Why would she do that?" Beauvoir asked.

"I have no idea. You'll have to ask Chancellor Roberge. My guess is she thought I'd be interested."

"Why would she think that?"

"Because Robinson's conclusions in her paper are inhumane and I'm a famous humanist."

Oddly, that was true. Again, not unlike Haniya Daoud, here was a renowned humanist who did not actually like humans.

"How do you and Chancellor Roberge know each other?" Gamache asked.

"We sat on a board together a few years ago."

"Which board?"

Gilbert crossed and uncrossed his legs and hiked himself further up on the sofa.

"I think it was some charity. I was on a lot of boards at one time. I am unstinting in my work for others."

"Think again," said Gamache. "Think harder."

His hackles up, Dr. Gilbert nevertheless caved to the inevitable.

"LaPorte."

"There," said Gamache. "That wasn't so hard."

Though he could see that it was. And he knew why. As did Beauvoir.

Dr. Gilbert had all but admitted he had a motive for killing Professor Robinson.

Jean-Guy knew LaPorte well by now. It was a community formed to support and protect men and women, boys and girls, with Down syndrome. The very people Professor Robinson thought should not exist.

What Gamache mostly found interesting was that both Colette Roberge and Vincent Gilbert had tried to hide this fact.

"I know you know this." Gilbert's voice was quiet now. He'd turned away from Gamache and spoke only to Jean-Guy. "With screening, fewer and fewer children with Down syndrome are being born. I'm not going to judge that choice. I suspect it's one I'd have made too, as a young parent. Fortunately, I wasn't faced with it."

Beauvoir, hearing the soothing voice, remembered being in this man's cabin. In this man's care. When he'd been hurt.

He'd felt, through the pain, this man's hands on his open wound, and knew he was with not just a doctor, but a healer. Someone who actually cared if he lived or died.

"*Ça va bien aller,*" Gilbert had whispered, as the pain and fear threatened to overwhelm Jean-Guy. "It'll be all right."

And he'd believed him.

"I didn't just sit on the board, I volunteered at LaPorte," said Gilbert. "And I came to see that maybe, maybe, instead of them being flawed, we're the ones with the defects. You know?"

He looked from Jean-Guy, to Armand, then back to Jean-Guy.

"They're kind. Content. They don't judge. They don't hide their feelings. There's no hidden agenda. Complete acceptance. If that isn't grace, I don't know what is. I'm not saying people with Down syndrome are perfect or always easy. That would be to trivialize them, make them sound like pets. What I am saying is that in my experience they make better humans than most." He smiled again. "Than me. And I think that's worth fighting for, don't you?"

There was a long silence before Gamache said, softly, "Worth killing for?"

Now Vincent Gilbert turned to him. "Have you ever arrested a person with Down syndrome for murder?"

"*Non.*"

"You?" he asked Beauvoir.

"*Non.*"

"No. And there's a reason for that. I aspire to be as decent, as optimistic, as forgiving."

Armand took a deep breath. And kept going. "I believe you. But to aspire to and to achieve are two different things. A person with DS did not murder Debbie Schneider. But someone looking to protect them might have."

"Me?"

"The Chancellor sent you Professor Robinson's research in hopes of stopping her campaign," said Gamache. "It focuses mainly on mandatory euthanasia for the terminally ill and elderly. But there are hints of something else."

"Of eugenics, yes," said Gilbert, his voice cold, abrupt. The clinical man was back. "Chancellor Roberge didn't say why she was sending it to me. She just did."

"And what did you do, after you'd read it?"

"I was appalled, but honestly, I didn't think anyone would take it seriously."

"Are you surprised the Premier has?" asked Gamache.

"Taken her report seriously? I didn't know."

And yet Gilbert didn't look like a man surprised. Though her meeting with the leader of the province was not secret, neither was it public. But there was one person who knew.

Colette Roberge.

And there was one person who could have told Vincent Gilbert.

Colette Roberge.

The Chancellor was proving a puzzle.

She was the one who'd suggested the lecture. She'd invited Abigail into her home. She'd brought her to the New Year's Eve party. And she was walking outside with the victim—

Gamache stopped himself there.

That didn't make sense. Colette Roberge was also the one person who could not possibly have mistaken Madame Schneider for Professor Robinson.

"How well do you know the Chancellor?" Gamache asked Dr. Gilbert.

"Not well. We might've met twice a year, if that. We were both busy. She was the Chancellor of the University, and I had scarlet runner beans to plant."

There was no mistaking the self-pity. Forgotten and embittered, Vincent Gilbert was a great man, fallen. The Cardinal Wolsey of the scientific world. Gamache could all but hear him lament, *Farewell! a long farewell, to all my greatness!*

But Wolsey had gone quietly. Gamache doubted Vincent Gilbert would.

Was he willing to do one last magnificent thing, to remind everyone of all his greatness? But the motive might not be just the Idolas of this world.

Gilbert could have another reason for wanting Robinson dead.

"Professor Robinson said you had no moral authority to judge her," said Gamache. "She even compared you to Ewen Cameron. What did she mean by that?"

Gilbert shook his head. "Not much subtle about our Abigail, is there? Whenever anyone wants to smear a McGill researcher, they drag out the bones of Ewen Cameron. Guilt by association. It just shows how desperate she is."

"She went on to say, 'Don't think I don't know.'"

"A terrible double negative."

"Yes. She meant that she does know something. What does she know?"

Gilbert laughed. "I'm not known as the Asshole Saint for nothing. She probably thinks she knows something that will embarrass me, not realizing I'm happy to own all the *merde*. But I've atoned for my sins. I live a quiet, blameless life now, deep in the woods. Away from the temptation, or even ability, to do anything immoral."

"But not illegal. Was she blackmailing you into supporting her work?"

He laughed again. "Oh, I do like you." He leaned toward Gamache. "Honestly? Do you think I can be blackmailed? Do you think I care what others think of me? I was once the most prominent medical researcher in Canada. The Order of Canada. The National Order of Québec. Invitations to speak at scientific conferences all over the world. Now I live in a log cabin in the middle of nowhere. *Non*, Chief Inspector, I have nothing more to lose. I gave it all away. A blackmail attempt would be amusing and diverting. It would pass the long winter days and nights. Nothing more."

And yet, thought Armand, as he looked into those bloodshot eyes, this was a very long and detailed denial for someone who had nothing more to lose.

What, Gamache asked himself not for the first time, had driven this ego-infested man into the forest? What had he done that demanded perpetual atonement?

And when he falls, thought Gamache, *he falls like Lucifer. Never to hope again.*

They went through the rest of the interviews quickly. Gabri, Olivier, Clara, Myrna. None of them saw, or heard, or knew anything.

There was one interesting exchange, though, when Beauvoir asked Myrna what she thought of Professor Robinson. He'd asked them all, but Myrna's answer was particularly penetrating.

"Did you notice that she went directly to the two people in the room who so obviously didn't want to talk to her? The Asshole Saint and you," Myrna said to Beauvoir. "There's something self-loathing about a person who does that, who keeps walking into a propeller blade."

"Then why do it?" Beauvoir asked.

"To punish herself. I think she puts on a hair shirt every day and goes out to spout crap she doesn't necessarily support."

"Wait a minute," said Beauvoir. "You think she doesn't believe in her own cause?"

"I think her head believes it, but I'm not so sure about her heart. Assuming, of course, she has one."

"Then why's she doing it?"

"Why does anyone do anything? Something's compelling her."

"Something? Someone?" asked Beauvoir.

"Either. Both. She's like an addict. So bound to something that she can't let it go, even though she knows it's self-destructive."

Jean-Guy Beauvoir nodded. He understood addiction and compulsion.

"You're a psychologist," said Gamache. "Do you think Professor Robinson wants to stop?"

Myrna sighed and glanced out the window. It had been a long, long horrible night. And that poor woman was still out there.

"If I had to guess, and it is just a guess, I'd say Professor Robinson is torn. I watched her try to ingratiate herself with the crowd, even you," she said to Beauvoir. "She wants to be liked, that much was obvious. And she is, actually, likable. But she's dragging around this big stinking albatross of an idea that repulses people. I think she'd love to let it go, but can't."

"Put down the cup," said Gamache.

She examined him for a moment, taking in the thoughtful eyes, and the ghosts swirling behind them.

Here was a man who understood the desire to put down the cup. The difference was, Abigail Robinson's cup was filled with bile.

"But why can't she?" Beauvoir asked. "Why keep going if she doesn't believe in it?"

"Oh, I think she does believe in it. And I think she hates herself for it. It's not a comfortable place to be. Someone like that might be very unstable."

"Might kill a friend?" asked Beauvoir.

Again Myrna smiled, but without amusement. "I have no idea. I'm presuming the murder wasn't planned, is that right?"

Gamache and Beauvoir glanced at each other and nodded. They hadn't had a chance, yet, to discuss the details, but it seemed obvious. When the murder weapon was a log, it probably wasn't premeditated.

"Then something must have happened in the party," said Myrna. "Was there a blowup between the friends? Did they argue?"

"Not that we saw," said Beauvoir.

"Well, you know more about murder and motives than I do, but I'd have to say someone who's desperate to be liked might not kill the only person who genuinely does like her."

"*Merci*, Myrna," said Gamache, getting up.

But Myrna paused, still sitting. "I'm not sure I should say this."

"What?"

Myrna took a deep breath. "What Abigail Robinson is proposing isn't new. It isn't revolutionary. It's evolutionary. It's already happening." When Armand went to talk, she held up a thick hand. "Québec was the first province to legalize physician-assisted suicide."

"With strict rules and oversight," said Armand. "That's a choice."

"But pulling the plug isn't. At least not by the person about to die. It's a choice made by relatives. And it's a cruel position to be put in.

Maybe we'd be better off if that decision was taken out of our hands. Off our conscience."

"Are you saying you agree with her?"

"I'm saying it's not so clear-cut. People have dug themselves into positions, but maybe we need to listen with a more open mind. I've had to pull a plug. I'll never get over the trauma. Killing my own mother. That's what it felt like. I'd have liked that cup taken from me."

Armand had also had to make that decision. It had turned out differently, but it was still traumatic.

"I'm not saying I agree with her," said Myrna, getting up. "I am saying I understand some of her points. *Bonne nuit*, Armand. Jean-Guy."

"Good night."

She was the last to be interviewed.

By just after four a.m. they were ready to leave too. Reine-Marie was alone in the living room, waiting for them. But there was one more thing the Sûreté officers had to do.

They'd had a text from the Scene of Crime officer.

Putting on their coats and boots, Armand and Jean-Guy walked into the woods. The wind and cold once again scraped their cheeks and stole their breaths.

They could see the tent, lit from the inside. Shadows were moving around like specters trapped.

After ducking in, they had a quiet word with the head of the forensics team. Then both Beauvoir and Gamache removed their tuques as Debbie Schneider was carried past them, on her way to the morgue.

CHAPTER 24

Isabelle Lacoste arrived in Three Pines early the next morning and went directly to the Inn.

The storm had dropped less than fifteen centimeters of snow, but it had all fallen sideways, creating huge drifts, packing snow up against homes, businesses, fences, trees. Doors.

After the bitter cold of the night before, the temperature had risen to –9 degrees Celsius. Practically balmy.

Flurries were in the forecast, and more snow expected in the coming days. Great for skiing. Not so great for a murder investigation, thought Isabelle as she walked around to the back of the Auberge.

What had been a nice cross-country ski trail winding through the woods now looked like a hiking path. With a tent incongruously pitched on one side.

Once in the tent, Inspector Lacoste bent over the imprint of the body in the snow. Like a mold.

Then she looked around. Over coffee at home that morning, long before the sun or her family rose, she'd watched the videos from Chief Inspector Gamache and Jean-Guy. And she'd read the preliminary reports.

She could see that they'd done well to protect what they could. But damage, in the form of nature and drunken kids, had been done.

After getting a sense of the scene, she returned to the Auberge to have a word with Dominique and Marc. It was decided that the Incident Room would be moved from the old gym to the new Inn.

They'd set up in the basement, away from prying eyes and paying guests.

Unlike the gym, this basement was brightly lit and clean and, best of all, it smelled of fresh paint, not jockstrap.

Jean-Guy joined her there a few minutes later, and while the technicians worked around them, he brought Isabelle up to speed on the events of the night before.

She'd read the reports, but they were skeletal. Now she listened closely as Beauvoir put flesh on the bones.

"Poor woman," she said when he'd finished. "Killed by mistake."

"We can't assume that," he said. "But yes, probably. What news on Tardif's brother?"

"I'm interviewing him at the local detachment in an hour."

"Good. We know he didn't have anything to do with the killing last night, but he might be able to clear up some things about the attack at the gym."

"So the two are unrelated?" asked Lacoste.

"Must be, don't you think?" He paused and looked at her. "What do you think?"

"Oh, I agree. They have to be unrelated, except maybe that one inspired the other. Les frères Tardif were both in custody, so someone else was responsible for last night."

Still, Beauvoir could see that Lacoste was uncomfortable. As was he, though he couldn't see how the two attacks could be connected in any way, except by the intended target.

"Where's the Chief?" asked Isabelle.

"Going over some things at home. He'll be here soon."

Jean-Guy looked around and wondered how the Chief would react to their new Incident Room.

Not well, he thought. Gamache, better than most, knew the wraiths hidden in this basement. He could even name them. Not actually an advantage, when it came to wraiths.

Stephen leaned against the doorjamb into the study. "You wanted to speak with me."

Armand got up from his desk. "I do, thank you. How are you doing?"

"Like everyone else," said the elderly man, walking stiffly to the straight-backed chair he always chose. "Sad and tired. It doesn't seem possible that actually happened."

He sat with a groan, then pointed to the desk. "I haven't seen that book in years. Is it the one I gave your father?"

"You gave it to him?"

"I did. Given what he was going through, I thought he might find it comforting."

Armand picked up the volume he'd found that morning in the bookcase in their living room. *Extraordinary Popular Delusions and the Madness of Crowds.*

"Chancellor Roberge was in the library of the Auberge last night reading it," said Armand. "I remembered seeing the same one in our collection. I was curious."

Opening it, he saw on the title page, *For Honoré, who knows a lot about the madness of crowds. Stephen.*

It was dated the year Armand had been born.

Honoré Gamache, Armand's father, had been a conscientious objector when Canada declared war on Germany. He gave impassioned speeches against conscription, arguing that Quebeckers shouldn't give up their lives to protect far-off imperial powers. He became the face of Québec resistance to the war.

He did, however, join the Red Cross and worked as a medic and ambulance driver.

But after going into the concentration camps, seeing what had happened, Honoré Gamache deeply regretted his stand.

Profoundly ashamed of himself for not recognizing his moral duty sooner, he spent the rest of his short life making amends. Including sponsoring two refugees. The woman, Zora, who would become Armand's de facto grandmother, and raise him after his parents died. And Stephen Horowitz, Armand's godfather, who defended Honoré at every turn. Pointing out to his detractors the great courage it took to be a medic. To be on a battlefield without a weapon. There to save lives, not take them.

And the great courage it took to admit a mistake.

Still, the name Honoré Gamache remained for a generation synonymous with cowardice, and Armand's father was often heckled when he gave speeches in support of the Red Cross and refugees. He took his son to the events, knowing what would happen.

He'd bend down and assure little Armand that *ça va bien aller*. That these people had a right to their opinion, and many had died for that right.

Armand, from a young age, knew a lot about courage, and a lot about the madness of crowds.

"I've never read it." Armand handed the book to Stephen.

"You should. It's about what happens when gullibility and fear meet greed and power."

"Nothing good?" said Armand, with a small smile.

"You're smarter than you look, *garçon*." Stephen tapped the cover. "People will believe anything. Doesn't make them stupid, just desperate. Interesting that the Chancellor would be reading this. She's friends with Professor Robinson, right?"

"It seems so."

"Delusion and madness," Stephen said, and handed the book back.

"I just need to ask you a few questions about last night," said Armand. "We believe Madame Schneider was killed between ten to midnight and a few minutes after."

"When we were all focused on other things," said Stephen.

"Exactly. Where were you?"

"In the living room, then Ruth and I went outside to watch the fireworks."

"In the cold?"

"Well, you never know."

Armand finished the thought. *When it will be for the last time.*

"Did you see Debbie Schneider in that time?"

"To be honest, Armand, I really don't know what she looked like. I knew the professor had arrived with Colette and someone else, but I didn't pay attention to the someone else."

"Did you notice anyone going into the woods?"

"No. We got back inside pretty quick once the fireworks were over."

They went over Stephen's impressions of the party. Like everyone else, he hadn't seen anything specific, but he had noticed the tension, erupting at times into acrimony.

"She and the Asshole Saint sure went at it," said Stephen. "You don't suppose he did it?"

"At this stage, everyone's on the list."

"Including me?" Stephen said with a laugh. But when Armand didn't laugh with him, he studied his godson. "You don't really think I'd kill Madame Schneider, do you?"

"Not her, no. But do I think you'd murder Abigail Robinson? Possibly."

Instead of taking it as an insult, as a slight on his moral character, Stephen Horowitz seemed to see it as a compliment.

"She needs to be stopped, it's true."

Armand leaned back and stared at his godfather. "Are you—"

"—confessing? No. Would I if I'd done it?" Stephen stopped to consider. "Yes, I probably would."

"Life in prison isn't such a threat."

Stephen smiled. "And I've seen the fireworks. You know, while the professional shows are spectacular, I prefer the little neighborhood ones. Seeing the children trying to write their names with sparklers. Waving them like magic wands."

Stephen moved his arm, as though conducting. Armand could see he was writing a name. Not his own. Stephen was writing *I-d-o-l-a*.

"I see that Madame Schneider's parents have been notified," said Isabelle Lacoste.

"Yes, the police in Nanaimo went to her parents' home last night." Jean-Guy looked at the large clock that had been placed on the wall. There was a three-hour difference between Québec and British Columbia. "We'll call in a few hours. Also need to speak to the head of Professor Robinson's department at the university."

Since they didn't yet know who the intended victim was, they were in the awkward position of having to treat it as though both Debbie Schneider and Abigail Robinson had been killed.

"Does the one hundredth monkey theory mean anything to you?"

Stephen had left, and now Armand and Reine-Marie were sitting quietly in the study, as they often did. Armand going over the reports and organizing his thoughts, and Reine-Marie sorting through the boxes of material from her client.

She removed her reading glasses and looked at him. Her eyes were bloodshot, with dark circles under them from lack of sleep. Where Armand, more used to murder, had fallen asleep quickly, Reine-Marie had lain awake thinking of the dead woman.

Seeing Debbie Schneider move about the comfortable living room of the Inn, oblivious to what was about to happen. Unaware that someone in that room was about to kill her.

If ever there was reason to lie awake, watching the curtains flutter, it was that.

Someone they knew was dead. Someone they knew had done it.

"One hundred monkeys, Armand? Are you saying there's actually a theory?"

"It's something Vincent Gilbert said last night when we were talking about the growing enthusiasm for Professor Robinson's findings."

He told her about the one hundredth monkey theory.

"That's pretty interesting," she said when he'd finished. "I wonder if it's true." She looked at the document on her lap. No monkey on that one, though there was one in the margin of an old letter she'd just read from Enid Horton's sister.

"I've lost track of how many monkeys I've found so far," she said. "Might be a hundred in total. Or more. Or less. I have one more box to open after this one. Can't imagine the number really matters."

"I agree," said Armand. "The idea is that there's a tipping point. There certainly seems to have been for Professor Robinson and her campaign."

"You think we've passed it, Armand?" she asked. "There's no going back?"

"No, I'm not sure she's gathered enough support yet. But I think she's close, thanks to publicity around the shooting. And then there's what happened last night."

"Yes, about that. Any idea . . . ?"

"Who did it?"

Armand talked openly with his wife about all his cases. Always had, always would. If he didn't trust her, why had he married her? And she him.

"It's so difficult. We need to work out whether Debbie Schneider was the intended victim, or if a mistake was made."

"How do you do that? Oh, wait. Don't you normally just ask Jean-Guy and Isabelle to do it?"

"While I sit around eating bonbons? Normally, yes. I'm not hopeful. I suspect they're up there getting facials." He smiled, then grew serious. "The thing about murder investigations is that the crime often begins long before the act. The killer starts down that path sometimes years earlier. Sometimes without even knowing it themselves."

"But something started it off," she said.

"*Oui*. There's always a reason, even if reason doesn't figure into it. It almost always starts with some emotion. A hurt feeling. A slight. An insult, a betrayal. It digs in like a hook, and festers. Dragging that person toward the cliff. It could take years, and for some it never goes that far. It becomes a low-level hum of anger all their lives. But for others . . . ?" He raised his hands.

"If it's that small, Armand, how do you find it?"

"We can't. Not the original offense. Not often anyway. Instead we collect evidence. We collect facts. But we also, along the way, collect feelings. Try to pick up the trail of unhealthy emotions. Of perceptions that are just slightly off. Like mariners at sea. If their course is off by a tiny amount at the beginning, by the end they're completely lost."

The same, he knew, was true of murder investigations. A misstep early on, now, could leave them so far off course they would either fail to find the killer or, worse, arrest the wrong person.

Or, worse still, delay things so much there was another murder.

"You look for someone lost?" she asked.

He smiled. "I guess so. The problem with that is that we're all lost at times."

Reine-Marie nodded. She knew that everyone in Three Pines, from Clara to Myrna, from Gabri and Olivier to Ruth and even Rosa, had found the village because they'd lost their way.

Even she and Armand. They'd come to live here when they were most adrift.

She knew, though, as did Armand, that not everyone lost was fortunate enough to be found. Some came to the end of the world, and kept going. To the place where monsters and madness lived.

She looked at the documents spread at her feet and wondered what had happened in Enid Horton's life to compel an elderly woman to draw monkeys on everything.

But she stopped herself. They weren't on everything. Only certain documents. And it wasn't an elderly woman who'd drawn them. Not all, anyway. She'd been a young woman, a young mother, when it had started.

As Reine-Marie had gone through the boxes, a picture had emerged of an absolutely normal woman of her generation. A woman who'd married young. Raised a family in the sixties and seventies. Who'd prepared Christmas and Thanksgiving meals, kept recipes and school report cards and gifts her children had made, that only a mother could find precious.

A woman who'd volunteered at the local hospital and had gone home, closed the door, and drawn monkeys on random letters and bills. Though Reine-Marie now wondered just how random they were.

"We also have to consider that the attack last night is connected to the shooting at the gymnasium," Armand was saying.

"You mean someone at the party tried to finish the job?"

"Could be. But I don't see how. The most likely accomplice was miles away in police custody. They're interviewing him this morning. The connection might be more nebulous. The first attack might have given someone the idea for the second. Emboldened them."

After he left, Reine-Marie decided to sort the papers, putting those with the odd drawings in one pile. Those without in another.

As she looked at the growing pile, Reine-Marie thought there might be one hundred monkeys after all.

Armand stopped in at Ruth's cottage on his way up to the Inn.

In summer the old home looked almost abandoned, with its rickety front porch and wobbly railing and the shutters half falling off. The paint was chipping, and her lawn was mostly crabgrass.

If Ruth had tried to make her home uninviting, she could not have done a better job. And there was a fairly good chance she did try.

Friends in the village had, more than once, offered to repair and repaint and weed, but she'd have none of that. Her home, it seemed, was a reflection of herself. Ramshackle. A little wonky. Definitely askew. She had no need of repair. And neither did her home.

"And for your information," she told Gabri when he'd shown up with gardening gloves and a trowel, "I like weed."

"Weeds, you mean," he said.

"Maybe," said the old poet.

He looked more closely at her garden and the healthy growth.

Armand was consulted and assured Gabri it was not marijuana. "Though that doesn't mean she doesn't smoke it."

Now he stood on the same spot and looked at the same little cottage.

In winter it was transformed. Covered in snow, with icicles dangling like crystals from the eaves, it looked like a gingerbread house. Made by happy children.

It went from the least attractive to the most attractive home in the village.

Such, Armand thought as he shoveled his way up the path, was the power of perception.

When he'd finished, and plunged the shovel deep into a drift, the front door opened a crack. "What do you want?"

"I need to speak with you, Ruth, about last night."

There was a hesitation. Then the door was opened wide, and he stepped quickly inside.

A fire was lit in the living room, fortunately in the fireplace. Almost everywhere he looked were books. It was the literary equivalent of a blizzard. They were stacked up against the walls, as though blown there. In some places they were four, five feet deep.

Books served as side tables next to the worn sofa, and stacks of books held up a plywood plank, creating a coffee table. Though in Ruth's home it was a scotch table.

Many of the volumes, Armand suspected, had been "borrowed" from Myrna's bookstore.

Ruth shoved a few off the sofa and pointed.

He was hot from his exertions and took off his parka and boots. Then he sat, slowly, carefully. Executing a controlled deep knee-bend, until he felt the cushion sag beneath him. He'd made the mistake, only once, of letting himself collapse into the sofa as he did at home. But this sofa had almost no springs, so he had hit the wood floor with a bruising bang and felt one lone spring where no spring should be. He'd leaped up. And never made that mistake again.

Rosa was nestled into a small dog bed by the fireplace, muttering in her sleep. It sounded, to Armand, like *"Merde, merde, merde"*—breath—*"merde, merde, merde."*

He wondered how long it would be before little Honoré or even Idola . . .

"So, speak," said Ruth.

"I meant you speak, I listen. How well do you know Abigail Robinson?"

The question surprised Ruth, and that wasn't easy to do.

"I see you've decided to start with a stupid question. Perhaps to set the bar low. What in the world makes you think I know her? I've never met her. We didn't talk last night. Or ever. Have you been harvesting my weeds?"

"And Debbie Schneider?" he asked.

"The woman who was killed." Ruth paused. She never took death, especially violent death, lightly. Perhaps she found it sobering, he thought, being one insult away from it herself.

Her rheumy eyes caught the reflection of the fire, and he saw, as he always did, intelligence burning bright.

"No. I didn't speak with her either. I spent most of the night talking with Stephen."

"Did you see anything that, given what happened, makes you wonder?"

Armand knew that while she claimed to be oblivious to others, it was an act. Ruth Zardo was keenly aware of others. Their presence and their feelings.

Whether she cared how people felt was another matter. But little escaped her. And most was rendered into poetry.

> Long dead and buried in another town
> My mother isn't finished with me yet.

Yes, he thought, as he watched her think, it took a special gift to write about the personal, and yet touch a near universal experience. He knew that his own parents, long dead and buried in another town, informed a lot of who he was and what he did.

He thought that was probably true of most people.

"I noticed the tension between that Robinson woman and the Asshole Saint," said Ruth. "What were they talking about?"

"It was an exchange of insults."

"Damn. And I missed it. Were they good?"

"Well, she likened him to Ewen Cameron."

Ruth's face hardened. "How did Dr. Gilbert take that?"

"He shrugged it off. Said it was a predictable insult. Anyone who wants to try to undermine a McGill medical grad throws Cameron at them. What is it?"

"Nothing. I knew a local woman, a few years older than me, who was apparently one of his subjects. Just rumor." She paused. "He was a monster, of course."

"Yes."

Armand felt inside his pocket and, bringing out what looked like a campaign button, he placed it on Ruth's scotch table.

"What's that?" she demanded, staring at it.

"It's being sold at Professor Robinson's events, to raise money for her campaign."

Before the shots had been fired and the gym had descended into near pandemonium, he'd considered buying one of the buttons from the concession, to show to Ruth. But he couldn't bring himself to give any money, however small, to that cause.

He'd found two of them on the floor among the other articles dropped in the rush to get out. They'd been gone over for prints and DNA. And then he'd taken them.

He watched as she picked it up. Looked at it. Then at him.

"This's mine," she said. He knew what she meant. Not her button, but what was written on it.

Or will it be, as always was, too late?

The angry chant of *"Too late! Too late!"* by Robinson's supporters momentarily filled the comfortable little sitting room.

It was from a poem, ironically, about forgiveness.

"I don't understand," said Ruth, holding up the button. "Why's my poem on this?"

"Professor Robinson didn't ask permission to use it?"

"No, of course not. I'd never . . ." Her voice trailed off.

"What is it?"

She'd turned to stare into the fire, her thin, blue-veined hand at her face. Then she got up and returned a minute later with her computer, opening it on her lap.

"Oh, shit."

"What?" He went over and bent beside her chair. The email was from a D. Schneider and dated a month earlier.

It asked permission to use that one line in a campaign to help raise money for the university's research into improving health care.

There was a return arrow.

"You replied?"

"I must have." She went to her sent file. Sure enough, there was her reply.

No fucking way. Sincerely, Ruth Zardo.

"Well, that seems clear." Armand straightened up. "But they did anyway."

That might explain, he thought, why both Robinson and Madame Schneider had, despite what Robinson claimed, avoided Ruth all night. It must've been pretty uncomfortable when they saw her at the party.

"Professor Robinson says they came from BC specifically to see you. That they'd arranged to meet you at the party."

"Bullshit."

"Are you sure?"

"You think I don't recognize bullshit?"

"I think you get a lot of requests, and it's possible in a moment of—"

"—madness?"

"—you agreed."

"To meet someone I'd already said no to? Why would I do that?"

"You might not have realized who they were."

She sat back and glared at him. "When was the last time I agreed to meet anyone? Especially to talk about my poetry?"

It was a good point.

Ruth hated discussing her work, preferring that it speak for itself. She was also secretly afraid that she could never really explain what she wrote, and why, and would come across as inarticulate and in need of repair.

She held the button between two fingers, her hand stretched out as though the object stank. "What do I do about this?"

"Not to worry," he said. "Easily handled. I can have a word with Professor Robinson and remind her of the email you sent. Can you forward it to me?"

"Yes. And tell her to donate any money she raised with my poetry to LaPorte," said Ruth.

He smiled. "I'll ask. If that doesn't work, contact your lawyer."

"I don't have the money."

"Don't worry about that. It'll be covered." He bent down and whispered, "You can always sell some of your weeds."

She laughed. "Not much of a market for dried Bishop's weed these days." Then she grew serious. "*Merci*, Armand."

They both knew that in doing this for her, he could be accused of a conflict of interest. But sometimes, he knew, as his father had before him, that conflict was necessary.

CHAPTER 25

Like Isabelle before him, Armand went around to the back of the Auberge first, before heading inside.

He walked down the trail he'd been on many times with friends, cross-country skiing on winter afternoons through the quiet woods. Just the *shhhhh shhhhh shhhhh* of the long, narrow skis on the tracks. Rhythmic, meditative. The sun breaking through the bare branches overhead.

Shhhhh shhhhhh shhhhhh.

They'd follow the trail for several kilometers, before bending back and ending up at the bistro. Unclipping their skis and leaning them against the building, they'd go inside to sit, rosy-cheeked, by the open fire and drink hot chocolate, or scotch, or hot rum toddies. And tease each other about their huffing and puffing.

But today his heavy boots crushed the narrow tracks as he made his way to the tent. Sûreté officers were combing the woods for the murder weapon or other evidence easier to see in the daylight.

When they heard someone approach, the senior agent had turned and was about to warn the curiosity seeker away. But when he, then the others, saw who it was, they stood up and saluted.

"*Bonjour,*" said Gamache. "*Bonne année.* Anything?"

"Nothing yet, *patron.*"

He went into the tent. It was eerily quiet in there. He stood at the spot where Debbie Schneider had lost her life and looked around. Then he closed his eyes briefly, taking in what couldn't be seen. Then he left and walked briskly back to the Auberge.

At the top of the stairs into the basement he paused and looked down. He saw not a well-lit, freshly painted stairwell but a crypt. In an instant he was propelled back to the first time he'd chased ghosts through the Old Hadley House right into that hellhole.

He saw the thick cobwebs, he saw the skeletons of rats who'd been poisoned and had crawled into a corner to die.

He smelled again the decay, the rot as he'd followed the beam of his flashlight deeper into the darkness. He felt the thick electrical cords dangling from the beams overhead. They brushed his head. His face. His shoulders.

And then they'd moved. And he'd realized the basement was infested with snakes.

Then came worse.

But, he told himself, that was in the past. This was a different time. A different place. And yet, as he descended, he felt the chill rising like floodwater up his ankles, to his knees. To his torso, his chest.

It reached his neck, then spilled over his head. And for a moment Armand felt he was drowning in a memory.

"*Patron,*" called Jean-Guy from what seemed like very far away.

Armand felt a hand on his arm.

"You took your time getting here," said Jean-Guy, his voice light but his grip tight. "Isabelle thought you'd gone back to bed, but I defended you. Said you'd probably forgotten where we were."

"*Merci.*"

They both knew this wasn't genial kidding, it was a rescue. Thanks to Jean-Guy, the wraiths were shoved back into the walls. Back into memory. Where they belonged. He was once more in control of re ality.

Though as he walked deeper into the basement, Armand could see the bumps in the rough stone wall, like the features of trapped creatures. Longing to get out. As monsters from the past always did.

The atmosphere in the bistro was muted. By now even those who hadn't been at the party the night before were well aware of what had happened.

Gabri had decided not to wear his frilly pink apron, the one he put on just to annoy Olivier, who still wanted to pass as straight.

"In case his father ever drops by unannounced," said Gabri. "Like he ever does."

"Are you saying Olivier has never come out to his family?" asked Clara.

"Not in so many words."

"And how does he explain . . ." She wagged her finger at Gabri.

"I'm a little afraid to ask."

"What's Olivier afraid of?" Myrna looked across the bistro to the handsome, perfectly groomed, slender man reorganizing the candy jars on the bar.

But the psychologist in her could guess.

Olivier was afraid of disapproval. He hated disapproval even more than he wanted approval. A vestige of childhood, Myrna knew. How horrible it must have been when the boy realized he was gay and destined for a lifetime of judgment.

At that moment, as though summoned by a promise of judgment, Ruth arrived.

She tossed a button onto the table, then sat on the sofa facing the huge fieldstone hearth with its blazing fire.

"What's that?" Clara asked, picking it up. "Oh, I see. It's a line from your poem 'Alas.'" She closed her eyes and tilted her head back in an effort to remember. *"Her voice, resigned, comes ragged from my throat / and in my heart her anger smolders still / amid the ashes—"*

"Enough," snapped Ruth. "We all know how it goes."

"—of residual guilt," Clara finished and opened her eyes. "A poem about your mother."

Such a good way of putting it, thought Myrna, *the ashes of residual guilt.*

Though sometimes the ashes were in fact embers, waiting to leap back into flames. To do even more damage.

They all had it, residual guilt, though some were able to brush the ash off and move forward, while others were smothered by it. Like those poor souls caught in the eruption of Vesuvius. They had human form but were, in fact, hollow.

Myrna looked at the button. *Or will it be, as always was, TOO LATE?*

"That horrible woman is selling these," said Ruth. "To raise money for her campaign."

"Abigail Robinson?" asked Myrna.

"Amelia Earhart," said Ruth. "We found her. She and Jimmy Hoffa are shacked up down the Old Stage Road. Yes, Abigail Robinson. Who else?"

Isabelle Lacoste put the mug of strong coffee down in front of Alphonse Tardif and introduced herself.

She'd made sure Édouard had seen his brother arrive. She'd watched as they resolutely refused to look at each other. The one walking between two Sûreté officers. The other behind bars.

Maître Lacombe was again there.

"Are you representing this Monsieur Tardif too?" asked Isabelle.

"Only until charges are laid, or not."

Isabelle started off discussing conditions for snowmobile trekking in the Abitibi. She knew the area well and spoke knowledgeably. And apparently aimlessly.

She knew that the longer she took to get to the point, the more stressed the man in front of her would become. He was powerfully built, like his brother. But this Tardif was short and stocky and had the lined, puffy face and moist eyes of someone who drank too much.

Isabelle continued to ask him innocuous questions about trails and snow conditions, until finally Alphonse Tardif cracked.

"Look, I know why I'm here. But we didn't mean to do anything. Not—"

"Please, Monsieur Tardif," said Maître Lacombe.

"No, I want to talk." No listening to the lawyer for this one, thought Isabelle.

"Were you involved in the attack on Abigail Robinson at the gymnasium two days ago?" she asked.

"Ye—no." He sighed. "We didn't mean for anything to happen."

"So the gunshots were an accident?"

"They were never meant to hurt her. Just stop the talk. Maybe scare her. But not kill her. Look, Édouard's a great shot. If he'd wanted to hit her, he would have."

"Is that what he told you when he asked you to hide the gun?"

"Don't answer that, Monsieur Tardif," said his lawyer.

"They already know. I just want this over with. Yes, I hid the gun."

"And the firecrackers?"

"And them. In the bathroom, while Édouard distracted the caretaker. That was the plan."

"Were you supposed to be there?"

"No. Édouard told me to get far away. So I did."

"Have you seen what happened, at the event?"

"No. There's no internet that deep into the Abitibi. But I heard about it. No one was killed."

"No thanks to you or your brother." Isabelle's phone was on the dented metal table, and now she hit play on the video.

As he watched, his breathing became labored. When the firecrackers went off, and the crowd began to panic, his brows drew together.

And then the shots.

"The stupid shit," he snapped. "But he missed. Like we planned."

"Barely." Lacoste clicked off her phone.

"Someone must've shoved his arm."

"Who else was involved in the plot?"

"No one."

"Why would you do this, Monsieur Tardif?" Isabelle's voice was soft, calm. Clearly trying to understand. "You have no record. You and your brother are hardworking, decent members of the community. Why suddenly decide to do this? Even if the plan was just to scare Professor Robinson, you must have known the shots could cause a riot. Several were in fact hurt. One man had a heart attack."

"Oh, God, I'm so sorry. We didn't think. Is he going to be okay?"

"We think so. No thanks to you."

Alphonse Tardif was angry, now. Furious in fact. "What an asshole."

"Who?"

He seemed to struggle with himself. "Me. We just wanted to scare her. That's all."

Alphonse Tardif gave details of exactly where he'd been the day of the shooting. Who he'd been with. The cabins they'd stopped at.

And then he was charged with being an accessory to attempted murder.

In the basement of the Inn and Spa, Armand and Jean-Guy were consulting.

"Forensics came to the same conclusion we did," said Beauvoir. "The murder weapon was a log, cut for firewood. Agents are looking for the weapon in the woods."

"I just had a word with them. To be honest, I doubt they'll find it. I think it was thrown onto the bonfire. Billy Williams had doused the flames to embers, but the young man who discovered the body—"

"Jacques Brodeur," said Beauvoir.

"—said when he threw the stick into the bonfire, there were flames. Now, the wind had picked up and it's possible there were embers under the ash and they came back to life, but I think they were helped along."

"By the murder weapon," said Beauvoir.

When Isabelle arrived back a few minutes later, she told them about the interview with Alphonse Tardif.

"It all fits," she said. "So we can at least put that to bed."

"Yes," said Gamache.

One less investigation, one less complication, was always good. But—

"Is something bothering you, Isabelle?"

"It just seemed a bit too easy. Alphonse Tardif didn't have to say anything. He sure didn't have to confess. We have no proof. If he'd just sat quietly listening to his lawyer, we'd have had to let him go."

"Maybe he wanted to confess," said Beauvoir. "Some do."

"Maybe."

"But?" said Beauvoir.

"I don't know. It just seemed too quick, too pat. And when I showed him the video, he got really angry, like it was all a surprise."

"It was. He wasn't there," said Beauvoir.

"No, he said he was angry at himself, but I think he was furious at his brother, for doing it. That's what it seemed like to me."

"What're you thinking?" asked Gamache.

"Nothing really. I suppose they're exactly what they seem. Two local guys who got caught up in something. Who didn't think it through."

"Do you think they meant to kill her?" asked Beauvoir.

"Well, I've charged him with being an accessory to attempted murder, but I'm not so sure. I wish we had a clearer video."

"Let's keep looking for one," said Gamache. "In the meantime, we have an actual murder. Let's concentrate on that."

"So far we've been assuming that Abigail Robinson was the intended victim last night," said Jean-Guy. "But I think we need to consider that maybe she wasn't."

"But who'd want to kill Debbie Schneider?"

"Maybe they didn't. There is another possibility." Beauvoir looked from one to the other. Waiting to see if they saw it. "Chancellor Roberge. She holds a senior position at the University. Someone could have a grievance against her or the University. A professor or student, or a worker who was fired."

"But no one knew she'd be at the party," said Lacoste.

"Exactly. This murder wasn't premeditated, we know that. So someone there sees the Chancellor and snaps."

"You're saying this might have nothing to do with Professor Robinson and her studies."

"I'm saying it's possible," said Jean-Guy. "But there's another possibility. A fairly obvious one."

Gamache nodded. He'd thought of that too. It was the most obvious solution. "Colette Roberge killed Debbie Schneider while on their walk. But why?"

Isabelle barely suppressed a smile. A few weeks earlier, she and her family had been visiting the Gamaches. She'd gone into the bookstore in Three Pines and found Myrna and Clara drinking brandy eggnog and listening to *A Child's Christmas in Wales*, read by Dylan Thomas himself. He talked about the gifts he'd been given, as a boy.

. . . And books which told me everything about the wasp, except why.

The Chief Inspector had just used exactly the same almost plaintive tone. Why?

"Why would anyone, never mind the Chancellor, want Debbie Schneider dead?" asked Gamache.

"And why now?" added Isabelle.

Why did Debbie Schneider have to die at that moment? Why not the day before, or after?

"Suppose," said Beauvoir, thinking out loud, "suppose the killer supported what Professor Robinson was preaching. Suppose they saw that she was now more useful dead? A martyr to the cause. Isn't that what Haniya Daoud suggested last night?"

Gamache nodded. Haniya had said that ideas could grow, flourish, fertilized by the body of a martyr. Yes, that could be it. An idea bloated by blood, made all the more potent.

"And Debbie Schneider was a mistake," said Isabelle.

Or . . .

"Suppose she wasn't a mistake?" Gamache said, leaning forward. "Suppose all this was set up by Professor Robinson? She got the idea after the attempt the day before. Suppose there was another attempt? A murder so obviously meant to be her, but tragically killing her best friend and assistant instead? Robinson would get international publicity for her campaign, without the inconvenience of having to die."

"But does she really care that much? Would she kill her best friend?" asked Jean-Guy. "If she wanted publicity, wouldn't she be more likely to kill the Chancellor? Remember what Myrna said last night? Abigail Robinson wants to be liked. So the last person she'd kill is the only person who genuinely likes, even loves, her."

"True," said Gamache, sitting back again.

"There's something I found strange in your report, *patron*," said Isabelle.

"Oh, no. What did I write? It was late. Probably a typo."

She smiled. "Could be. You mention in passing that Debbie Schneider called the professor Abby Maria."

"Yes."

"It probably doesn't mean anything, but her middle name's Elizabeth, not Maria."

"It was just a nickname," said Jean-Guy. "Maybe an inside joke."

"Like 'numbnuts'?" said Isabelle, and saw Jean-Guy's eyes narrow. "Your nuts aren't actually numb."

"They were last night."

"Let's divide up tasks," said Gamache, before this went too far.

Beauvoir would follow up with Debbie Schneider's parents and the university. Lacoste would go to the arraignment of the Tardifs and see what more she could find on that front.

Armand would speak to Abigail Robinson and Colette Roberge again.

Reine-Marie looked down at the pile of monkeys.

Most were cartoonlike figures drawn on documents, but some were stuffed dolls. There were two porcelain figurines and one children's book, *Curious George*.

Oddly, there was no record by the Monkees.

Humming "Last Train to Clarksville," she put the loose papers into an archival box, then called Enid Horton's daughter and drove to the home two villages over.

Édouard Tardif was formally charged with attempted murder, for which he pleaded not guilty, then was arraigned for trial.

His brother, Alphonse, was charged with being an accessory.

Once again, the two brothers didn't speak. And while Édouard tried to catch Alphonse's eye, the younger brother resolutely looked away.

What did come out was that Édouard and Alphonse Tardif's elderly mother was in a nursing home, having been severely disabled by a stroke. Her mind was clear, but her body was crippled.

The elderly woman, having survived the pandemic, would not survive Abigail Robinson's "mercy."

Love, as much as hate, had pulled the trigger. And luck had intervened.

As Édouard was being led away, Lacoste said to him, "There was another attempt on Abigail Robinson's life last night at the Auberge in Three Pines."

"The Inn and Spa?" he asked. "What happened?"

"The wrong woman was killed."

"Killed?"

She saw his surprise. But it went beyond that. Édouard Tardif was terrified.

"Do you know who did it?" he asked.

"No. Do you?"

Tardif shook his head, and was led off.

Jean-Guy Beauvoir found the caretaker, Éric Viau, in the basement of the old gym wiping everything down with disinfectant.

"I'm sorry," said Beauvoir. "Did we leave a mess?"

"No. Habit."

"I need your help with something. What can you tell me about Chancellor Roberge?"

"The Chancellor?" Viau stopped what he was doing. "I don't know her, not well. I've seen her at big University events, like convocation."

"Is she liked?"

"Yes, very. She always has a kind word, always seems cheerful. Never heard anything against her. But you do know she's not really involved in University life. Not day-to-day stuff." He paused. "I heard about what happened at the party last night. Terrible."

"Out of interest's sake, where were you last night?"

"We always have a fondue on New Year's Eve. The kids stayed up for midnight, but my wife and I were in bed by ten."

Thanking Monsieur Viau, Beauvoir walked across the campus to the pretty little fieldstone building where he'd arranged a meeting with the President of the University.

"Chancellor Roberge?" said Otto Pascal, as though he'd never heard of her before. Then, dragging his head out of ancient Mesopotamia, he said, "No, we have no grievances filed against her. Her role is ceremonial. She doesn't have much contact with professors or students, though she does give two lectures a year, to first-year mathematics students. A sort of introduction to statistics. I've been to some. Quite fun, really."

That seemed unlikely to Beauvoir, and unhelpful. As he left, he paused in the entrance to check the alert that had just come in on his phone.

A new video from the event at the gym had been posted online. Not, he noticed, sent to them, but put up on YouTube. With commercials. So far it had more than five thousand hits.

He almost didn't watch it since the gunman had been arrested and charged, as had his accomplice. But Beauvoir was in no hurry to plunge back into the cold, gray winter day. He found a chair and clicked play.

He could see from the first few frames that this video would be different.

"Little shit," he muttered.

It was taken from the back balcony of the auditorium. Recorded, Beauvoir knew, by the lighting technician who'd sworn he'd done no such thing.

Armand turned off the engine and sat in his warm car in the driveway of Colette Roberge's home.

Light flurries were just beginning. They drifted, nonchalant, from the clouds, landed on his windshield, and lived there for just a moment before melting.

Bringing out his phone, he read messages, replied, then made his way to the front door.

Reine-Marie placed the archival box on the living room floor.

Most of the furniture had been removed. Cardboard boxes sat on the worn carpet, some taped up, some waiting to be filled.

Susan Horton dragged her sleeve across her face, pushing loose hair back from her forehead.

"Did you hear the news?" she asked Reine-Marie.

"No, what?"

"About the murder, over in Three Pines. Mom used to go there, to the church."

Reine-Marie did not say that she lived in the village and had been at the party.

"I found something among your mother's things," she said instead. She heard moving about below them, in the basement.

"Something valuable?" There was no mistaking the hope in the weary voice.

"Well, no, not really. More puzzling."

"Puzzling how?"

"Can we sit down?"

They found two boxes of books, sturdy enough to sit on, then Reine-Marie took the lid off the box she'd brought.

Susan looked in, then leaned back. "Dolls?"

"Monkeys. Lots of them." *Maybe a hundred*, she thought but didn't say. "Do you have any idea why your mother might have so many?"

"Monkeys? Well, she probably liked them. People collect things all the time."

"This wasn't a hobby." Reine-Marie brought some papers out of the box and showed the daughter. "You see? She didn't just collect monkeys, she drew them."

Susan seemed genuinely perplexed. "Does it matter?"

"Probably not, but you did ask me to go through her things and try to bring some order to them. This is something that seemed important to your mother."

"Maybe. It is strange, but she did get strange in the end."

"Well, that's what I wanted to talk to you about. This didn't start in old age, it started when she was quite a young woman. So far, the earliest I've found is from the mid-sixties. She'd have been quite young. It was on a bill for a hotel in Montréal. Did something happen around about then?"

"I was a baby," said Susan. "I have no idea if something happened. Maybe she went to a zoo and fell in love with monkeys."

Reine-Marie considered the woman in front of her, just slightly older, she thought, than herself. "Did your mother ever read *Curious George* to you?"

"What? No. It's a book?"

Reine-Marie brought out the book with its yellow cover and happy little monkey. It was unopened and unread.

"Now why would your mother buy this but not read it to you?"

Reine-Marie turned it upside down and shook. She'd found quite a few things hidden between the pages of books donated to the Bibliothèque et Archives Nationales du Québec. Documents. Letters. Even money.

Both women watched, but nothing fell out.

Putting the book down again, Reine-Marie said, "It looks to me like your mother hid all this from you. Can you think why?"

"Sorry. This's the first I've heard of it."

"Do you mind if I have a little look around?"

While surprised, Susan said, "Knock yourself out. I need to keep packing."

Twenty-five minutes later, after going through the rest of the house, Reine-Marie stood next to Enid Horton's bed. Her deathbed, as it turned out.

Glancing around to make sure no one was looking, she got onto it, rolled on her side, and lifted her arm.

Her hand, finger out like a pencil, touched a rough patch in the rosebud wallpaper. It wasn't a flaw. It was a scratch.

"What're you doing?" came a man's angry voice from the door.

CHAPTER 26

Judging by the dark circles under their eyes, and the lethargy, neither Abigail Robinson nor Colette Roberge had slept the night before. Both looked stunned, shell-shocked.

But that didn't mean one of them wasn't the killer. It seemed to Gamache that whoever murdered Debbie Schneider hadn't started the day, or even the evening, planning to kill.

It was probably as much a shock to him, or her, as to everyone else.

The three of them sat, once again, around the fireplace in the kitchen. All very much aware of the empty chair.

"Any progress, Armand?" Colette asked.

"We're gathering evidence, information. And I need more information from you, Professor Robinson."

"Yes. Anything."

"Why did you really come here?" It felt like the hundredth time he'd asked that.

Abigail Robinson had been expecting some question about Debbie Schneider, and was momentarily stumped.

"I told you already. It was to see Ruth Zardo."

"And yet you didn't speak to her at all last night."

He placed the button on the table between them, then sat back and watched as color returned to Professor Robinson's face.

"Yes, exactly. I came to thank her for letting us use that line from her poem."

"'Alas,'" he said.

"Excuse me?"

"It's the name of the poem."

"Yes." Abigail smiled. "Sorry. I'm tired. Debbie had read in some bio of Madame Zardo that she lives in a village called Three Pines. That's why we went to the party. Hoping she'd be there. But she didn't look at all interested in being approached, so I didn't."

"You travel thousands of miles just to thank her, then when you're feet away you stop?"

"Yes."

He lifted his phone. "This was Ruth's reply one month ago to Debbie Schneider's request to use that line from her poem."

No fucking way. Sincerely, Ruth Zardo.

Abigail looked at him. "She didn't agree?"

"Seems pretty clear she did not. Was Madame Schneider in the habit of not sharing important information with you?"

"No, not at all. At least I didn't think so. But Debbie might not have wanted to upset or disappoint me. She might've thought that, once here, she could convince Madame Zardo to let us use her quote."

"And yet she didn't approach Ruth either. Just so I'm clear about this. Madame Schneider lied to you."

Beside him, Chancellor Roberge shifted and seemed about to say something when Gamache's sharp look stopped her.

"No. Well, yes, but you have to know Debbie," said Abigail, flustered now. "She'd never do it to hurt, she'd do it thinking she was helping. Protecting me even."

"If Madame Schneider misled you about the quote, are there other things she could have lied about?"

"Like what?"

"Well, like the meetings with the Premier. Like the income from sales of merchandise. It seems Madame Schneider was very involved in the day-to-day details of your campaign."

"Not just the campaign. My life. Maybe, I guess. I'll have to check."

She looked around. For Debbie Schneider. To help her check on Debbie Schneider.

"I'd like access to all your papers," said Gamache. "Documents, finances, everything. To see what she might have been up to."

"Is that necessary?"

He looked at her with some sympathy now. "A murder investigation is, by nature, invasive, and I'm genuinely sorry about that. By the time this's over we'll know far more about you, about everyone involved, than we should. But I can promise you, if the information isn't pertinent, it will be forgotten."

"Really? You have that ability, Chief Inspector? To just forget? Lucky you."

They held each other's eyes. No one with gray in their hair got there without things they'd prefer to forget. But could not.

Armand finally broke the silence. "Madame Zardo asks that you stop using her poetry, and certainly stop selling the buttons."

"Of course, I'll get . . ." Abigail's voice petered out. Get who? "I'll make sure it's done."

"And she wants any proceeds already collected to go to LaPorte."

"Where?"

He looked at the Chancellor, who had no reaction. Gamache chose to say nothing either, except "Perhaps the Chancellor here can help with that." Then he turned back to Abigail. "Who's Maria?"

"I'm sorry?"

"Debbie called you Abby Maria. But your middle name's Elizabeth, not Maria. So where does that come from?"

"It's a nickname. From childhood. My God, you're never going to find out who did this to Debbie if these are the questions you're asking."

Her eyes shifted, quickly, briefly, to Colette. She must've given her some subtle signal because Abigail exhaled in an exasperated sigh.

"You'll find out soon enough. I had a sister. Maria. Younger than me. She was born severely disabled. She died when she was nine."

"Abby Maria," he said and glanced at Colette Roberge.

She knew. And yet Gamache remembered, when he'd asked her directly if Abigail was an only child, she didn't disagree.

"My mother used to call us that, from the moment they brought her home. I knew what it meant."

"What?"

"That we were linked. Not two individuals but one person. Abby Maria. Dr. Gilbert was right last night. It was a reference to Ave Maria. A play on words. An attempt to make it seem a good thing. A gift from God."

"It wasn't?"

Abigail didn't answer. Instead she looked down at her fingers, twisted together in her lap. Not two separate hands, but one mass. Impossible to tell which fingers belonged to which hand. Where one ended and the other began. Not stronger for being pressed together. The one held the other so tightly both were useless.

Armand knew that the "Ave," in "Ave Maria," translated into "Hail." Though it could also mean "Be well."

But all had not been well.

Alas.

It was just a split second. So quick Beauvoir only caught it the third time through the video.

Because of the vantage point, he could see almost all the audience, as well as the stage. Granted, he only saw their backs, but it was enough.

He'd suffered through Abigail Robinson's talk again and again, with its odd combination of dull facts building to an electrifying conclusion.

"Too late! Too late!" half the auditorium chanted, while the other half jeered.

And then the firecrackers went off.

Gamache strode to center stage and tried to calm everyone, but couldn't be heard above the growing panic. Grabbing the microphone, his voice clear and commanding, he managed to settle everyone down.

Then Beauvoir saw the man in the middle of the auditorium raise his arm and point the gun. Even though he knew what happened next, it was still shocking.

The podium between Gamache and Robinson exploded.

Then the second shot rang out. How it missed them, Beauvoir couldn't guess. Thankfully, agents tackled the gunman before he could get off a third shot.

Beauvoir watched it again, slower this time. Focusing on the firecrackers. On who might have set them off.

His view of that moment was blocked by a man in a Montreal Canadiens tuque. Beauvoir began to wonder if, maybe, he was the one who'd set off the firecrackers, not Tardif.

The man had his back to the camera, of course. Beauvoir moved the video forward, frame by frame. Just as the shots were fired, the tuque man ducked. And as he did, he turned his head just enough for Beauvoir to see who it was.

"Holy shit," he whispered, looking at the face frozen on his screen.

"I'm sorry," said Reine-Marie, getting off the bed as quickly as though it was on fire. "I was told it was all right to look around the house."

"And to lie on my mother's bed?" the man at the door demanded.

Reine-Marie smoothed her slacks and felt her cheeks getting warm. "No, I just wanted to see something."

"Who are you?"

"Reine-Marie Gamache." She walked toward him, her hand extended. "I'm the archivist."

"Archivist?" he said, staring at her. Angry, but also perplexed.

"*Oui*. You're James Horton? Madame Horton's son?"

"Yes."

"Your sister contacted me and asked if I'd help her sort through your mother's papers. She found boxes of things in the attic and she wasn't sure what should be kept for the family records and what could be thrown out. I understand the house has been sold and there's a time issue."

"She had no right to do that without asking me. Those are personal, private family papers." He looked at her. "And?"

"And?"

"What did you find?"

She knew she should tell him. Knew his sister probably would. But something in the way he demanded to know told her not to say anything.

"So far just bills and pictures. Mother's Day cards. The usual."

"Why were you on her bed?"

"I am sorry. I hadn't planned to, but I saw something on the wall and wanted to check it out."

"What?"

She took him there and pointed.

"I don't see anything."

"It's a few lines scratched into the wallpaper between the bed and the nightstand."

"What business is that of yours?" he asked.

"You're right. None."

And he actually was right, Reine-Marie knew. It was none of her business.

James Horton escorted her out and insisted the archival box of their mother's things stay with them.

"Send us your bill," he said, while Susan stood behind her brother, her face full of embarrassment and apology.

"No need. I wasn't much help."

It was snowing more heavily now, but not blowing. It was a heavy fall of light snow.

Reine-Marie brushed off her car and thought about Mrs. Horton on her deathbed. With the last of her strength, she'd drawn a monkey.

This was becoming less amusing by the moment.

She almost felt bad that she hadn't mentioned to Susan or James that their mother had another box, as yet unopened, that sat in the study of the Gamache home.

On her way back to Three Pines from speaking to Édouard Tardif at the courthouse, Isabelle Lacoste's phone buzzed. It was a message from Jean-Guy.

Making sure not to get stuck in a snowbank, Isabelle pulled over and read, *Vincent Gilbert was at Robinson's talk.*

"The official biography on your website doesn't mention a sister," said Gamache, looking into the bloodshot eyes of Abigail Robinson.

"No. I try to keep my personal life private."

"Private, or secret?"

"What do you think would happen if it comes out that I had a severely disabled sister? People would think that influenced my findings. My conclusions."

"Did it?"

"You don't think I've asked myself that? It was painful, yes. I saw what having a severely disabled child did to my parents. Their exhaustion, their constant worry. But I loved my sister. My findings, my research, have nothing to do with Maria, and everything to do with the future of the social safety net in this country. We don't have enough resources to go around and—" She put up her hands, and smiled. "There I go again. You know my arguments. It's statistics. Cold hard facts. It has nothing to do with Maria."

Gamache turned to Colette. "You knew about the sister?"

"Yes. Abby's father told me. Her death was obviously devastating. It wasn't a secret, Armand. It was a private family tragedy." She looked at him. "You don't talk about the death of your parents."

"True. But I do talk about their lives." But that reminded him of something. He turned back to Abigail. "I've heard about your father, but not your mother."

"She died when I was quite young. Before Maria died."

"I'm sorry. That's difficult. Can you tell me how she died?"

There was a pause, and he was pretty sure one of them would ask to know how it could matter. And he knew he couldn't answer that. Because it probably did not.

"A heart attack. She was only in her mid-thirties. That left my father and me to look after Maria."

He could sense the resentment, still smoldering after all these years.

Not against her sister, he thought. But the mother. For leaving them behind, even if it wasn't her choice.

A wild thought passed rapidly across Gamache's mind. Like some feral idea.

Or maybe it was. A choice.

> And then shall forgiven and forgiving meet again,
> or will it be, as always was, too late?

CHAPTER 27

   ⌒

Isabelle Lacoste turned her car around.

   Within twenty minutes she was again talking to Édouard Tardif.

She showed him the image Beauvoir had sent from the video and saw him squint, raise his brows, then shake his head.

"Who's that?" he asked.

"You know who that is."

"I don't. Never seen him before."

Lacoste placed her phone on the table, angled so that it looked like Vincent Gilbert was staring at Tardif.

"Is he your accomplice? Did he set off the firecrackers?"

Tardif shook his head and repeated, "I've never seen him before."

"How well do you know Vincent Gilbert?" Gamache asked.

His phone had buzzed with the message from Beauvoir. He'd glanced down just long enough to take it in.

"Dr. Gilbert?" said Abigail Robinson. "I hadn't met him before last night."

"But you knew of him? You even compared him to Ewen Cameron. An infamous, even notorious, doctor and researcher."

Abigail gave a single snort of laughter. "I did, didn't I."

"Why?"

"It just came out. I was angry. It's the worst thing any researcher can be accused of. Being as morally bankrupt, as cruel as Cameron. Are you familiar with his work?"

"Yes."

"Then you know."

"What I don't know is whether you believe Vincent Gilbert is also morally bankrupt."

"What's this got to do with Debbie's death?"

"You had a heated argument with someone. Then, less than an hour later, your friend and assistant is killed in what looks like a failed attempt on your life. Questions must be asked. And answered."

"You think Gilbert tried to kill me?" Her astonishment was real. "We had a disagreement, but I can't believe he'd go that far."

"Your final words to him sounded like a warning. A threat. You said that you know. What do you know about Vincent Gilbert?"

"I know how sensitive our egos are. Scientists might seem rational, but we're among the most fragile people in the world. Maybe because most of us never learned to control our emotions, so we're always at their mercy. I wanted to push his big, bloated ego over the edge. I wanted to hurt him back. And there's no better way than comparing him to Cameron."

"Or maybe when you said, 'I know,' what you meant was that you know he was at your talk the other day."

With that, he saw something interesting. Not Abigail Robinson's surprise—she didn't seem to care. But Chancellor Roberge did.

"Why do you think Gilbert was at Professor Robinson's talk the other day?" Gamache asked Colette as she walked him to his car.

He wanted to get her alone, figuring he had a better shot at the truth away from Abigail.

Snow was coming down thicker now. But while it was heavy, it was also gentle. Like feathers out of a broken pillow.

The world seemed muffled. Quiet, quiet. Except for the soft crunching of their boots.

"How should I know? I barely know the man."

"Now, that's not true, is it." He stopped to look at her. The

Chancellor's cheeks were rosy. Probably from the cold. Maybe from something else. "You withheld information from me last night. You failed to say you and Vincent Gilbert sat on the same board."

"So? I sit on a lot of boards but don't know the other members well."

"This particular one is LaPorte, an organization created to protect men and women with Down syndrome."

"True. I didn't think it mattered."

"Oh, for God's sake, Colette. Of course it matters."

"All right, that was a mistake. I didn't want to tell you because I knew you'd read more into it than is there."

"Like?"

"That Vincent and I are colluding. That we have a shared agenda. That we've taken our desire to protect people with Down syndrome to insane lengths and might even be involved in the attempts on Abigail's life. That we're some sort of secret assassination society."

"Well, with the exception of that last part, you have to admit, it's not exactly a stretch."

They'd begun walking again toward his car.

"That I'd kill—" she started to say, her voice raised, then she looked around and lowered it. "That I'd kill someone? You don't really believe that, Armand."

"The only one I know for sure didn't kill Debbie Schneider is me." He paused to consider. "And maybe Reine-Marie."

Her snort of laughter came out in a stream of vapor that incinerated the young flakes in its path.

"I know you have to consider everyone, it's your job. But don't waste your time on me. I didn't do it."

"But maybe Vincent Gilbert did. How well exactly do you know him?" On seeing her rosy cheeks get redder, a thought struck him. He stopped again and turned to her. "Wait a minute, Colette. Are you two involved?"

She took a deep breath, then glanced toward the house.

"No. Were we attracted to each other? Yes. In an intellectual way. He's brilliant and unconventional, and it's stimulating to be around him. But there was never anything physical."

"A meeting of the minds, not the body?" he said.

"Yes."

"You also lied when you said Abigail was an only child."

"*Non*, you said that and I didn't disagree."

He cocked his head. "You're better than that. Are you really going to hide behind some technicality?"

"The loss of Maria was years ago and private to the family. I couldn't see how it could matter."

"Then why not tell me?"

"I should have. I'm sorry."

"What else aren't you telling me? Now's the time."

"Nothing. There's nothing more to say."

They'd started walking again and had reached his snow-covered car.

"You've been very careful up to now to tread a fine line," he said. "Or, really, to stand on the fence. But I need to know. Do you support Professor Robinson or not?"

"I won't tell you that, Armand."

"Why not?"

"Because I'm the Chancellor of a university and my personal and political views need to remain private so I don't influence any student or staff."

"That sounds to me like you support her. And yet . . ."

"*Oui?*" she said.

He'd handed her a brush, and was using one himself to clear snow off his side of the car.

"And yet," he said, stopping to look at her, "I can't believe you would support such a terrible proposal. What amounts to mass murder."

"But you think I'm capable of one murder? So I'm either on Abigail's side, and happy to support mass murder, or I'm against her, and involved in only one murder. An improvement, I suppose. What a mind you have, Armand. I respect you, but I don't envy you. Living with that view of humanity."

He started again to sweep the rest of the snow off the windows and roof.

"Not all of humanity. Just a select few. Be careful, Colette. I'm not the only one paying attention."

As he drove away, he looked in the rearview mirror. Colette Roberge was standing on the path, watching him. And behind her, unseen by the Chancellor, Abigail Robinson was at the window. Watching.

CHAPTER 28

The autopsy report came in just as Gamache arrived back at the Incident Room. It showed nothing they didn't already know or suspect.

Deborah Jane Schneider's life ended at approximately midnight between December 31st and January 1st.

Cause of death: blows to the back of her head. Weapon: a length of wood, almost certainly a split log.

Isabelle Lacoste had returned, and now the three sat at the long conference table in the basement, watching the video. Not the whole thing, just that section. Over and over. Then Beauvoir froze it, on Gilbert's face.

Gamache sat back. "What do you think? Is Vincent Gilbert an accomplice?"

Isabelle shook her head decisively. *"Non."*

"He was there," said Jean-Guy. "Standing right beside the guy."

"But Tardif hadn't planned to stand there," said Isabelle. "He wanted to be much farther forward. He only moved back when he saw us. I've talked to Tardif a few times, and I can tell you there's no way Vincent Gilbert would choose him as his accomplice for anything, never mind murder."

"Why do you say that?" asked Beauvoir.

"Because Gilbert would be sure to find someone who knew what they were doing. Édouard Tardif's a nice, hardworking man, a decent man pushed to an extreme. He's not exactly a criminal mastermind."

"He was calculating enough to almost pull it off," said Beauvoir.

"But not get away with it," Lacoste pointed out. "Gilbert would never agree to a plan that saw his co-conspirator immediately arrested."

"True," said Beauvoir, nodding slowly.

"I don't think Tardif would choose Gilbert either," Isabelle went on. "They're not compatible. An arrogant academic and a naïve woodsman?"

"You like him," said Gamache. "Tardif."

Lacoste considered. "I understand him."

"And sympathize?" asked Gamache.

She nodded slowly. "My mother's getting on too. I'd feel the same way."

"Don't," said Gamache. "Édouard Tardif didn't suddenly pick up a gun and shoot. He planned it. Over days. Setting up a diversion. Almost causing a riot. This isn't a *crime passionnel*. This is cold-blooded attempted murder that put hundreds of lives in danger. Let's not romanticize Monsieur Tardif and his motives or his actions."

It worried him that his hardheaded lead investigators were doing exactly that.

This case was triggering all sorts of strong emotions, in them all. Including himself.

"*Désolée, patron,*" said Isabelle. "But there is a problem. While I don't think Dr. Gilbert was the accomplice, I'm not convinced the brother, Alphonse, is either."

"Why not?" said Beauvoir.

"Like I said before, he gave in far too quickly, and he was shocked by what he saw on the video. It didn't seem he expected it. I want to speak to him again."

"I don't think we can rule out the Asshole Saint," said Jean-Guy. "He might not be the accomplice, but he misled us about his relationship with the Chancellor. He didn't tell us he was in the auditorium, and he was at the party last night. He's the only one who was at both attacks."

"Except Robinson herself," said Gamache.

"And you." Isabelle narrowed her eyes at Jean-Guy. If there was one thing she enjoyed, it was needling him.

"Don't make me have to sit between you," said Gamache. "I think it's probable the two attacks aren't related. The first was planned. The second was not. And we still don't know if Debbie Schneider was the intended victim."

"I spoke to her father," said Beauvoir. There was no need to describe the man's shattered mind. Or broken heart. "He tried to be helpful but couldn't remember much. He did confirm that Debbie and Abigail had been friends since childhood."

"Did he know about Abigail's sister, Maria?" Gamache asked.

"I didn't know about her when I was talking to him, so I didn't ask."

"Can you call him back and ask if Abigail had a sister?"

"*Absolument.*" Beauvoir made a note. "Monsieur Schneider said he couldn't think of anyone who'd want to hurt his daughter, and since she'd never been to Québec, he couldn't see why anyone here would."

"Her ex-husband?" asked Lacoste.

"She hadn't seen him in years and they parted on friendly terms. Doesn't seem to be anything there. I also spoke to the head of Professor Robinson's department."

Gamache leaned forward.

"What came through, though he never actually said it, is that he's incredibly disappointed in Professor Robinson. He said she's brilliant. They were very proud when she was chosen to do the post-pandemic statistical study for the Royal Commission. But after he read her preliminary report, he asked her to stop. Explained that the math was right, but her conclusions were wrong."

"But she didn't, of course."

"No. Caused a real shit storm in the department."

"His word?" asked Isabelle.

Beauvoir smiled. "He was actually quite complimentary. Said she had a quicksilver mind."

Gamache grunted. "Clever."

"Yes, isn't that what he meant?" said Lacoste. "A clever mind?"

"But 'quicksilver' is also the nickname for mercury. Which is a poison. He couldn't think of anyone Professor Robinson had specifically hurt?"

"No. There was just the general sense that she was harming the reputation of the department, of the university, with her work. But I can't see him getting on a plane and coming here to kill her with a fireplace log."

"Didn't Abigail's father also work at the university?" asked Isabelle.

"Yes. They knew each other. They were associate professors together. He said Paul Robinson was"—Jean-Guy checked his notes—"a superb mathematician. Worked mostly on probability theory. Was well-liked by his colleagues and students. Collaborated a lot. His death came as a shock."

"So, back to last night," said Isabelle. "It looks like Professor Robinson must've been the target. Someone who was at the party has a mother or father who'll be affected if her recommendations are accepted, saw their chance and took it."

"Or a child," said Armand. There was a pause that threatened to become awkward before he broke it. "Or grandchild."

"My God," said Jean-Guy. "You've actually seriously considered me?"

"Not seriously, no."

"But you did wonder."

Gamache held his son-in-law's eyes. Then smiled. "Only to the extent that someone else might. But did I think you'd picked up a log and hit her from behind in a moment of insanity? No. Any more than you considered me." Again the awkward pause. "Did you?"

Jean-Guy smiled. "Did I wonder if you could have? Given not just Idola but what happened in the pandemic? Yes. Did I suspect you, even for a moment? No."

"Well, that's two we can strike off the list," said Isabelle. "That leaves about fifty others."

"There was someone in that room last night who I think has killed before," said Gamache. "And would again, without remorse, given the right motive. And the right motive was also in the room."

"Haniya Daoud," said Beauvoir.

"*Oui.*"

"I'll speak to her," said Beauvoir.

"*Non*, let me," said Lacoste. "I want to meet her, and I have no preconceived ideas—"

"Take along your mace," said Beauvoir. "You're about to be mind-fucked."

"—like that one."

Gamache got up and the others rose too. "While you do that, I'm going into Montréal. I want to see what I can find on Vincent Gilbert's career. If he's hiding something, it'll be in the Osler Medical Library at McGill. Might see if Reine-Marie wants to come along and help. She's familiar with their archives."

"I'll talk to the Asshole Saint," said Beauvoir. "See why he was at Robinson's event, and suspiciously close to the shooter."

As they walked down the corridor toward the stairs, past the creatures, past their features in the stone wall, Gamache stopped.

"You know, I'm thinking it might be best if you go into McGill, Jean-Guy."

"Good idea, *patron*. Assign me to an English medical library. At least we'll have the element of surprise."

Lacoste laughed. "Your vast well of ignorance is finally paying off."

"Now, just one question," said Jean-Guy. "What's McGill again? Ha, McGilligan. An Irish Gilligan's isle." He seemed inordinately pleased with himself.

Gamache laughed and held Beauvoir's eyes, bright with amusement and intelligence. He did love the young man.

"You'll do fine. Shouldn't take more than three hours."

Beauvoir laughed. "Why the change, Skipper?"

"I want to talk to Vincent Gilbert. I think he'll be more open with me."

Both Isabelle and Jean-Guy suspected that was true. One of the many features of the Asshole Saint was his snobbery.

Jean-Guy found his mother-in-law in the bookstore discussing Enid Horton's monkeys with Myrna.

"I agree," said Myrna. "If you can find where she drew the first monkey, that might help understand where it came from."

When asked if she'd go to McGill with him, Reine-Marie said she was more than happy to. She liked the Osler. It was a hidden treasure, considered by those in the know as the finest medical library and archive in North America. And just about completely unknown by everyone else.

To be polite, Jean-Guy asked Myrna if she'd like to come along. Dr. Landers was, as it turned out, very familiar with the library, having spent hours there as an undergrad.

And so the little party set off.

Armand spotted Vincent Gilbert in the living room of the Auberge, sitting in front of the fire, reading. All evidence of the party the night before had been cleared away.

"*Bonjour*, Vincent," said Armand. "I'm looking for a lunch companion. Would you join me?"

"On you?"

"On the Sûreté."

"That means you'll be grilling me?"

"At least," said Armand, as they made their way across the hall. "Maybe even puréeing."

Vincent smiled.

They passed Isabelle, who was at the front desk asking after Haniya Daoud.

"Last I heard she was in the stables," said the front desk clerk.

"*Merci.*" Inspector Lacoste hesitated, then asked, "Are Marc or Dominique Gilbert around?"

"The owners?" the young man said. "Madame Gilbert's in the office. Would you like to see her?"

"I'll just go in," she said, before the clerk could stop her. Though to be fair, he showed absolutely no desire to try.

CHAPTER 29

———

"The langoustines are excellent," said Vincent Gilbert, as they took their seats by the window.

On a clear day there was a splendid view of the village below and the hills beyond, rolling into Vermont. But the falling snow both obscured and softened it, giving the landscape a dreamlike quality.

To Dr. Gilbert, looking at the vista behind his companion, it was like something out of a storybook. Peaceful, calm.

But Gamache was looking in the opposite direction, and had a very different view. He saw the Sûreté agents, and the tent in the woods, and the crime scene tape.

To him it looked like something out of *Grimms' Fairy Tales*, or one of the darker fables of La Fontaine.

How closely the two perspectives existed, coexisted, he thought. Side by side. The border between Heaven and Hell a sliver. Murder and mercy. Kindness and cruelty. And how very difficult it was, sometimes, to tell them apart. Or to know on which side of the border you stood.

"They brush them with garlic butter, then grill them over coals," said Dr. Gilbert, taking the menu from the young man and grunting what might have been thanks.

"What a coincidence," said Armand, scanning the menu. "Exactly what I plan to do with you."

Gilbert laughed. "I doubt I'll be as tasty, or as tender. Any progress on the murder last night?"

"Some." Armand waited until they'd ordered and the young server poured Vincent a glass of Chablis. "But before I get into that I have a question about the other attack, the one at the auditorium."

"Oui?"

"Why didn't you tell us you were there?"

Vincent had reached for one of the rolls, still warm from the oven, and was tearing it in half, when he paused. Then continued, though now, as he twisted the roll, it looked like he was wringing a neck.

"Admit I was there when both attacks happened? Do I look that stupid?"

"It's a matter of how you act, not how you look. You're smart enough to know that."

Vincent Gilbert, who was fairly sure he was smart enough to know nearly everything, smiled thinly.

"I was curious. I'd read her paper and knew the Royal Commission had refused to hear her. An extraordinary decision, given the study was commissioned by the federal government. I wanted to see just how crazy she and her followers are."

"You could've watched one of the online videos. You didn't have to go to the rally."

"It's not the same as being there. You're smart enough to know that."

Armand grinned. No one collected, and, when necessary, manufactured, resentments quite as efficiently as the Asshole Saint. But few, Armand knew, were kinder.

Kindness and cruelty, side by side. In the same person. The Asshole Saint.

"And?"

"And they're pretty squirrelly."

"What was it like, to be in the middle of the crowd?" Armand asked, after the waiter put down his bowl of cider-and-onion soup and Vincent's grilled langoustines. "I was off to the side of the stage, so my experience was different."

"Yes, I saw your experience."

He squished a piece of bread into the garlic butter and considered.

"It was frightening. All those people chanting. Supporting her. Supporting killing others so they could be safe. How did it come to this?

Were people like this before the pandemic, or did that bring it on? A long-Covid of fear? I don't know, Armand. It made me sick. And sad. And glad I live far—"

"From the madding crowd?"

Vincent Gilbert smiled and nodded. "Yes. I peek out every now and then, then scuttle back to my little cabin, where I hope so-called civilization won't find me."

"Has it, though, Vincent? Found you?"

Armand's companion was silent, dropping his eyes to his plate.

He slowly looked back up and sighed. "It's hard, Armand. When you care, but try not to. Pretend not to. As long as I didn't hear about anything, see anything, I was okay. I lived through the pandemic in my own little bubble. Safe from the world. But then Colette sent me the research paper, the statistics on what happened, and . . ."

He opened, then closed his hands.

"Your bubble burst." Armand lowered his voice and asked again, softly, gently, as though coaxing a wounded fawn out of hiding. "Why did you go to her talk?"

"I needed to assess the damage she'd done. The damage I'd done by not trying to stop it when I had a chance. If I'd said something after reading her paper."

"Professor Robinson's university tried to stop it and couldn't."

"At least they tried. I didn't. I just retreated into my little home and hid from the world."

"But then you came out." Armand paused. Examining the lean, leathery man in front of him.

"And found a plague of another sort, but just as deadly. Abigail Robinson isn't just spreading death, she's spreading despair. That chant of 'Too late, too late.' It needs to be stopped. You see that too. I know you do."

"What did you decide to do about it?"

When the Asshole Saint was silent, Armand brought out his phone, swiped once, then tapped the screen a few times and hit play before turning it around.

The sound was off. No need to disturb the other diners.

Anyone who was watching the two men by the bay window would

have seen the younger and sturdier of the two holding out a phone and the other staring into it, the blood draining from his face.

It would have been disturbing.

Jean-Guy drove over the new Samuel de Champlain Bridge, the Montréal skyline ghostly through the snow.

Within minutes they were at McGill University. The campus buildings circled a parklike setting, right in the middle of Montréal. Thanks to Reine-Marie's contacts, the head of the Osler Library met them at the main door into the McIntyre Building and let them in.

"*Bonne année,*" said Mary Hague-Yearl, as the women kissed on both cheeks.

"*Bonne année,*" said Reine-Marie. "Thank you for opening the library for us."

"You said it's important."

Reine-Marie introduced her companions. "This is Myrna Landers. Dr. Landers is—"

"A prominent psychologist, yes, we've met," said Dr. Hague-Yearl, taking Myrna's hand.

"I'm sorry, I don't remember."

"It was at a cocktail party in the library to celebrate the naming of a chair in Women's Studies," said Dr. Hague-Yearl. "It's wonderful to see you again. I'd heard you'd retired to the country but didn't realize you knew the Gamaches."

"Neighbors. Friends," said Myrna.

Reine-Marie introduced Inspector Jean-Guy Beauvoir, of the Sûreté.

"So this's about the attack on Abigail Robinson at the Université de l'Estrie a few days ago," said Dr. Hague-Yearl, leading them up to the third floor of the modern building.

"And the murder last night," said Inspector Beauvoir.

Dr. Hague-Yearl paused in the corridor outside the entrance to the Osler Library. "Murder? Someone killed her?"

It was impossible not to see the mix of disgust at the violence and relief at the victim.

"You haven't seen the news?" Reine-Marie asked.

"No. I try not to on holiday. What happened?"

"It wasn't Professor Robinson who was killed," said Beauvoir. "It was her assistant and friend. A woman named Deborah Schneider."

They'd paused in front of the closed doors that led into the library.

They were immense, more suited to a fortress than a library. Fifteen feet tall at least, and made of heavy, worn wood. They were in stark contrast to the rest of the concrete-and-glass building.

This was, Beauvoir knew from watching movies late at night, how most horror stories began. With naïve people standing in front of huge, old, locked doors.

How often had he whispered at the screen, *Don't go in, don't go in?*

But of course, they always did.

Dr. Hague-Yearl unlocked the doors, and in they went.

The Asshole Saint sat back in his chair and pressed his bony knuckles against his lips.

Armand had paused the video and lowered the phone. Dr. Gilbert stared past him and out the leaded glass window, to the forest and hills spread out before them.

"Finished, Dr. Gilbert?" The waiter startled Vincent, bringing him back to the present. He looked down at his empty plate.

"Oui."

When the young man took their dishes away, Vincent Gilbert refocused on Gamache.

But he said nothing. Not because he was waiting for his companion to speak, but because he didn't know what to say. Where to start.

He opened his mouth, took a deep, deep breath, sighed. Then closed it again.

Finally, when the coffee had been poured, he spoke.

"I was there."

It was, Armand knew, not said to state the obvious. It was the pause before the leap.

"What I said earlier was true. I didn't go to her talk with any particular agenda. Certainly not to cause harm."

Do no harm. For years Armand had thought that the phrase was part of the Hippocratic Oath all doctors swore. It was only recently he learned that wasn't true at all.

Do no harm was part of Hippocrates's writing, but from a different text. On epidemics.

"You know what the video shows," said Gamache. "Not just that you were there."

"Yes."

The video that Jean-Guy had discovered, taken by the lighting technician in his booth above the floor of the old gymnasium, showed quite clearly what had happened.

They could see Vincent Gilbert, Canadiens tuque shoved far down his head to hide his identity as much as possible. When the fireworks went off right next to him, he ducked. Clearly surprised.

Then he stood back up and looked at the stage, along with the rest of the crowd, as Gamache calmed them, reassured them it was not gunfire.

And then those telltale few seconds.

The man beside Gilbert raised his arm. Slowly. And in his hand, seen clearly on the video, was a gun.

Everyone else was still staring at the stage. At Gamache.

Except Vincent Gilbert. He was looking at the gun. Then he turned his head, to look at the man holding it.

Aiming it. Taking his time before he pulled the trigger.

And firing.

The Asshole Saint had seen it all. Been close enough to reach out and knock the hand up. So that the shot missed.

"It's not that you did no harm," said Armand. "It's that you did nothing."

CHAPTER 30

—

O n the drive into Montréal, Reine-Marie and Myrna had talked about the Osler while Jean-Guy drifted in and out of the conversation. Taking in some details.

Basically, what he heard was that the library was named after some long-dead prominent Anglo doctor who had donated his papers and books to McGill more than a century ago.

Blah, blah, blah.

Jean-Guy Beauvoir hadn't much seen the use of libraries, though he'd never have said that to Annie or her parents, who saw *les bibliothèques* as sacred places.

He hadn't grown up going to one, and now, with the internet and easy access to information, he couldn't imagine why libraries still existed. That is, until he'd gone with Annie and Honoré to a children's hour at their local library. He'd seen the wonder in his son's eyes as the librarian read to them.

He'd seen Honoré's excitement at getting to choose books himself to take out. How he clutched them to his chest, as though he could read with his heart.

Through his infant son, Jean-Guy discovered that libraries held treasures. Not just the written word, but things that couldn't be seen. Like *le Petit Prince* said, in the book Jean-Guy had first read as he'd read it to Honoré.

What is essential is invisible to the eye.

Knowledge, ideas, thoughts. Imagination. All invisible. All lived in libraries.

But few knew better than the homicide investigator that not all ideas and thoughts, not everything imagined, should be held tight to the chest.

As the great doors to the great library swung open, Jean-Guy's jaw actually dropped.

Dr. Mary Hague-Yearl stepped aside so he could take in the soaring ceiling and oak paneling. The tall glass-fronted bookcases and stained-glass windows and quiet corners, and long tables with reading lamps. They'd stepped out of the twenty-first century and into the 1800s.

"Sir William Osler was a McGill grad," said Dr. Hague-Yearl, leading them through the vast room. "He's considered the father of modern medicine. This's been reconstructed from his original library."

Beauvoir could believe it. It was like walking into a Victorian gentleman's home.

Dr. Hague-Yearl nodded toward a long oak table.

"If you stay here, I'll see what I can find on Vincent Gilbert. We should have some documents. He's quite prominent."

All three grinned, knowing how annoyed the Asshole Saint would be at the qualifying "quite." Within minutes they each had a pile in front of them.

"All this?" asked Beauvoir.

"Yes." Dr. Hague-Yearl seemed surprised herself. "We have some files going back a long way, to his residency. I didn't bring those, but can if you'd like."

"*Non, merci,*" said Beauvoir. "This is more than enough."

He squirmed on the hard chair and resigned himself to a long, dull afternoon. Though he remained alert. In case something, unseen, emerged from the files.

Isabelle Lacoste had spoken to Dominique and been given a list of staff members.

She'd had a thought.

Édouard Tardif had a son and daughter, Simon and Félicité. They'd been interviewed, along with Tardif's wife. All had alibis for the day of the event, and could add nothing to the investigation. According to the investigator conducting the interviews, they seemed stunned and naturally upset.

Both Tardif kids were in their early twenties. As Isabelle Lacoste had looked around the Inn, she realized almost all the employees were also in their early twenties. The chambermaids, the waiters, the front desk clerks.

Suppose . . .

But there was no Tardif on the list.

It was only when she was almost at the barn to find Haniya Daoud that she had another thought. Turning around, she retraced her boot prints in the deepening snow and once again knocked on Dominique's door.

"Do you hire extra staff for the New Year's Eve party?"

"Yes. We give a lot of our regular employees time off around Christmas and New Year's."

"Do you have a list of those who worked the party?"

Five minutes later she walked into the dining room and spotted the Chief Inspector deep in conversation with Vincent Gilbert.

"Would you believe me, Armand, if I said when I saw the gun I was shocked? Too stunned to act?"

Armand shook his head. "In almost anyone else, I might believe it, but you're a doctor. A surgeon. You spent your career dealing with the unexpected. I suspect you also spent shifts in Emergency."

Gilbert nodded.

"Your whole training is to react quickly," said Armand. "And yet you didn't. Or"—he examined the man in front of him—"more likely, you did react. You just didn't act. You saw what was about to happen and let the gunman fire."

"I'm not going to admit that, not to you. But I think I owe you some possible explanation, since what happened could've cost you your life. That was never ever intended, and I'm sorry."

And he looked it.

"What was intended, Vincent?"

He took a while to answer. When he finally did, Gilbert could not look Armand in the eyes.

"I was a coward. During those long months of the pandemic, I stayed in my cabin. People brought me food and drink. Supplies."

"*Oui*. Reine-Marie among them."

"Is that right? I never looked out. I was too afraid."

"Of what? The virus didn't spread by sight."

"No, but shame does. As long as a bag mysteriously appeared, I could pretend I wasn't hiding in there. But if I saw someone helping, when I should also be, then . . ."

Then.

"I'm a doctor. I should've been treating the sick. Administering tests. Doing something useful. But I hid."

"You're in your seventies," said Armand. "You're in the age group ordered to shelter in place. You couldn't have helped."

"But I didn't try." Vincent raised his voice, angry now. "So when I saw the gun, aimed at Abigail Robinson, aimed at the person convincing others that the sick and the elderly, and now even babies, should die, as they had in the pandemic, well . . ."

Well . . .

"*Patron?*"

Both men looked up.

"*Désolée*, but may I see you for a moment?" Lacoste asked.

"Do you mind?" he asked Vincent, who shook his head.

Dominique joined Lacoste and Gamache in the far corner of the dining room and pointed.

When their waiter took their bill to the table, Armand broke away and rejoined Gilbert.

"It's on me, remember?"

After handing his credit card to the young waiter and getting it back, Gamache said, "*Merci*. Monsieur Tardif."

The young man stiffened, and for a moment Gamache thought he'd try to run away. But he didn't.

"Might we have a word?"

Vincent Gilbert looked perplexed but relieved. It was someone else's turn to be grilled.

And puréed. The waiter walked between Gamache and Lacoste, down into the basement of the Auberge, and took the seat indicated, at the long table.

"You are Simon Tardif?" asked Isabelle Lacoste.

"*Oui.*"

"Your father is Édouard Tardif?"

"Yes."

Simon Tardif was small. Slender. His face pale, pasty. He looked like a baby bird balancing on the edge of the nest, and about to be pushed out too soon.

Too soon.

"Where were you on the afternoon of December thirtieth?" Lacoste asked.

"With friends. I can prove it."

"Not with your father, at the University gym?"

"No."

"Did you work the New Year's Eve party last night, here at the Auberge?" Gamache asked.

The two locked eyes.

Gamache could see that Simon Tardif was tempted to lie. But he could also see there was intelligence there, though not, he thought, cunning.

"Yes," said Simon. "But I didn't do anything. I didn't hurt that woman. I—"

The Chief Inspector stopped him there. "You need a lawyer. Do you have one?"

The boy looked like he was about to cry. "No. I'm sorry. I—"

Gamache leaned forward and said, "Say no more. It'll be all right. Look at me. Look at me." The third time he said it, Simon Tardif did. He looked into the deep brown eyes, and his shoulders slumped. In resignation. And relief.

It was over.

*   *   *

"Nothing," said Reine-Marie, sitting back.

Beside her, Jean-Guy had taken off his glasses and was rubbing his eyes.

It was mid-afternoon and already getting dark outside. All the lamps in the huge library had been lit. It made the place feel more intimate. Though as the natural light faded, what had been aisles of books started to resemble tunnels. And it was possible for Jean-Guy's vivid imagination to conjure all sorts of unnatural things awakening.

So far all they'd found was what they pretty much already knew. Dr. Vincent Gilbert was a gifted thoracic surgeon. The one you wanted with his hands in your chest. But not the one you wanted standing beside your bed.

And certainly not the one you wanted as a chief, if you were an intern or resident. The file was full of letters of complaint from young medical students about his manner.

Those were accompanied by other letters, from patients and their families, thanking him for saving their lives. And from other interns and residents, saying what a wonderful teacher he was. How much he had helped them. His innovations, his challenging them to think for themselves. Yes, he was harsh at times. But so was life in a critical care unit.

The Asshole Saint emergent.

"We need to look at the early documents," said Beauvoir, resigned to his fate.

"When he was an apprentice asshole," said Myrna.

"A baby saint," said Reine-Marie. She was curious to see what they'd find there. Had he started his medical career as a saint, or as the other? Had something happened that changed him?

Twenty minutes later Myrna said, "Look at this. Before starting medical school here at McGill, Vincent applied for, and got, a grant."

"Really?" Reine-Marie leaned over and read the application.

Gilbert's father had died, and his mother took in boarders and did laundry.

"But it's pretty small," said Myrna. "Did he also get a scholarship?"

Beauvoir found it. "Yes. But it's not very much."

Together, grant and scholarship would not be nearly enough to cover medical school at McGill.

"So how did he do it?" Beauvoir asked.

"He must've gotten a part-time job," said Dr. Hague-Yearl. "Lots do, at the student pub, or the cafeteria. In the library shelving books. That sort of thing. Let's keep looking."

They didn't realize it yet, but they'd just come across the first hint of the creature, unseen, that was waiting patiently in a tunnel of documents. To be found.

Twelve minutes later, it was.

"He did get a job," said Myrna, holding up a slip of paper. "He earned extra money looking after the lab animals."

"Yech," said Reine-Marie. "Terrible."

She assumed the look of revulsion on Myrna's face was because she too hated the use of animals in experiments. Which she did.

But it wasn't that.

Dr. Hague-Yearl took the slip, read it, and looked stricken. "Not that. Not again."

"What?" asked Jean-Guy.

She handed him the piece of paper. It was a receipt for delivery of lab animals to the Allan Memorial Institute of McGill.

She placed a finger on a name at the top.

"Who's Ewen Cameron?" he asked. The name was familiar. Then he remembered that Gamache and Gilbert had talked about him.

"Wait a minute." Reine-Marie took the paper and studied it. "Vincent worked with Ewen Cameron?"

"We don't know that," said Myrna. "Just that he looked after the animals that Cameron used."

"Who is he?" repeated Beauvoir, growing more agitated.

Dr. Hague-Yearl had disappeared, as though the name itself was enough to incinerate the librarian.

Jean-Guy was beginning to think his instincts about those huge closed doors were right.

They were partly to keep intruders out, but also to keep something in.

Something, or someone.

A legal aid lawyer Gamache knew well showed up within the hour.

Ten minutes later, after private consultation, Simon Tardif confessed that he'd been involved in the plot at the auditorium.

The boy insisted that the plan was to just scare the professor, not hurt her.

No, he hadn't thought about the hundreds of other people who'd be in the auditorium.

No, he hadn't been there himself. His father had insisted he be with friends at the time.

Yes, he was surprised his uncle had confessed. As far as Simon knew, he wasn't involved.

Yes, the plan was that while his father distracted the caretaker, he hid the gun and firecrackers.

Yes, there were bullets with the gun, but they were blanks. Weren't they?

When Chief Inspector Gamache showed him the video, Simon Tardif broke down.

"I didn't know. I didn't know. Dad couldn't have .. ."

His lawyer laid a hand on his arm to stop him.

"And last night?" Gamache asked, once Simon had recovered.

"I didn't do anything. I didn't even know that professor woman was here. I have no idea what she looks like."

"You have no idea what the person your father was targeting looks like?" asked Isabelle, clearly incredulous. "You didn't want to know why? We can check your search history."

"No, don't do that." The boy blushed, and both investigators and the lawyer could guess why. It wasn't just a university professor he was googling. "Yes, okay, I did look at her videos. And I could see why Dad would do it. But I spent most of the time at the party last night in the kitchen preparing the trays. I didn't know she was there."

"You came up for the countdown to the New Year, didn't you?" Gamache guessed.

"Yes."

"And what did you see?" Isabelle asked.

"Almost everyone went outside to the bonfire."

"Did you see anyone go into the woods?"

"No. I wasn't watching. I just wanted the night to be over and get home. All I could think of was my father. Of what was going to happen to him. And me."

Chief Inspector Gamache stood up and said to Lacoste, "Charge him."

"With what? Accessory to attempted murder?"

Gamache stared at the frightened young man. Thrown out of the nest by an obsessed father. To land, splat, in the arms of the Sûreté du Québec.

"Mischief."

It was a misdemeanor. If convicted it would not ruin the boy's life. But it still kept the options open to charge Simon Tardif with a more serious crime. Like murder.

They interviewed Alphonse Tardif again. He admitted he knew his nephew had been involved and confessed in order to protect the young man.

After weighing a charge of obstruction of justice, Gamache ordered that Alphonse Tardif just be released.

CHAPTER 31

⌒

"Ewen Cameron was a psychiatrist," said Myrna. Her voice was calm and steady. Warm, as always. Almost musical. "He studied human behavior, but his specialty was memory. He went to Nuremberg and assessed the Nazi Rudolf Hess. Cameron's diagnosis of amnesia got Hess out of a death sentence."

"Didn't Hess later admit he'd faked the amnesia?" asked Reine-Marie.

"Yes. Cameron went on to develop theories of society, placing people into two categories. The weak and the strong."

> Thus human courts acquit the strong,
> And doom the weak, as therefore wrong.

Mary Hague-Yearl had reappeared with several books. She opened one to a black-and-white photograph and placed it in front of Beauvoir.

"That," she said as she thrust her forefinger onto the face, "is Ewen Cameron."

A slender, middle-aged man with gray hair and glasses smiled up at him.

Trustworthy. Benign. Caring. He looked like something out of central casting.

Marcus Welby, M.D.

The line under the photo said Dr. Cameron had been the President of the American Psychiatric Association. The Canadian Psychiatric Association.

The World Psychiatric Association.

"But it was his work with the CIA, here at McGill, that made his name," said Myrna.

Jean-Guy Beauvoir looked up. "The Central Intelligence Agency?"

"Yes. This was back in the fifties and sixties. The height of the Cold War. He was hired by the CIA and others, including the Canadian government, to study brainwashing. How to do it. How to undo it. And to do that, he needed not just animals but human subjects."

"Prisoners?" asked Jean-Guy.

It was a repugnant, immoral practice that had apparently continued long after it was declared illegal.

"No," said Reine-Marie. "They were men and women from across Canada who came to him for help. Most had minor complaints, like we all do at times. Insomnia, headaches, anxiety. Some for depression. Young mothers with postpartum. It was a great thing, to be seen by the eminent Ewen Cameron. They had no idea what they were in for."

"What did he do?" Beauvoir looked down and met those kindly gray eyes. *What did you do?*

"It was called MKUltra," said Dr. Hague-Yearl. "Sounds almost laughable now. Like bad science fiction. You'll find the details in those pages . . ." She motioned to the stacks of paper she'd brought over. "We also have the testimony of some of his victims."

Not patients. Not clients.

Victims.

"They were guinea pigs," said Myrna. "He used drugs like LSD. He tied them up and shot electricity through them. He used sleep deprivation. He put them into comas, sometimes for months—"

"My God," said Beauvoir. "And no one stopped him?"

"No. No one even questioned him," said Dr. Hague-Yearl.

"But he tortured them," said Jean-Guy, unable to comprehend.

"Yes," said Reine-Marie. "Ewen Cameron took men and women who'd come to him for help and he tortured them. Here. At the Allan Memorial Institute. At McGill University. For years. In full view. And no one stopped him."

"Apparently the CIA was pleased with the results," said Myrna. "They turned his findings into psychological torture methods they still use today."

"Oh, my God," whispered Jean-Guy.

He dropped his eyes to the smiling father figure in the photograph. And had it confirmed, yet again, that most monsters looked exactly like that.

They didn't hide in dark alcoves. The distinguished monsters sat among them. Secure in the knowledge that no one would condemn them, even if they knew.

"*The Prince of Darkness is a gentleman,*" said Mary Hague-Yearl, following his thoughts and his eyes to the photograph.

Jean-Guy spent the next hour reading about the victims of Ewen Cameron. Their stories. How they showed up in his office complaining they couldn't sleep and returned home months later unable to speak.

Unable to recognize their husbands and wives and children.

Unable to hold a job, or hold their bladders, or hold their babies.

He read about how Cameron would strap them down and send electricity through them so strong they could smell their flesh burning.

How he kept them awake for days at a time, or put them into comas for months and filled them with drugs.

Until their brains were so washed they'd lost their minds.

And then he sent them home, addled. Clutching bills for the treatments. Then Dr. Ewen Cameron went on to the next, and the next.

"And Vincent Gilbert knew about it?" said Beauvoir. "Helped him?"

"We don't know that," said Myrna. "All we know is that the receipt for the animals, sent care of Dr. Vincent Gilbert, is authorized by Cameron. It's from the mid-sixties. Gilbert must've been young, just starting out."

"Come on," said Beauvoir. "He must have known."

Reine-Marie saw Vincent Gilbert sitting at the old pine table in their kitchen after dinner, as they'd had coffee and cognac and swapped stories.

Had the same hands that had held her grandchildren held men and women down while Cameron tortured them?

Jean-Guy Beauvoir asked for copies of some of the more damning documents, including the receipt for the animals. They thanked Mary Hague-Yearl, then left for home.

The car was quiet, everyone lost in their own thoughts. The wipers lazily, rhythmically, sweeping the freshly fallen snow from the windshield.

As the city disappeared into the rearview mirror and the peaceful countryside slipped by, Reine-Marie opened the file on her lap and looked again at the damning receipt for the rats and monkeys and actual guinea pigs.

There would be people still alive who'd suffered Cameron's torture. And the silence of his colleagues.

She leaned her head against the cold window and stared out at the acres and acres of snow. At the lights just beginning to show in homes. At the forests and fields and mountains. At the wilderness. And Reine-Marie Gamache longed to get home to Three Pines.

Isabelle Lacoste found Haniya Daoud in the stables.

She had a currycomb in one hand and a brush in the other.

Lacoste stood in the wide aisle and watched as Haniya, a borrowed parka over her long abaya, made slow circular motions with the currycomb, then brushed the horse's flank down.

Then did it again, and again. In long, flowing, rhythmic movements.

And as she did it, Haniya muttered something Isabelle couldn't make out, though she knew if she could, she probably wouldn't understand the words. But she would understand the meaning.

It was a prayer. A meditation. An invocation.

It was, Isabelle felt, very calming. Between the whispered words, the fluid motions, the occasional toss of the horse's mane and tail, the musky scent of horse and hay, the warmth of the barn, Lacoste could feel herself relax.

"Do you know horses, Inspector?" asked Haniya, without stopping.

"A bit. I rode as a child, but I could never figure out the bridle."

"It is complicated." Haniya moved to the other side of the horse and could now see Lacoste. "The leather and metal bit and straps. The means of control."

The horse was leaning against Haniya Daoud. Not in a threatening way. It seemed to like the contact. As did she.

"Billy Williams tells me the owners of the Auberge saved these animals from the abattoir," said Haniya. "This one's a former racehorse who was no longer useful. So it was going to be killed and ground up. Turned into dog food and sweet treats for children."

She looked over to another stall, where Billy was just putting a large harness on an immense animal.

"I'm not totally sure that's a horse," she confided in Lacoste.

"No," said Isabelle, glancing over. "That's Gloria. We think she might be a moose."

Haniya snorted in some amusement and looked around. "What a strange place."

"It grows on you," said Lacoste.

"So does a mole."

Putting down the brushes, Haniya traced the lattice of whip marks on the horse's flank.

"We haven't actually met. My name's Isabelle Lacoste, I'm with the Sûreté. But you already knew that."

"Yes, you work with Monsieur Gamache. I've seen you around."

"Can we talk?"

Haniya looked behind her. "Monsieur Williams is just hitching up the sleigh to take the children out, but he's offered to take me on a short ride first. I suppose you might as well come along."

Not the most gracious invitation Lacoste had had, but far from the worst.

A few minutes later, a heavy blanket tucked around them, they were ensconced in the back seat of the big red sleigh looking at Gloria's immense rump. Billy sat high in the driver's seat, his back to them, muttering to Gloria, who seemed to understand his incantations. His invocations. And maybe his prayers.

She meandered across the road and into the woods. Away from the Auberge. Away from the crime scene.

Haniya tipped her head back, letting the huge flakes land on her face. She was almost smiling.

This close to the woman who would probably be named the winner of the Nobel Peace Prize, Isabelle could see two things. How young Haniya Daoud actually was, and the scars all over her face. It looked like a jigsaw puzzle, imperfectly assembled.

"I can't get used to snow," Haniya said, her eyes closed, her face tilted and moist.

The small bells on Gloria's bridle jingled merrily. The rails of the sleigh slid along the snow making a soft sound. *Shhhh.*

"Tell me what happened to you in Sudan."

"You don't want to know," she said to the sky.

"I do."

"Why?" Haniya asked the snowflakes. Then lowered her face and opened her eyes and looked at the homicide investigator. "Oh. You want to know how damaged I am. And if I've killed before. Let me give you the shorthand. I am damaged, *beyond repair,* as your lunatic poet would say. And yes, I've killed." She studied Isabelle. "I think you know how both feel."

"I do."

"So, I'll make you a deal. I'll tell you if you tell me."

Isabelle sat quietly for a moment, looking into the naked woods. Only in the winter was it possible to see both the forest and the trees. Homicide, she thought, was a perpetual winter.

"Agreed."

So with the swish of Gloria's tail for accompaniment, and the *shhhhh* of the sleigh, Haniya told her.

About being kidnapped at the age of eight, when her village was attacked and destroyed. Her crime? Being a member of an ethnic minority. She was beaten and whipped and slashed with machetes. Staked naked in the dirt. And left there. Given just enough food and water to be kept alive. For the men to rape. Day after night after day.

To the tune of the sleigh bells, Haniya told her about giving birth at twelve. The baby taken from her.

Then again at thirteen, and fourteen. And every year until she'd escaped. Expelling babies from her body. Some dead. Some screaming. Never to be seen again.

"They told me that the meat I was eating was the flesh of my dead children," she told the pine trees as they passed.

Isabelle felt herself grow faint, and thought she might pitch forward, out of the sleigh.

"But I didn't believe them," Haniya said to Gloria's swaying back. "I know they're alive."

They glided through the silent woods.

As the rails of the sleigh requested silence, *shhhhh*, Haniya spoke. "One night a particularly drunk soldier raped me, and then, as he beat me, his machete fell from his belt. When he passed out, I was able to saw through the rope. Took a long time, but I did it." Haniya turned to face Isabelle. Her eyes steady, her voice soft, almost kindly. "I killed him. Then I killed them all. Then I released the others, and we escaped, taking their machetes with us."

She paused then. "They had child soldiers guarding the camp." Haniya stared ahead, at the pristine landscape. "Have you ever heard of brown brown?"

"*Non.*"

"When children are abducted, that's how they turn them into soldiers. They're given brown brown. It's cocaine mixed with gunpowder."

Isabelle inhaled deeply but said nothing. *Dear God*, she thought. *Dear God*.

"It . . . it . . . turns them into something else," said Haniya. "When we went to get away, a boy tried to stop us. I could see that look in his eyes. His brown brown eyes."

"What did you do?" Isabelle whispered.

Shhhhh went Gloria's tail. *Shhhhh* went the rails of the sleigh.

"I'm here, aren't I?" said Haniya.

Almost, thought Isabelle, and wondered how much of herself Haniya had left behind at the boundary.

"We finally crossed the border. And were safe." Now Haniya smiled. "But you know as well as I do, Inspector, that no place is safe."

Haniya Daoud tipped her head back again, closed her eyes, and let the cold snowflakes melt into her scars. To the sky she said, "I'm alive because of my children. I had to survive, to save them. Every woman and child I save is my baby."

Isabelle wondered, but didn't ask, if Haniya Daoud, once out, had turned her machetes into plowshares. But she was pretty sure she knew the answer.

Haniya opened her eyes and looked around, as though surprised to see the thick Québec forest, and the trees. Then her eyes came to rest on Isabelle.

"Your turn."

CHAPTER 32

When Gloria stopped in front of the bistro, Haniya and Isabelle got out.

The village children crowded around, and while some wanted to get into the sleigh, others were far more interested in Gloria. Reaching up as she bent down, they rubbed her huge silky nose.

"Just a moment," said Billy, laughing, as kids pushed and shoved to climb onto the sleigh. "Everyone'll get a turn. I promise."

It was, perhaps, not completely surprising that children understood every word Billy Williams said, while adults struggled.

Gloria started off, pausing to let the car pass as it came slowly down the hill into Three Pines. Billy touched his tuque, in a salute to them. But mostly to Myrna, who also understood him.

Then, with a cheerful jingle, they set off again.

"Papa," Florence, Zora, and Honoré shouted a minute later as they passed their grandfather. He was walking from the Auberge back into the village and had stopped to wave to them. Then he continued, his hands behind his back, his head down. Thinking.

Haniya Daoud stared at the door that connected the bookstore to the bistro. A door she'd been through a few times. Then she looked at the long, beamed room with its wide-plank floors cut from trees that grew within sight of the building.

At the huge stone hearths at either end, made of rocks pulled from nearby fields.

At the men and women sitting there, including the demented poet and her fucking duck. Sons and daughters of Québec, whether born there or not.

Haniya Daoud, the Hero of the Sudan, had listened as Isabelle Lacoste told her what had happened. There. In this quiet place, in this quiet village.

Shhhhh.

The gun placed at the base of her skull. The push through the bookstore door. Catching Gamache's eye as he sat in the bistro, and that instant of mutual recognition. Of what she was about to do. Of what he had to let her do.

She was about to die. So that others in the bistro—including Armand and Jean-Guy, including Ruth and Gabri and Olivier—might have a chance.

Shhhhh. But Isabelle continued.

She told Haniya about that moment, frozen in time, as she held Armand's eyes, and thought of her children. Then Isabelle braced and shoved with all her might, so that her body slammed into the gunman behind her. Throwing him, for one precious moment, off guard.

The last thing she saw, the last thing Isabelle believed she'd ever see, was Gamache lunging forward, toward the other gunmen.

She hoped he'd survived. Hoped Jean-Guy had. And the others.

Because she knew, as she felt the explosion, that she had not.

And then she described things she didn't know, but had herself been told. How Ruth had, in the midst of the bedlam, crawled across the floor of the bistro, to hold her hand. So that she would not die alone.

How her husband, her colleagues, her friends, had taken turns at the hospital, holding her hand and reading to her.

Haniya listened, and wondered if someone, anyone, would hold her hand when her time came.

"Things are strongest where they're broken," she said, and wondered where that had come from.

"Yes."

Neither woman had described their long, long journey back. But both recognized it had led them there. To that moment. In this quiet place, in this peaceful village.

Shhhhh.

The Hero of the Sudan looked around the bistro, at the villagers. At the friends and families. There were small cracks between them. She knew that because she could see the light.

Armand met Reine-Marie, Myrna, and Jean-Guy outside the bistro.

"How did it go?" he asked.

But he could tell by their expressions that it hadn't gone well. Or, perhaps, "well" was not the word.

"Let's go inside and talk," he said. Putting his hand on Reine-Marie's arm, he searched her eyes. "You okay?"

She nodded, but without conviction. "Actually, I'd like to go home. I want to go through that last box. With the kids on the sleigh ride it'll be quiet."

The truth was, she was a coward. Vincent Gilbert might be in the bistro, and she was terrified of what she might say, what she might do, if she met him. Home was the only safe place.

"Do you want company?" Armand asked.

"*Non, merci, mon coeur.* You need to hear what they have to say."

He looked at Jean-Guy and Myrna, grim-faced. He probably did need to hear it, though he doubted he wanted to hear it.

While she went home, the rest headed into the bistro. Isabelle was sitting by the fire with Haniya, Ruth, and Clara. They got to their feet when the others arrived. Except Ruth, who took the opportunity to switch her empty scotch glass for Clara's almost full one.

"Looks like you have things to talk about," said Clara. It didn't take a portrait painter to understand their expressions. "Why don't we go back to my place?"

"What? We have the best seats in the house, right in front of the fireplace," said Ruth. "Why would I leave to walk through a blizzard to your shack?"

Rosa, in her arms, nodded agreement and gave Clara the stink eye.

Clara glanced outside at the softly falling flurries. Hardly a maelstrom. "Well, I have a bottle of single malt."

"So does Olivier."

"I have chocolate cake."

Ruth used Rosa to gesture toward the cake stand on the long bar.

"I'll let you critique my latest work," said Clara.

Ruth became more interested. Finding fault was just about her favorite thing to do.

As they left, Ruth paused in front of Armand. "Did you speak with her?"

"All sorted. Professor Robinson will stop using the quote and donate whatever they've raised to LaPorte."

"Thank you, Armand," she whispered.

At the door, Clara and Ruth looked back. Haniya was standing in the middle of the room, between the groups.

"Well?" demanded Ruth. "Do you need the king of Sweden to invite you? Dumb shit."

Haniya paused, then walked across the bistro to join them. She was not totally sure, but she suspected being called "dumb shit" by Ruth Zardo was almost as good as winning the Nobel Peace Prize. Though it was possible the old poet was calling the king of Sweden a dumb shit.

As they trudged through the snow toward Clara's pretty little cottage, Ruth lost her footing. Haniya grabbed her before she fell. She held Ruth's hand for the rest of the way, and wondered if maybe the key was not in being held, but in holding.

Gabri put down a pot of tea. "It's already steeped, just as you like it." Then he threw a birch log onto the fire, and stirred it, before leaving them.

The white bark caught and curled as embers popped and chased each other up the chimney.

Armand poured the tea while Isabelle talked.

Within minutes, Jean-Guy, Myrna, Isabelle, and Armand had left the cheery bistro and were in the Sudan. Looking down, helpless, at the women, girls, staked to the dirt.

Armand clamped his jaw so tight he thought his molars might shatter. But if he didn't, he was sure he'd vomit.

And still, Isabelle talked.

Jean-Guy saw his sisters, his mother. Annie. Staked there. And thought he might pass out.

And still, Isabelle talked.

Myrna felt the rawhide straps cutting into her wrists and ankles, the flesh now growing around the bindings. She saw the men approaching. Drunk. Angry. She saw them draw their machetes. And she looked up at Armand. At Jean-Guy. At Isabelle. Watching. And she pleaded with them. Begged them for help.

The world had been watching. And had done nothing.

And when Isabelle got to the part where Haniya escaped and killed her attacker, Armand unclenched his jaw.

When Isabelle got to the part where Haniya freed the other women and girls, Jean-Guy wanted to leap up and cheer.

When Isabelle got to the part where they approached the barbed-wire fence, to freedom, Myrna wanted to sob with relief.

When Isabelle got to the part where Haniya confronted the child soldier, she stopped.

"What is it?" Armand asked. "What happened?"

"Brown brown," said Isabelle.

And she told them what happened, when Haniya had a choice to make. And made it.

There was a long silence as their breathing mingled with the smoke and crackling fire and the images that had invaded the peaceful bistro.

Haniya was right, of course, thought Isabelle. No place was safe.

"Isabelle?" Armand finally said.

She looked at him. Not even the amber glow from the fire could disguise his pallor.

She knew what he was asking.

"Yes. I have no doubt she would kill again, if it meant saving lives. I'm not sure if it's heroic or psychotic, but Haniya Daoud seems to see every innocent man, woman, and infant in the world as her children. She's driven to save them. Obsessed even."

A few years ago, Jean-Guy might not have understood that. Now he could. Every parent, he was sure, became slightly insane the moment their children were born.

Armand nodded. He too understood.

He'd assumed Haniya Daoud had survived, where so many had given up and died, out of hatred. An all-consuming need for revenge. But something even stronger had kept her going.

Love. The love of her children. The need to save, not the need to destroy, had kept her going. And still fueled every step Haniya Daoud took.

But to have to kill one child to save others? What did that do to a person? What had that done to Haniya? And did it make every other killing so much easier?

Would Haniya Daoud murder Abigail Robinson to save men, women, and children?

In a heartbeat.

Reine-Marie poured herself a red wine, dragged the box from the small study into the living room, lit the fire in the hearth, and turned on the Christmas tree lights.

Stephen and Gracie, who she now thought might be a guinea pig, were having a nap in his bedroom. Daniel and Roslyn were at the sales in Sherbrooke, and Annie had taken Idola to visit friends in the next village over.

Henri and Fred were curled at her feet.

She had the place to herself.

Before dipping into the last box, she sat back on the sofa, put her feet up, and quietly sipped her drink, staring into the fireplace, the lit tree in the background.

They'd take it down, along with the other decorations, on January 5th. The eve of the Twelfth Night.

Neither she nor Armand were particularly religious, though both had a steadfast and private belief in God. But they loved tradition, and taking down the Christmas tree every year on that day was one they'd both grown up with.

Besides being the night before Epiphany, when the Three Wise Men recognized the Christ Child, it also saved their Hoover from needing to pick up too many dried pine needles. And burning out. Again.

In the meantime, Reine-Marie relished the tree, the decorations, the quiet.

She closed her eyes, feeling the warmth of the fire on her face. But her peace was invaded by Ewen Cameron. His kindly face looked down at her, assuring her all would be well, *ça va bien aller*, even as he tied her wrists to the posts.

Her eyes flew open, and she sat up so quickly wine slopped from her glass onto Henri, asleep by the fire. He didn't stir. With Ruth such a constant visitor, he was used to it.

Reine-Marie put down her glass and got to work, while over in the bistro Jean-Guy sat in front of the fire and told his horror story.

"Ewen Cameron?" Armand's eyes moved from Jean-Guy to Myrna, then back again. "Vincent worked with Cameron?"

"Who?" asked Isabelle. Like Jean-Guy, she was too young to know the name. But it was about to become one she would never forget.

They told her, while Armand sat back, his hand to his face, listening, thinking.

When they'd finished, Isabelle had quizzed Jean-Guy and Myrna, unwilling to accept that this had actually happened. In Québec. In Montréal. At McGill. Within living memory. And no one had stopped it. Stopped him.

"And Vincent Gilbert was part of it?" she asked.

"There's no actual proof of that," said Jean-Guy. "We know he looked after the lab animals. If he'd been part of the experiments, wouldn't there be papers in his file?"

"Evaluations of Gilbert by Cameron or others," said Myrna. "You'd think."

"Still," said Armand, sitting forward. "It's hard to believe Dr. Gilbert wouldn't have at least known what was going on. By then Cameron had been at it for almost a decade."

The Asshole Saint had gone, they noticed, from "Vincent" to "Dr. Gilbert," as Gamache put distance between them.

He turned to Myrna, but before he could ask her to leave, she got up. "I'm off. Work to do in the store."

When she'd gone, Jean-Guy said, "Didn't Cameron's name come up last night? You mentioned it to Gilbert when we interviewed him."

"Yes," said Gamache. "I've been trying to remember the exact words Robinson used. She didn't make a direct accusation. It was more subtle than that. She'd been talking about monsters and mentioned Cameron. And then she'd intimated that Gilbert was no better than him. That's why I wanted to know what was in Dr. Gilbert's files at McGill. But I never thought . . ."

Who would?

"But if she knew something definite," said Beauvoir, "wouldn't she come right out and say it? Why just hint?"

"She could've been toying with him," said Isabelle. "Like a cat with a wounded bird."

Armand could not see the Asshole Saint as a wounded bird. He was more likely the cat. Still, it was a good point. And a possible motive.

"You found nothing definite?"

"No, nothing," said Beauvoir.

"They'd still be alive," said Isabelle.

"Who?" asked Beauvoir.

"Cameron's victims. Gilbert's victims. Most must've been from Québec. Maybe even from around here."

"They'd be quite old by now," said Beauvoir. "This was years ago."

Armand looked toward Clara's home. Where Ruth had gone. Ruth?

> Who hurt you once so far beyond repair
> That you would greet each overture with curling lip?

Did they have their answer?

"When I had lunch with Dr. Gilbert," said Gamache, "he admitted he'd been at Abigail Robinson's talk in the gym."

"Could hardly deny it," said Beauvoir.

"True. He also admitted that he saw the gun in Tardif's hand. He says he froze."

"But?" said Isabelle.

"When pressed, he all but admitted he wanted it to happen, wanted her to be killed," said Gamache. "It was a split-second choice. He hadn't done anything to protect people in the pandemic. He saw his chance to make up for it."

"Not just in the pandemic," said Isabelle. "He didn't do anything to protect people from Cameron. Seems like a pattern in his life."

Gamache was nodding. Had Gilbert finally decided to act?

Like a battlefield surgeon, had he, last night, decided to amputate the leg in order to save the body? Kill Abigail Robinson in order to save thousands?

Or was the motive, as it often was with Gilbert, far more complex, more selfish? Was it to protect himself? To stop Abigail Robinson from revealing his one great secret. His great shame.

"Of course," said Beauvoir, "it's possible he didn't stop Tardif from shooting because they were working together."

"I have news on that," Isabelle said to Jean-Guy. "While you were in Montréal, we found the accomplice. Not Gilbert, not the brother. The son."

She brought Jean-Guy quickly up to speed about Simon Tardif.

Beauvoir immediately understood the important detail. "He also worked the party. Kids were going in and out of those woods all night long. One more wouldn't be noticed. Simon Tardif could've tried to finish the job his father started."

"The thing is, I'm not convinced," said Lacoste. "I don't think he'd have the nerve."

"Neither do I," said Gamache. "But I've been surprised before."

CHAPTER 33

—

Within moments of taking the lid off the final box, Reine-Marie knew that this contained the motherlode. The earliest items from Enid Horton's life.

No more report cards, Mother's Day cards, Christmas cards from her children.

These cards were from, and about, Enid herself.

The world receded around Reine-Marie as the librarian and archivist stepped from her life into Enid's.

There were cracked and faded photos of her as a child, running in an immense snowsuit and dragging a long, frozen wool scarf behind her, outside an old Québécois chalet in the Laurentian Mountains.

Photos of her sitting between two siblings. An older sister and younger brother.

A little white Bible was dedicated to Enid Blythe, on the day of her christening. Given to her by a godmother.

And there were letters. Lots of them.

Taking out a pile and smoothing them on her lap, Reine-Marie picked up the top one and wondered, not for the first time, what the next generation of archivists and biographers would do. No one wrote letters anymore. No one had printed photographs and albums for historians, or even family members, to pore over. Everything was in a cloud and needed a password.

But that wasn't her concern, not today at least.

At first Reine-Marie read every word of the letters, but then she started to skim.

Here was Enid, growing up with all the natural questions and insecurities of a girl. Of a young woman. Of a young bride. Of a young mother. But . . . then . . .

Reine-Marie turned the page and looked at the next letter.

Her eyes first went to where it was from. Then who it was from.

And then they stopped. At the doodle in the margin.

She almost shoved the paper off her lap, as though some snake had landed there.

But it wasn't a snake. It was a monkey.

Ruth stood in the middle of the studio staring at the canvas on the easel.

Without turning around she said, "What is it? Oh, wait, don't tell me. Is it a bunny?" Before Clara could answer, Ruth had cocked her head and raised her hand for silence. "No, I've got it. It's a car. It's a bunny in a car."

She turned astonished eyes on Clara, who was standing, arms crossed, at the door to her studio.

"You're exhibiting signs of creativity," said Ruth. "It's still shit, of course, but at least it's unexpected *merde*."

"If I paid you to kill her," Clara said to Haniya, "would that cost you the Peace Prize?"

"I doubt it. I'm up against a brutal dictator and a man who ordered that refugees be separated from their children and put into cages."

"You're kidding," said Clara. "For the Nobel Peace Prize?"

"I think it's not about how much good a person's done, but how much worse they could have been."

Clara, who knew who Haniya was talking about, muttered, "Not much worse."

"No, wait," said Ruth. "Rosa thinks it's a Bundt cake. Are we getting close?"

"I think," said Haniya, "it might even work in my favor."

Clara smiled and turned away. "Tea?"

They walked back into the large country kitchen. "Why do you put up with her?"

"Ruth?" said Clara, putting on the kettle and opening a tin with butter tarts. "Maybe she's my peace prize. It's not about how good she is, but how much worse she could be."

The truth was, Clara had put that especially horrible canvas up just for Ruth. It was a running joke between them. Each morning Clara would work on her actual painting. Then, just before stopping for the day, she'd put the other canvas up and slop paint on it, choosing colors and brushstrokes at random.

The real painting would be carefully placed against the wall of the studio, hidden under a sheet. Clara was very protective of her works, and even more so since those scathing reviews of her last exhibition had all but destroyed her career.

She heard the front door open and still, to this day, half expected it to be her husband, Peter. Instead a familiar voice called out, "*Bonjour? Clara?*"

"In the kitchen, Armand."

He greeted the two of them, then looked around. "Where's Ruth?"

"In my studio."

"Do you mind?" he asked, cocking his head toward it.

"Not at all."

He found Ruth staring at a canvas propped against the wall. She turned quickly, dropping the sheet so that it fell back over the painting.

"What do you want?"

"I'd like to talk."

"About?"

"About Ewen Cameron."

There was a pause, then Ruth said, "*I smell blood and an era of prominent madmen.*"

"So do I," said Armand.

Jean-Guy Beauvoir hung up from the first call, made notes, then placed the second.

After a few questions, he thanked the head of the mathematics department and hit end call.

Sitting back in his chair in the basement Incident Room, he thought for a moment. Then, after placing a third call to British Columbia, he finished his notes and went upstairs to wait for the Chief Inspector.

He saw Vincent Gilbert sitting by the fire in the living room. Relaxed, cross-legged, reading a book. He wore gray flannels, a cashmere sweater with a crisp white shirt and tie. His white hair was trimmed and his glasses were round tortoiseshell.

A professor.

A doctor. Right out of central casting.

Jean-Guy Beauvoir returned to the basement.

Reine-Marie Gamache stared into the flames, then looked down at her fist.

She was clutching the paper, the letter. Crushing it in her hand. Opening it, she smoothed the paper out, read it again, then got up.

She had to find Armand. Had to show him this.

He was, she knew, at the bistro.

Putting on her coat and boots, she tried to explain to Henri and Fred that she'd take them out soon, but not now.

They didn't understand.

"Join the club," she muttered, as she shoved her hat down over her ears and went out into the snowy evening.

She got partway to the bistro when she heard her name through the flurries. "Reine-Marie!"

She saw Armand jogging across the road from Clara's home. They met in front of the pines, their faces lit by the Christmas bulbs.

"I have to tell you . . . ," they both began.

"You first," he said.

"No, you."

"I was just talking to Ruth. It took a while, she didn't want to tell me, but finally she did. That woman whose documents you've been going through, Enid Horton—"

"She was a patient, a victim of Ewen Cameron," said Reine-Marie. "I just realized that myself. I have to show you something."

Armand and Reine-Marie sat in the small study off their living room.

Beyond the closed door they could hear Stephen greeting Daniel and Roslyn. They could hear Annie return home with Idola.

The comforting sounds of normality. Of a family doing what families did. Just outside the door.

While inside, Armand and Reine-Marie looked at the paper Enid Horton had kept and Reine-Marie had found.

It was on Allan Memorial letterhead. A fairly polite but firm request that an earlier bill be paid. It was for the services of Dr. Ewen Cameron. For twenty-three days of inpatient treatment of postpartum depression for Enid Horton.

In the margin was a doodle. A monkey. As yet barely formed. Just taking shape. The first crude attempt. The head, ears, curling tail. And the wide, terrified eyes.

The letter was signed by Dr. Vincent Gilbert.

"Monsieur Tardif," said Isabelle Lacoste, as the prisoner was led into the interview room.

His *avocat* had been summoned and had had a brief word with the Sûreté Inspector before they joined Édouard Tardif.

"We've arrested your son," said Lacoste.

There was a long silence as Édouard Tardif opened his mouth, not to speak, but to catch his breath.

"It's not his fault," he said, softly. "He didn't know. He thought . . . I told him . . . He believed the gun had blanks. I told him I just wanted to interrupt her talk. He didn't know."

"And your brother?"

"He had nothing to do with it."

"Then why did he confess?"

"He must've guessed that Simon had helped me, and he wanted to protect him."

Isabelle nodded. This was a close family. A loving family. That had, inadvertently or not, colluded in attempted murder.

"Don't say anything," said Maître Lacombe. She turned to Lacoste. "Monsieur Tardif was in extreme distress. His mother was in a home where more than twenty elderly residents had died of Covid. She'd survived. But he was afraid she wouldn't survive Professor Robinson. He was protecting his family. Or thought he was. Surely you can see that."

"I have sympathy, but the fact remains, your client shot a gun in a crowded auditorium. Barely missing the professor and a Chief Inspector of the Sûreté."

"Yes, he has to face the consequences," agreed the *avocat*, while Tardif looked on. "But he wasn't of sound mind."

"Simon didn't know," Tardif repeated.

"He was at the Inn last night. He was working the party when Professor Robinson's assistant was murdered."

"He was?" Then his eyes widened. "You can't believe Simon did that."

"Given he was your accomplice in the attempted murder of Professor Robinson, it's hard to believe he didn't."

"But he never . . . he couldn't. He doesn't have it in him. He was just doing what I asked. He has his whole life ahead of him. Please, for God's sake, believe me. Let him go. Charge me with anything you want, but let him go. Don't ruin his life."

"I'm afraid I'm not the one who's ruined his life."

"So," said Beauvoir, looking up from the letter, "this proves it. Vincent Gilbert did know what Cameron was doing. And was part of it."

"Yes," said Gamache.

He'd walked up to the Auberge and gone in the back way to avoid running into Gilbert.

With each mention of Ewen Cameron, the faces in the basement wall seemed to grow more prominent. Pushing forward.

Was Cameron himself in there? Had he been summoned from Hell? Gamache knew this was fantasy. And yet . . .

"We need to have another word with Dr. Gilbert," he said.

Beauvoir got up. It had been a while since he'd so looked forward to an interrogation.

"But first," said Armand, motioning him to sit back down, "I want to hear what you found out from your calls out west."

"Oh, right. Seems they all knew about the second daughter, Maria," said Jean-Guy. "She was no secret. Her death had been especially hard on her father. He blamed himself."

"Why?"

"The little girl choked on a peanut butter sandwich. One he gave her for lunch."

Armand took a long, deep breath. Imagining, and trying not to imagine, what that would be like. The minutes when it happened, and the years that followed.

"I also called the coroner's office in Nanaimo," said Beauvoir.

"Why?"

"Well, it just seemed to me there were quite a few deaths in that family. First Abigail's mother, then her sister, and finally her father."

Gamache frowned, then slowly nodded. "Good idea. Anything?"

"Not yet. I asked for the death certificates and any autopsy reports."

Armand pushed himself out of the chair. It was time.

CHAPTER 34

Vincent Gilbert watched as Chief Inspector Gamache closed the door to the library. That was expected, in a private conversation. What happened next was not.

Gamache turned the key in the lock. And pocketed it.

Jean-Guy Beauvoir sat in one of the leather chairs across from Gilbert, while Gamache took the other.

A chill crept over the doctor and he looked at the hearth. There was no fire. Not even one laid and ready to be lit. Instead it was just a dark hole, with ash in the grate and a slight smell of burning.

Gamache brought a piece of paper from his jacket pocket and handed it to him.

Gilbert unfolded it, saw the letterhead, and let it go. It fell to the coffee table, unread. Had there been a fire in the grate, he might have tried to throw the letter in. Consign it to where it belonged. Though he wasn't sure it would burn.

But there was no fire. There was no escape. Not into an illustrious career. Not onto boards of charities. Not deep into the woods.

Vincent Gilbert had known for years, decades, that this day would come. That one day he'd be found.

He'd been through the files in the Osler and quietly, over the years, removed all reference to his time with Ewen Cameron. But he couldn't retrieve the letters sent to the patients. He just had to hope they'd destroyed them. After all, who would keep something that grotesque?

But at least one person had. He glanced down at the name. Enid Horton.

It meant nothing to him.

But this Enid Horton had found him. And brought the head of homicide with her.

"You knew" was all Gamache said.

Gilbert nodded. "Yes. I knew what Ewen Cameron was doing."

He could have left it at "yes." But he had to say the words. To say out loud what he had never even admitted to himself.

I knew what Ewen Cameron was doing.

"Tell us," said Gamache.

Jean-Guy Beauvoir shot a glance at the Chief Inspector. Surely, he thought, there were specific questions to be asked. Ones that would nail Gilbert. Trap him and lead to his arrest. Because that was where this was heading.

Vincent Gilbert killed, or tried to kill, Abigail Robinson not to save others, but to save himself. To stop her from revealing the one thing he'd spent his life hiding from. His complicity in the torture of hundreds of men and women. Then sending them home crippled, shattered. With a bill for their services.

The Asshole Saint. What, Beauvoir wondered, were saints called in Hell?

He remembered now, from his brief time in Sunday school before the nuns expelled him, that there was a concept of the "wicked angel." The idea had stuck with little Jean-Guy. Somehow, for a binary-minded boy who thought in black and white, the idea that an angel could be wicked was terrifying. Because it suggested chaos.

Were they locked in with, trapped with, not an Asshole Saint but a Wicked Angel?

And Jean-Guy understood, in a moment of complete clarity, why Armand Gamache had not asked a question, but had simply invited Dr. Vincent Gilbert to explain.

It was perhaps to trap the Wicked Angel.

But more likely to free him. To give him an opening, one last shot at redemption.

"Like so much else," Gilbert began, "it started innocently. I needed a part-time job, and all the good ones were taken. No one wanted to work in that place, and no one wanted that job. Looking after lab animals at the Allan." He stopped and looked directly at Gamache. "Have you ever been there? To the Allan Memorial?"

When Gamache shook his head, Gilbert looked at Beauvoir, who also indicated he hadn't.

"It's in what used to be called Ravenscrag, this old stone mansion on the top of Mont Royal, built by one of the robber barons. They say it's haunted and I can believe it. If it wasn't before Cameron, it was after. Terrible place. Probably still is. Terrifying. Caretakers were afraid to go into the basement. I wouldn't stay there at night."

He lowered his head as the shrieks of the animals mixed with the screams of the people, until they were indistinguishable. They'd chased him down the hallways and out the door. They'd chased him into the gathering darkness. They'd chased him all over the world. And finally, they'd chased him deep into the woods.

Beauvoir could feel the hairs on his forearms rising and glanced at Gamache, who looked perfectly calm. As though suspects told them ghost stories every day.

"But I kept the job, because it paid well and I was learning a lot. I was a resident and Dr. Cameron was a god. The God. The eminent head of psychiatry. Doing important work, vital work. They were beginning to understand how the mind worked. Not the brain, but the mind. It was exciting."

Jean-Guy's lips pressed together in an effort not to say something, and he noticed that, beside him, Armand's hand was moving, very slightly. His fingers were caressing the leather chair. And then Gamache slowly closed his right hand into a fist.

And Jean-Guy knew why. It was to stop the trembling that had plagued Gamache from that moment in the factory. From the moment his whole body had been lifted off the ground, as though levitating, propelled by the bullets.

And then slammed back down.

Gamache had had the scar at his temple from that day forward. And a slight limp and a tremble in his right hand, whenever he was stressed or fatigued. Far from being a mark of weakness, Jean-Guy Beauvoir understood it was, in fact, a sign of strength.

"It was a terrible job," Vincent Gilbert was saying. "But it didn't take long before I discovered something far worse. What was happening on the other side of the wall. In the next room, and the room beside that. And so on and so on."

"Ad nauseum," said Gamache.

Gilbert gave a curt nod. "We'd heard rumors, of course, of the CIA involvement. But we'd thought that was a myth. And if we believed it, it just added to Cameron's luster. It seemed romantic. That he was helping the Free World in its fight against Communism. Against the Red Tide. It seems laughable now, but it was real back then. You have to remember, this was right around the Cuban missile crisis. The world was on the brink of nuclear war. Anything that could be done to prevent that was considered fair."

He looked from one to the other of them, to judge their reactions. But all he got were stares.

Gilbert took a deep breath. "That's what I told myself, anyway, when I realized what Cameron and the others were doing to those men and women."

He sat back and folded his hands together on his lap, interlocking the fingers. Then he brought them to his face so that his chin rested on the top of his clasped hands. Like a child at prayer.

Now I lay me down to sleep, I pray the Lord my soul to keep.

"Most of Cameron's experiments had to do with brainwashing and sleep deprivation," said Gilbert. "He'd keep them awake for days at a time. Part of my job was making sure they got food and water."

"Them? They?" asked Gamache, his voice terrifying in its calm. "The animals or the people?"

"Both," Gilbert said, quietly. "The people begged me to let them sleep. To untie them. To let them go home. But I didn't."

If I should die before I wake, I pray the Lord my soul to take.

"Not because I thought what Cameron was doing was right. I knew it wasn't. But because I was afraid if I said or did anything I'd be kicked out of medical school. He was that powerful." He stared at Gamache for a moment before saying, "And I was that weak."

Vincent Gilbert screwed his eyes so tightly shut they all but disappeared into his face.

"I spent the rest of my life trying to make amends," he said, his eyes still shut. "I was still an asshole." He opened his eyes and smiled. "That, I'm afraid, is hardwired. But I'm hoping I'm also . . ."

Gamache now let his feelings, his thoughts, be known. In the sickened expression on his face as he greeted this sally by Vincent Gilbert. Who seemed to be inviting them, him, to agree that besides being an ass he'd also, magically, become saintly. His soul cleansed of an early misdemeanor.

Armand Gamache was having none of that. Though he remained mute.

And now Jean-Guy Beauvoir saw what he was doing. He was giving Vincent Gilbert rope. To either escape his prison or hang himself.

Gilbert, by his last statement, appeared to be fashioning a noose.

"I did try, Armand," said Gilbert, softly. Pleading for forgiveness that was not Armand's to give.

"Did you know Mrs. Horton?" Gamache asked, his eyes not wavering from Gilbert's face.

There was a pause. Then Gilbert shook his head. "I can't remember. Maybe if I saw a photograph . . ."

"Why the monkey?"

"Pardon?"

"The drawing on the letter," said Beauvoir. "What does it mean?"

"How should I know?"

"I think, Dr. Gilbert," said Gamache, "you've proven there's a great deal you do know that you're not admitting. Madame Horton died recently. In the attic the family found boxes filled with, among other things, monkeys. Dolls. Books. Drawings. Why this fixation on monkeys?"

Gilbert was silent for a moment. Sullen. But as the silence went on, his expression changed. His face opened, in realization.

"There was a woman in the room next to where the animals were kept. She was part of the sleep-deprivation trials. She must have heard . . ."

They looked down at the drawing, the first one. Of the terrified animal with the human eyes.

The monkeys, their screaming, must have, in her muddled near-demented state, become part of her nightmares. Become part of her. The lab monkeys had fused to her shattered mind and stayed there.

In drawing them, she freed them. An act of compassion that the great Dr. Gilbert could never achieve.

"Do you also hear them?" Armand asked.

Had Gilbert also conflated the animals and the people? And convinced himself it wasn't people he'd heard screaming? Begging for help. Searching, with wild eyes, for one decent person to free them.

"Not monkeys, no." Gilbert paused before going on. "Have you ever heard a blue jay shriek?"

And they had their answer. Vincent Gilbert thought he'd find refuge, peace, deep in the forest. But all he'd done was go deeper into the nightmare. Where all the wild creatures, the forest itself, screamed at him. Every day and all night long.

But if he could just do one magnificent thing, maybe he and they would be free.

Maybe, thought Beauvoir, *the Wicked Angel would be redeemed.*

Maybe, thought Gamache, *the era of prominent madmen would end.*

"When Abigail Robinson threw Ewen Cameron in your face last night," he said, "what did you think?"

"I thought she knew."

"And?"

"And I was afraid."

"And?"

Gilbert shifted in his seat. "And you want me to say I tried to kill her? To keep her quiet? But that I killed her friend by mistake?"

"Tell us, Vincent," said Gamache, leaning forward.

"The truth? Yes, I saw a chance to redeem myself. Not because she knew about my work with Cameron, but because what she's proposing is wrong, on every level. It was too late to stop her with intellectual arguments. I'd missed my chance. I should have done something when Colette sent me the paper. But now I could make it right. I'd failed to save those men and women years ago, I'd failed to help in the pandemic. I'd failed to condemn her work when I first read it, but now, maybe I could make up for it. Abigail Robinson has to be stopped. I knew that. You know that." He stared at Gamache.

Beauvoir looked over at Gamache. They had him. It was over.

"And?" said Gamache. They needed to hear him say it.

"And nothing. Someone got there first. Except they messed it up. Killed the wrong person." He held Gamache's eyes. "I wouldn't have made that mistake. I'm not the one you're looking for, Armand."

"Were you and Colette Roberge in this together?" Gamache asked. "Did she know what you had planned?"

"All she knew is that I was determined to stop Professor Robinson."

"She brought Professor Robinson to the party so you could kill her," said Beauvoir.

"No, no. It was Abigail Robinson's idea to go to the party, not Colette's. But we decided it was a good idea. It would give me a chance to try to reason with Abigail. Get her to stop this madness. Colette thought, I thought, that the reason she wanted to meet me was because she respected me. Not . . ."

"So Colette Roberge also wanted Abigail Robinson stopped? And she's alone with Professor Robinson?" said Gamache.

"No. Well, yes, but she didn't know how far I was willing to take it."

"And maybe you don't know how far she's willing to take it," said Gamache.

He turned to Beauvoir, who grasped the situation immediately. Getting up, he took a few steps away and placed a call.

"You're coming with us," Gamache said to Gilbert.

Gamache grabbed the letter off the coffee table and put it back in his pocket before taking Gilbert's arm and maneuvering him to the door.

Jean-Guy had reached the agents guarding the Chancellor's home and told them to go inside and find Professor Robinson.

"And stay with her. We're on our way."

The flurries had stopped, and the stars were just coming out while around them the creatures in the dark forest watched.

CHAPTER 35

⁓

Chancellor Roberge's eyes widened, slightly, when she saw Vincent Gilbert at her front door.

She was expecting the Sûreté investigators, but not him. And not him with them. Though she quickly recovered herself.

"Welcome," she said. This time Colette did not lean forward to kiss Armand. The lines, and boundaries, were now clear. "Your people are here, Chief Inspector. They're in the kitchen with Abigail."

"*Merci.*"

They followed her into the house. The Chancellor paused at the door to the now familiar kitchen. Armand could feel warmth radiating off the woodstove.

The agents behind Abigail Robinson stood a little taller when they saw the senior officers.

"*Patron,*" they said.

Beauvoir went to step into the kitchen, but Chancellor Roberge stopped him.

"I thought since there are so many of us, we should sit somewhere else."

After passing through the gracious living room, Colette Roberge stopped at the room that was as far from the kitchen as possible.

Gamache quickly took in his surroundings, instinctively checking for any escape route.

The Chancellor had taken them to the solarium. The sofa and armchairs were covered in fresh botanical prints. Gamache could see that the room, with its three walls of windows, would be magnificent in the daylight.

But now, lacking both light and warmth, it felt as though the dark panes of the windows were made of ice.

Dr. Gilbert had taken the seat next to Chancellor Roberge on the sofa, while Abigail Robinson took one of the armchairs.

Beauvoir indicated to the agents that they should stand just outside the door, in the living room. Out of sight, but ready should anything happen. Then he and Gamache brought over two incidental chairs and sat.

Armand contemplated the Chancellor. A woman he admired, respected. Liked. And now distrusted.

She held his thoughtful gaze.

"What's your role in this?" he asked, going straight to the point.

"This?" Her voice was almost amused. "What 'this,' Armand?"

But even as she said it, she recognized her mistake. It was childish. Worse, she'd placed the power back in Gamache's hands after he'd offered her a chance to frame the events herself.

"The conspiracy, Madame Chancellor, to stop Professor Robinson, by killing her if necessary."

"That's not true," protested Colette Roberge, outraged.

"What?" said Abigail, almost laughing. Then, seeing Gamache's serious expression, she turned to Colette. "What's he saying?"

"Nothing. He's taking leaps of logic. Making spurious correlations."

"He's saying," said Beauvoir, "that your former mentor, your friend, has been involved in a plot to murder you."

"That's not possible," said Abigail, though they could see her hesitation now. "Is it?"

Vincent Gilbert put his hand over Colette's. To stop her from saying anything more? But Gamache didn't think so. It was an intimate gesture. Meant to support and comfort.

Colette was shaking her head. "All I wanted to do was change your mind about your campaign. I tried to talk you out of it."

"You never did," said Abigail. "I sent you my preliminary research and you thanked me. You never said you disagreed. You invited me here. You set up that talk. You told me I could meet with Dr. Gilbert."

"Is that why you came to Québec?" Gamache asked. "Not to see Ruth Zardo, not even to see Chancellor Roberge, but to meet Vincent Gilbert?"

Abigail Robinson hesitated, then nodded. "To get him to publicly endorse my work. The Royal Commission would listen to him."

"What made you think he'd do that?" Gamache asked.

"Because when Colette showed him my report, he didn't disagree with it. He has a reputation for brutal honesty, so I assumed that meant he, you, agreed." Gilbert dropped his eyes. "So I came here to see you. To ask for your help." She turned to her former mentor. "But you actually planned to kill me? Colette?"

"No. We planned to talk you out of it. When you called and said you wanted to visit, we saw our chance. I offered you the event to make sure you'd come. I had no idea so many would show up. That only strengthened our resolve."

"To kill me?"

"To stop you," said Gilbert. "The Royal Commission was right not to hear your submission. Even if your findings are correct, they aren't right. There're human factors."

"You'd say that? To me?" demanded Abigail, rounding on him. Sneering at him. "You'd lecture me on what's right? On human factors?"

Gamache watched this with intense interest and was tempted to interrupt. To ask his question. But once again he remained quiet, to see where this would go.

"Damn right I will," said Gilbert, leaning toward her. "I was there, at your rally. You whipped them into a frenzy with your patented mix of facts and fear. Like some snake oil salesman at a fairground, trying to get gullible people to buy your poison. First you scare them, then you offer them your false hope. It's disgusting. But it works. And now the politicians, familiar with the power of fear, have bought your potion wholesale."

"You'd give me a sermon on morals, then murder me?"

Abigail looked from Gilbert to Colette.

"No," said Gilbert. "She had no idea what I had in mind. I didn't even know, not until I saw your rally at the University. Colette wasn't there. Clips on television or social media couldn't fully capture the atmosphere. I saw what you did. I saw your face as your supporters chanted. You weren't triumphant, you were smug. You knew exactly what you were doing. And I knew there was no stopping you."

Gilbert failed to mention that he'd also seen Édouard Tardif raise the gun to shoot Abigail Robinson. And had done nothing.

It was Vincent Gilbert's first attempt at the murder of Abigail Robinson. Perhaps not in the eyes of the law, but in a higher court, almost certainly.

Professor Robinson's eyes widened as she followed the logic, the steps, the evidence, until she reached the only possible conclusion.

"You killed Debbie."

"No."

"Yes, you killed her thinking it was me."

"No, no, I didn't. I'm not that stupid."

It was not, they could all see, much of a defense.

Gamache shifted slightly and all eyes went to him.

It was time to ask his question.

After her interview with Édouard Tardif, Isabelle returned to the basement Incident Room.

It was dinnertime and she was hungry, especially walking by the dining room of the Inn and smelling the rich, earthy scent of Québécoise winter cuisine. The soups and sauces, the stews and pies, both savory and sweet.

But she forced herself onward. Downward.

Once at her desk, she checked messages. She'd been copied on Beauvoir's request to the coroner in Nanaimo, and now she opened it.

No autopsy had been done on Abigail's mother or father. The attending physician had put down heart failure. Abigail's sister, Maria, had choked to death on a piece of peanut butter sandwich, lodged deep in her throat.

It was tragic, but straightforward enough. Still . . . Lacoste called Nanaimo.

"Heart failure" was what doctors put on reports when they either didn't know what someone died of, or knew and wanted to protect the feelings of the family.

"How did you know that Dr. Gilbert once worked with Ewen Cameron?" asked Gamache.

"He did?" Abigail Robinson asked, eyes wide.

Gamache smiled pleasantly. "Come now, Professor. You all but accused him of it last night at the party, and again today." He paused before dropping his voice deeper into the inky void. "We know."

He didn't say what they knew. The truth was, they knew almost nothing.

He could see her quickly examining the various options. Struggling to find a way out that did not involve the truth.

"I'd hoped to torment you a little longer," she said, giving up and turning to Gilbert. "But I see the time has come for the truth. A fact, if you prefer. I'd asked Debbie to research you so I'd be prepared for our meeting. She came across some documents suggesting that you worked with Ewen Cameron."

Gamache kept his focus on Professor Robinson, but he also, in his peripheral vision, watched Chancellor Roberge's reaction.

There was none.

She knew, he thought. She knew he worked with Cameron.

"What were the documents Madame Schneider found?" Beauvoir asked.

"Just vague references."

"Like the ones you're making now?" he said. "We went through your files. We also searched what Debbie Schneider brought with her. There were all sorts of papers, but nothing about Dr. Gilbert."

"Really? That's surprising. Something must have happened to them."

"How were you planning to use those documents?" asked Beauvoir.

"Well, once I got over the shock that he was involved in something so hideous, I thought they might help convince him to support my work, if he was reluctant. He's still a nationally recognized scientist."

"Internationally," said Gilbert, instinctively.

"Blackmail?" said Beauvoir, but Abigail ignored that.

Her brows had drawn together in thought. "I wonder if Debbie showed you what we'd found. Is that what happened? Did she meet you outside and show you the proof? Did you kill her and take the papers?"

It was something that had occurred to Gamache. The one reason Gilbert might have killed Debbie. To destroy the damning evidence.

But there were other possibilities.

Beauvoir's phone had vibrated with a message, which he ignored. Now it rang. Looking down at it, he glanced at Gamache, who nodded.

Beauvoir walked into the next room, taking the call while Gamache turned to Colette Roberge. "Ewen Cameron would have needed a statistician in his work, wouldn't he?"

"Yes, that's true. Are you accusing me?"

"No. You'd have been far too young. Cameron would have made sure to use the best, even if the best was all the way across the continent. In, let's say, British Columbia."

He turned back to Abigail Robinson. They all turned to her.

"Is that what you found?" Gamache continued. "Is that why you were reluctant to come right out with it? Debbie Schneider said you were going through your father's papers. Is that where you found the proof that Dr. Gilbert was involved in Cameron's experiments? Because your father was too."

"No, never," said Abigail. "My father would never have done that. He was a good man. A caring man."

Beauvoir came back and flashed his phone for Gamache to see the four-word message.

Gamache paused, quickly putting things together. He'd been wrong. Gone down the wrong path. But now, thanks to Lacoste and Beauvoir, he could see where they needed to be.

He turned slowly back to Abigail Robinson, who'd looked from Beauvoir's phone, though she couldn't see the message, back up into Gamache's eyes. And she saw there that he knew the truth.

"Are you going to tell me, or do you want me to say it?"

Her silence stretched on. He gave her thirty seconds, which seemed an eternity. The room felt like a sensory-deprivation chamber. No movement. No sound. No light outside the windows. Not even the ticking of a clock.

Armand Gamache gave Abigail Robinson another thirty seconds.

But the only thing that happened, the only movement, was the thinning of her lips, as she pressed them together.

"Your mother killed herself."

That had been Lacoste's message. What the coroner had written in his notes, but did not include on the death certificate.

Mrs. Robinson committed suicide.

Still, Abigail didn't speak. So Armand did.

"She'd been suffering from insomnia and postpartum depression since your sister Maria's birth."

He stepped carefully, feeling his way forward. Backward. Into the past. He had no proof of what he was saying, but finally the pieces fit.

His voice was deep, gentle. "Your father didn't work with Cameron. That was wrong. He knew of Cameron's work, though not the exact nature of it. Your father loved your mother and wanted the best treatment." As he spoke, he kept thoughtful eyes on Abigail. Watching, gauging, her reaction to his words. "He arranged for her to go to Montréal for treatment." He paused. "With Ewen Cameron."

Vincent Gilbert's mouth went slack. Dropped open.

But Gamache kept his attention on Abigail. Her breathing was rapid, like someone hiding in a closet from an intruder.

"She came back worse," Armand said, quietly. He and Abigail were alone in the room now. In the world. This dreadful world where such things happened. "Broken, beyond repair. A short time later she took her life."

"No. Cameron took her life. And him." She narrowed her eyes to stare at Gilbert.

Vincent Gilbert paled, as though her gaze was drawing the blood from him.

"And then, to add insult," said Gamache, "Dr. Cameron sent a bill. That's how you knew Gilbert worked with Cameron. Because he signed the demand for payment. And you found it among your father's papers."

From his breast pocket he brought out the paper Reine-Marie had given him, unfolded it, and placed it on the table in front of Abigail Robinson.

"This is what you found. A letter like this."

She bent down and studied it. Looked at the name. Enid Horton.

"Exactly like that." She looked at Vincent Gilbert. "A form letter?" Gilbert stared at his hands. "You couldn't even be bothered to write individual letters? By the time Dad got this, my mother was dead. But he paid anyway."

"And you came here not to get Vincent Gilbert's endorsement, but for repayment."

"Yes."

CHAPTER 36

"Well, we now know why Abigail Robinson came to Québec," said Lacoste, slicing the baguette. "To kill Vincent Gilbert."

They were back in the Incident Room. Dominique had brought down dinner. A large pot of her winter *spécialité*, a hearty *pot-au-feu*.

Jean-Guy ladled it out, while Armand poured beer for himself and Lacoste, and gave Jean-Guy a ginger ale.

Abigail Robinson had come back to the Inn with them, as had Vincent Gilbert. They were now under the same roof, but on different floors, restricted to their rooms.

"She doesn't admit that," said Gamache, tearing a thick piece of baguette and dipping it into the stew. "It would be helpful if we had any evidence, like the letter Gilbert wrote and Abigail found among her father's things."

"I think Abigail got that much right," said Isabelle. "Debbie threatened him with it, he panicked and killed her, then burned the letter along with the murder weapon. He admits he destroyed every other document connecting him to Cameron. And he was in the library before the attack. He could've taken a piece of firewood without anyone seeing."

"So they were going to kill each other?" asked Jean-Guy. "Like gladiators in the ring?"

"Not quite," said Armand. "But close. I think Abigail's plan was more subtle, more layered. I think she was going to blackmail Gilbert into publicly supporting her campaign—"

"Then she'd release the evidence anyway, that Gilbert had collaborated with Ewen Cameron," said Jean-Guy. "Why kill the man outright when you can torture him first? Give him some of his own back. Let him watch everything he'd spent a lifetime building up come crumbling down."

"He was far beyond his depth, in his sea of glory," said Gamache.

"A quote?" asked Beauvoir. The rich stew and sleepiness had lowered his resistance, and the question popped out before he could stop it.

His eyes widened in fear, some mock, some real, that the Chief would now regale them with the full poem.

He did not. Gamache only smiled and said, "Why is it when I say something profound you assume I'm quoting someone else?"

"Were you?" Beauvoir asked, and could have kicked himself. *Stop it. Stop giving him an opening.*

Gamache gave a small grunt of laughter. "How well you know me. Yes. Wolsey's farewell, from Shakespeare's *Henry VIII*. I've thought of it a few times when I've considered Dr. Gilbert in this whole thing. His ego propped open the door to his enemies."

"I've been thinking of eunuchs," said Isabelle.

"Eunuchs? As in—" Jean-Guy made a gesture over his lap.

"Exactly. Some men in China intentionally castrated themselves in order to rise to a position of power."

Jean-Guy's eyes widened. He'd heard of the practice, but had assumed it was a punishment, not a choice. Who would . . . ?

Armand, though, was nodding. "Yes. That might be closer to the truth. What people do for power. How they're willing to mutilate themselves, physically, intellectually, morally, for power and position."

"You think that's what Gilbert did?" asked Jean-Guy, fighting to get the quite vivid image out of his head.

"I think some people would do just about anything, say just about anything, stay quiet about anything, to attain, then hold on to power," said Armand. "We've seen a lot of that in the last few years. Why not Vincent Gilbert? A boy from a poor family, gifted with remarkable intellect, but crippled by a lack of resources and conscience. His brains got him into medical school in McGill, and his faulty moral compass allowed him to stay there."

"All he had to do was turn a blind eye to torture," said Isabelle.

"And when, years later, having achieved international recognition as a doctor and humanitarian he was threatened with exposure, his core instincts come out."

"So you do think Vincent Gilbert killed Debbie Schneider," said Jean-Guy. "To get those papers off her. To stop the blackmail."

"I think we finally have a motive for her death. He'd clearly gone to huge lengths to erase any evidence of his work with Cameron, destroying all the paperwork in the files in the Osler Library."

"But he couldn't get those demands for payment back," said Lacoste. "They were in private hands."

"He must've assumed, as time went by and the victims died, that he was safe. That those papers were lost or destroyed," said Gamache.

"Or that no one would notice, or recognize, the signature of a minor research assistant," said Lacoste. "But Abigail Robinson did. And she came here to make him pay."

Jean-Guy was nodding, thinking. Imagining it.

Debbie Schneider had had Dr. Vincent Gilbert's balls in her pocket. And he meant to get them back.

"Though Chancellor Roberge could've done it too," said Jean-Guy. "Maybe even more likely. She and Debbie went for a walk. Alone. In the dark. Debbie could have shown her the letter and, thinking she was a friend and ally, told her what they had planned. Roberge realized how damning the letter was and lashed out. Then burned the paper in the bonfire."

"But why would she do that?" asked Isabelle. "Kill someone to get a letter back that had nothing to do with her? She wasn't named in it."

Gamache realized that Isabelle hadn't been at the meeting at the Chancellor's home. Hadn't seen that small gesture, Gilbert's hand on Roberge's. But Jean-Guy had.

"Because Colette Roberge loves Vincent Gilbert," said Jean-Guy.

"Really?" Isabelle considered that, then said, "But do you really think the Chancellor would kill to protect his reputation? His life, maybe, but his reputation?"

"Have you met the man?" asked Jean-Guy. "His reputation is his life. All he has left."

"I think it's fairly clear that Abigail, probably with the help of Debbie Schneider, planned to, at the very least, blackmail Gilbert," said Armand. "To avenge her mother."

"And maybe her father," said Isabelle.

"Why do you say that?" Armand laid down his spoon and fork.

"When his wife died, Paul Robinson lost a life partner, a companion, and a helpmate. His death certificate also says heart failure, just like hers. Vague. I doubt it tells the full story, the real one. There was no autopsy."

"You think he killed himself too?" asked Jean-Guy.

It wasn't all that hard to imagine.

Suppose, he thought, Annie died? Suppose she'd been tormented into it? And he was the one who'd put her into the monster's hands? And then Idola dies, and once again it's his fault. He'd given her the peanut butter sandwich that lodged in her throat.

Jean-Guy suspected his broken heart would give out too. Crushed by grief and guilt.

"He waited until his other daughter was grown," he said.

"*Oui*," said Isabelle. "Out of the house. She'd just gone away to Oxford."

"And was in the care of his friend Colette Roberge," said Armand. It fit. If he could follow the sequence of events, Abigail Robinson certainly could.

"The specter of Ewen Cameron hangs over this case," said Gamache. "As do the ghosts of all his victims. Including both of Abigail Robinson's parents."

A few years ago, when Agent Beauvoir had first arrived in homicide and the Chief Inspector said things like that, he'd roll his eyes and smirk.

Gamache had ignored him and waited. And waited. Until one day Jean-Guy Beauvoir understood that when people died, they didn't go away. They were very much alive in the minds, in the hearts, in the vivid memories of those left behind.

And they were not always easy to live with. Some ghosts had demands.

"How old was Abigail when her sister died?" Armand asked.

"Fifteen," said Isabelle.

"And her father was alone with Maria when she died?"

"As far as we know. Because of the manner of her death, the coroner did a full autopsy."

"May I?" Gamache held out his hand, and Lacoste gave him the autopsy report. "Both, if you don't mind," he said. "And Paul Robinson's death certificate."

Putting on his glasses, he started to read. Nodding every now and then.

He was not, they saw, skimming. He was reading every word.

"Can you send me the electronic versions?" he asked.

When she did, he attached the reports to an email to Sharon Harris. Their coroner and colleague.

Taking off his glasses, he heaved a sigh. "Are you staying over, Isabelle?"

"Yes. I've got my room at Olivier and Gabri's B&B."

"Good." He looked at his watch. It was past eleven. "Time for bed I think. We won't get an answer until the morning."

Beauvoir drove his car back down the hill, but Armand felt the need for fresh air, as did Isabelle. Instead of going straight down into the village, Armand asked her, "Do you mind?"

She shook her head and followed him, knowing where they were headed. They stopped at the bench and swept off the fluffy snow that had accumulated during the day. As she did, Isabelle reached out and caressed the back of the seat. It was too dark to see the words etched into it, but she could feel them.

Armand and Reine-Marie had put the bench there so that friends and strangers could rest from the journey. Could sit and contemplate the vista, then drop their eyes to the homes below. The wood smoke rising from their chimneys and the buttery light spilling from their mullioned windows. They could watch the huge pine trees sway, wave, on the village green.

The three pines in a cluster that gave the village its name was an old United Empire Loyalist code to tell war-weary refugees that they were safe. At last.

But while Armand and Reine-Marie had put the bench there, the words etched into it remained a mystery. They'd just appeared. First one phrase, then, below it, another. No one admitted to doing it, but Armand had a feeling that it had been Billy Williams, who, while often enigmatic, still managed to make himself understood.

Written on one of the weathered slats was part of a prayer.

May you be a brave man in a brave country.

And underneath that, *Surprised by Joy*.

The night was completely still. Isabelle and Armand sat side by side, their breaths coming out in puffs.

And in one of the puffs were the words "How are you, Isabelle?"

"Better," she said.

"Better than?"

"Before." She smiled and sat in peace for a moment before speaking again. "The day after I got home from the hospital, you came over. You made us tea and brought treats from the bistro and we talked. Do you remember?"

"I'll never forget."

"You told me that you were stronger than you had been before you were wounded a few years earlier. I could see that was true. For you. But I was afraid I'd never get there. I could barely speak or move on my own. I had to have help feeding myself."

How well she remembered the Chief, sitting beside her, tearing the flaky croissant into bite-sized pieces. Then, instead of feeding her as everyone else did, he placed a small piece into her hand, and closed her fingers over it, until she gripped it.

Then, as tears of embarrassment streamed down her cheeks, he gently lifted her hand to her mouth. It took a couple of tries. The bread kept slipping from her grasp, but the tears had stopped. As she concentrated.

And finally, they had it.

They cheered. As though she'd done something remarkable. Which she had.

They did it again. And again. Until the croissant was all eaten.

It tasted better than anything she'd ever had before, or since.

From then on, that was how she asked her husband, her parents, her carers, her children, to do it. It took far more time, and was often frustrating, even humiliating. But finally she could do it on her own.

She turned to him now. His face was outlined against the stars. The deep scar on his forehead was invisible. But if she reached out, she'd be able to feel it. Etched there.

"I still have days when I struggle," she said.

He nodded. "Me too. When I'm tired."

"I search for words," she said. "And when I find them, I slur. But that just reminds me how far I've come."

"I'm sorry you've had to make that journey, Isabelle."

Her actions had saved not just his life, but the lives of most of the villagers. She'd been shot, almost killed, right there. In the bistro. In the safe place.

But they, better than most, knew that no place was really safe from physical harm. Anything could happen to anyone, at any moment. What made a place safe were the people. The caring. The kindness. The helping. Sometimes the mourning. And often the forgiveness.

"I am stronger, in every way," she said. "But I feel badly for my children. I tell myself it's made them stronger too, more resilient. They saw that it's possible to overcome. But . . ."

But.

"They were wounded too," he finished her thought.

"Oui."

They sat in companionable silence, breathing in the thin, cold air. Breathing out words unspoken. Until Isabelle spoke.

"I've been thinking about Abigail. What happened to her mother is something a child would never fully get over."

She saw Gamache nod, then he got up. Together they walked past the New Forest and into the village. Both of them limping slightly.

Daniel was out with the dogs, the last walk of the day. Armand joined him, while Isabelle headed to her bed in the B&B.

"Dad?"

"Oui?"

"Do you think Professor Robinson will be successful? In her campaign, I mean."

Armand turned to his son. Large, sturdy like his father. Strong and kind. And sensitive. One day it might fall to Daniel to make that decision. To pull the plug, to remove the respirator. To let his father die. To let nature take its course.

But what "nature" were they talking about? Human nature? Was that what Abigail Robinson was relying on? Armand knew it was not always pretty. Or compassionate. Or brave.

If human nature was allowed to take its course, unchecked, what would happen?

He remembered the smear on the window. The elongated handprint. And had some idea. Though he also had an overriding belief in the decency of people. While he'd seen the worst, Armand Gamache had also seen the best. And he believed the best would prevail.

"I hope not." But was hope enough?

"Would it be such a bad thing if Professor Robinson died?" Daniel asked.

Armand looked at his son, hardly believing what he heard. "You can't mean that."

"I do." Daniel examined his father for a moment. "Do you regret saving her life?"

No one had, as yet, asked him that. Not directly. "I had to try."

"I understand," said Daniel. "But do you regret it? Do you wish you'd failed?"

Armand breathed in, and out, unable to answer.

"Would you do it again?" Daniel asked, quietly.

Over his son's shoulder Armand could see the hill out of Three Pines where the bench, invisible in the darkness, sat. And on that bench, the words, unseen, were etched.

May you be a brave man in a brave country.

Armand Gamache realized he no longer knew what bravery might look like. What "the best" might be.

CHAPTER 37

⌣

D r. Sharon Harris was having a café au lait and brioche in the bistro when Armand, Jean-Guy, and Isabelle arrived.

"I thought you'd email the answers to us," said Armand, sitting down after greeting Gabri and Olivier. "Or call. I didn't expect you to actually come here."

"Though we're not complaining about meeting you in the bistro," said Jean-Guy. He'd slept in and missed breakfast. Now he ordered French toast, with maple-smoked bacon and syrup from the *cabane à sucre* down the road.

The other two had coffee.

It was a few minutes past eight on this crisp January morning. The sun was just coming up, and the bistro was just filling up. Children were beginning to hit the rink. Some literally. As parents stood in the snow, rubbing their arms, stamping their feet and glancing longingly at the bistro.

"I wanted to talk it over," said the coroner. "The reports you sent on the three deaths in the Robinson family are . . . suggestive."

"Of what?" Isabelle asked.

"Of something more going on," said Sharon Harris.

"Like?" said Jean-Guy.

"I think you already know."

Gamache held her steady gaze and said nothing.

"All right, I'll tell you," said Dr. Harris. "I think the doctor's notes are right. Kathleen Robinson, the mother, killed herself. The drugs she was prescribed are consistent with depression. The report says she'd given birth a few years earlier, so it might've been a prolonged, extreme case of postpartum. In an unusual death like this, it would be normal to do an autopsy. But none was performed. I'm guessing it's because the doctor and coroner knew exactly what she died of." She glanced around the table. "You don't look surprised."

"We're not," said Lacoste. "We think it was . . ." She searched for the word. "Provoked."

"How?"

"She came to Québec to be treated for her depression, by Ewen Cameron."

Sharon Harris's eyes widened and she gave a short sharp inhale. "I see."

And what she saw was an otherwise healthy, happy woman suffering temporary, though acute, depression put into the hands of a monster. To be cured.

What she saw was that after months of torture, Kathleen Robinson was sent home to her husband and children. She'd left depressed, she returned in despair.

And killed herself.

"I see."

What Sharon Harris saw was that it wasn't really suicide. It was morally, if not legally, murder.

"If you knew all this, why send me the reports?"

"I think you already know," said Gamache, with only a slight smile.

Dr. Harris gave a small grunt of amusement. "*Touché.*" She glanced down at the printouts. "It wasn't about Madame Robinson's death, was it? That was for context. It's about the others. The husband and daughter. The report on the man's death, Paul Robinson, also says heart failure. You're wondering if there's more there?" She exhaled. "Might be, but it's impossible to tell. In his case it could really have been heart failure. He was in his early fifties, so a heart attack or stroke aren't out of the question. Equally, he could have killed himself. Like his wife's, the report on his death is vague."

She hesitated, then looked directly at the Chief Inspector. "But you're head of homicide, not head of suicide. What do you suspect, Armand?"

"You tell me."

She dropped her head and muttered what sounded like "bastard."

"All right," she said, when she looked up again. "I'll tell you, but this isn't official. It can't be. And I doubt at this point it can ever be proven."

The three investigators waited. Sharon Harris shuffled the papers in front of her. Bringing one to the top.

"I think the child Maria Robinson's death wasn't an accident."

"Meaning?" Isabelle leaned forward.

"Meaning I think she was murdered. I think her father killed her, then later took his own life."

"But the deaths are years apart," said Isabelle.

"True. But there can be a delayed reaction."

"Of years?" she asked, clearly not buying it.

"When you investigate a murder," said Dr. Harris, "don't you go back into the past? To find some wound that festered? That erupted years later in murder? I've heard you talk about that. Why not self-murder? Suicide. Paul Robinson must've been deeply scarred by what happened to his wife. And then the pressure of caring for a severely disabled child alone. The mind can warp and twist and land in a very dark place. Chalk another one up to Ewen Cameron."

"Wait a minute," said Beauvoir, holding up his hand. "You think Robinson killed his own daughter? A defenseless little girl? Wh . . . wh . . ."

"Why do I say that?" asked Dr. Harris. "Because of this."

She placed her finger on a word. One single word buried, intentionally or not, among so many.

Beauvoir bent over, studying it as though examining a tiny body.

Petechiae.

He looked up at Lacoste, who'd also bent to see the word. Then they both looked at Gamache. Who had no need to read it. He'd seen the word the night before.

That was why he'd sent Dr. Harris the reports, without comment. To see what she'd think. If she'd see what he saw.

Petechiae.

Tiny red dots on the girl's face. Like freckles, only not. They were, the homicide investigators knew, signs of strangulation or smothering.

"She choked on a peanut butter sandwich," said Jean-Guy. "That's how she died. It says it right there. The hemorrhages were caused by that. Not . . ."

He could feel his hands and feet grow cold, as though he'd been on thin ice all along. And it had given way.

He fought for control. Fought to give the impression all was fine. *Ça va bien aller.*

But he was overcome with the thought that if it could happen to Paul Robinson, a loving father, it could happen to . . . anyone.

"The child's condition had deteriorated," said Dr. Harris, watching him closely. "She'd be on puréed food by then. No parent would give her a peanut butter sandwich."

"But maybe a carer did," Beauvoir said, his voice rising, even as his heart sank. "Someone unfamiliar with her."

"The report says she was alone with her father," said Dr. Harris.

Armand shifted his eyes from Dr. Harris to Beauvoir. He knew what fear looked like. Had seen it often enough in young agents. In experienced investigators. As they'd prepared for an especially dangerous action.

He saw it now in his son-in-law. And he could guess why.

"It looks to me like Maria's father smothered her, probably with a pillow, then shoved the sandwich down her throat postmortem," the coroner was saying.

"*Non. Non,*" said Jean-Guy, shaking his head. "No father would do that."

And there it was.

"Most wouldn't," said Armand. *You wouldn't.*

It was the nightmare, the worst fear. Not just that his child would die, but that he'd somehow be responsible for it. Even, God help him, do it. In a moment of madness.

"We've seen it before—" Isabelle began.

"Yes," snapped Jean-Guy, cutting her off. Not wanting to be reminded of the terrible things they'd seen. What happened when human nature went feral.

Yes, sometimes they discovered that a parent had killed their child, though it was more often the other way around.

"Let's leave it there," said Armand. "Thank you for coming here, Sharon, and walking us through what might've happened."

"You saw that in the autopsy, didn't you, Armand," Dr. Harris said, as she got up. "Petechiae. That's why you sent all three reports to me."

"Yes. But as you said, it's a long time ago. There's no way to prove any of this."

"I can't see how it can relate to the murder of Deborah Schneider on New Year's Eve," said the coroner, pulling her coat off the back of the chair.

"Neither can I," admitted Gamache. "We're just assembling the pieces. Most are not helpful."

Dr. Harris turned to Beauvoir. "You might be right. It could've been an accident, not murder at all. With no way to prove it either way, maybe we choose to believe that."

"*Excusez-moi.*" Without waiting to be excused, Beauvoir put his coat on and left.

"Forget something?" Stephen asked. He was holding Idola on his lap and reading to her. From the *Financial Times*.

"Yes. I just need to . . ." He held out his arms, and Stephen, a little surprised, handed the child to her father.

Jean-Guy felt Idola's breath on his neck, and felt her supple body conform to his. And he knew he could never, ever hurt her.

In fact, he'd hurt anyone who tried.

That's what he'd forgotten. For one horrific moment. That he would die before he'd let anything happen to either of his children. In fact, he would kill.

So what had happened to Paul Robinson?

Jean-Guy carried his daughter into the study and sat at the desk. On the laptop he looked up Paul Robinson. Not much came up. But there was a photograph from a conference he'd been at.

It showed a middle-aged man. Slender, geeky, with glasses and graying hair and a bow tie.

He was standing in front of an easel with a poster on it and smiling into the camera. He looked a little goofy.

Was Paul Robinson, at that moment, contemplating murdering his daughter?

Maria. Beloved, vulnerable. Ave Maria. Blessed Mary.

But there was another daughter. The Abby to her Maria.

Bright. Brilliant even. So like her father in so many ways.

Abby Maria. Conjoined sisters. Not by some cartilage or artery. They didn't share an organ, they shared a father and a fate. That bound them forever.

He looked down at Idola, and when he made eye contact, she laughed.

Her flat features no longer said Down syndrome.

They said daughter.

As he left the house, Jean-Guy saw his father-in-law standing on the far side of the frozen pond. Watching the children play.

Armand looked up, and their eyes met. He'd been waiting. Patiently. In the cold. For him.

They didn't speak as they walked through the bright sunshine, up the hill to the Auberge. Past the chapel. Past the New Forest. Past the bench.

May you be a brave man in a brave country.

Reine-Marie was more than halfway to Enid Horton's home, the box in the back seat of her car, when she slowed down. Stopped. And turned around.

Parking at the Inn, she went in and found Haniya standing at the window, looking out over a field of snow, her arms wrapped around herself.

Without turning she said, "It's so white. And cold. Everything looks dead. I don't know why anyone lives here."

She coughed, and Reine-Marie stopped where she was. And had to remind herself that a cough was no longer a threat. A sneeze wasn't an attack.

The vaccine had worked. It was one of the great global shared experiences. The plague and the cure. But still, she had to force herself forward, to stand beside the young woman with the sniffles.

"Voltaire described Canada as *quelques arpents de neige*," said Reine-Marie. "A few acres of snow. It was, of course, dismissive. An insult."

"No offense. I didn't mean to insult your home."

Reine-Marie smiled. "I think you know the difference between an insult and a compliment." Then she too looked out the window. Where Haniya Daoud, and Voltaire, saw a few acres of snow, of misery, she saw tobogganing. Skiing. Snowshoeing. Hockey games on frozen lakes. Sitting by a fire with a hot chocolate, while a blizzard pounded the windows and walls. Was there anything more comforting than being safe and warm inside during a snowstorm?

"Each snowflake is unique, you know."

"Really?" It would be impossible to convey less interest.

"*Oui.* A fellow named Snowflake Bentley proved that, more than a century ago. He was a Vermonter. Lived not far from here. A backwoods man who was fascinated by the new invention of photography. He figured out how to take a picture of a single flake. Sounds easy, but just try to capture one, never mind take a picture of it. His photographs are amazing. Beautiful. It was only then that scientists confirmed what they suspected. That each snowflake is different. Trillions and trillions." She turned to Haniya. "All unique. All exquisite. Each a work of art. Imagine that."

"His name was Snowflake?" asked Haniya.

"His name was Wilson. Snowflake was an affectionate nickname." Reine-Marie returned to the view. "Without that thick layer of snow, the crops, the flowers, even many of the animals would die. It's insulation against a killing frost. Then in the spring it melts. Liquid gold, the farmers call it. They pray for as much as possible. Perception's an interesting thing, *non?*"

"What?" said Haniya. "I wasn't listening. Are you still talking about snow? I've been here three days and all you people seem to talk about is the weather."

"And murder."

"The two seem to dovetail, yes."

Reine-Marie heaved a long sigh that fogged up the glass in front of her. Fully realizing she might be making a terrible mistake, she did it anyway. "I have a delicate, maybe even unpleasant task to perform, and I'm wondering if you'd like to come along."

Haniya's brows all but disappeared into her bright purple hijab. "Why?"

It was, of course, a very good question.

Why? Reine-Marie asked herself.

"Because I don't think you should be alone. Because you might be a distraction."

"Because I'm Black?"

"Because you're annoying. It'll make me look more reasonable."

Haniya laughed, then considered. "Might as well. Nothing else to do except look at that." She gestured toward the acres of snow.

As she followed Reine-Marie to the car, Haniya scooped up some snow. She stared at the flakes in her mitten. Then tried to separate one from the pack. But couldn't. She leaned close, trying to see the patterns of each individual flake, but her breath melted them before she could see.

She raised her head and looked at the snowbanks and snowdrifts. At the snow balancing on tree limbs and sitting on the roof of the Inn, and the cars, and the stone walls.

Acres and acres.

As she got into the still warm car, Haniya realized that when Reine-Marie Gamache said she wanted her company, there was one reason she hadn't given.

Because I like you.

Haniya had been called brave. She'd been called remarkable. She'd been called tireless and inspirational. She'd been called a hero. All of which, she knew, were true.

But no one had called her friend.

On the way over, Reine-Marie brought Haniya up to speed about Enid Horton and the commission to help the family sort Mom's things before the sale of the home.

"You said it might be unpleasant. Why's that? Did you find something?"

That's when Reine-Marie told her about the monkeys. About the strange collection. The books and drawings. The etching on the bedroom wall.

But not about Ewen Cameron. She felt she should tell the family first.

"Monkeys?" said Haniya, shaking her head. "And now you have to tell the family that their mother was crazy. And you brought me along as an example of crazy?"

Reine-Marie pulled into the brick bungalow on the outskirts of Cowansville. "I've brought you along as proof that terrible things can happen, and we can still heal."

"You think I've healed?" said Haniya, with a laugh. "You think I'm whole?"

She turned in her seat and stared at Reine-Marie. "No. What you see is a mockery, a mimic. I'm made up of bits and pieces left on the ground, from other broken people. An arm here, a leg there. A memory, an aspiration, a desire. Sewn together so that I look human, but am not quite."

"The creature from *Frankenstein*," said Reine-Marie.

Haniya laughed. "And here I thought you'd comfort me. Tell me I'm wrong. That I'm fully human and beautiful. Instead you call me a monster."

"The creature wasn't the monster," Reine-Marie said, quietly. "The doctor was." She smiled at her companion. "I told you this was going to be unpleasant, and you came anyway, to keep me company. If that isn't whole, I don't know what is. You are beautiful. And you are brave."

And, and, Haniya waited, *you are my friend.*

When Reine-Marie didn't say it, Haniya turned away and looked out the window.

"You say that your snow covers all sorts of wonderful things. Keeps them alive. But I suspect it covers terrible things too. Things that are better off dead, or at least hidden." She turned back to Reine-Marie. "Perception. Who's to say who the monsters are? And where they're buried."

Reine-Marie got out of the car and wondered if she was about to make a mistake, in telling the Horton family the long-buried truth she'd uncovered. About their mother. And the monkeys. And the modern monster.

Maybe Haniya was right. Some things don't need to be brought into light. Some truths can remain unspoken.

CHAPTER 38

"I think I know what happened," said Jean-Guy, taking a seat at the conference table.

They were once again in the basement of the Auberge. Snow from the day before had blown up against the windows, blocking out the sun.

As Jean-Guy spoke, the rough stone walls of the Old Hadley House seemed to lean closer. The specters trapped there eager to hear how a father might murder a helpless daughter.

"*Oui?*" said Armand. He too leaned forward.

"I think Paul Robinson didn't kill his daughter."

At that Armand's brows drew down. Worried for Jean-Guy, but willing to listen.

"Go on."

"I think he saved Abby." Jean-Guy looked from Armand to Isabelle and saw skepticism, and not a little bewilderment. He hurried on. "At least that's how he saw it. It came to me just now when I was with Idola. He'd never have hurt Maria—"

"Do you mean you could never hurt Idola?" asked Armand.

Jean-Guy turned to him in frustration. "No, well, yes, partly. Look, I admit, it's hard to separate my feelings for Idola from what Paul Robinson might've been going through. And I'm not saying he didn't do it."

"What are you saying?" asked Armand, confused now.

Beauvoir regrouped. "I'm saying that I agree with you. Paul Robinson was exhausted. Drained. I think he saw that Maria was failing and in his confused state he did something that made sense at the time but that he immediately regretted. I think in a moment of sheer madness, he didn't see it as killing her, but as freeing her. And her sister. Separating them, finally. No more Abby Maria. I'm saying he saw it as releasing both his daughters. One to peace, the other to a full life."

He looked from one to the other, trying to read their expressions.

There was silence as Armand and Isabelle, both parents, imagined that moment when Paul Robinson looked into the abyss.

It wasn't completely unknown. Not just with parents and suffering children, but with adult children and frail parents. With spouses. With friends. When there was interminable pain. Terrible suffering. When the end was inevitable but taking too long.

Plugs were pulled and respirators turned off. Hands were held, and prayers and promises and goodbyes whispered.

But what happened when the suffering continued? Or when there were no plugs to pull? Just a loved one wracked with uncontrollable pain and begging for help.

What happened when nature was taking its time to take its course? When the necessary permission for assisted suicide hadn't been given in time?

Was a nudge necessary?

Did mercy sound like a soft footstep in the middle of the night? Did it look like a syringe? A pillow?

But was it always mercy?

If looked at from a certain angle, in a certain light, did the kind angel become wicked? Dispatching not a tormented loved one, but an inconvenience. Wasn't that the debate they were locked in now, thanks to Abigail Robinson and her campaign for mandatory euthanasia?

The word "burden" was never used, but it hung in the fetid air. Only a fool would refuse to see it. To hear it.

Only a fool was deaf to the whispers in the halls of power, now emboldened by Professor Robinson's success, that most of those who died in the pandemic had underlying conditions. They'd have died soon anyway.

Perhaps, they whispered, it wasn't such a bad thing. Perhaps it was a blessing. Perhaps the pandemic had, inadvertently, done them all a favor. Freed some to peace, freed the rest to get on with their lives.

Everyone was quick to say what happened was heartbreaking. But really, privately, they considered the tragedies of the pandemic a cull. Of the weak.

Armand Gamache was no fool. He heard the whispers. And he'd witnessed the so-called mercy. Smelled it. He'd seen the handprint on the window. The streak. An arc, like some mockery of the rainbow children worldwide had drawn.

And Armand Gamache knew that the underlying condition, the infirmity everyone talked about, did not lie with those who died, but with those who had allowed it to happen.

And now it was about to move from a tragic miscalculation to calculation.

Where was mercy now, he wondered, and what did it look like? Where was courage now, and what did it look like?

"You're saying that Paul Robinson killed his daughter out of kindness?" asked Lacoste.

Beauvoir nodded, then shook his head. "No. Well, partly. Yes. I think that was the justification he used. But really, it was exhaustion. He just couldn't go on."

While Beauvoir looked down at his hands, and Gamache remained silent, Lacoste worked her way through what might have happened.

"So he smothers Maria," she said. "Then years later kills himself. A kind of execution. A self-imposed death penalty for what he'd done?"

"*Oui*," said Beauvoir. "He still had Abigail to raise, so he waited until she was settled in Oxford. Away from home. Safe with Colette Roberge."

At the sound of that name, Gamache looked up. But remained quiet. Thinking.

Finally, he lifted his hands.

"We have no idea what actually happened. Did Professor Robinson's father kill Maria? Maybe. We can never know for sure. Let's focus on the murder we do know about."

And yet, as the morning progressed, Gamache couldn't quite shake it. This convergence of events. And the thought, the feeling really, that it did matter. That, thanks to Beauvoir, they were onto a continuum. That each step mattered. And had brought them here. To a basement, investigating the brutal murder of Debbie Schneider.

But he also felt there'd been a misstep along the way. Something off. And that was why it hadn't brought them straight to the murderer. Straight to what had happened two nights ago, as they'd watched fireworks light the sky, while a woman was being bludgeoned to death just meters away.

The prearranged video call from Nanaimo came through for Isabelle, and she excused herself. Returning to her desk and putting on her headset, she answered.

"Inspector Lacoste?" A middle-aged man in plain clothes appeared. "It's Sergeant Fillmore. Barry."

"*Salut*, Barry. It's Isabelle. Thank you for doing this."

"No worries. Should we begin?"

The Nanaimo investigators had already been through Debbie Schneider's house once, but Isabelle wanted to see it for herself.

She always found it interesting, and often revealing, to see the private space of a victim, or a suspect. Actually, she just liked looking at people's homes, often going for walks with the kids around their neighborhood in the evening, hoping to get a peek into lighted living rooms.

Now she hit record and watched as Sergeant Fillmore took her through the modest bungalow in Nanaimo. Two bedrooms. Galley kitchen. There was a TV in the living room and what looked like good, but dated, furniture. Probably inherited from parents. Framed photographs sat on side tables and bookcases.

The home was tidy. Comfortable. Left by someone expecting to return.

The final stop was what Isabelle really wanted to see. The second bedroom had been made into an office. That was less tidy.

Fillmore panned around, then turned to the desk. "The top drawer was locked when we found it. We had to break in."

"But there wasn't much in it, from what I remember."

"No. We emptied it onto the top of the desk." He pointed his phone at the collection of items.

There were birthday cards, assorted office supplies. An agenda sat on top of a partially obscured photograph.

"Can you get a clearer picture of the photograph, please?"

He pulled it out and Isabelle's face softened. There, unexpectedly, was Maria.

And not just Maria. There was young Debbie and Abby and a man who could only be Paul Robinson. All gathered around the wheelchair. Smiling.

"Can you box up the things from her desk and send them to me, express?"

"Fine." Though he sounded less than pleased.

"*Merci.*"

After hanging up, Isabelle went back over the video, pausing at the photograph. She took a screenshot and printed out copies. Then she contemplated it.

The picture was taken at the oceanfront, one sunny summer's day.

Isabelle guessed that Abigail and Debbie were about fifteen and Maria would have been nine.

Lacoste looked closely at the little girl with the huge brown eyes and twisted body. Was this the last year of her life? The last month? Week? She'd died on August 27th, the coroner's report said. On a sunny summer's day?

Isabelle sat back in her chair and stared. Now why, she asked herself, was this photograph hidden away and not up with the others? It seemed innocuous enough. It looked pretty much like any family photograph. The very pedestrian nature of it fascinated her.

Paul Robinson was bending down, his face close to Maria's. Smiling. This was not, Isabelle thought, a man on the verge of nervous collapse. He didn't look exhausted and spent. And contemplating the unthinkable.

He looked happy, carefree even. Though Isabelle knew that while a picture might be worth a thousand words, many of them were lies. Or at least misleading.

She'd smiled in pictures but had been seething inside. Or sad. Or bored. People were programmed to smile for pictures. To say "Cheeeeeze." It meant next to nothing.

But still, there was an ease about this image.

Paul Robinson had one hand resting casually on the back of Maria's wheelchair, the other on Abigail's shoulder. Protectively.

Three of the four people in the photograph were now dead. One apparently accidental death, one perhaps by his own hand, and one had been murdered not two days ago.

One thing Inspector Lacoste did not doubt was that everything had begun with two people not in this picture.

The tragedies had started with the mind control, the mind-boggling experiments conducted in full view at one of the continent's great universities. By a prominent madman. And by an intern who'd go on to become one of the nation's leading academics. A healer. A humanitarian.

And when she found among her father's things the old letter from the Allan Memorial signed by Vincent Gilbert, Abigail Robinson knew it too. And while she couldn't get at Cameron, she could get at Gilbert.

And had he, with one swing of his arm, attempted to rid himself of that threat?

Isabelle got up and started to pace.

Jean-Guy was at his desk, tipping back in his chair, so that its two front legs were off the concrete floor.

He balanced there, absently pulsing back and forth. Back and forth. Rocking himself and staring at his blank screen.

Why was Debbie Schneider murdered?

Why not Abigail Robinson, or the Asshole Saint? Why kill Debbie?

That must've been a mistake. Robinson must have been the target.

But suppose she wasn't? Suppose Madame Schneider was the intended victim? Suppose she knew something? Saw something? Possessed something?

The only viable theory so far was that Vincent Gilbert, desperate to get back the letter proving his connection to Ewen Cameron, had killed Madame Schneider, then burned it along with the weapon.

But that didn't make sense to Jean-Guy. There were other letters out there. They'd already found one, among Enid Horton's things. More would probably come to light as victims died of old age and attics were cleared out.

Besides, Debbie wasn't the only one who knew the connection. Abigail Robinson did too. She was the driving force. Killing Debbie would solve nothing.

No. Vincent Gilbert might be a little eccentric, but the man was far too smart, far too cunning, had far too great a survival instinct, to go killing someone for that reason. For essentially no reason.

If Debbie Schneider was the intended victim, it would be for a whole other reason. One they hadn't yet thought of.

Beauvoir stood up and started to pace.

Abby Maria. Abby Maria.

The words haunted Gamache, breaking into his thoughts as he went back over the murder of Debbie Schneider.

He pushed the words away and refocused, studying what they knew. What they had.

Abby Maria. There it was again. There she was again. The little girl.

Finally, in frustration, he took off his reading glasses and admitted defeat. Getting up from his desk, he started to pace the room, his hands behind his back.

Abby Maria. Ave Maria. Hail Mary. What am I missing?

There was, he realized, one person in the case that he hadn't fully considered. In passing, yes, but not seriously. Now it was time.

Colette Roberge.

She was the unlikely linchpin. The person around whom all this moved.

She'd known Abigail's father well enough to be entrusted with his daughter.

She'd acted as more than a mentor, she was a surrogate parent to the girl so far from home. And had offered comfort when news of her father's death arrived.

Years later Abigail had trusted Colette enough to send her an advance copy of the controversial report for the Royal Commission.

The Chancellor had then given it to Vincent Gilbert. And while both professed to be appalled by her recommendations, neither had done anything about it.

As he paced the basement, his mind traveled down this new path. One he'd all but ignored, in favor of the more obvious thoroughfares of Abigail Robinson and Vincent Gilbert.

But now he felt he was finally getting closer. Closer. To the truth.

The Chancellor had not just invited Abigail to Québec, she'd invited her to speak. She'd invited her to stay at her home.

Abigail and Debbie.

And then she'd taken that last necessary, fateful step. Colette Roberge had invited them to the New Year's Eve party.

To lure her into Gilbert's hands so he could stop her crusade for mass euthanasia by stopping the woman?

Kill the woman. Kill the idea.

Haniya Daoud had protested her own innocence by saying that she knew that killing a person did not kill an idea. Often it only strengthened it, by making the person a martyr.

Maybe, in desperation, Vincent Gilbert thought it was the only option now open to him.

So why was Debbie Schneider dead and not Abigail Robinson? Was it mistaken identity? Or was she the intended victim all along?

There was, of course, the issue of the letter, the possible blackmail, as a motive.

Gamache shook his head. No. Gilbert would realize that even if Debbie had the paper on her, killing her would solve nothing. Abigail still knew about his work with Cameron.

And other letters still existed and would come to light. Like the Horton letter.

Debbie Schneider should not be lying dead. It should have been Abigail Robinson, because of her campaign. Or Vincent Gilbert, killed by Abigail in revenge.

This didn't make sense. Only it did.

He was missing something. He'd blinked, or been looking in another direction, distracted, and had missed some small signpost.

The only thing that did seem clear was that without Colette Roberge, none of this would have happened. Abby and Debbie would be in Nanaimo, looking forward to a new year.

Gamache closed his eyes. He was deep in a dark cave now. He could hear scrambling, as the truth skittered away.

But it was in here with him, and he was close. He felt it. In his heart and in the hairs on the back of his neck. In the stale clammy air on his skin.

He tipped his head back, his eyes still closed in concentration. Taking a long, deep breath, he held it for a moment, then slowly released it. As he did, Abby Maria floated back.

Abby Maria.

A name first uttered by their mother, who'd bound the sisters together.

And then, decades later, uttered by Debbie Schneider at the gym, then again at the Chancellor's home after the attack.

Another deep breath. Hold it. Exhale. Hold your ground. Don't back away.

What's in that cave with you? What's scurrying around? Its claws scraping the walls. To get out.

Abby Maria was.

Debbie had said it again at the New Year's Eve party. And, worst of all, Vincent Gilbert had picked up on it. Mocking the clear reference to Ave Maria. Hail Maria. Be well, Maria.

Was that why Debbie was killed? To keep Maria a secret? To not reveal an unwell, terribly disabled sister, and therefore hinder Abigail's campaign?

But you don't kill your best friend because she was letting something inconvenient slip out, something that anyone who went looking could find easily enough. Maria Robinson was no family shame locked away in an attic. Plenty of people in the community knew about her.

No, there was a secret, but it wasn't Maria's life. It was her death.

Was that it? Was that the secret Abigail was desperate to hide? That her beloved father was a murderer? And with each mention of Abby Maria, Debbie was inadvertently revealing it?

What would happen if the media began digging? Got hold of Maria's death certificate. Saw that one word.

Petechiae.

And started asking questions. About her father. About what had really happened.

Lost in thought, lost in the cave, Gamache felt something slide across his face. And he suddenly remembered where he really was.

His eyes flew open, half expecting to come face-to-face with a snake.

But all he saw were pipes. And a cord hanging from a lightbulb in the ceiling. His heart thumping, he dropped his head and caught his breath and stared at the rough wall in front of him. And it stared back. Taunting him. Mocking him. The Old Hadley House seemed to be asking which of them was really trapped.

He turned away and tried to remember what he'd been thinking.

Was it about Colette? No. Not really. Maybe.

Striding back down the long room, he grabbed his coat. "I need some air."

As he made his way outside, Armand tried to find that thread of a thought.

The sun hit his face, and he turned to it, taking a deep breath of the crisp, fresh air. Up from the village came the sound of children laughing. From the brow of the hill, he heard screams, as toboggans were launched.

And on those rapturous cries he found it. What he'd been thinking. Abby Maria.

The one sister freed of her torment. The other freed to live her life.

The thread was tenuous. Thin and frayed. Armand had the sense that if he pulled too hard, or too soon, it would fall apart.

But if he was very, very careful, the other end could be tied to a killer.

CHAPTER 39

Reine-Marie and Haniya shared a box while Susan and James Horton each had their own.

They sat in the living room of the Horton home, surrounded by packing crates and newspaper and tape.

"I should have brought this back sooner," Reine-Marie confessed, placing her hand on the file box filled with their mother's things. "But to be honest, I was curious."

"About the monkeys," said Susan. "We opened the boxes you left, and James looked at the side of Mommy's bed."

Her brother was quiet. And quietly seething.

Did he know? Reine-Marie wondered. Was he old enough to remember his mother before, and his mother after?

Did he know what was in the box in front of them? The family secret that had somehow, as secrets often did, morphed into a shame.

"Why did she do that?" asked Susan. "Why draw monkeys? Even when she was dying? I don't understand."

Haniya Daoud shifted, trying to get more comfortable. But to do that, she was nudging Reine-Marie closer to the edge.

She'd introduced Haniya, but hadn't explained who she was. It seemed, by his expression, that James vaguely recognized her, but couldn't quite place her.

Susan, though, just stared at her. Unable, it seemed, to see beyond the disfigurement.

Now brother and sister waited for Reine-Marie to say something constructive.

Armand had allowed his feet to choose the path, this freed his mind to also choose its own way forward.

He was in the woods now, his boots sinking into the soft snow of the trail. It was quiet in there. Peaceful.

Abby Maria. Ave Maria. Hail Maria, full of grace.

Be well, Maria.

He allowed his thoughts to roam free, untethered by logic.

Ça va bien aller. All shall be well. Maria.

Gamache stopped, looked up, and saw where his feet, where the thread, had taken him. Up ahead was the hermit's cabin. The home of the Asshole Saint.

A thick layer of snow lay on its roof. There was no smoke from the chimney. No light at the windows.

No sign of life. And yet it didn't feel abandoned, or empty. It felt as though it was waiting for Vincent Gilbert to return. Home.

Gamache had visited Gilbert there a few times.

They'd sat on the porch in the summer sipping lemonade. They'd harvested vegetables in autumn, from the garden out back by the stream. He'd skied to the log cabin in winter. They'd drunk tea and eaten bread and honey Armand had brought from the village, while Vincent fed wood into the stove.

They'd talked about all sorts of things. Family. Paris. Emerson. Auden and Keller.

They'd talked about choice and chance and fate.

One of Gilbert's favorite quotes was from Henry David Thoreau. *The question is not what you look at, but what you see.*

And Armand had told Vincent one of his favorite Thoreau stories.

When Thoreau was arrested for protesting an injustice, Ralph Waldo Emerson had visited him in prison and said, "Henry, what are you doing in there?" And Thoreau had replied, "Ralph, what are you doing out there?"

Vincent had laughed. As had Armand. But both appreciated what Thoreau was saying.

Came a time when people of conscience had to take a stand.

Had that time come for Vincent Gilbert? Had a crisis of conscience moved him from looking to seeing to acting?

Would he have to arrest the Asshole Saint for that act? And when he did, would Vincent Gilbert ask him what he was doing "out there"?

But Armand knew the answer to that. He was bringing a murderer to justice.

He heard footsteps behind him. Had heard them almost from the moment he'd veered off the road, onto the path through the woods.

Now they were close. Almost upon him.

"You don't really believe what you said, do you?" said Armand. "About Paul Robinson. That he killed his daughter."

The footsteps stopped. And there was silence for a moment. "Yes. I do."

Armand turned and faced Jean-Guy. He smiled. He'd known from that first footfall who it was. He recognized the gait. And, more than that, he knew that Jean-Guy would, if he could, always be there. Close by.

Isabelle Lacoste barely noticed the gloom in the Incident Room anymore. She was preoccupied with her thoughts. With her questions.

She picked up the phone.

"Barry? It's Isabelle. You know that photograph that was in Debbie Schneider's desk? Can you see if anything's written on the back? A date or something?"

"It's packed away in the boxes, ready to be shipped to you."

"Can you find it?"

He heaved a sigh. "Yes. It'll take a little while."

"Please, as soon as you can."

He must have finally heard the urgency in her voice. "I'll go down now."

"And can you send a list of the other items in the drawer with it?"

"I have it here on my computer. There were some staples. Two printer cartridges. A ruler, an agenda, some birthday cards, a box of paper clips, and that picture. I'll forward you the list."

"*Merci*. When you find the box, can you also scan those cards?"

She hung up and stared ahead.

"You don't believe Paul Robinson killed his daughter," said Armand. "I do."

"The truth, Jean-Guy."

"I think Paul Robinson killed his daughter. He regretted it, and he tried to justify it, but yes, I think he did it."

"Think. You think that. But what do you feel? What do you believe, in here."

Gamache tapped Beauvoir's chest. The gesture, the insistence, infuriated Jean-Guy. He hated it, hated it, when Gamache pushed him like that. Not physically, but pushed him to consider feelings. Beliefs. Emotions. When Gamache insisted that they could possibly be as important as thoughts. As facts.

Jean-Guy Beauvoir had strong feelings about feelings, and Gamache knew it. But insisted anyway.

"All right. You want to know what I feel? This's what I came to show you."

He pulled out his phone, tapped, and shoved it into Gamache's face, almost hitting him.

It was the image of Paul Robinson that Jean-Guy had found when he'd googled the man. Robinson was at a conference, standing in front of a poster showing a bunch of graphs. He was smiling, in an exaggerated, silly sort of way.

"Look at the banner behind him," demanded Jean-Guy. "This's the week before, maybe days before, Maria died. That's not the face of a father in such despair he's considering killing his youngest daughter."

Gamache took the phone and examined the picture. Then handed it back.

"This proves nothing, Jean-Guy. Like you said, if Paul Robinson smothered Maria, it was in a moment of madness. A psychotic break."

"You're right," said Beauvoir. "That's what I think too. But you asked me what I feel. And I feel that man did not go home and put a pillow over his daughter's face."

Armand stared at his second-in-command. His son-in-law.

"Then who did?"

Isabelle Lacoste was at her desk going over the latest forensic reports when a text came in from Beauvoir asking her to meet them in the bistro.

She found the Chief and Beauvoir in a private corner. Heads together, deep in discussion. Perhaps about the case. More likely, she thought, about what to order.

"Are you here to see me, *ma belle*?" Olivier asked, kissing her on both cheeks.

Try as he might, every time Olivier saw Isabelle, he first saw her lying on the floor of their bistro. Bleeding. Dying. As shots exploded all around them.

Now, when she walked into the bistro, it felt like a resurrection.

"Of course, *mon beau*," she said, and whispered, "Getting to see you is the only reason I stay in the Sûreté."

He laughed, took her coat, and nodded to the corner. "You know where they are. What would you like?"

"A tisane and—"

He held up a hand. "I know. They're just out of the oven. You can probably smell them. You're like a bakery hound."

The bistro was quiet. It was between meals, and only a few tables were taken by parents and children having hot chocolate, something the parents would soon regret. The Sûreté officers had the place virtually to themselves.

Isabelle pulled up an armchair and waited until Olivier had brought her chamomile tea, with honey, and put a plate of fresh baked brownies on the table. Once he'd withdrawn, she placed copies of the photograph in front of each of them.

"This was found in the search of Debbie's home. Locked in her desk drawer."

There were Debbie and Abigail, young teenagers. Side by side. As though attached at the hip. On the other side of Abigail was her father. But the center of the photograph, the center of attention, was the little girl in her wheelchair.

This was the first time they'd seen Maria.

She was eight, maybe nine years old. Thin. Her arms bent and rigid, her hands and fingers twisted, as was her mouth. But there was no denying the pleasure, the gaiety, in her expression. In her bright brown eyes. Nor was there any mistaking the intelligence.

Whatever had caused her physical disabilities had clearly not affected her mind.

Here was a happy, inquisitive girl.

Armand moved his gaze over to Paul Robinson, whose expression was calm, his smile relaxed. A father enjoying a day out with the family.

One hand was resting on Maria's chair, and the other was on Abigail's shoulder.

Abigail's left hand was on Maria's shoulder in a sisterly, protective gesture.

Debbie was looking at Abigail, her hands holding Abigail's arm. Both girls were laughing. One of them had just said or done something funny.

It looked like any one of a hundred pictures each of them had of their own families. It was both heartwarming and disturbing, given what would soon happen.

"Is it dated?" Beauvoir asked.

"I don't know," said Isabelle. "I've asked the Nanaimo detective to see if anything's written on the back."

"You say this was locked in Debbie's desk?" said Gamache.

"*Oui.*"

The victim, Armand realized, had gone from "Madame Schneider," to "Debbie Schneider," and now "Debbie." It was a sort of watershed, as they got to know her better and better. A relationship had developed with the dead woman that was far more intimate than they'd ever have had with a live Debbie Schneider.

"What else was in the drawer?"

Isabelle brought out her phone and read from the inventory.

"Staples. Two ink cartridges for a printer. An agenda. A ruler. Some birthday cards and a box of paper clips."

"Birthday cards?" asked Beauvoir. "Why keep those locked away?"

"Why lock away any of it?" asked Isabelle.

"Were there other pictures of Maria in the house?" Gamache asked.

"No. Ones of Abigail, and of Debbie's family, but none of Maria."

Just then her phone beeped with a text. "It's from Nanaimo." After reading it, she said, "The birthday cards are from Debbie to Abigail."

"Unsent," said Gamache. "And the picture?"

"No date, but someone wrote, *The last one*. It doesn't seem to be in Debbie's handwriting, judging by the writing on the cards. He sent a photograph of one of the cards."

She showed it to them.

Dear Abby. Happy seventeenth. Love, Debbie.

A heart had been drawn over the *i* in "Debbie."

"Doesn't say much," said Jean-Guy.

"The handwriting doesn't match," agreed Gamache, comparing the card with the back of the photograph. "We must have examples of Abigail's writing somewhere."

Beauvoir found a sample and they compared. It didn't match her writing either.

"So who wrote, *The last one*?" asked Jean-Guy. "The father?"

"Must be." Isabelle clicked her phone off. "But why would he give that picture to Debbie? And why did she lock it away?"

All three looked down at the photograph of the happy family. The last one.

"I have a picture to show you," said Jean-Guy. He produced the one of Paul Robinson at the conference.

Isabelle studied it. "The conference ends the day Maria died." She looked up at her colleagues. "He doesn't look like he's about to—"

"No, he doesn't," said Gamache. "Now here's a question, Isabelle. If Paul Robinson didn't kill Maria—"

"Then who did?"

"Any theories?" Gamache asked.

"Hello, numbnuts."

Beauvoir almost jumped out of his skin. He'd been so deep in thought he hadn't seen Ruth coming, and had not crossed his legs.

She grinned at him before turning to Armand. "I was just at your home."

Ruth went to sit down, but a look from Armand stopped her.

"You'll have to show me how you do that," Jean-Guy muttered.

"I wanted to see Reine-Marie, but apparently she's returning the last box to the Horton family. Took the crazy lady with her."

"I don't think that's true," said Jean-Guy.

"If you see her, can you let her know I was asking for her? I wanted to talk to her before she spoke to Enid's kids."

"Why?" asked Armand. "Is there something she needs to know?"

"No. It's more a matter of not needing to know."

She turned and left. Through the window, Armand could see the elderly poet trudge slowly up the snowy road, her head down, bent forward. Rosa tucked protectively inside her coat.

She walked past her home and up to the white clapboard church on the side of the hill. St. Thomas's. Named after Doubting Thomas. The skeptic who needed proof before he'd believe in the miracle of the resurrection.

Armand returned his gaze to Jean-Guy and Isabelle. He was no skeptic. But then he had help. He saw proof of resurrection every day.

"Any thoughts?" he repeated to Isabelle.

"Okay. If Paul Robinson didn't kill Maria, that leaves two others. Abigail or Debbie. Is that what you're thinking?"

"Not thinking, exactly," said Beauvoir. "More like feeling."

He leaned forward. Isabelle assumed it was to take one of the still-warm brownies, but instead he picked up the picture she'd brought, and stared at it. Then at her.

"What do you think?" he asked.

"Honestly? I think it's taking us off base and away from the crime right in front of us. The murder of Debbie Schneider."

"You don't think the two are connected?" Beauvoir asked.

"I don't see how. They're decades apart. We don't even know for sure that Maria was murdered. There's one word in an autopsy report done by a coroner who's now dead."

Gamache was nodding, his lower lip thrust out in thought. "Fair enough. And you're probably right. But I think it's worth a few minutes of our time to try to work out how this child died. Don't you?"

He looked at her. The reproach mild, but clear.

"*Oui*," she said. Chastened, but unconvinced.

"If not the father, then my money's on Abigail," said Beauvoir. "Especially given that she's traveling the country arguing that anyone with severe disabilities is an unnecessary burden. She's trying to justify what she did. Making it legal, even moral, in retrospect."

"What're you thinking, *patron*?" asked Lacoste.

He was looking at the photograph. His eyes narrow in concentration.

"How did that picture get into Debbie's possession?"

"Maybe Paul Robinson made copies, so each of them could have one," said Isabelle.

"Maybe," said Gamache. "Then why hide it away? I'm not so sure it was Abigail who killed Maria. You can see the affection she has for her sister. In fact, this looks like three members of a close-knit family"—he hovered his finger over Abigail, Maria, and their father—"and one outlier. Someone who didn't quite belong."

His finger stopped, pointing directly at Debbie Schneider.

"What're you saying?" asked Isabelle. "That Debbie did it?"

"Why would she?" asked Jean-Guy.

"Jealousy maybe. Look at her hands. She's not just holding Abigail's arm, she's gripping it. As though trying to drag her away. Everyone else is looking at Maria, but Debbie is focused on Abigail."

"And then there are the birthday cards, also locked in the desk," said Jean-Guy. "That's pretty strange. Remember they said they'd drifted apart at one stage? Maybe it was more than a drift. Maybe Abigail also suspected and broke off the friendship. And it was during that time that Debbie wrote the cards, but didn't send them."

"But if Abigail did suspect that her friend killed her sister, would she ever reconcile?" asked Isabelle. "And why would Paul Robinson tell the coroner that he'd given Maria the peanut butter sandwich when it wasn't true? He sure wouldn't cover up for Debbie."

"No," agreed Gamache. "But he might for someone else."

Isabelle stopped. "Abigail? He thought Abigail had done it? So he took the blame."

Gamache inhaled deeply, then exhaled. "It's possible he came home, found Maria dead, and realized one of the two girls must have done it. Maybe he even suspected Debbie, but he couldn't take the chance."

"But the coroner must've known, or suspected. The police must've been called," said Isabelle.

"And found what?" said Gamache. "A severely disabled child who'd died and a distraught father explaining about a sandwich."

"But wouldn't they ask questions?" Beauvoir asked.

"Have you ever heard of the Shipman murders in England?" Gamache asked.

They shook their heads.

"Look it up. I was at a reunion in Cambridge when the arrest was finally made. He was a doctor convicted of killing fifteen of his patients."

"Fifteen?" said Jean-Guy. "Fifteen?"

"It gets worse. A subsequent inquiry found he almost certainly killed more than two hundred. All his patients."

They stared at him. From anyone else, they wouldn't have believed it.

"Didn't anyone suspect?" asked Isabelle.

"Yes, there was even an investigation. But he was a doctor, a respected member of the community, his explanations for the deaths were reasonable. The junior investigators assigned to the case didn't take the allegations seriously. And do you know why?"

"Because he was a doctor?" asked Isabelle.

"Partly that, but there was another reason. The vast majority of those who died were elderly." He let that sit there. "Close to death anyway, it was felt. It wasn't worth the effort to investigate. And before we get all high and mighty, let's remember what happened here not long ago in the pandemic. Let's remember what happens when a street worker, a gay or transsexual man or woman, a Black man or woman, an indigenous man or woman or child is killed. There's hardly a great outpouring of attention or resources. Or grief."

As he spoke, they could hear the outrage simmering just below the surface. Gamache, as head of homicide and, for a time, head of the entire Sûreté, had worked to change all that. But it was the work of a lifetime.

"So, you're saying when they saw a badly disabled child, and were given a story by a prominent member of the community, they chose to believe it?" asked Jean-Guy.

"It's possible," said Gamache. "Especially if they had sympathy for him and could see no benefit to digging deeper. Yes. I can see it happening."

"But Paul Robinson had his doubts," said Isabelle. "His suspicions. He was covering up for Abby, but he actually suspected Debbie, is that what you're thinking?"

"It's one way that picture got into Debbie's possession," said Beauvoir. "He might have sent it to her as a warning. An accusation."

"Could be," said Gamache. "But if so, why would she keep it? And for so long?"

They stared at each other. There seemed no answer and yet, obviously, there was one.

"And why would Debbie have killed Maria?" asked Isabelle, breaking the silence.

"Jealousy?" said Beauvoir. "Maria was taking up too much of Abigail's time and attention."

Isabelle could see that he might have a point. Fifteen-year-old girls weren't famous for having the best grasp on their emotions, and jealousy was an especially toxic one.

They turned to Gamache, whose eyes had narrowed. What he was thinking, what he was feeling, went against all his beliefs.

"I think it's possible Debbie did it out of love, not jealousy. Not hate."

"Love?" said Beauvoir. "Of Maria? To free her?"

"No. Love of Abigail. To free her."

Armand Gamache believed with all his soul that love could never, ever kill. Not real love. A counterfeit one, something that masqueraded as love, yes. But real love? Never.

Was he wrong? he asked himself. Could love murder? Could it put a pillow over a helpless child's face?

This was the second time in two days it had been justified as a motive.

Haniya Daoud had killed, in cold blood, apparently out of love. Out of a mother's driving need to protect and free her "children."

And now Debbie might have killed Maria, out of love. To free Abigail.

And Armand Gamache was forced to finally see something he didn't want to. That the only thing that could possibly drive him to murder wasn't hate.

It was love. For his family.

So why not Haniya?

Why not—he looked down at the photograph—Debbie? If she thought that Maria threatened Abigail's life. Not her physical life, but her intellectual, her emotional life.

Then he noticed something else. "What's the photograph sitting on?"

Isabelle bent closer. "Looks like the agenda that the inventory mentioned. It must be Debbie's."

"No. She had her agenda on her phone," said Beauvoir. "Why would she need another one? Especially a book. That's pretty old school."

He gave a sly glance at Gamache, who still used a handwritten agenda. He had reminders on his phone, but kept his daily appointments in a book.

Isabelle smiled, recalling the last time Beauvoir had teased the Chief about his ring-binder agenda. They'd been in a meeting at Sûreté headquarters, not long after the lockdown lifted but before the vaccine. They were sitting six feet apart and were masked.

"Less likely to be hacked," Gamache had said, laying a hand on the open book on his desk.

"Thank God," said Beauvoir. "Because your dentist appointment is of national interest."

"Maybe not the dentist, but the barber?" Gamache said. "What the Russians wouldn't do . . ."

"Your hair did look a little Soviet era, during the lockdown."

"Ohhh, Einstein," Isabelle had said to Jean-Guy. "Are you sure you want to bring up the subject of Covid hair?"

She herself had been shocked by the amount of gray that had come in. At thirty-three she felt she was still far too young. But a bullet in the head left more than a scar.

"Why would Debbie have two agendas?" said Gamache. "And why not bring it with her? Why leave it behind, locked in a drawer?"

"Are you saying she had a hidden agenda?" asked Isabelle, proud of the double entendre.

While the men groaned, she called Nanaimo with yet another request. After verbally prostrating herself, she hung up. Grimacing.

"He'll go back down to shipping and find the agenda. He says the box might've left already." She put her phone down on the table and focused on the Chief. "Even if Debbie did kill Maria, which can never be proven now, where does this lead us?"

"It leads us," said Jean-Guy, "to Debbie Schneider being the intended victim all along, and Abigail Robinson the murderer."

"How do you figure that?" asked Isabelle.

"Revenge. Abigail finally realized what Debbie had done."

Isabelle stared at him. "Really? Forty years later? And even if that's true, why murder her at a party? Abigail could hardly have chosen a worse place. I think we've gotten way off track. We need to go back to our first, most likely suspect, victim, and motive. Vincent Gilbert killed Debbie mistaking her for Abigail Robinson. He had any number of motives." She lifted a finger as she counted them off. "He despised her campaign. He realized she knew about his work with Ewen Cameron and was blackmailing him. He was making up for failures of the past. Any one of those would be enough."

Gamache was nodding, deep in thought, then he came to a decision. "The fact is, we don't know. So we follow all lines of inquiry. *D'accord?*"

"*D'accord,*" said Jean-Guy.

Gamache looked at Lacoste.

"*D'accord, patron.*"

"*Bon.*" He got up and they followed suit.

"Back to the Incident Room?" asked Jean-Guy.

"You go ahead," said Armand. "I have a stop to make first."

At the door, Jean-Guy suddenly turned around and returned to their table.

"The brownies?" Isabelle asked as they left the bistro. Her nose never lied.

They walked together as far as St. Thomas's.

While they climbed the hill, he climbed the steps and turned around. From there he could survey the village.

When he'd first visited Three Pines, he'd had the impression the four roads radiating off the village green formed a sort of sundial. Which had struck him as ironic. To have a huge timepiece in a place that was so clearly timeless. But soon he'd realized the roads were a compass. Each one corresponding exactly to north, south, east, and west.

With Three Pines in the center.

And again, the irony was not lost on him. A compass for a village not on any map. Only found by those who were lost. But then maybe it wasn't ironic.

He stood there and considered what might have led to the murder of Debbie Schneider. Could love really have been at the heart of it, the start of it?

If I have the gift of prophecy and can fathom all mysteries and all knowledge, he thought, *and if I have a faith that can move mountains, but have not love, I am nothing.*

Was he looking for someone who was nothing? A shell? Or was he looking for someone whose love was so great it had moved them to murder. Could love really do that?

"Close the fucking door" came the shout from the body of the chapel, followed by a muttered "Fuck, fuck, fuck."

Armand was pretty sure it wasn't the voice of God. At least he hoped not. Though he suspected God might want to, at times, scream at them.

He did as he was told.

Ruth was in her usual pew, bathed in the bright reds, blues, and greens of the three stained-glass boys. Brothers. Marching forever into a battle from which they would never return.

Armand crossed himself, by habit, even though this was not a Catholic church. And he no longer considered himself Catholic. Or Protestant. Or Jewish. Or Muslim.

He was, in the words of Abu Ben Adhem, *one who loves his fellow man*. Though the duck, he had to admit, took some effort.

"Sit in the last pew," Ruth said, at least her tenth command of the day. "The one to the left of the door."

Again, Chief Inspector Gamache did as he was told. It took him a few minutes, but he finally found out why he was there. A small figure was etched into the wood on the back of the pew, hidden by a Book of Common Prayer.

He got up and joined Ruth.

"What do you know about the monkeys?"

Ruth's face was in profile as she stared ahead. And stroked Rosa.

"I know they weren't drawn by a crazy woman. Enid came here most afternoons. So did I. She was here when I arrived, and here when I left. We never spoke, barely acknowledged each other. Not because we didn't like each other, but we'd both come here for peace. One day I heard scratching. Now, as you know, it's not in my nature to be critical, but I just thought I'd point out that this is God's damned house and she should fucking stop desecrating it."

"Amen," said Armand, and saw her smile.

"If you can believe it," said Ruth, turning to him, "she took offense, and left. So I looked at what she'd done."

"The monkey."

"No, the stained-glass window. Of course the monkey, Clouseau. When I saw her next, I asked her what that was about."

"And?"

"And it took her seven years to tell me. We sat in silence all that time. Every day. She in her pew, me in mine. She didn't draw any more monkeys, but she seemed to get some sort of comfort from that one. Then one day she just blurted it out."

"What did she say?"

"That she'd been a patient of Ewen Cameron." Ruth studied him. "I already told you that."

"But you didn't tell me about the monkeys."

"No. Reine-Marie found something in those boxes, didn't she. I thought she might."

He nodded but didn't tell her about the letter from Vincent Gilbert.

"Ruth," he asked softly. "What do you know about Ewen Cameron?"

She took a deep breath. But didn't break eye contact. They could have been there for ten seconds or ten minutes, or a lifetime, before she spoke.

"My mother took me to him. To fix me. She thought that I was broken." She tried to smile but could not. "She wanted to leave me there, but he didn't have any beds. By the time one had freed up, I'd changed."

"Changed?"

"I'd learned what she wanted me to be. I learned to pretend. So I wouldn't be sent to that place. I learned what it would take for my mother to love me. But—" Ruth raised her hands, then dropped them back. One to her lap, the other to rest gently, protectively, on Rosa. "That was a long time ago."

"*My mother isn't finished with me yet,*" he said and saw her smile. Just a little.

"Probably true."

Armand glanced at the demon duck and knew that, if and when the time came and Rosa was in distress, Ruth would do what was necessary. So great was her love.

"Enid wasn't so lucky," Ruth continued. "She was a young mother and was having trouble sleeping. She'd begun having anxiety attacks. So she went to Cameron for help. She came home . . ." Ruth looked around. "She found peace here. At least for a little while each day."

"And the monkeys? Did she ever explain them?"

"She said when she was in the Allan she could hear them. She knew she wasn't alone. It was comforting."

"And she never told anyone?" he asked.

"Not as far as I know. Just me. When she died and her house was sold, I was worried that her kids would find something among her things. And it would be upsetting."

"That's why you suggested that Reine-Marie help to sort through things. So if there was anything to find, she'd get there first."

"Yes. Imagine finding out that your mother had been tortured. If Enid had wanted them to know, she'd have told them herself. Explained. Answered their questions. But now . . ."

Now, thought Armand, there were no answers. How do you explain a Ewen Cameron? A Harold Shipman? How do you explain what happened to Haniya Daoud? How do you begin to explain brown brown?

Not just that it could happen, but that so many could know about it and do nothing.

What are you doing out there, Ralph?

"Why did you want to speak to Reine-Marie?"

"I wanted to say that the truth doesn't set everyone free. For some it becomes a burden. A stinking albatross. I wanted to ask Reine-Marie if it was necessary to tell them."

Armand stood up and, reaching into his parka pocket, he brought out a linen napkin.

"From Jean-Guy."

Then he bent down and kissed her cheek.

Reine-Marie looked down at the box. Full of things collected over a lifetime. Including one small slip of paper. On Allan Memorial letterhead. Explaining everything.

She opened her mouth, but before she could speak, Haniya said, "Can I ask you a question?"

When Susan and James nodded, she said, "Was she a good mother?"

The question took them by surprise. Susan said, "Of course." But it took James longer to answer.

"Yes. She could be impatient, sometimes a little unpredictable. But she was great."

"Did you know that you were loved?"

"Why are you asking this?" asked James. "Why're you even here?"

"I—"

"I asked her along," said Reine-Marie.

"Why?" said Susan. "Is there a problem?"

Reine-Marie started to answer, but Haniya gave her a shove and she almost fell off the packing box.

"I remember my mother," said Haniya. "But not well. I remember her trying to protect me when the soldiers came. I was eight. I tried to find her years later, but the village was gone."

She paused then and thought of the other village. The one covered in snow, in the valley. Frozen, it seemed, in time.

"I think she was killed," Haniya whispered. She spoke directly to Enid Horton's children. "Protecting me. I imagine your mother protected you too. In her way."

"She tried, yes," said James. He turned to his sister. "Remember when the smoke alarm would go off?"

Susan laughed. "She wasn't a very good cook and it went off at least once a week. She'd come running into the living room where I was watching TV and shove me outside."

James laughed. "I remember."

"'Get out! Get out!'" they both screamed, clearly imitating a hysterical woman.

"She went back in." Susan looked at her brother. "I hadn't thought about that, until now. She thought the house was on fire, but she went back in. For you."

James looked stricken. "That's true. We thought it was funny. We teased her about that relentlessly."

"She loved you," said Haniya.

"But the monkeys?" asked Susan.

They looked at Reine-Marie. Who knew the answer. Knew their mother had been tortured. Had been kept awake for days on end, listening to the shrieks of monkeys. Maybe even seen the panic in their wide, knowing eyes.

Now was the time to tell her children.

"Your mother loved you. That's what's in the box," she said.

She laid a hand on the top of the container, as though to say goodbye. Then, reaching out, she helped Haniya up.

CHAPTER 40

"Still no word from your friend in Nanaimo?" asked Gamache, as he took off his tuque and, shoving it and his gloves into the arm of his parka, he hung them up.

"No," said Isabelle. "I'm afraid the evidence from the desk might've already shipped. I'll call him back in a couple of minutes. Unless you'd like to?"

He laughed as he tried to smooth his hair. "I wouldn't deny you the pleasure. Any news?"

"None," said Jean-Guy, then went back to making phone calls.

Isabelle sat forward and said to the Chief, "I've been thinking about what you said in the bistro. About the possibility it was Debbie who killed Maria, then Abigail killed Debbie."

"*Oui?*"

"I think, *patron*, that you're off base."

"How so?" He sat down and swiveled his chair to face her.

"I think you and Jean-Guy are fathers and you don't want it to be Paul Robinson who smothered his daughter."

Gamache paused, absorbing what she said before speaking, quietly, reasonably. "I've arrested fathers for the murder of their children before, Isabelle."

"Yes, but this one's different. This has Abigail Robinson in the mix. And a disabled child. You asked me what I think, and I'm telling you. I think both you and Jean-Guy want Abigail to be guilty of the murder of Debbie."

"Are you saying you think that I'm ignoring, even twisting evidence, in order to build a case against Abigail Robinson? Because I don't like her or her views?"

Put so starkly, Lacoste didn't quite know what to say. But the fact was, that was exactly what she thought. That they'd pivoted away from the obvious suspect, Vincent Gilbert, and the obvious motive, in favor of the least likely.

It would be so much better all around if Abigail Robinson was arrested and convicted of the crime.

"Not intentionally," she began.

He lowered his head and glowered at her. "By mistake?"

Now she was confused. Clearly, the Chief Inspector, the head of homicide, the man who'd recently headed the entire Sûreté du Québec, did not do things by mistake. He might make mistakes, but his actions, his decisions, were well thought out.

"I think," she began, gathering her thoughts, "I think you're going after Abigail Robinson on purpose. Not because you really believe her to be guilty, but because you want her to be guilty."

Armand Gamache couldn't believe what he was hearing. He stared at her, speechless.

Isabelle Lacoste had, in the past, disagreed with him. They'd sometimes argued over evidence, or suspects, over an arrest even.

And yes, he could be wrong, and had been wrong in the past. But neither Lacoste nor anyone else had ever questioned his motives. Until now.

"You think I'm railroading Abigail Robinson out of prejudice? My own personal agenda?"

"No, I'm just—"

"You think I'd turn my back on solid evidence and arrest someone for a murder I knew, I knew, they didn't commit?"

His voice instead of rising had dropped to a whisper so that she had to lean closer.

"Because it sounds like that's what you're accusing me of. It's one thing to disagree with a line of inquiry, Isabelle. It's another to accuse me of wanting to arrest someone I knew to be innocent."

Her cheeks were burning so hot Isabelle wondered if she might melt. She also wondered if she'd crossed a line that could never be uncrossed. If she'd gone far too far.

And now she faced a choice. To scramble back and beg forgiveness. Plead a sugar high from the four brownies she'd eaten.

Or . . .

"No one has more respect for you than I do, *patron*. I don't think I need to prove that. We've been through too much together. But you're human. Jean-Guy is human. Lots of what we do is science, but a lot is driven by intuition. By emotion. You say so yourself. And you're no different than the rest of us."

She watched him as he watched her. His eyes astute. And hurt.

"You have a granddaughter you adore and whose future concerns you. You see Abigail Robinson threatening that future. And . . ." She hated to do this, but felt she had to. "And I saw some of the footage you took inside that nursing home."

"What's that got to do with it?"

She had a lump in her throat now. Remembering those images.

That experience in the pandemic would become part of their DNA. His DNA. Part of every perception, every sight, every sound, every meal, every celebration. Every moment.

Every decision. For the rest of his life. Including this one. Couldn't help but.

"You beat yourself up for not being there earlier. I know you do. And now I think you'd do just about anything to make up for it. I think you see Abigail Robinson threatening tens of thousands of people, including, maybe, Idola. And, like Dr. Gilbert, you want to stop her. You can't kill her, but you can imprison her."

Armand could feel his rage trying to claw its way out. Becoming outrage.

From an adversary, and he had plenty, this charge would be insulting enough, but from a trusted ally? A colleague he'd brought not only into the department, but into his life. His home. His family.

He stared at her, speechless. No, not speechless. Afraid to say anything, for fear of what he might say.

And to her credit, though he wasn't yet willing to give her any,

Isabelle Lacoste did not back away. She sat still, in the full force of his glare. And waited.

"*Merci*," he finally said.

"*Patron*," she began, sensing that something precious had just torn. "I—"

"Thank you," he said, turning away.

She'd been dismissed.

But . . .

But her words had not been. As he stared at his screen, he knew that what he was really feeling wasn't anger, it was fear.

He was afraid that what she said was true. That he wanted to stop Abigail Robinson and the only weapon he could use was his office. As head of homicide.

He could arrest her for murder. Whether she committed that actual crime or not would be immaterial. She was in the process of planning hundreds, thousands, of murders. And he wouldn't let her.

He would act. He would protect Idola. He would protect Stephen and Ruth. He would protect those unborn, and those born long ago.

Was that really it? Was Isabelle right? Was he trying to make up for his earlier failure, in the pandemic, to protect the most vulnerable?

Gamache stared straight ahead, straight at the thing uncurling before him. Was it the truth? Or was it residual guilt?

And then his eyes focused, and he realized that what he was really staring at was the photo Jean-Guy had found from the conference just days, maybe hours, before Maria had died. He was staring into the eyes of Paul Robinson. And then his gaze shifted and he leaned closer to the screen, narrowing his eyes and zooming in.

Beauvoir interrupted his thoughts. "*Patron?*"

"Yes, what is it?" Gamache looked up.

Jean-Guy had pulled up a chair. "Let's say Abigail did kill Debbie in revenge for the death of her sister, why did it take so long? Maria died years ago."

Chief Inspector Gamache looked from Beauvoir to Lacoste. Here was his chance. To change course. All he had to do was tell Beauvoir to drop that line of inquiry. That the death of Maria was sad but not pertinent. They were going to focus on the most likely suspect in the murder of Debbie Schneider. Vincent Gilbert.

Beauvoir waited. Lacoste looked up.

Except . . .

"I think Ruth gave me the answer to that."

Jean-Guy turned to Isabelle. "This should be good."

Gamache pushed away from his desk, away from Paul Robinson's stare. He'd been slow to see it, and only now did it all come together.

"She and I were talking about Reine-Marie's work, going through Madame Horton's possessions, and the fact that when someone dies it falls to family to sort through their things."

"Right," said Jean-Guy. "All the crap in closets and drawers."

"Attics and basements," said Isabelle.

"Exactly. There are hundreds of decisions to be made. Often painful ones, deciding what to keep and what to get rid of. Items become charged with emotion, with memories. So relatives often just pack the stuff up and put it away. That's what happened when Paul Robinson died. Abigail was young, in shock. She packed up his things and put them in the attic, and didn't think of them again until her home was sold."

"Six weeks ago," said Jean-Guy. "That's when she found the letter from Ewen Cameron demanding payment for the treatment."

"That's when she realized what had happened to her mother," agreed Gamache. "And that Gilbert had been part of it. But suppose she also found that photograph."

He nodded to the one on his desk. The one of the four people at the seashore.

"But if Abigail found the picture, why did Debbie have it?" asked Isabelle. "And why would she lock it in her desk?"

"There must be something incriminating in it," said Jean-Guy. "Something that proves Debbie killed Maria."

They stared down at the photograph. But it still just looked like a happy family, and a friend.

"If there is something there that we can't see, but they can, why would Abigail give it to Debbie? And why choose the New Year's Eve party to kill her?"

"Something must've provoked it," said Jean-Guy.

"'Abby Maria.'"

They looked at Gamache. "I'm sorry," said Jean-Guy. "What?"

"Debbie kept repeating it, then had to apologize since it so clearly upset Abigail. But why the anger? Why the apology? She said it again at the party, this time in front of the worst possible person. Vincent Gilbert. That was just before she was killed."

"But Abigail already explained that," said Isabelle. "She didn't want anyone to know about Maria. She thought it would undermine her arguments."

"That was a lie. Maria wasn't a secret. Lots of people knew about her. No, there's another reason it upset, angered, Abigail."

"You think Debbie killed Maria," said Beauvoir. "And every time she used that pet name it felt to Abigail like she'd been stabbed."

"I think it's possible. Something provoked the attack that night."

"What provoked it was Abigail threatening Vincent Gilbert," said Isabelle. "And he killed her, or rather, he killed Debbie by mistake. It had nothing to do with Maria or her death."

"Okay," said Beauvoir, "but maybe it does. Suppose Abigail has her suspicions of Debbie but nothing concrete. All this talk of Abby Maria pushes her past the breaking point. She needs to have it out with Debbie."

Since Isabelle wasn't encouraging, he turned to Gamache, who was listening closely.

Beauvoir leaned forward. "Abigail goes outside, and when the Chancellor leaves, she catches up with Debbie and confronts her. Demands the truth about Maria. And Debbie admits it. Probably knew it was coming. Ever since Abigail gave her the picture."

As Jean-Guy spoke, Armand found himself standing in the snow, just off the path. In the dark. In the woods. Watching the two women, while Roman candles burst overhead and children stood around the bonfire, trying to write their names in sparkles.

He watched as Abigail Robinson demanded the truth and Debbie

Schneider admitted her crime. She might have even been relieved to finally tell Abby.

Would she show remorse? Beg forgiveness?

Or maybe she did neither.

"If Debbie really did kill Maria," said Gamache, "I think it's possible that she believed she'd done Abigail a favor. Freed her to go to Oxford to pursue her dreams. Maybe she even convinced herself she'd done Maria a favor. But she misjudged. Abigail loved her sister. You only have to look at the photograph to see it." He picked it up and looked at it again. "I think that's why it was locked away. Not because Debbie felt guilty and couldn't look at Maria, but because she didn't want to see the love there."

"Now we just have to prove it," said Beauvoir.

"Not quite so fast," said Gamache. "There's a problem."

Not just one, thought Lacoste, but managed to restrain herself.

"I've cross-country skied down that trail," said Gamache. "There aren't any handy pieces of wood lying around."

"It's a woods, *patron*," said Beauvoir. "There're trees everywhere. Trees are made of wood."

"*Merci*, Jean-Guy. But Debbie wasn't hit with a tree. Or even a branch. And any that had fallen would've been covered with snow. No, according to the coroner, Debbie was hit with a fireplace log, cut at a certain angle."

Gamache created the wedge with his hands.

"Where did Abigail get the log?" asked Isabelle.

"Exactly."

Beauvoir thought for a moment. "There's a stack by the fireplace in the living room, and there was a pile by the bonfire. The problem is, both are pretty public. I think someone would notice if Abigail Robinson picked up a log and walked away with it."

"There is another place," said Isabelle. "The library has a fire. And it's private."

"That would mean the killer took the weapon with them," said Jean-Guy. "And that would make it premeditated. You don't just stroll around with a log."

"Well, not very pre-," said Gamache. "But yes, it wasn't the sudden lashing out we'd assumed. The killer approached Debbie prepared, if not actually committed to killing her." He turned to Isabelle. "There was someone alone in the library at that time."

Lacoste threw her mind back over the interviews they'd done. "Vincent Gilbert."

"Yes," said Gamache. "He said he'd gone in there for some peace and quiet."

"Gilbert might've seen who he thought was Abigail out the library doors," said Isabelle. "And saw his chance. He picked up the log, followed her into the woods, and killed her. Only it was Debbie Schneider. Are you saying you now believe it was Vincent Gilbert?"

"I'm saying what I've said all along. We need to look at everyone. Which brings me to something I wanted to show you two."

He woke up his laptop and Paul Robinson again popped onto the screen. He was in a suit and bow tie, standing proudly, almost comically, in front of a poster of his work. An exaggerated look of delight, like a showman at a carnival.

"We've seen that, *patron*," said Isabelle. "It was taken the week Maria died."

"Yes, but did you notice what he's standing in front of?" Gamache zoomed in tighter.

Lacoste and Beauvoir leaned closer.

On the poster was a series of graphs showing comparisons of statistical studies.

Isabelle stood up and turned to the Chief. "Is this a joke?"

The top graph showed that there was a direct correlation between the per capita consumption of mozzarella and civil engineering doctorates awarded.

"I'm not the one joking, if that's what you mean," said Gamache.

The next graph showed a correlation between people who drowned after falling out of a fishing boat and the marriage rate in Kentucky.

Lacoste and Beauvoir looked at each other.

"But this's ridiculous," said Beauvoir. "It doesn't make sense."

"Exactly," said Gamache. "They're spurious correlations, you can just make out the title of the poster. And I'm willing to bet Paul Robinson had a coauthor. The person taking the photograph. I think it's Colette Roberge."

"The Chancellor?" asked Lacoste.

"Yes. Chancellor Roberge mentioned the phrase 'spurious correlations' several times."

"Including last night," said Beauvoir.

"She also said they'd collaborated on several studies," said Gamache.

"Could that really be called a study?" asked Isabelle. "It's more like a joke. How could this be important?"

"If she was the coauthor, it means she was with Paul Robinson around the time his daughter died. She might have even been there."

"Are you saying you think the Chancellor killed Maria?" asked Jean-Guy.

"They spent time coming up with jokes," said Isabelle. "That shows a closeness. Even, maybe, an intimacy."

Beauvoir was tapping away on his laptop and now turned it around for them to see. "There's a website called Spurious Correlations. It's by some guy named Tyler Vigen."

Gamache got up to look closer but stopped. The name meant something. Something. And then he gave one small laugh.

"What is it?" asked Isabelle.

"Tyler Vigen. It's the name Chancellor Roberge used on the request form when reserving the gym for the event. Is he a real person, or an alias Colette and Paul Robinson used?"

They huddled around the site.

"Looks like a real person," said Beauvoir. "At the bottom he credits two professors, Paul Robinson and Colette Roberge, with giving him the idea."

"I think in repeating the phrase Colette was trying to guide me to this," said Gamache. "If not the site, then the concept."

"What concept?" asked Isabelle.

"That Abigail Robinson's conclusions were no more legitimate than the connection between"—he bent down and read off Beauvoir's screen—"per capita cheese consumption and people who died after being caught up in their bedsheets."

"Really?" Beauvoir leaned closer. He himself often woke up in the night, entangled. And he liked cheese.

Gamache now wondered if the Chancellor had also been trying to warn him about making connections that did not exist. It was, of course, the bane of any investigator. To misinterpret, to overinterpret.

Was he connecting two things that were not related? The death of Maria Robinson and the murder of Debbie Schneider forty years later. Was he making a spurious correlation?

He didn't know. What he did know was that yet another thread led back to the Chancellor.

"We need a search warrant," he said as he moved to the door. "For Colette Roberge's home."

It was time to give that thread a tug.

CHAPTER 41

⌒

"Colette?" said her husband. "Who are these people? Why're they searching our home?"

He stood in the kitchen, a seventy-six-year-old man, bewildered.

Armand, who hadn't spoken to Monsieur Roberge in a few years, and had only seen him from a distance in his recent visits, looked from him to Colette. It was clear that Jean-Paul Roberge, who'd risen to the top of a large Montréal accounting firm, was now living with dementia.

"I didn't know," Armand said to Colette.

"Would it have changed anything if you had?" she asked.

"It might have."

While Inspector Beauvoir led the search, Armand went for a walk outside with Jean-Paul and Colette, getting the older man away from the activity that was so clearly agitating him. Armand was on one side of Monsieur Roberge, taking his hand, while Colette took the other. Holding him steady and upright in case of ice underfoot.

Armand listened as Jean-Paul told him about his recent visit with his mother. And his plans to take Colette to Prague for their honeymoon.

Jean-Paul stopped and turned bright blue eyes on Armand. "Are you my brother?"

"No, sir. I'm a friend."

"Are you? Really?" asked Monsieur Roberge.

Standing beside her husband, Colette stared at Armand, clearly asking the same thing.

"I hope so," he said. He could see Beauvoir at the door, his hand up to get his attention. "Perhaps we should go inside."

"Yes," said Jean-Paul. "We should pack."

"Good idea," said his wife. "I've put the suitcases on the bed. Maybe you can start."

When they got inside, Armand gestured to Beauvoir to wait a moment while he walked with Monsieur Roberge to their bedroom. He was surprised to see that suitcases really were on the bed.

"It gives him something to do," Colette explained, as they watched Jean-Paul take socks out of a chest of drawers and carefully place them in one of the cases. "When he goes to bed, I unpack."

"I'm sorry," said Armand.

"Don't be. He's not doing any harm and it makes him feel useful." She watched her husband for a moment. "We're the lucky ones."

Armand followed her back down the hall and into the living room, where Beauvoir was waiting.

"We found this." He handed Armand a book.

Extraordinary Popular Delusions and the Madness of Crowds.

"Yes, I've seen it," said Armand, a bit perplexed.

"But have you seen this, *patron*?"

Beauvoir opened it to the title page. "*For Colette, with love and eternal gratitude, Paul.*"

He looked at Colette. "Paul?"

"My husband, Jean-Paul."

"My name is Jean-Guy. No one calls me Guy."

"And I've never heard you call your husband Paul," said Armand. "Even now, it was Jean-Paul."

"It was a joke between us," she said. "Long ago. May I?" She reached out and Beauvoir gave her the book.

Armand gestured toward a seating area by the window. There was activity all around them as Sûreté officers went through the home.

"Who's Paul, Colette?"

"I've already told you."

"We can do a handwriting analysis you know."

She considered for a moment, looking at the book, closed on her lap. "Paul Robinson. As I think you guessed."

"So why lie?"

"Because I can see what you're thinking. He and I were close, but not that close."

"He signed the book, *With love*."

"Don't you love your friends?"

"Why was he eternally grateful? What had you done?"

"I looked out for Abigail at Oxford. He appreciated that."

"Eternally?"

When she didn't reply, Armand nodded toward Jean-Guy, who showed her the picture on his phone.

She smiled. "I haven't seen that for years. Look at him. So happy. He always wore a bow tie, you know. A *noeud papillon*." She stared at the photograph, mesmerized. "That was taken at the conference in Victoria. His last happy day, last happy few hours."

The last one, thought Armand. "Before?"

"Before going home and giving Maria a sandwich for dinner. She choked to death on it. But you knew that too. You're not thinking . . ."

"What?"

She cocked her head to one side and studied him. "Why're you interested in Paul? In that picture?" She paused. "You're not thinking that there was more to it? You think Paul did it deliberately?" When both Gamache and Beauvoir continued to watch her, she gave a bark of laughter. "You think I did it?"

"Did you take that picture?" Beauvoir asked.

"I did. Paul and I worked on the poster together. We had a lot of fun doing it."

"You know what I see when I look at this photograph?" said Armand. "I see a happy, relaxed man looking at a woman he loves. Who loves him. I see an amusing, even silly, poster made for a serious scientific conference. About spurious correlations. A phrase you've repeated several times. Why did you do that?"

"I wanted you to know that statistics can be manipulated, misinterpreted. They can be made to say anything."

"I already knew that," said Armand. "I think most people do, don't you? I think you wanted us to find this." He nodded toward the phone and the photo.

"Why would I do that?"

"To muddy the waters," said Armand. "To confuse us—"

"You don't seem to need my help for that."

"—to make us question, doubt, the connections we were making. Between the death of Maria Robinson and the murder of Debbie Schneider. Between Abby and Maria."

"The connection," Beauvoir said, "between you and Paul Robinson."

"There was a connection," Colette said. "A very deep one. But there was no affair. He was older, a mentor. Like with Vincent, there was a powerful intellectual attraction, but that's all. And yes, I loved him. And he loved me. But—"

"Colette?" called Jean-Paul Roberge from somewhere in the house.

She jumped to her feet, the book almost falling to the floor. She put it on the table, then took a step toward the voice, before turning to them. Both men were also on their feet.

"But he"—she looked behind her—"is my soul mate. The only man I've ever wanted to be with. And still do."

They watched her go, but only after Armand asked her to leave the book.

"Keep looking, Jean-Guy."

"You don't believe her, *patron?*"

"I think she's telling the truth when she says there was no affair, but I think there's a lot she isn't saying. Like what she did that made Paul Robinson eternally grateful. Notice the date above the inscription."

"A day before he died," said Jean-Guy.

Isabelle Lacoste asked the young man at the reception desk if he'd seen Professor Robinson.

"I think I saw her go into the living room."

Lacoste looked in there. A few guests, including Vincent Gilbert, were relaxing. Most reading. They looked up at her, then away. Not wanting to catch the cop's eye.

Only Dr. Gilbert continued to stare. Interested but not worried. But then he wouldn't be, she thought as she left the room. He thinks he's smarter than everyone else.

She got a few steps away, stopped, turned, and returned to the living room.

"May I join you?" she asked.

He half rose, in a halfhearted invitation. "Please."

"Dr. Gilbert, can I confide in you?"

He closed the magazine and set it aside. "Of course."

"Chief Inspector Gamache has asked me to interview Professor Robinson again because, well, we have our suspicions."

Gilbert raised his bushy gray brows. "Like?"

"I think you can guess," she said, lowering her voice and looking at the other guests, too far away to hear.

"You think she killed her friend?" he also whispered.

"I'd rather not say, but before I speak with her yet again, I'm wondering if you know anything that could be helpful?"

"Like?"

"Like anything about her father, for instance."

Now the brows drew together. "Her father? Don't you mean her mother? And Cameron?"

"No, we already know about that. I mean her father and her sister."

"She had a sister?"

Lacoste smiled tightly, "Yes. Badly disabled. She died under strange circumstances."

"Poor one," he said, by rote.

"And then the father, it seems, might have taken his own life."

"Really? A tragic family."

"Yes. It all seems to go back to the mother being in treatment with Cameron and her own suicide."

"That seems a bit of a leap."

"A spurious correlation?"

He studied her. "Yes, I suppose so. Why're you telling me this?"

"I just wondered if Abigail said anything to you," said Lacoste. "Accused you of being responsible for the deaths of her sister and father, as well as her mother."

Now he glared at her. "She did not. Are you?"

"Blaming you, sir? No, of course not. You can't be held responsible for what someone does decades later and thousands of kilometers away. And all you really did at the Allan Memorial was look after the monkeys, is that right?"

"All the animals, yes. I was never involved in the actual experiments."

"But you knew what was happening."

"What's this got to do with your suspicions about Professor Robinson and the death of her friend?"

She got up. "You've been very helpful, sir. *Merci*."

Isabelle Lacoste left Vincent Gilbert looking far less smug than when she'd arrived.

Jean-Guy Beauvoir found it an hour later. Not in the basement of the Roberge home. Not in the boxes in the attic.

It was in plain sight and, as a result, completely overlooked.

When he realized what it was, he placed it in a plastic cover and took it to Gamache, who was in the process of opening and shaking out the thousands of books in the Roberges' collection.

It was something he'd learned early on in his career with the Sûreté. Not from his first Chief and mentor. He'd learned it from his fiancée, Reine-Marie Cloutier.

The trainee librarian had told him that people put all sorts of things between the leaves of books. Stashes of money. Dried and pressed flowers. Letters.

Some they want to keep. Some they want to hide.

"Where did you find it?" Armand asked, taking the letter in the plastic sleeve and putting on his reading glasses.

"In this." Jean-Guy held up the book. "*Extraordinary Popular Delusions—*"

"*—and the Madness of Crowds*," said Armand, grinning and shaking his head. He looked around at all the volumes he'd just spent an hour shaking out. Having ignored the most obvious one.

"It was at the beginning of a section on 'The Drummer of Tedworth.' About a ghost."

Jean-Guy looked anything but pleased about the find, and as Armand read it, over by the window in the natural light, he knew why.

When he'd finished, he slowly removed his glasses, heaved a sigh, and turned to Jean-Guy.

"Where is she?"

"In the kitchen with her husband."

They found the Roberges having a cup of tea, heads bowed over a jigsaw puzzle. It was, Armand saw, the one he'd assumed was for the children.

The image was a basket of puppies.

"Can we have a word, please?" he asked, and held the document in such a way that the Chancellor would see it.

She pressed her lips together, paused, then got up. Kissing her husband on the top of his head as he bent over the puzzle, engrossed, she said, "I'll just be over by the woodstove."

He didn't answer.

Once they sat down, Armand handed her the letter in the plastic cover.

"So you found it."

"Inspector Beauvoir did."

She looked at him, and for some reason Jean-Guy felt he'd done something wrong.

"Evidence, Armand?" She sounded almost amused as she noted the tag.

"Would you like a lawyer?"

Now she did laugh. One humorless grunt. "No need."

"Tell us about the letter."

"Isn't it self-explanatory?"

"Please, Colette."

She looked at it, then carefully placed it on her lap and folded her hands over it.

"I haven't seen this in years. Not since he died. Well, that's not completely true." She looked directly into Armand's eyes. "I got this in Oxford, along with the book. It arrived the day after Paul died. The mail was much faster then, but not fast enough. Have you read it?"

Armand nodded, as did Jean-Guy.

"Then you know what it says. Paul admits to killing Maria. Smothering her with a pillow while Abigail and Debbie were out riding their bikes. Then he put a peanut butter sandwich down her th—" She stopped and took a series of short breaths, but seemed unable to catch it. She dropped her eyes, then slowly, deliberately, with trembling hands she moved the letter off her lap, to the sofa. Banished.

With what seemed a supreme effort, she raised her eyes. "He loved that child. Can you imagine?"

She managed to take a deep breath, while across from her the two men tried not to imagine.

Tried to remain police officers, while the father in them fought to get out.

It was a losing battle. The father would always win. And both were swept away by the thought, the very idea, of doing what Paul Robinson had done that day. Putting a pillow over their child's face. But perhaps especially, grotesquely, the sandwich.

It was what they'd suspected happened, since seeing the word "petechiae" in the autopsy. That the sandwich was postmortem.

That Maria's death wasn't some terrible accident.

Gamache had toyed with the idea that either Abigail, or more likely Debbie, had done it. But the letter made it clear. Maria's own father, driven by desperation, had killed her.

To read it in his own handwriting, stated so simply without embellishment, made it all the more horrific.

Colette removed her glasses and wiped her eyes, then startled slightly when a hand landed unexpectedly on her shoulder.

"It's all right. I'm here," said Jean-Paul. He turned mild eyes on their visitors. "Have you upset her?"

Colette put her hand on top of his. "No. They're friends. Here to help."

"With the packing?"

She smiled at him. "Never. That's your job. No one does it better. Please, come sit."

"Are you sure?" asked Armand.

"Jean-Paul knows it all, don't you?"

"Yes."

His eyes were kindly, but blank.

"You said the letter reached you the day after Paul Robinson died?" said Beauvoir.

"Yes. It came with the book. I knew what it was after the first line. It was so clearly a suicide note, admitting that he killed Maria and couldn't live with himself any longer. As he says, he'd known the moment it happened that he'd have to take his own life, but he also knew he'd have to wait until Abigail was grown and out of the house. He sent her to me at Oxford, and asked that I look after her."

"Which you did," said Armand. "And earned his eternal gratitude."

"*Oui*," she said quietly. "Jean-Paul and I had rented a cottage in nearby Lower Slaughter. Abby came every weekend and stayed until after Sunday roast. She'd often bring a friend. Abby was a bright, happy young woman. Ambitious, but most at that level are. And then this"—she glanced at the letter—"happened."

"What did you do when you read it?" Armand asked.

"I called him. I thought maybe . . . But it was already done. A neighbor answered and told me Paul was gone. It looked like a stroke or heart attack, but of course, I knew."

"And didn't say anything."

"No, why would I? If he'd wanted people to know, he'd have left a note there, but he didn't."

"But he did send one to you. Why was that?"

"I've wondered myself. The closest I can come is that he felt the need to confess. To tell someone who loved him, and might even understand, what had happened."

"But," said Armand, leaning forward, "he also says at the end that you should let Abigail read the letter."

"Yes."

"Why? Why would he want her to know what he'd done to her sister? Surely that's something he might, at a stretch, want you to know, but not his other daughter."

His eyes were imploring her to explain it to him.

Colette smiled a little, a sort of grin. "You didn't know Paul." She looked at her husband, who was pulling tissues from the Kleenex box and folding them methodically.

"He was a scientist. Meticulous in his research, in his notes, his files. Always neat and clear. He was dedicated to the truth. I think he wanted someone to know."

"Someone, yes," said Armand. "But Abigail?"

"She's cut from the same cloth. You can see that, in her insistence that her findings get a proper airing, no matter how foul. I think he knew she'd want the truth. It's possible he thought she already suspected, and wanted to end her speculation, so she wouldn't spend the rest of her life wondering."

Armand sat back and considered. It wasn't what he'd want. To burden, to hobble one of his children with such a truth. Some things really did not have to be said.

But then Colette was right. He didn't know Paul Robinson. He'd learned long ago the folly of expecting others to behave, to feel, to think and make the same choices as he would.

"And did you?" Beauvoir asked.

"What?"

"Did you tell Abigail about the letter?"

"She did more than that," said Jean-Paul Roberge, his voice strong, his eyes clear. "She showed it to her. She was very upset."

"Abigail would be," said Beauvoir.

"Not Abigail. The other one."

"*Bonjour*," said Isabelle. "Do you mind if I join you?"

She'd found Abigail sitting alone in the library.

"I didn't think cops asked." Abigail closed her laptop.

"My mother raised me to be polite. And the Chief Inspector gave me a gun, in case that doesn't work."

Abigail smiled. She looked wan. Tired.

Lacoste took the armchair across from her so that they were sitting on either side of the lit fire. She cast a glance toward the stack of wood, where Vincent Gilbert, two nights earlier, had found a murder weapon.

"Are you hiding?"

"Not a great hiding place if I am. You found me."

"I don't think I'm the one you're hiding from."

Abigail heaved a sigh. "I needed to get out of my room, but I didn't want to see him. I don't trust myself."

"You think you might finish what you came here to do?"

Abigail smiled again and shook her head. "I came here to humiliate him. To scare him. To wound his ego but leave his body intact. So that he'd spend the rest of his life writhing. Like my mother."

"You've already done that. So what are you afraid you might do now?"

"Kill him. We all know he killed Debbie, thinking it was me. Gamache and the other one as much as told me that the night Debbie died. Debbie was killed by mistake. But I didn't take it in." She rubbed her forehead, hard enough to leave red marks. "Is there always a delayed reaction?"

"Often, yes." Isabelle leaned forward. "Can you tell me about the day your sister died?"

"I'm sorry, what?"

"Maria. What happened that day?" As she asked her question, her phone pinged with a message from Beauvoir and a photo of a letter. She'd read it later.

"Why do you want to know that?" Abigail asked. "It was a long time ago."

"Please, just tell me."

Another sigh. Not of exasperation, but of exhaustion.

"It was a Friday. Dad had just come back from a conference—"

"Was he alone?"

"Yes. He'd been there with Colette, but she didn't come to Nanaimo with him." She paused. "I always wondered if she and Dad . . . But I guess not. And then the thing happened, and they almost never saw each other again."

"Huh," said Lacoste, her mind moving quickly. "Where were you when your sister died?"

If Abigail heard a slight suspicion in the question, she didn't show it. "Debbie and I were looking after Maria. But we'd gone out for a bike ride—"

"And left Maria?"

"She was asleep. We wanted to go to the store, and I knew Dad would be back soon. Debbie decided she'd rather go home, so I went to the store alone. By the time I got home Dad was there, but Maria was . . ."

"What did your father say?"

"Nothing, not then. He was working on her. Trying to bring her back. She was on the kitchen floor and he had his fingers down her throat. I must've shouted because he turned and looked at me. I'll never forget his expression."

"Yes?"

"He looked terrified. Panicked. He told me to leave. To call nine-one-one. Then all sorts of people arrived and I was pushed out of the way."

"Was Debbie there?"

"No, like I said, she'd gone home."

Lacoste leaned forward and her eyes and voice became intense. "Think carefully. Before you left to go to the store, was Debbie alone with Maria?"

"No, why would she be?"

"Were you together the whole time?"

"Well, I went to the bathroom, and Debbie wasn't with me." She smiled, then it faded. "Why're you asking?"

"Could your sister's death have been more than a terrible accident?"

"No."

"Are you sure?"

"I'm positive. Why are you asking? What does any of this have to do with Debbie's murder?"

"Have you seen this picture before?"

Isabelle handed her the photograph of the four of them. The last one.

As Abigail stared down, her chin puckered and she took a deep breath. "Yes. But not for years. Where did you find it?"

"At Debbie's home. It was locked in her desk."

Abigail's brows drew together. "But why would it be there? Why would she have it?"

"We don't know."

What Isabelle did know, and suspected all along, was that their theory was wrong. Abigail hadn't found the photo among her father's things and given it to Debbie, starting a chain of events that led to murder.

No. The picture of that happy day had probably sat in Debbie's desk for years, forgotten. Debbie Schneider's murder had nothing to do with the picture, or what had happened to Maria.

Her phone dinged again. Another message from Beauvoir, asking if she'd read the letter.

Not yet, she typed and hit send.

She turned back to Abigail, but was interrupted by a call.

"Yes, what is it?" she demanded. "I'm in the mid—"

"Read the damned letter," he hissed, and hung up.

Gamache looked at Beauvoir and raised his brows.

Jean-Guy smiled tightly. "All's well."

"That bad?" said Colette.

Gamache turned back to the Chancellor and her husband. "You said the other one was upset by Paul Robinson's letter. Who was that?"

Jean-Paul had gone back to the tissues, but Colette answered. "Debbie Schneider."

"She was with you when you showed Abigail the suicide note?"

"Yes."

"When was this?"

"Shortly after Paul's funeral. It's my understanding Abby and Debbie had had a falling-out, but they reconnected at the service. Abby returned to Oxford, and Debbie went with her for support. They stayed with us for a weekend, and I decided if I was ever going to show Abby the letter, it would be then, when she had a friend with her."

"What was the reaction?" Beauvoir asked.

"What you'd expect. Abby was shocked, she didn't believe it, couldn't believe that her father would do that to Maria. As you read, he explained in his letter that it was to free them both. Maria from her misery and Abigail from her obligation, her burden. She was freed to live her life."

The letter had been deeply disturbing and painful, even for a stranger to read. A father trying to justify killing his daughter. But what had struck Jean-Guy, and he suspected Armand too, was that last bit.

Even if it was true, why lay some of the motive, and therefore indirectly the blame, for the murder on the other child? How could she not, then, spend the rest of her life feeling guilty? Her sister had been sacrificed so she could have a better life.

Did that explain Abigail Robinson's headlong pursuit of terminating pregnancies of children who'd be born less than perfect? So no other parent need make that choice?

"Debbie's reaction to the letter was even stronger than Abigail's?" asked Gamache.

"Yes, well, she seemed to show emotions that Abigail felt. They had a strange, almost symbiotic relationship. One was reason, one was intuition. Head and heart."

"Was it an unhealthy relationship, would you say?" Gamache asked.

"You mean sexual?"

"No, I don't consider that at all unhealthy. I mean codependent. So that it's impossible for them to distinguish where one life ends and another begins."

Colette thought about it. "I'm not sure. What I do know is that there was a deep love there. Certainly on Debbie's part. She was devoted to Abby. You could see that."

"You were with Paul Robinson that week. That day. The man in that picture doesn't look like he was about to kill his child."

"I agree, but if we could tell by looking at someone that they were about to commit murder, we wouldn't need you, would we, Chief Inspector?"

"That's a good point," said Gamache. And it was.

Even after a murder was committed, he could be sitting right in front of the killer and not know it.

Isabelle Lacoste lowered her phone. She'd stepped across the room, away from Abigail, to read the letter Jean-Guy had sent.

Abigail was staring into the fire, still. Like a waxwork. No longer fully human, no longer fully functioning.

Lacoste pulled her chair up so that she was sitting close to Abigail. Then she began to read out loud, off her phone. Three words in, Abigail sprang to life. Standing up so suddenly her laptop crashed to the floor.

"Where did you get that?"

"I see you recognize the letter," said Lacoste. "You lied to me."

After a moment's struggle to bring herself under control, Abigail sat. "Wouldn't you? If your father had done such a thing? Why drag that up? My God, what're you people doing? What're you doing?"

Abigail Robinson stared at Isabelle Lacoste, partly in rage but mostly in bewilderment.

"Why would you do this?" she said. "Drag up what happened to Maria? To my father. Why? This has nothing to do with Debbie's death. How can it?"

"When people lie, we need to know why."

"Do you? How can it matter?"

"I'll tell you what the Chief thinks," said Lacoste. "He thinks Debbie killed your sister and in clearing out your father's things you came across evidence of that and took your revenge."

Abigail stared at her. "You think Debbie killed Maria? And then I killed her, forty years later? But that's insane. Why would Debbie hurt Maria? And if she did, why would my father confess to something he didn't do? And what possible evidence could there be among his things? None of this makes sense."

The problem Isabelle had was that it didn't make sense to her either. She had no answers, so she just sat back and tried to look knowing.

Abigail's eyes narrowed. "You don't believe it either, do you. You said this was the Chief Inspector's theory, not yours." Professor Robinson leaned forward. "What do you really think happened to Debbie?"

"Jean-Paul and I have been patient with you, Armand, as you turn our home upside down," said Colette. "But don't you think you owe us an explanation?"

"Perhaps we should talk in private." Armand looked at Jean-Paul, who was organizing the tissues in neat rows on the coffee table.

Colette hesitated, then said to her husband, "You know, it would be really helpful if you could finish the puzzle. That way we'll be able to see the whole picture."

She walked with him back to the table, got him settled, whispered a few things in his ear, then straightened up.

"Let's go into the next room. He'll be fine for a while."

When they arrived in the living room, Gamache indicated a seat, but she refused, preferring to stand facing him. Staring at him. Waiting.

"All sorts of people have a motive for killing Abigail," he said. "And one theory we have, the leading theory, is that Debbie Schneider was mistaken for her."

"Yes, I know."

"So if Abigail was the target, who had motive and opportunity?"

As he looked at her, she began to smile. "Me?"

"You invited her to Québec, set up the talk, had her stay at your place, and then took her to the party. Without you, none of this would have happened."

"Setting aside the question of why I'd want Abigail dead, aren't you forgetting something? I'm the only one who knew for sure it wasn't Abigail in the woods. What're you hoping to find with all this?" Her arm swept the room, taking in the Sûreté agents continuing the search.

"Evidence."

"Of what? That in a fit of madness I mistook Debbie for Abby and killed her? Search away. I had no reason to want either of them dead, and certainly not Debbie Schneider. I barely knew the woman. Certainly not enough to hate her."

"No, I don't think hate was the motive. I think love might've been."

"Now you have lost me."

Armand gestured toward the book. "Paul Robinson asked you to watch over his daughter. He gave you his eternal gratitude. You couldn't kill her, but you had to stop Abigail's campaign of mandatory euthanasia. It was bad enough when you saw how much support she was getting, but then you realized at the party that she had something to hold over Vincent Gilbert."

"His work with Ewen Cameron," said Beauvoir. "You knew about it, but no one else did. Except now Professor Robinson had found out."

"So I murdered Debbie to protect Vincent Gilbert? How does that make sense?"

"You're a problem solver, a rational thinker," said Gamache. "You probably worked out that if Abigail was going to accuse him of that, as she essentially did at the party, she'd have some proof. And that proof would have been carried by Debbie, like she carried all the papers."

"Ahh, I see it now. I knocked her on the head, stole the papers, and burned them. Is that what you're thinking?"

Gamache opened his hands, in agreement.

"You've made a few leaps of logic. If you were one of my students, you'd get a fail. The biggest leap is that my love of Vincent Gilbert is so great that I'd actually kill to protect his ego."

"No. Not protect his ego, protect him from his ego. You were afraid that Gilbert would bend to the blackmail. Would lend his support to what Abigail was advocating."

"Politicians are already climbing on board," said Beauvoir. "More and more people are voicing support."

"A prominent scientist, a renowned humanitarian publicly supporting Professor Robinson's proposal could be the hundredth monkey," said Gamache.

"The what?"

"The tipping point. You couldn't take that chance. You'd do anything to protect the one you love."

"Vincent Gilbert?" She laughed.

"*Non.* Not Gilbert. You knew that if Abigail was successful, Jean-Paul would be in line, one day, for a mercy killing."

Colette stood up straighter. Raised her chin. But said nothing.

"The real motive, the final push, was to protect him," said Armand. "It was for love."

CHAPTER 42

So Abigail admitted to knowing about the letter from her father," said Beauvoir.

They were once again in the basement of the Auberge. Shut off from the rest of the world, in their own bubble of suspects and suspicion.

It was a pretty crowded place.

"Not happily, but when I showed her your message she could hardly deny it," said Isabelle.

"At least we know now what happened to Maria," said Beauvoir. "That's no longer a motive in the murder of Debbie Schneider."

"Do we know?" asked Isabelle.

Armand and Jean-Guy turned to her.

"Well, yes," said Jean-Guy. He pushed the plastic encased letter from Paul Robinson across the conference table. "There is a small clue in the suicide note."

"But is it a confession?"

Now Beauvoir laughed, then looked at her with suspicion. "Of course it is."

"What are you thinking, Isabelle?" asked Gamache.

"Something's been bothering me about this." She pulled the letter toward her.

Gamache moved around the table until he was beside her, while Beauvoir moved to her other side.

"Why didn't Paul Robinson leave a note with his body?" asked Isabelle. "Most suicides do. Not all, but most. Or he could've easily made a copy of this note and left it in a safety-deposit box. In case the other got lost. Everyone describes him as a methodical scientist. Wouldn't he make sure there was a copy of something so important? And why write to Colette, but not Abigail? It's not like she was a child. She was twenty."

"Maybe he wanted to make sure there was someone with her when she read it," said Gamache.

"Could be, but he could've included a separate letter to Abigail in the same envelope, just saying he loves her and is sorry. What's it going to do to a young woman, knowing she was the reason her father killed her sister, then took his own life? Did that really need to be said?"

"The whole thing seems strange," admitted Jean-Guy. "I mean, why confess at all, so many years later?"

"That's the other thing, though," said Isabelle. "He doesn't really confess."

"But he does." Gamache pointed to the letter. "It's right there."

"No, it isn't."

As one, the three of them bent their heads over the letter.

Isabelle could feel Jean-Guy's shoulder touching hers, and she could smell the Chief's faint scent of sandalwood with a hint of rose. The bit of his wife he carried with him always. Like breath.

"I'll be damned." Gamache stood up and, bringing his hand to his mouth, he stared at the page.

"You're right," said Jean-Guy. "Nowhere in this does he come right out and say, *I killed Maria.* What he does say"—he reached for the letter—"is that he's responsible. That it's his fault, that he can't live with what he did." Looking up again, he stared at the other two. "Knowing it was a suicide note, we filled in the blanks."

"And he still might have done it," said Isabelle. "But it just struck me that he never actually says it."

"He also says," Gamache read out loud, "*It wasn't deliberate. I know that.*" Gamache looked at Isabelle and Jean-Guy. "Isn't that strange wording?"

They nodded. Slowly.

"Wouldn't he leave it at, *It wasn't deliberate*?" asked Jean-Guy.

They all, in unison, went back to staring at the letter.

Gamache, his eyes narrow in concentration, was trying to think it through.

Why didn't you clearly confess? he asked a man long dead but still very much present. *Why did you send the letter to Colette Roberge? Why did you say you knew Maria's death wasn't deliberate?*

Why did you really kill yourself?

In the gloom of the basement, an idea was forming.

"We need to have that"—he nodded toward the letter—"fingerprinted and checked for DNA." He handed it to Isabelle. "And have the handwriting analyzed."

"*Oui, patron.*"

He watched as she made a copy. Then, putting it into a secure envelope, she gave it to an agent to take to the lab in Montréal.

As the letter left the confines of the basement, Armand's thoughts chased after it.

Did you really kill Maria?

Did you really kill yourself?

He walked over to the large board, placed in the Incident Room by the technicians. Photographs had been pinned up there. Of the murder scene. Of the body. There were schematics of the crime scene, the trail, the Auberge. The bonfire. Movements and relationships between various people.

Down the side of the board were other photographs.

From the shooting in the old gym.

The mug shots of a stunned Édouard, Alphonse, and young Simon Tardif.

The portrait of Ewen Cameron.

And now, two more had been added. Paul Robinson in front of the silly pseudo-scientific poster of spurious correlations, and *the last one*, of Maria, Paul, Abigail, and Debbie.

Picking up a black felt pen, he turned to the others.

"Let's try to clarify. We have several scenarios. One. The intended victim on New Year's Eve was Abigail Robinson."

As he spoke, he wrote her name, under the heading, *Victim*.

Then, next to that, under *Motive* he wrote, *Mass Euthanasia Campaign/ Blackmail.*

Under *Suspects* he wrote: *Vincent Gilbert, Colette Roberge.*

"With a possibility being Simon Tardif," said Isabelle. "Though he's pretty far down the list."

"Agreed. The other scenario," Gamache continued, "is that Madame Schneider was the intended victim all along."

"And the motive?" asked Jean-Guy. "We'd thought maybe she'd killed Maria, but with the letter from Paul Robinson . . ."

"We don't know for sure it is a confession," said Isabelle. She leaned forward, putting her elbows on the conference table.

"Abigail believed all this time that her father killed Maria," said Gamache. "But we're back to the other theory. Maybe, in clearing out his things, she finds something that tells her he hadn't. That tells her the truth."

"That Debbie did it," said Beauvoir.

Armand pointed the pen at him, then turned and circled Debbie's name.

"And the motive?" he said. "In Abigail's mind, Debbie not only killed a sister she loved, but also, by association, her father."

"He sent the letter to Madame Roberge," said Beauvoir, "and told her to show it to Abigail, believing she'd killed Maria. He wanted Abby to know she was safe."

"Except she didn't do it," said Isabelle. "Can you imagine how she'd feel if she realized her father had lived with that belief for so many years? That he believed she'd killed her sister? Then he'd taken his own life for no reason. How she'd feel about Debbie?"

"She'd hate her," said Beauvoir.

Isabelle, though, was shaking her head.

"I think we're making this much more complicated than it needs to be. I think the motive has to be something that's recent."

"But it is recent," said Beauvoir, "for Abigail."

"Go on," Gamache said to Isabelle. "What do you think happened."

"I think your first scenario is right. Abigail was the intended victim. I think someone saw her at the party. They hated the agenda she's pushing. They saw their chance to stop her, and they took it."

"Anyone in mind?" asked Beauvoir.

"Vincent Gilbert, maybe with Colette Roberge's help," said Isabelle. "They had motive and opportunity."

Gamache turned around and studied the board, the pictures, the schematic. Something didn't fit. Some small piece.

Then he walked to the table and reread the letter. He was beginning to see what.

"There's someone else, *patron*," said Jean-Guy, taking Gamache's place at the board.

Picking up a red felt pen, he wrote, *Haniya Daoud*.

Gamache's brows rose. How could he have forgotten her? Was it because while the others were standing in plain sight, practically jumping up and down for their attention, Haniya Daoud was sneaking up. Machete in hand. Unseen in the dark.

He wondered if the young woman had had one last killing left in her. And then, *ça va bien aller*. All would be well. She could put down the machete. Put down the cup.

He put down the letter. "I think it's time for dinner."

To avoid an Auberge crawling with suspects, they returned to the Gamache home.

Armand went into the kitchen to look for Reine-Marie, while Isabelle and Jean-Guy made themselves comfortable in the living room.

As he entered, Armand saw Haniya Daoud, a long blade in her hand. She was pointing it at Reine-Marie, whose back was turned.

He felt his heart skip a beat, and his muscles tense. The world slowed down, in a rush of terror and adrenaline. And then, as quickly as it came, it passed.

A vestige of the job. Fireworks were gunshots, and all knives were weapons, especially when pointed at someone he loved.

"I didn't know you were here," he said to Haniya.

"Clearly. And I can see your delight."

He smiled. "No, you just saw my surprise. You're always welcome."

"Oh, hello, Armand." Reine-Marie turned around. "I asked Haniya to stay for dinner. She was kind enough to come with me to the Horton place to return the last box."

Armand kissed her lightly, then grabbed a wooden cutting board, a baguette, and a knife.

The kitchen smelled of simmering coq au vin and fresh basil, which Haniya had torn and placed on a platter, with the tomato and the burrata she was slicing.

Daniel and his family, along with Annie and the children, had gone back to their homes in Montréal. They'd offered to stay on, but both Reine-Marie and Armand had said it would probably be best if they returned when there wasn't a murderer among them. Which, in Three Pines, might prove problematic.

"What else can I do?" Haniya asked.

"You can put that platter on the table," said Reine-Marie. "Then pour yourself a drink and join the others in the living room. Dinner's in about twenty minutes."

Haniya placed the burrata and tomato on the pine table, but didn't go into the living room. Instead she wandered down to the far end of the kitchen, pausing on the way to look at the art on the walls. Some portraits, some naïve works. Some landscapes.

And one modest little frame.

"Is this . . . ?"

"It is," said Reine-Marie. "Took a long time to track one down. It's an original."

"One of a kind?" asked Haniya, leaning close to the small photograph of a single crystalline snowflake.

"How'd it go with the Hortons?" Armand asked.

As Reine-Marie told him, he watched Haniya. She'd made herself comfortable in one of the large chairs by the woodstove and was staring into the night.

"You didn't tell them about their mother and Ewen Cameron?"

"No. Not all truths need to be told. They have the box, they can look into it if they want. I think they know there's something in there, but this way they have a choice." She looked at their guest and lowered her voice. "I think she wants to stop."

"Stop what?" he asked. *Killing?*

"Being the Hero of the Sudan. Look at her. She's barely more than a child. I think she wants to have a peaceful life. To wake up and meet

Clara in the bistro for breakfast. To discuss books with Myrna. To drop by here for tea or dinner, and not have to worry about all the girls, all the women, out there waiting for her to rescue them."

"To put down the cup," said Armand.

She watched him put the kettle on. *If only that were possible.*

While Reine-Marie returned to the living room, Armand took a cup of tea to Haniya.

"May I?" He nodded toward the armchair across from her.

"Of course."

As he sat, he mused that Haniya Daoud seemed to own every room she was in. And yet she never seemed to belong.

"Did you kill Debbie Schneider?"

Haniya's brows disappeared into her hijab. "Small talk, Chief Inspector?"

He smiled, but said nothing.

"Or is this how you investigate a crime? Ask that question over and over until someone says yes?"

"Or it's time for bed, *oui.*"

She laughed. It was full-throated and seemed to surprise even her.

"Well," she finally said, "all I can say is your investigation must be a real shit show if you still suspect me. That is the expression, isn't it? 'Shit show'? I learned it from Ruth. She was describing Clara's career as an artist."

"Well, that's one expression, yes. You haven't answered my question."

"Oh, you were serious?"

He was no longer smiling. His eyes on her were thoughtful, searching.

"No. I didn't kill her. What I told you before is true. Killing the person does not kill an idea. And if I had wanted to do away with Professor Robinson, I wouldn't have been stupid enough to kill the wrong person. I've never done that."

There was a crackling silence between them.

"We all make mistakes. In the cold and dark, in a hurry. It's possible."

"True," she said. "But not that mistake. Human life is sacred. That's another thing I learned in the camps. When you see so much death, you come to value life. When you see so much cruelty, you come to value kindness."

"But do you recognize it? Because it's out there." He gestured toward the next room. "And you're in here." He put down his cup. "I'm going into the living room. Will you join me?"

"No. I'm just fine out here."

He nodded. "If you change your mind . . ."

What are you doing out there, Ralph?

But he had some idea what Haniya Daoud was doing.

CHAPTER 43

~

"C ouldn't sleep?" asked Armand.

Though it was almost three in the morning, the voice hadn't surprised Jean-Guy. He'd heard the slippered feet approaching the kitchen and recognized the gait.

"I haven't really slept since Honoré was born," he said.

"Tea?" Armand turned around, kettle in hand.

Beauvoir was about to decline, then realized that yes, a nice cup of tea . . .

Dear God, he thought, *I've been infected*. "Yes, please. Did you hear that?"

Jean-Guy half rose. His face alert, his body tense. There'd been a sound from the front of the house.

"It's okay," said Armand, turning off the tap. "I was just about to tell you—"

"Is it morning already?" asked Isabelle. Her cheeks were red from the short walk from the B&B. She carried a plate covered with a checked dish towel and was wearing polka dot flannel pajamas under a plaid flannel robe.

"You look like something out of Dickens," said Jean-Guy.

"I don't think we want to get into what each of us looks like, do you?"

In sweats and unshaved, he looked like some bedraggled mess cops on an overnight shift brought in. And kept downwind.

Putting the plate on the counter, she greeted Gamache, who looked pretty much as he always did. Or at least a variation on the same theme.

A university professor woken up out of a deep sleep. Also unshaven, his beard would be almost completely gray, she saw, if he chose to grow one again. Unlike Jean-Guy, he'd at least made an effort to brush his hair, but one side still stood up.

"I saw Isabelle's light on over at the B&B," Armand explained, pouring milk into a jug, "and texted her to join us."

It was 2:53.

Lacoste took off the towel to reveal an assortment of breakfast pastries. "Courtesy of Gabri and Olivier."

"Do they know how generous they're being?" asked Armand.

"Not yet."

While the tea steeped, Armand went into the study and returned with the documents he'd brought from the Incident Room. Jean-Guy spread them out on the kitchen table. Mugs in front of them, the three Sûreté officers ate *pain au chocolat* and studied the pages.

It was like Jean-Paul Roberge's jigsaw puzzle. Though, when correctly assembled, this would not show a basket of puppies.

The problem was, they seemed to have a few puzzles mixed together.

There was Vincent Gilbert's involvement in Ewen Cameron's experiments on innocent men and women. Including Abigail's mother.

There was the question of Maria's death.

There were the violent reactions to Abigail Robinson, and the people, including Gilbert and maybe the Chancellor, who'd do anything to stop her campaign for euthanasia.

And then there was the outlier. The puzzle that was their visitor. Haniya Daoud. Who talked of moral courage and committed murder under cover of darkness.

Were they separate puzzles, Gamache wondered, or all part of the same picture? One part forest, another sky, some water, some buildings? Appearing unconnected, spurious even, but combined they formed a single image.

Or maybe he had the analogy wrong. Not a puzzle, but what he'd thought earlier. One long thread. That started with Cameron and ended decades later with the body of Debbie Schneider.

The tug he'd given earlier had revealed Colette Roberge. The recipient of Paul Robinson's oddly vague letter. And his eternal gratitude.

Had she earned it for looking after his daughter when the suicide note arrived, or was it more expected? Was the commitment ongoing?

Picking up his mug, Armand strolled over to the windows at the far end of the kitchen and gazed out. "Why was Paul Robinson so grateful to Colette?"

His words formed steam on the cold window.

Turning around, he looked back at Beauvoir and Lacoste. This was far from the first time they'd found themselves sleepless and poring over a homicide in their pajamas.

"He was grateful to her for looking after Abigail," suggested Isabelle.

"Possible, but 'eternal' gratitude? That seems excessive." After rekindling the fire in the woodstove, he returned to the table and brought the copy of the suicide note closer to him. "It'll be interesting to get the handwriting and DNA analysis."

"You think he didn't write it?" Jean-Guy asked.

"I'm wondering, not thinking."

"But if he didn't, who did?"

"Abigail and Colette were both in Oxford when he died," said Isabelle. "Who does that leave—" She stopped. "Debbie Schneider? Why would she?"

"Maybe Paul Robinson found evidence that she'd killed Maria," said Jean-Guy. "The evidence Abigail might have found among his things a few weeks ago."

"You're saying he confronted Debbie," said Isabelle, "and she killed him? How? Then she writes a suicide note and mails it with a book to someone she doesn't even know exists?"

"Do you see a problem with that?" Armand asked, and smiled. "I suspect if she had done that, she'd have made the supposed confession a lot clearer. I also think if the letter wasn't in his handwriting, Colette or Abigail would have known. So Paul Robinson wrote that letter to Colette and his daughter, then took his life. But"—he looked down at it again—"it seems an unnecessarily cruel letter, and he doesn't seem like a cruel man. Just the opposite really. By all accounts, he had a loving relationship with Abigail."

"And with Maria," said Isabelle. "We know where that ended."

As one, the three of them looked at the photograph of Debbie, Abigail, Paul, and Maria, with the vast Pacific stretching out behind them, sparkling in the sunlight.

The last one.

That photograph, Armand knew, must have been precious to Paul Robinson, so what was it doing locked in Debbie Schneider's desk?

Armand sat slowly back in his chair and stared into the distance. Trying to see something just beyond his grasp.

If he pulled the thread, gently, maybe. Maybe . . .

Unexpectedly, Reine-Marie's elderly mother appeared.

He sat forward and turned to them. "You haven't lost a parent yet, have you?"

They shook their heads, surprised by what seemed a non sequitur.

"Then you haven't had to clear out their home, go through their things. It's a terrible job. We did it after Reine-Marie's mother died a couple of years ago. It's sad and exhausting and incredibly tedious at times. All the things they didn't know what to do with, they just put in closets and piled in the basement. Every paper and photograph needs to be gone through, and decisions made. We were lucky, we had Reine-Marie's seventy-eight siblings to help."

Isabelle and Jean-Guy smiled. Each time the Chief mentioned Madame Gamache's enormous family, the number went up. They actually had no idea how many brothers and sisters there were. It was unclear if Reine-Marie even knew.

"But what happens when you're an only child?" he asked. "Or there are too many things and not enough time?"

"You get help?" suggested Isabelle. "Like what Reine-Marie does for people."

"Exactly. That's what I should have seen."

He was animated, annoyance at himself replaced by excitement at finally seeing clearly.

"You get someone in who isn't as emotionally attached to help sort things out. So when faced with a deadline, and loads of her father's things to go through, who would Abigail turn to?"

"Debbie Schneider," said Jean-Guy. "*Merde*."

"Debbie found the photograph. Not Abigail," said Isabelle, her eyes gleaming. "That's why it was in her desk. That's why Abby was surprised. She hadn't seen it in years."

"But why lock it away?" asked Jean-Guy. "What's in it that we can't see?"

He leaned over and once again saw the devotion on Debbie's face as she looked at Abigail. And saw the devotion on Abigail's face as she looked at Maria.

Paul Robinson was looking at Maria. He appeared calm. Content. Happy.

Then Jean-Guy looked at her.

The little girl, her body twisted, had her mouth open, joining in some joke. Her hair gleamed in the sunshine. Her complexion was pink and healthy. Her clothes were clean, and covered with cheery daisies.

But mostly it was her eyes that Jean-Guy noticed. They were bright, amused. Alert and aware.

There was no pain. No despair. No sign Maria was failing. This was not a little girl with no quality of life and this was not a family struggling to keep their heads above water.

"Is that what was hidden in full view?" he said. "A happy family?"

"*Non*," said Armand, his voice certain. He too had been staring at the photo, and what he'd seen wasn't a happy family. "Did the evidence box from Madame Schneider's home arrive?"

Isabelle checked the tracking on her phone and shook her head in frustration. "Yes and no. They sent it to Sûreté headquarters. Not here. It's sitting in my office."

"Get one of the agents on duty to drive it down. Right now."

"On it."

As she put in the call, Armand turned to Jean-Guy. "It was there all the time, for us to see. And we did. We even talked about it, but didn't pursue it."

"What?" said Jean-Guy.

"That." Armand pointed at the photograph.

They'd been so focused on the picture of the four people that they'd failed to notice they were actually looking at a screen shot of Debbie Schneider's desk.

The picture of the happy people, the last one, was sitting on top of the other things that had been locked in the drawer. The ink, the cards, the staples . . .

"The agenda," said Jean-Guy.

"Yes," said Gamache. "The agenda. That's what Debbie found. That's what Debbie hid."

The evidence box arrived at the Auberge within the hour.

By then they'd showered and changed into warm clothes. Armand had wound a bright red cashmere scarf around his neck and tucked it into his parka, to better protect himself against the biting cold.

The night was impossibly clear, the sky awash with stars.

It was preternaturally quiet. Still. Peaceful.

The only sound was the rhythmic crunching of their boots on the snow-covered road as they made their way past St. Thomas's, past the New Forest. Toward the only light visible. Toward the Old Hadley House, at the top of the hill.

It was like a beacon, thought Gamache. A lighthouse.

Except a lighthouse was a warning, of shoals, of rocks. It was not a destination. No mariner would steer toward one, he knew, as their steps took them closer and closer.

Once there, they found the agent sitting on a straight-backed chair in the lobby, the box on her knee and her arms around it.

"Agent Lavigne, isn't it?" said the Chief Inspector.

"*Oui, patron.*" She stood up so quickly the box almost fell to the floor. When Inspector Lacoste took it, the young agent turned to Gamache.

"If you don't mind . . ." She was holding out a receipt.

Beauvoir pressed his lips together and made a mental note to buy her a coffee. If not for good sense, then for valor.

She left with a receipt signed, *Armand Gamache*. And they were left with the box.

Putting it on the conference table in the Incident Room, Beauvoir handed around sterile gloves. Gamache put them on, trying not to show the nausea he still felt as the memories came flooding back, carried on the scent of latex.

Lacoste brought out her phone to record the proceedings.

Breaking the seal, Beauvoir picked up the various items, dictating as he went. All went into bags and were labeled.

The last three items he placed on the desk.

"Four birthday cards."

Isabelle opened them. "For Abigail's sixteenth to nineteenth birthdays. All signed, *Love, Debbie*. So now we know exactly when the falling-out happened."

"Not long after Maria died," said Gamache.

"Here's the photograph," said Beauvoir. Turning it over he saw, neatly written, *The last one*. It was the same handwriting as the suicide note.

There was only one item left, sitting all alone at the bottom of the box.

"An agenda," he said, for the recording. But it was, they all knew, far more than that.

He opened the front cover to reveal the name and year. Then he handed it to Chief Inspector Gamache. "Paul Robinson's."

Gamache closed his eyes for a moment and exhaled. He'd thought maybe, but until Jean-Guy had said that, he hadn't been sure.

"From the year Maria died?" asked Isabelle.

"*Non*," said Jean-Guy. "From the year he died."

Armand sat down, put on his reading glasses, and opened it.

"Debbie Schneider found it when they were going through his things," said Isabelle.

"Just weeks ago," said Armand, looking up. "*Oui*. I think that was the catalyst."

They'd come around and now hung over his shoulder as he turned to the day Paul Robinson died.

"It's blank," said Isabelle. Though disappointed, she knew he was hardly likely to put in a reminder to kill himself.

"I think when Debbie found it, this picture"—Gamache held it up—"was in that page. You can just see where some of the resin from the gloss has come off. We'll get it analyzed."

Armand turned the pages. All the ones going forward were blank.

Then he turned back. One page. Two. And there was the entry. The last one.

Letter to Colette. Copy.

And there it was. So matter-of-fact. Not the word "letter," but the other one.

"*Copy*," said Armand, nodding. "You said it, Isabelle. You even did it." He looked over at the scanner. "You made a copy of the letter. So why wouldn't he? It's been bothering me. Everyone describes Paul Robinson as a methodical scientist. Wouldn't he make a copy of something so important?"

"And he did," said Isabelle. "So where is it?"

Smiling, Armand turned the book upside down and shook, waiting for the letter to flutter out.

But it did not. Nothing came out.

"*Sometimes the magic works*," he said with a sigh.

Jean-Guy smiled, recognizing the quote from *Little Big Man*.

"Okay," said Isabelle, "let's say Debbie found the copy of the suicide letter among his things. Where is it? And how could it matter? She already knew what was in it. She'd read the original when Colette showed it to them. I agree that what started this all off was something they found when going through Paul Robinson's things, but I don't think it's that." She pointed to the agenda. "That was the ninety-ninth monkey."

"And the hundredth?" asked Jean-Guy, also taking a seat.

"Was something Abigail found. The letter from Gilbert, demanding payment for torturing her mother. That's what started all this."

Gamache removed his reading glasses, the better to study her. "Go on."

"That letter from Gilbert must've been explosive. It changed everything for Abigail, but it also explained everything. Cameron's experiments led to the deaths of her mother, her sister, and her father."

Isabelle leaned forward, her arms outstretched on the table, trying to get them to embrace her scenario.

"Abigail is smart. She realizes that it's a personal tragedy, but also a professional opportunity. Vincent Gilbert, the great humanitarian, was involved in the most shameful event in Canadian medicine. What would he do to hush that up? She was in the middle of a shit storm of controversy. She needed allies. She admits she came to Québec to try to blackmail Gilbert into an endorsement. But suppose it's more than that?"

"You're saying she came here to kill him," said Gamache.

"We talked about that, yes. Doesn't that make the most sense? Maybe she didn't start off with that idea, maybe it did start as only blackmail, but when she came face-to-face with him at the party, it changed. He was smug, arrogant. Mocking. She snapped. This wasn't a murder with a whole lot of thought. A whole lot of planning."

"So how does Debbie Schneider end up dead?" asked Jean-Guy.

"Because Gilbert gets there first. He had a whole lot of motives." Isabelle ticked them off on her fingers. "To protect his reputation." One tick. "To make up for what he didn't do before." Another. "In self-defense when he realizes what she probably has in mind for him." A third. "He just made one mistake."

"He killed the wrong person?" said Beauvoir.

"Did he? Maybe he knew, or suspected, that Debbie Schneider had the letter from Cameron, the proof. He had to get it back. And there was something only he could do."

Isabelle looked from one to the other. It all seemed so obvious. Couldn't they see it?

To his credit, she thought, the Chief Inspector did seem to be trying. There were deep creases across his forehead and his eyes had the thoughtful, slightly unfocused look of someone struggling to see something in the distance.

"The firewood," she finally said. "Vincent Gilbert was alone in the library on New Year's Eve. He was just about the only one who could pick up a log and—"

"Come on, Isabelle," said Jean-Guy. "This's all circumstantial. You have no evidence that Gilbert did it. But there is evidence that Debbie Schneider—"

Like a man warding off an attack, Gamache put up his hands and turned his head away, dropping his gaze. Asking them to give him a moment.

Instead of pulling on the thread, now he was trying to follow it. The answer was right there. He was sure of it. Gently, carefully, quietly, he traced it back.

From Debbie's body. To Abigail's confrontation with Vincent Gilbert at the party. To the attack in the gym.

From Abigail's controversial research into the pandemic. To clearing out her father's home, and finding Ewen Cameron lurking there. And, by association, Vincent Gilbert.

The agenda. The photograph. And, maybe, the copy of the strangely but carefully worded suicide note.

And finally, again and always, he came face-to-face with Abby Maria.

He stood up. "We won't find the truth sitting here. We need to go back to the Roberge home. I think Paul Robinson trusted the Chancellor to keep his secret. To help him hide the truth. I think that was his eternal gratitude."

"You know what that is?" asked Lacoste, getting up too. "The truth?"

"No. But I think Colette Roberge does."

CHAPTER 44

It was just before six when she opened the door. She was in her house-coat, and while surprised to see them, Chancellor Roberge did not look shocked.

After she took them into the now familiar kitchen, and offered coffee, they sat at the table.

Without prelude, Armand said, "Paul Robinson trusted you with the truth, and now we need to hear it."

"No. What Paul trusted me with, Armand, was Abigail. He loved her. He loved both his daughters more than life itself. That's the only truth you need to know."

"If he loved her so much, why would he tell you to show her his suicide note?" asked Isabelle. "Why would he hurt her like that?"

The Chancellor crossed one arm over her lap and rested her other elbow on it, bringing her hand to her mouth. She could not have been more armored if she'd been wearing chain mail.

Gamache could see Isabelle's frustration, shared by Beauvoir. Shared by himself. But he also felt a frisson of elation.

This was the question.

Why would Paul Robinson write such a letter, then ask Colette to show it to his daughter? What was he trying to tell her? What was that precise man, that loving father, trying to say?

Why couldn't he make this last connection? What couldn't he see?

"Tell us again about that weekend in the Cotswolds," Gamache said. "When you showed Abigail and Debbie the letter."

Though still guarded, the Chancellor relaxed, slightly. "I remember it was Saturday afternoon. Dreary. We'd been on a long walk and stopped for lunch at a pub. Sat in front of the inglenook and had a ploughman's."

Though not a lot of that sentence made sense to Beauvoir, he followed the gist. "You remember that much detail?"

Colette turned to him. "I couldn't tell you what I had for lunch the day before, or after. I remember because I knew what I was about to do. I had the letter on me, and as we sat with our pints, chatting, it seemed the perfect time to show Abigail. Everyone was relaxed. Comfortable. I actually had it in my hand, then put it back in my pocket. It was too public. By the time we left it was drizzling. One of those cold, damp English days."

Armand remembered them well, and with fondness, from his time at Cambridge. Sitting in the pub by the fire with a pint, studying, as a heavy mist settled outside.

"When we got home, I made tea and took the tray into the living room. Jean-Paul was laying the fire while the girls got into warm, dry clothes. I knew it was time."

She paused. Reliving that moment. What she was about to do.

Armand knew what it felt like. He again had the sense of standing in front of the closed door. Two inches of wood between the family inside and catastrophe.

He saw his hand lift. Made into a fist. Ready to rap on the door and change a life, end a life. He'd look into those mild, inquiring eyes. *I'm sorry, but I have news about your daughter. Son. Husband. Wife. Mother.*

Father.

"I brought out the letter," said Colette, "and gave it to her."

"What was her reaction when she read it?" asked Jean-Guy.

"I watched her face, of course," said Colette. "I could see exactly where she was in the letter. When she came to the part about him killing Maria, she crumpled it in her lap and made a noise. Sort of deflated."

"Did she say anything?" asked Jean-Guy, quietly.

"She whispered, 'Oh, God. Daddy. You did that?'" Colette shook her head. "I've asked myself a thousand times if I did the right thing, in showing her. It seemed . . ." She searched for the word.

Cruel? thought Jean-Guy.

Unkind? thought Isabelle.

"Unnecessary?" suggested Armand when Colette seemed stuck.

She looked at him. "Yes. That was it. I couldn't understand why he'd want or need her to know. But he did. And it wasn't for me to question. I was like the executor of his will, with a small *w*. Paul had his reasons, and he knew his daughter better than I did."

"And Debbie?" Armand asked. "Jean-Paul said she reacted even more strongly when she read it."

"Yes." Then her brow creased in an effort to recall. "But she never actually read the letter."

"*Pardon?*"

"She reached for it, but Abigail did this." Colette mimed turning away and clutching something to her chest, protectively.

"So how did she know what was in it?" Isabelle asked.

"Abigail told her."

"Read it to her, you mean?" asked Armand. It was important, vital at this stage, to be precise.

"No. She described the letter."

"Accurately?" asked Isabelle.

"*Oui.* Debbie started to cry. Abigail didn't. At least, not that I saw. I think she was just too shocked."

"Did you and Abigail have a chance to talk about the letter privately?" asked Armand.

"Yes. I told her that her father loved both his daughters. And that it was his choice, his decision. And not her responsibility."

"And you kept the letter," said Armand.

"I asked Abby if she wanted it, but she didn't. So yes, I've had it all this time."

"And as far as you know, Debbie never actually read it?"

"That's right. Why?"

"Paul Robinson made a copy of it. I'm wondering where it went."

Now Colette smiled and nodded. "Yes, I can see him doing that. I'd do that."

"I imagine you'd also be clearer, Colette."

Her smile flattened and she stared at him, then at the other two. "You noticed that, did you?"

"You did too?"

"Not at first, but I read it again a few years later, and it struck me that he never really came right out and said he'd killed Maria. It's near impossible to read it and not come to that conclusion. And yet . . ."

"Why didn't he just say it?" Armand asked.

He thought back to the notes he'd written before heading into an action he was leading. One he knew could go very badly. The scribbled words of love. And then sliding his wedding ring off and sealing it in the envelope, to be left in his desk drawer.

In case.

There was no ambiguity about those few words. And neither should there have been about Paul Robinson's. He'd had, after all, time to consider. Years in fact. To choose each word.

Armand Gamache had no doubt that Robinson had indeed killed himself. And he had absolutely no doubt Robinson had written the suicide note. But what was he saying?

And to whom?

Colette Roberge? Abigail?

"What was he trying to say, Colette? I think you know."

"All I know for sure, as I said before, is that Paul Robinson loved his children. Everything he did, he did for them."

"Including killing himself?" asked Jean-Guy. "How could that be for his one remaining child? To be left alone, and then told everything that happened was partly her fault?"

Colette shrugged. Not dismissively, but to show she had no answer.

"How does Debbie Schneider figure into this?" asked Armand. When Colette said nothing, he pressed. "Did Paul Robinson kill Maria?"

"He says he did."

"No, he doesn't," said Armand. "We've just been through this. As a precise man, he is shockingly, glaringly imprecise in his final letter. And yet I think his message is clear. To someone."

"Well, when you figure it out, Armand, you let me know."

"I'll let that go, Madame Chancellor, because I know you're not used to your work having real-world consequences. But ours does. A little girl was killed decades ago, and then days ago a grown woman was murdered. The two are connected, and I think you know how."

"Are you sure you haven't stumbled into a spurious correlation?"

He leaned forward. "Why was Paul Robinson eternally grateful to you? What were you doing for him? Keeping his secret? Protecting his daughter? Are you still protecting her?"

The color rose up Colette's neck and into her cheeks. "I need to make sure Jean-Paul's all right."

She got to her feet.

Gamache also rose. "You saw the vague wording of the letter and knew it wasn't really a confession. He couldn't possibly put a pillow over his daughter's face. But someone else could. Someone else had. And he thought he knew who."

"What I know is that Paul Robinson loved his children."

"More than life itself."

"Yes."

Gamache considered the calm, serious woman in front of him, and weighed his options, considered the consequences. And made his choice.

"When Paul Robinson returned home from that conference, he found Maria already dead, isn't that right? And all his subsequent energies, including that letter, went into covering up what happened."

"And that was?" But they could see that she knew. Or suspected.

"That Paul Robinson believed his other daughter had done it."

Colette Roberge gave a single whoop of laughter. "You're kidding. That's nonsense. Abigail loved Maria."

"Yes. I agree. I'm not saying he was right."

"What are you saying?"

"He could see that Maria had not died naturally. Suppose in his shock he leaped to the worst possible conclusion, and had to act on it. In case it was true."

He knew he'd hit the open wound that Colette Roberge had gauzed over for decades. But that had continued to weep, to seep, until it became septic.

"The coroner at the time noted petechiae on Maria's face. Tiny—"

"I know what that is, Armand."

"Then you know what they indicate. I think the coroner might have suspected. But there was the overwhelming evidence of the sandwich lodged in the girl's throat."

"Wait." Colette put up her hand to stop him. "You said suppose Paul got home, found Maria dead, and assumed Abby had done it. But you also said suppose he was wrong. So if not Paul, and not Abby . . ."

Her voice trailed away, and her eyes drifted out the window to the acres of snow, just beginning to catch the first light.

Then she turned back and searched Gamache's face. And found a disconcerting quietude. A patient man waiting. His hand holding a worn thread.

"Debbie?" she asked.

She began to nod. Began to see.

"Debbie was so devoted to Abigail. She could see that Maria would always hold her back. But no. I think if she did such a thing, it would be far more personal. They were fifteen. It's a difficult age. She had complex, maybe even confusing feelings for her best friend . . ." She looked at Armand. "Jealousy. She was devoted to Abby, but Abby was devoted to Maria."

"Perhaps."

"Is that why Paul sent not just the letter, but the book? *Extraordinary Popular Delusions*. Was he telling me that what he'd written was a lie? That he hadn't killed Maria? He thought Abby had done it in a moment of madness, and he wanted me to protect her." She hesitated, working her way through this. "But you're saying he got it wrong? It was Debbie? But there's no evidence, is there? Why would you think Debbie killed Maria?"

"Because she's dead."

"And you think Abby found out what happened and killed her?"

The sun was just up now, the sky a soft morning blue behind Chancellor Roberge. Armand stepped toward her and shook his head.

"Me?" she said, in astonishment. "Why would I do that?"

"So that Abigail wouldn't have to. I think you're still working to earn that eternal gratitude." He paused. "Go check on Jean-Paul, then get dressed and call someone to be with him. You're going to have to come with us."

"Are you arresting me?" she asked, half laughing.

"Not yet."

Like Paul Robinson before him, he'd chosen his words carefully. To be both clear, and ambiguous.

CHAPTER 45

———

It was just after half past six when Jean-Guy Beauvoir went over to the Sûreté agent in the vehicle outside the Auberge.

"Has anyone gone in or out?"

"*Non, patron.* Only the staff. Day shift starts at six thirty."

"If anyone comes out, stop them. It might not be from the front door. They could come around the side. Your partner?"

"Patrolling the outside, like you ordered. We're taking turns."

"*Bon.*"

Once in the lobby Isabelle had the front desk clerk call Haniya, Abigail, and Vincent in their rooms. And invite them down for breakfast.

The receptionist got through to Haniya, but there was no answer from the other two.

"Probably in the dining room," said Isabelle. But she returned a minute later. "Not there."

"Did anyone come down?" Gamache asked the receptionist.

"No."

"Can we have the keys to their rooms, please."

Beauvoir took the stairs two at a time while Lacoste asked, "Is there a staff entrance?"

"Yes, around the side."

She went off quickly to check it and returned at the same time as Beauvoir.

"Not in their rooms," he reported.

"There're back stairs, for the staff," said Lacoste. "And an exit. Gilbert would know about both."

"Search the place," commanded Gamache.

While they did, he made some calls. His first was to the bistro, to make sure neither Vincent Gilbert nor Abigail Robinson was there. Olivier answered and said they were not.

Next, Gamache called Gilbert's son, Marc, who had a home a couple of kilometers away.

As he listened to the phone ring Armand saw Haniya descend the sweeping stairway into the lobby, wearing a royal blue abaya and embroidered hijab.

"Marc? It's Armand Gamache. I'm wondering if your father's with you."

"No, he should be at the Inn. He said he'd be leaving this morning but not until later."

"Leaving for where?"

"His cabin. Why? Is there a problem?"

"Did you speak to him last night?"

"Yes, we had dinner there. Why?" Now his voice had risen.

"How did he seem?"

"How does Dad ever seem?"

"So the same as always?" asked Armand.

"Yes. What's this about? Is something wrong?"

"I just need to speak to him."

"At"—there was a pause—"twenty to seven in the morning?"

"*Merci*, Marc. Nothing to worry about."

Move along, nothing to see here. Though there always was.

Just asking questions. No real reason. Though there always was.

Nothing to worry about. Though . . .

"Nothing," said Beauvoir, when Gamache hung up.

Isabelle appeared from the other direction and agreed.

"What's going on?" demanded Haniya, who was standing in the lobby beside Chancellor Roberge.

"Look outside," Gamache said to Beauvoir and Lacoste, then turned to Haniya.

"Did you see or speak to Professor Robinson or Dr. Gilbert last night when you got back from our place?"

"No. I went right to my room."

"And this morning? Did you hear or see anything?"

"I was asleep until you called. What's happened?" She looked from the Chief Inspector to the Chancellor, who seemed troubled.

Beauvoir arrived back. "The agent saw the night shift leave at six thirty but didn't check them."

"There're boot prints leading into the woods," reported Lacoste, breathless.

"Toward the crime scene?" asked Gamache.

"No. Toward the cabin. Two sets."

"Damn." Gamache looked at his watch. "That was seventeen minutes ago." He turned to Colette. "What's his plan? What's he going to do to her?"

The Chancellor was pale. Her breathing rapid. Her mind working. "Nothing. I'm sure of it."

But of all the things she seemed, "sure" wasn't one of them.

"There're snowmobiles in the garage," Gamache said to Beauvoir and Lacoste.

While they sprinted out, he turned to Colette and Haniya. "Stay here. Don't follow us. I mean it, Colette. Do not follow us."

They heard engines revving outside.

"Chief?" Lacoste called from the door.

At the door Gamache put on his gloves, then said to Colette, more gently now, "Paul Robinson was wrong. You know that."

More revving.

"Was he?"

"Don't follow us."

The Chancellor noticed the emphasis and tilted her head.

Gamache pointed at Haniya. "Stay."

She was clearly outraged at being spoken to like that. He couldn't blame her. But it had to be done.

He plunged back into the cold, and after speaking quickly to the Sûreté agent in the car, he hurried over to Beauvoir and Lacoste, each astride their own snowmobiles.

"Are you armed?" he asked, his voice raised above the roar.

When both shook their heads, he opened his glove to reveal a gun. "Here, take it."

"Not yours," said Beauvoir, zipping it into a pocket of his parka.

"*Non.* The agent's. For God's sake, don't lose it. Gilbert has a rifle. It's licensed. He has it for protection in case a bear attacks, though I doubt he's ever fired it."

"Only because he prefers bears to people," said Lacoste.

Gamache got on the lead machine and, gunning it, he crossed the road and headed deep into the woods. With Beauvoir and Lacoste right behind.

The wind was full in their faces. Their eyes teared and their cheeks froze as they hunched over their machines. Banking around corners, and racing ahead, desperate to get to the cabin.

Just before the last curve, Gamache stopped and dismounted. As did the others.

They ran the rest of the way, slipping and skidding on the snow and ice. When one fell, the others ran back and dragged them up.

Sunlight bounced off the reds, blues, and greens of their coats, as the three of them plunged forward.

They could smell the cabin before they saw it. A fire had been lit in the hearth and the scent wafted to them through the thin air. Rounding the corner, they slowed to a walk. Then, at a signal from Gamache, they stepped off the path and into the woods. Their boots sank knee-deep into the snow as they waded through it, catching glimpses of the cabin through the forest.

It sat at the far side of the clearing, a wisp of smoke coming out the stone chimney. A propane lamp had been lit, throwing soft light from inside onto the pristine snow.

It was a peaceful scene. Like a Christmas card, or a snow globe before being shaken.

But it was time to shake it up.

Gamache pointed, and together they sprinted across the clearing, skidding to a stop at the cabin. Pressing themselves against the logs, they held their breaths.

Nothing. They hadn't been heard.

Lacoste craned her neck and glanced through the window. Then ducked back down.

"They're sitting by the fire," she whispered. "One on either side. Talking."

"Talking?" asked Beauvoir. He had his hand on his pocket. He hadn't yet unzipped it, but he could feel the comforting outline through the goose down.

"*Oui*. I can't see the rifle."

She looked again, then ducked down quickly. "Gilbert's gone."

"Get back," said Gamache. As Beauvoir and Lacoste went to scramble around the corner, the cabin door opened.

Armand threw out his arm, as a father did to instinctively protect a child in the passenger seat, when something unexpected happened.

They froze.

Vincent Gilbert stepped onto the small porch and looked around. He held something in his hands. Something long and metallic.

At the small sound of a pocket beginning to unzip, his eyes swung around and landed on Gamache.

Armand stood up and faced Gilbert.

"What're you doing in there, Vincent?" he asked.

"What're you doing out there, Armand?"

The Sûreté officers followed Vincent Gilbert into the cabin.

Gamache saw Jean-Guy's hand on his still sealed pocket and made a small gesture.

Not yet.

Isabelle was the only one who hadn't been in the Asshole Saint's home before. She quickly took in the single room.

A brass bed, separated from the rest of the cabin by bookcases, was at one end. A small kitchen with worn wooden counters and an old pine table was at the other. And in between was a sitting area around a woodstove, which Gilbert was now tending with the poker he'd been carrying.

The cabin was warm and smelled of sweet pine and herbs. It smelled of the forest. As though the log walls were an illusion. Like so much else about this case.

Propane lanterns had been lit, and a coffeepot was perking on the woodstove.

It would have been a perfect domestic scene, if not for the rifle on the coffee table among the mugs, the cream jug, and the sugar bowl. Like a still life in Appalachia.

Two oversized armchairs were in front of the fire. *One for solitude. Two for friendship.*

Neither Henry David Thoreau nor Vincent Gilbert had anticipated so much society. Nor could the two people who'd been in the chairs be considered friends.

"May I?" Gamache asked, stepping forward and pointing to the rifle.

"Perhaps not," said Gilbert, sitting back down, still holding the poker. "As you know, I have a license for it."

"True, but you're not licensed to point it at people."

"It's just sitting on the table, Armand. Not doing any harm."

Not yet.

"Are you all right?" Lacoste asked Abigail.

"Yes."

"Why wouldn't she be?" asked Gilbert.

Isabelle looked from Gilbert to Abigail. She couldn't make out who was the hostage and who was the taker. And she could see that Gamache and Beauvoir were having the same difficulty.

While Gilbert held, gripped really, the poker, the rifle was actually closer to Abigail.

"We were just talking," said Abigail. "Two scientists comparing notes. But looks like the time has come for some sort of conclusion, don't you think, Dr. Gilbert?"

"I do, Professor Robinson. Armand, you look worried."

In fact, he was hyper-alert. Trying to fathom what was going on.

This extreme *politesse* was masking a brutal aggression, he could tell that much. Violent emotion was radiating off both Abigail and Gilbert. The place might smell like the forest in high summer, but it felt like a courtroom, nearing the end of a long and dreadful trial.

What had Abigail said? Scientists might appear rational, but they were in fact completely at the mercy of their emotions. Because most never learned to face them.

And it seemed to Gamache that, now faced, their emotions would have no mercy. Not today. Not in this courtroom.

"Why did you come here?" asked Gamache.

"We wanted to talk in private," said Abigail. "No one was forced. There were things that needed to be said."

"And done," said Gilbert. "We hadn't expected company."

"What did you expect?" asked Beauvoir.

He slowly, carefully unzipped his pocket. He could feel the weight of the gun and knew that he could get to it long before either Abigail or Gilbert could grab the rifle.

He hoped it would be Abigail Robinson who tried.

"We expected to finally have it out," said Abigail. She turned to Gilbert. "What's that line from Ruth Zardo's poem? I'm sure you know it."

"*Or will it be*," he said, "*as always was, too late?*"

"No, though that would fit too."

"*And now it is now*," said Beauvoir, "*and the dark thing is here.*"

Abigail shifted to him and nodded. "That's the one."

Gamache and Lacoste were staring at Beauvoir in disbelief.

"Why are you here?" asked Gilbert.

"For the same reason," said Gamache. "To have it out."

They'd collected the evidence. The facts. Now they needed the feelings.

The dark thing.

There was a sound outside, and then, incongruously, a polite knock on the door.

Gilbert started for it, but Gamache stepped in front of him and nodded to Lacoste, who opened the door.

"Oh, thank God." Colette Roberge practically fell inside. Her face was bright red, her eyes and nose running, and her speech slurred by frozen lips and cheeks.

"What the hell are you doing here?" demanded Gilbert.

"I couldn't stay away." She stomped her feet to get the circulation back and glared at Vincent for a moment before turning to Gamache. "But you knew that. Did you tell the agent in the car to let us by?"

"Us?" asked Isabelle. She opened the door again and saw Haniya Daoud trudging to the porch. Her head down, her beautiful blue abaya sodden and dragging behind her, like a long teardrop.

Pushing past Lacoste, she muttered through chattering teeth, "Fucking snow." Once inside she shivered uncontrollably and looked around the cabin. "Fucking Canada."

Colette had gone straight to the woodstove and stood with her hands outstretched toward the warmth.

"You got your meeting after all, Armand," she said, rubbing her hands together. "Though maybe not where you'd planned."

She stood almost exactly midway between Abigail and Vincent. Her allegiance as yet undeclared.

"We're used to adjusting when things don't go as we planned," said Gamache.

"I wonder." Her eyes were shrewd, calculating. "Was this your plan?"

"How could it be? I had no idea Professor Robinson and Dr. Gilbert had left the Auberge."

"True, but once that was clear, I think you manipulated both Madame Daoud and me. You wanted us here, all together, but you also needed time to manage the situation."

Gamache raised his brows. "I'm not sure you could call this 'managed' and I doubt either of you is that easily manipulated."

"Everyone can be manipulated. Even you."

There was a stillness in the air, and Gamache wondered if that was what had happened. What was happening still. Was he being manipulated?

He looked again at the rifle and thought maybe he had been, this whole time. From the first moment that call had come through, asking him to provide security for an obscure little event. All the way along. To this moment.

The case was bookended by this woman, Chancellor Roberge. Who'd requested he head up security at the gym, and now stood warming herself by the woodstove.

"You could've had that agent in the car stop us, but you didn't,"

Colette said. "Instead you pivoted. Moved the meeting to here. By your emphasis to me, and your tone to Haniya, you knew we'd come. Very clever. That flexibility, that creativity, is something not encouraged in scientists. We plod along, following facts to a conclusion. Then we stick the landing."

"Maybe if statistics carried guns, you'd learn to pivot," said Haniya.

Colette smiled. "Probably true."

"But statistics are a weapon," said Gamache. "Isn't that why we're here?"

"I wonder how much you really know about why we're here," said Abigail.

"I know," said Haniya. "I know that Gilbert brought you here to finish what he started."

"And what was that?" asked the Asshole Saint.

"To kill you," Haniya said to Abigail.

"Why would he want to do that?"

"Why did I slit men's throats in the middle of the night? To prevent an even bigger outrage."

Half the people there gaped at Haniya in surprise.

"You did?" asked Abigail.

"You make it sound noble, Madame Daoud, the Hero of the Sudan," said Gilbert. "The truth is, you did it to escape. To survive."

"Of course I did. Who wouldn't," said Haniya. "You think it's easy? It's sometimes a necessity, but that's all. You can't tell me you haven't sighted another person and pulled the trigger. Was it easy? Or did it add another measure of bile to your cup?"

Isabelle Lacoste began to speak, to defend him, but Gamache raised his hand to request quiet. To let Haniya continue. To see if she'd plunge right over the edge. She might take him with her, but at least then they'd know.

"I warned you, when we first met," said Haniya. "That it takes courage to stop a monster. Courage you clearly don't have."

"But you do."

"Why do you think they're going to give me the Peace Prize? It's for the courage to do what's necessary. There's no peace without courage."

Isabelle couldn't take it anymore. "What works at night with a machete in Sudan doesn't work here. There's no moral high ground in Canada for murder."

Haniya turned to Isabelle, her stare intense.

"Because you're so much more civilized, is that it? The true north, strong and free. You just bash each other over the head at parties. And shoot each other in bistros. Must be nice to be so evolved. But just so you know, your high ground is actually a hole."

"Jesus," said Abigail. "Do we live in the Dark Ages? Where a scientist is condemned to death for telling the truth? I'm just compiling statistics from the pandemic. The study was commissioned by the federal government, for God's sake."

"So was Ewen Cameron's," said Gilbert.

"Yes," said Abigail, turning to him. "Let's talk about Ewen Cameron. He killed my mother, my sister, my father. And you're just as guilty of their deaths."

As she spoke she leaned closer to Gilbert, closer to the rifle. Beauvoir moved his hand to his pocket and rested it there.

Come on. Come on.

"Did you come to Québec to kill Dr. Gilbert?" Gamache asked her.

"No. I came here to look him in the eye. To make him admit what he did."

"You came here to ruin him," said Colette.

"He's already ruined," said Abigail. She looked around the cabin. Outside, they could hear the blue jays shrieking in the morning sun. "I came here to expose him. I wanted the rest of the world to see what a monster he really is."

"And to blackmail him," said Beauvoir. "To force him to support your work."

"This whole thing started a few weeks ago, didn't it?" Gamache said to Abigail. "When you found the letter Dr. Gilbert wrote to your father demanding payment. That's when you realized what had happened to your mother."

"And that he"—she glared at Gilbert—"was part of it. Yes."

"You brought the letter with you, of course," said Gamache, feeling his way forward now.

She nodded. "Debbie had it. I didn't even want to touch it."

Gamache turned to Gilbert. "How did you know she had it on her?"

"I didn't. I had no idea that letter still existed. Not until we were at Colette's and you brought out the other letter. The one sent to the local woman. That's when she"—he nodded toward Abigail—"said she'd found a similar one. Before that I had no idea her mother had been part of Cameron's experiments." His gaze moved on to Colette. "Aren't you going to say something? You're going to let them accuse me of a crime you know I didn't commit?"

"Do I know that, Vincent?"

"Of course you do." The Asshole Saint was beginning to lose it.

Colette was quiet for a moment, then turned to Gamache.

"You said that this started a few weeks ago, when Abigail found the letter from Vincent among her father's things. That might've been, to use your analogy, the hundredth monkey. The final push. But it started long before that."

"*Oui*. I see that now. I've made a few mistakes. Some in judgment." He held her eyes. "And some in logic. I thought of the murder of Debbie Schneider as a puzzle, like Jean-Paul's. A jigsaw. I watched him do what we all do with jigsaws. We separate out the pieces, into colors, into patterns that match. Then we frame it. But this seemed to be two or three different puzzles mixed together. It didn't make sense, until I changed the analogy. Until the rational puzzle became a thread of emotions. One end is tied to Debbie Schneider, the other to Ewen Cameron. And the thread that runs through everything that happened in between has a name. Abby Maria."

Abigail sat back in her chair and stared at him. "Did Colette tell you?"

"*Non*. She kept your father's confidence. All Colette would say is that he loved both his daughters, equally. More than life itself. I didn't see it, couldn't quite get there, even after we found the note he wrote you."

Abigail turned to Colette. "You showed them?"

"No. They searched the house and found it."

"It seemed to contradict what everyone said about your father," said Gamache. "The letter appeared cruel, even vindictive. It seemed to lay part of the blame on you. You were, he said, part of the reason for what happened to Maria, and for his own suicide. He did what he did to free you." Gamache shook his head. "I couldn't reconcile the two. A loving father who kills one child and burdens another with a lifetime of guilt? How could this be love? How could love, real love, ever be a reason to murder?"

"I know how," said Haniya.

Gamache looked at her and nodded. "Yes, you do. You survived for love. And you did what you did for love. And now, I think, I also understand."

"*Now it is now, and the dark thing is here,*" said Gilbert, quietly.

"*It's not dark yet,*" said Gamache. "*But it's getting there.*"

Haniya gave a snort of laughter. "A cop who quotes Bob Dylan. You are dangerous."

"Colette was right," Gamache continued. "What Paul Robinson did, he did for love. But it wasn't murder. Inspector Beauvoir here understood that before anyone else. He knew Paul Robinson could never kill his daughter. In fact, he died protecting his family. Abby Maria."

Colette Roberge nodded. "Abby Maria."

"Are you saying 'Abby Maria' or 'Ave Maria'?" asked Haniya. "I don't understand."

"My mother called us that," said Abigail. "Abigail and Maria. Abby Maria. It was a nickname, a term of endearment."

Colette muttered something, and when everyone looked at her, she spoke up. "It was more than that. It was a bond. It bound you."

"Yes. It meant our fates, our lives, were intertwined. I thought it could be broken, but I was wrong."

Abigail looked exhausted. Drained. An animal tired of the plague. Of what had been plaguing her for decades.

"What's this about Maria?" asked Haniya. "What happened to her?"

"Maria is, was, Professor Robinson's younger sister," Colette explained. "She was severely disabled. After Maria was born, Madame Robinson suffered postpartum depression. Her husband, Abigail's father, was a scientist and had heard that Ewen Cameron was the best psychiatrist in the country, doing landmark research. So he got his wife in."

"What Paul Robinson didn't know," said Beauvoir, "was that Cameron was conducting experiments on his patients, for the CIA and the Canadian government."

"What sort of experiments?"

"Mind control. Brainwashing. He used LSD. Sleep deprivation. Electric shocks."

Haniya's mouth dropped and the scars deepened, as though maws had opened across her face. "He tortured his patients? This was allowed? Here? In Canada?"

"Tortured them, then sent them a bill," said Lacoste. "Signed by Vincent Gilbert. One of Cameron's residents."

Haniya turned to Gilbert. "You knew?"

Vincent Gilbert stared at the planks of his floor.

"Madame Robinson, Abigail's mother, eventually took her own life," said Colette.

"Madame Robinson would refer to her daughters as Abby Maria," said Gamache. "As though they were one person. It was meant as a sign of affection. And perhaps slightly more than that. She was, I'm guessing, a devout Catholic."

"Yes," said Abigail.

"And she committed suicide?" said Haniya. "Isn't that a mortal sin?"

"Yes," said Gamache, when Abigail didn't answer. "A testament to just how broken she was. To the pain she suffered. She'd been driven out of her mind, out of her faith. She'd been driven to despair."

"By you." Abigail glared at Vincent.

In a swift movement, Gilbert bent down and grabbed the fireplace poker.

While everyone was momentarily distracted by that, Abigail picked up the rifle. And aimed it at him.

CHAPTER 46

B eauvoir brought out his gun.

"*Non*," commanded Gamache.

Beauvoir didn't lower the weapon. Holding it steady in both hands, he kept it on Abigail. Prepared to fire. Longing to fire.

Come on, come on. One little movement, please. Come on.

"There's something you don't know," Gamache said to Abigail. His arms were out, trying to restore calm.

She was breathing heavily, the muzzle of the rifle lifting and falling with each breath. But she was so close to Vincent Gilbert she couldn't miss. It was just a question of inhale or exhale. Chest or head.

"Your father made a copy of his suicide note."

"So? You found the original at Colette's." She kept her eyes on Gilbert. "You've read it."

"But Debbie hadn't. I don't think you wanted her to."

Now Abigail's eyes darted to Gamache. "Yes, she did. At the cottage, when Colette gave it to me."

"You read it, Abby," said Colette, taking a small step forward. "And you told Debbie what was in it, but she never actually read it."

"How could it matter? What more was there?"

"A great deal more," said Gamache, his voice calm. Calming. "I think she found the copy of the letter among your father's things when she was helping you clear them out. It was probably in his agenda along with this." He nodded to Lacoste, who placed the old photograph on the table, then backed away.

Abigail glanced at it. "How can any of this matter? Gilbert killed Debbie to get back the letter that he wrote Dad. He did it to protect himself. This has nothing to do with what Dad did. With what happened to Maria."

"It has everything to do with it," said Gamache. "When Debbie read the suicide note your father left, she realized it wasn't quite the same as you'd said. Inspector Lacoste saw it too. She pointed out that Paul Robinson never actually confesses to killing Maria."

"He does," said Abigail. "He says it. He did it for me. So I wouldn't have to look after Maria for the rest of my life. So that I could go away to university, do my research. He did it for her too. To free her too. And then he killed himself, to free himself of the guilt. And yes, whether he meant to or not, he put that guilt on me. Do you know what that did to me?"

"It made you write a report on the pandemic that suggested euthanizing the frail and vulnerable," said Gamache. "It made what happened to your sister no longer murder, but a mercy killing."

"That's a lie." Her voice rose higher, strained, her breathing heavier now, more rapid.

Chest, head. Chest, head.

If Gamache had come to the cabin looking for emotion, he'd found it.

"But suppose your father didn't kill Maria," he said.

"What do you mean?" asked Abigail.

"Why would he confess to a murder, to killing his own daughter, for God's sake," said Haniya, "if it wasn't true?"

"Ahhhh," said Gamache. "And that's where we come to it. You might be here for your own reasons, but that's why we're here. To answer that question."

"Answer it if you want, if you can. But it's too late," said Abigail. "Too much damage done. The only truth that matters is that he"—she shoved the rifle toward Gilbert—"helped Cameron kill my mother, my sister, my father. And now he's killed Debbie. It stops here. Now. Nothing else matters."

She hiked the rifle up.

Gilbert took a step back and stumbled on the chair behind him, while Beauvoir warned Abigail. "Don't!"

"Your father's letter wasn't written out of guilt," said Gamache, taking a small step forward. His voice was soft, almost mesmerizing. "It was love."

He could see her hesitating.

"It was love," Gamache repeated, his voice dropping, forcing her to listen. "He didn't kill Maria. The letter was to you, always to you. He didn't want you to be alone, to be afraid, when you read it. That's why he sent it to someone he knew he could trust. With his life and with yours."

Gamache glanced at Colette, who gave a small nod of acknowledgment.

"When your father got home from the conference that day," he continued, "Maria was already dead, wasn't she? He could see she'd been smothered. He knew it could only have been you or Debbie. I think he had to assume the worst."

"The worst?" asked Haniya. She looked at Abigail. "You? You killed your sister?"

Colette shook her head. "No, she didn't. But Paul had to assume she had, in case it was true. So he covered it up. And took the blame."

Jean-Guy tried to keep his focus on Abigail. Tried to erase an image that would never completely go away. Of Paul Robinson hurriedly making the peanut butter sandwich, while one daughter called for help and the other lay dead. And then, picking up the sandwich, he . . .

"No," said Abigail, adamant. "My father would never think that of me. He'd know I couldn't do such a thing. I loved my sister."

And yet, Gamache considered, Paul Robinson had thought exactly that.

"Your father lost his mind," said Colette. "He was overcome with a sort of fugue, a temporary insanity. All he could think of was protecting you."

"But I didn't—"

Once again Gamache held up his hand. "He was a careful man. He'd close all holes, make absolutely sure there could never be any doubt. He wrote that letter, then took his life as his final act of love, to make absolutely sure you'd never be accused of the crime. But his confession was worded in such a strange way."

He brought the letter out of his breast pocket. It was warm from sitting against his rapidly beating heart.

"He writes"—Gamache found the place—"*It wasn't deliberate. I know that.*" He looked up. "He's writing to you. To tell you that he knows you didn't really mean to do it. He wants you to know that he forgives you, and that you're free now, to live your life. To continue your studies at Oxford. To fulfill your potential. He wanted you to know that you're safe."

"That's why he sent it to me," said Colette. "He wanted me to know the truth. And to watch over you. To carry on his work of protecting you. I did it from far away, but I was always there. Always watching."

"That was his eternal gratitude," said Beauvoir.

"Yes."

"No, that's not the truth, I didn't kill Maria," said Abigail, exasperated. "And how can this have anything to do with what happened to Debbie?"

"That was the question," said Isabelle Lacoste. "If your father didn't kill Maria, and you didn't, then who did?"

A silence descended on the cabin, broken only by the shrieking birds outside.

"Debbie?" suggested Gilbert, tentatively. "She did it?"

"Debbie?" demanded Abigail. "Why would she hurt Maria?"

The rifle was getting heavy, the tip dipping, then lifting.

Chest, abdomen. Chest, abdomen.

"Jealousy," said Lacoste. "That picture says it all." She nodded toward the photograph on the table. "Debbie locked it away in her desk because she didn't want to see it. She didn't want to see the little girl she'd killed, and she sure didn't want to see how much you loved her. Look at it." They did. "Look at Debbie's expression. Look at how she's tugging your arm. She's practically ripping you away from your sister. You must've known."

"I knew she was possessive, yes. That's part of the reason I wanted to cool the friendship. She was smothering me."

If Abigail realized the word she'd just used, she didn't show it.

"There's another reason Debbie might've killed Maria," said

417

Gamache. "The same one your father wrote in his letter. To free you of a burden."

"No, Maria was never a burden."

"I'm telling you what Debbie might have thought. Is that what she told you, when she confessed?" he asked. "That she did it for love?"

"Confessed? What're you saying?"

"What are you saying, Armand?" demanded Colette.

"You know what I'm saying." He hadn't taken his eyes off Abigail. "She confessed, and you killed her."

"No!"

"Yes." His voice was grave. Sad. There was no triumph.

"Armand." Colette reached for him, but Lacoste stepped between them.

"When Debbie found and finally read your father's suicide note," said Gamache, taking another step forward. He saw Abigail grip the rifle, steady the rifle. He saw, in his peripheral vision, Beauvoir brace himself, to take the shot. "She realized your father blamed you for what happened. She decided to tell you the truth."

"No!"

"That night, New Year's Eve." He had her full attention now. "When Colette left Debbie and returned to the Inn, you went out to look for her, to tell her you were leaving. You found her on the trail. She told you then. That your father hadn't killed Maria, she had. I think she had both letters with her. The one from Gilbert to your father. The one you wanted to threaten Gilbert with. But she had another. The one from your father."

"None of this happened," snapped Abigail.

"Did she try to explain that it was done for love? Did she beg forgiveness?" Gamache studied her. "I don't think so. I think she genuinely believed you'd be pleased. Grateful even. You might even thank her. Is that what pushed you over the edge? That there was no remorse? No recognition of what she'd done?"

"No! This's absurd."

And in a flash he saw she was right. He'd made another mistake. His mind had traveled too quickly and overlooked one vital detail.

The murder weapon.

The scenario he'd just described depended on Debbie confessing, and Abigail lashing out. But if so, how did she get a fireplace log in her hand? As Beauvoir said, no one was likely to have been walking around with one.

And no one had a chance to get one. Except . . .

He looked at Vincent Gilbert, who was staring at Abigail and gripping the poker.

Gamache's mind rapidly backtracked. Going back over images. Statements. And then he had it.

"Your coat," he said to Gilbert.

"What of it?"

"You had it on. You came outside during the fireworks and you were wearing your coat."

"Yes. So?"

"How did you get it?"

"What's this got to do with anything?" asked Haniya. "Did she kill her friend or not?"

But Gamache wasn't listening. He was staring at Gilbert.

"I went up to my room, of course."

"When?"

"Just before midnight."

"But you told us you only left the library at midnight."

"Well, I guess it was a couple of minutes before."

"And you"—he turned to Colette—"say you got to the library just after midnight?"

"Yes. The fireworks were already going off."

That was the window, the time when the murderer could get the weapon.

But that would mean . . .

Almost there.

"No," Gamache said, taking another step forward. "I was wrong. When Debbie read your father's letter, she saw it wasn't a confession. She knew that your father hadn't killed Maria. But she also knew that she hadn't." He stared at her. "That's it, isn't it."

He'd finally stuck the landing. It took the rest of them an elongated moment to see it.

"You?" said Gilbert, staring at Abigail.

"That's the answer to our question," said Gamache. "Why your father would confess to a terrible crime, and one he didn't commit. He didn't believe it was you. He knew it was. He knew you. Where he was selfless, you were selfish. Where he was sincere, you were manipulative. Where he put family first, you put your ambitions first."

"Far from the tree," said Beauvoir.

Armand nodded. "You fell far from the tree. But he loved you and wanted to protect you. When Debbie found the copy of his suicide letter and finally read it for herself, she could see what he was really saying. When did she tell you that she knew? Was it before you even traveled to Québec? Did she promise your secret was safe with her?"

"My God," said Abigail. She looked at the others. "Can't you see what he's doing? He wants me to be guilty."

"Is that why Debbie kept repeating 'Abby Maria'?" said Gamache, ignoring her outburst. He took another small step toward Abigail. On solid ground at last. "It was meant as reassurance. A sort of code between you. A secret you shared. But each time she said it, you heard a threat. A warning."

"This's bullshit. You're setting me up." She appealed to Colette. "He hates me because of my study. Can't you see that?"

"When Debbie said that your father believed that the truth should come out, no matter how unpleasant, that must have really set off alarms," Gamache continued. Unrelenting now. "Did panic set in?"

Abigail's face hardened. She was, he could tell, steeling herself to act. And he thought he knew what it might be. He'd seen that expression before. From men and women standing on a bridge, high over a river. Just before . . .

Abigail's breathing was steady now. Quiet.

"I don't think you woke up that morning intending to kill Debbie." Gamache's voice was calm now, reassuring. "I don't think you even went to the party with that in mind. But it was simmering. And then Debbie mentioned Abby Maria in front of Dr. Gilbert. It was a step too far. You knew then that you couldn't trust her. Whether intentionally or not, Debbie would let out too many hints and eventually someone would start digging."

"Armand," warned Gilbert. He could see that she was about to snap.

But Gamache had to keep pushing. They had no real evidence. His theory fit the facts, but an even moderately competent defense lawyer would get her off. They needed a confession. He could see that while Jean-Guy had the gun in his hand, Isabelle had her phone out. Recording.

"You're wrong, Armand," said Colette. "Debbie killed Maria. I know because she told me on our walk."

Gamache turned and looked at her. "Are you saying you then killed Debbie Schneider?"

"Yes."

"*Non.*" He shook his head. "You didn't. You'd never risk Jean-Paul's future like that. What would become of him, if you were arrested? No." He held her eyes. "You can stand down now. You've earned Paul Robinson's eternal gratitude. He just didn't realize what he was asking."

He turned back to Abigail. "You killed her."

"No." But her voice held little conviction.

Putting up his hands, he said softly, "Abigail—"

And then she did what he had feared. She swung the rifle away from Gilbert. To Jean-Guy.

"No!" shouted Gamache.

Beauvoir braced himself and pulled the trigger. But not all the way. Almost. Almost. Another hair . . .

"Do it," she shrieked. "Do it. Take the shot."

And he wanted to. With every fiber. Now was his chance. It wouldn't be murder, it would be self-defense. Everyone would see that. And then Idola would be safe. They'd all be safe.

"You want to," shouted Abigail. "I knew it from the start. You hate me because you agree with me. Your daughter should've been aborted."

"Abigail!" Colette made to move forward, but Gamache stopped her.

It was all Armand could do not to step between Jean-Guy and Abigail himself. But it was up to Beauvoir now. To resolve this. He held his breath, his eyes wide. His heart pounding.

"It's me or your daughter," Abigail screamed, and thrust the rifle forward.

Tears were streaming down Jean-Guy's face and he made a sound like a mortally wounded animal.

"Shoot, you fucking coward!"

He lowered his gun and shook his head. Isabelle stepped forward and grabbed the end of the rifle, lifting it to the ceiling.

"Do it," Abby begged, even as the rifle was twisted out of her grip and she slumped to the floor. "Please."

"Abigail Robinson," Jean-Guy began, "I'm arresting you—"

He could go no further. His knees began to buckle.

Armand grabbed him, holding him up. Holding Jean-Guy in his arms as he sobbed.

CHAPTER 47

T he chamber was full," Isabelle reported. "She meant to kill you."
"No," said Jean-Guy. "She meant for me to kill her."

He was slumped in the back of the car, utterly drained and still trembling. Not from the cold, but from exposure.

"Suicide by cop," said Gamache. It was one of the nightmares. One few cops had come out of without being forced to actually do it.

But Jean-Guy Beauvoir was far from the average cop.

They'd taken Abigail Robinson into the Sûreté station, where she was booked for possession of a dangerous weapon and assault on a police officer.

They hadn't yet charged her with the murder of Debbie Schneider, or Maria. They didn't know if they had enough evidence to convict. That might take some time. If ever. Though they still hoped for a confession.

By the time the booking was done, the statements taken, the paperwork completed, it was late afternoon.

Colette Roberge had been driven back home to Jean-Paul, and Vincent Gilbert and Haniya Daoud had returned to the Auberge.

Once there, Vincent had asked Haniya to walk down to the bistro with him, for a drink.

"I need some fresh air."

"We're going to walk?"

"It's just down the hill," he said. "You can see it from here."

"You can see the horizon too. Doesn't mean I want to walk there."

The two Asshole Saints bickered all the way down the hill and into the bistro, where Gabri got them a table away from polite company and pumped them for information.

He left with an order for a double scotch and a hot chocolate, but no information.

Isabelle drove the Chief and Beauvoir back to Three Pines.

Jean-Guy sat in the back seat and passed a shaky hand over his face. He wondered if they realized how close he'd come. He thought they probably did.

What he didn't know is why he hadn't fired. And whether he'd live to regret it.

"So you didn't take Abigail to your cabin to kill her?" Haniya asked.

"Me? Murder someone? I got a belly full of cruelty with Ewen Cameron. No. I asked Professor Robinson to join me, away from distractions, so I could apologize for what I allowed to happen to her mother. But I never got the chance."

He looked down at his veined hands, clasped together on the table. His scotch was untouched in front of him.

Haniya picked up her bowl of hot chocolate topped with peaks of whipped cream. She'd felt the need for something soothing. Never having had hot chocolate, but watching the pleasure it gave others, she felt it might be just the thing.

She wondered why she was so upset. After all, she'd been through worse. Done worse. But she'd never actually witnessed the fallout. She'd thought of the men she'd killed as inhuman. And she knew that she'd had no choice but to do what she did.

But now she was beginning to realize a greater truth. That those men and boys had families. Had motives, however flawed. Had wounds of their own. They almost certainly had not been born with the desire to rape, to torture, to torment and murder.

Now, sitting in the quiet bistro in the quiet village, Haniya Daoud accepted that while the men she'd killed were horrific, were monsters, they were also human.

And maybe, maybe, in realizing the truth, she could finally find some measure of peace. Maybe that was the real prize.

"Would you like to?" Haniya asked. "Apologize, I mean. Maybe you can try it on me."

Gilbert was about to dismiss the idea, but looking at her, he changed his mind.

"I'm deeply sorry for what happened to your mother. For my shameful part in it. I'm deeply sorry I didn't do anything to stop it. I should have, and I didn't. I'm sorry that it led to her death, and for what subsequently happened to your family, and all the families. I'm sorry for all the pain I've caused."

The elderly Asshole Saint searched the face of the young Asshole Saint and noticed that the scars had disappeared. Or rather, they were no longer the first thing he saw when he looked at her.

"I forgive you," she said quietly. "And I'm sorry too. That you were so hurt, driven mad with brown brown, that you did those terrible things. I'm sorry your life had to end as it did."

While Vincent Gilbert tried to figure out what she was talking about, and what brown brown was, Haniya lifted the bowl with trembling hands and took her first sip of hot chocolate. And immediately understood its powers to soothe, if not heal. She also understood why Canadians might love winter, if this warm drink came with the snow and ice.

She lowered the mug and smiled at Vincent.

He wondered if he should tell her about the whipped cream mustache but decided not to. Seeing it somehow lifted his spirits.

Once an Asshole Saint . . .

"Before you go, there's something I'd like to show you," Clara said the next morning.

She'd asked Haniya over to her home to say goodbye. When she arrived, she found Myrna already there in the now familiar kitchen. Going into the familiar living room, Haniya stopped at the threshold and stared.

Gabri and Olivier stood up and turned to her. As did Reine-Marie. Ruth, holding Rosa, stood next to Stephen. Jean-Guy and Isabelle were there. As were Annie and Honoré and Idola. They'd driven down to Three Pines, to see her off.

They were standing in a semicircle, facing her.

Haniya stepped back. Paused. Then took one step forward. Then another. And completed the circle.

Vincent Gilbert had declined the invitation to Clara's home, having had more than his fill of humanity to last him the balance of his life.

As he approached his cabin, he heard the blue jays shrieking. In the past he'd chased them off, or at least tried to. But now he stopped at his front porch and opened the sack he'd bought at Monsieur Béliveau's general store.

Scattering the black sunflower seeds on the white snow, he watched the birds swoop down and pick them up. He went inside then, lit the fire, made a pot of tea, and opened the book Colette had lent him.

Extraordinary Popular Delusions and the Madness of Crowds.

He settled in, and read about the South Sea bubble, and the tulip crisis, and the Drummer of Tedworth.

The birds still shrieked, of course. But now it sounded more like company.

"Oh, God," sighed Ruth. "Not that fucking painting again. Brace yourself," she said to Stephen.

At Haniya's request, Clara had made up a batch of hot chocolate with whipped cream. Stephen had poured brandy into his and Ruth's.

At least the two of them would be quite well braced.

Gabri was practicing saying, "It's wonderful. It's brilliant."

Even Reine-Marie was bracing herself. Like the rest of them, she'd been privy to Clara's latest effort. Their friend had taken to slapping layers of paint, apparently at random, onto the canvas. Occasionally breaking up the splatters with something hyper-recognizable.

The last one was a banana. Reine-Marie wondered if it was a reference to all those monkeys, but suspected it had no meaning at all. Behind her, Myrna was trying to coax Billy Williams forward, but like the donkeys he raised, he'd put his head down and was refusing to budge.

Smart man, thought Myrna, as she reluctantly followed the others into Clara's studio.

"How much did you know, Colette?" asked Armand.

The Chancellor and her husband were sitting in the Gamaches' living room. Since Jean-Paul was calmer away from crowds, they'd stayed behind while the rest of them had headed over to Clara's, to say goodbye to Haniya Daoud.

Jean-Paul was taking books off the shelves and stacking them neatly on the floor in front of the fireplace, while Armand and Colette talked.

"Paul never told me outright, but he knew that I knew. He'd never have given Maria a peanut butter sandwich by mistake. And if it was on purpose, it was murder. And I knew he wasn't capable of that. But I have to say, I'd always hoped it was Debbie Schneider who'd done it. Not Abigail. For Paul's sake. But when the letter came, I could tell that he thought it was Abby who'd done it. He knew his daughter. Knew what she was capable of."

"He wanted you to show the letter to Abigail, to let her know she was safe," said Armand.

Jean-Paul was holding a book and staring, then he walked over and gave it to Colette. He was now almost completely silent. Though he communicated in other ways.

"*Merci*," she said. "I've been looking for this."

He smiled and went back to work.

Colette squeezed her eyes shut, then opened them and put the book down on the sofa beside her.

"Vincent says you invited Abigail here so that you both could try to help her. To dissuade her from the path she was on."

"True."

"Did Vincent also plan to tell her about his involvement with Ewen Cameron?"

"No. He didn't realize her mother had been one of Cameron's victims. Not until she told us."

"With Abigail's arrest, will that end the debate over mandatory euthanasia?" Armand asked.

"You'd think," said Colette. "But I'm afraid the barb has gone in. She's scared enough people into believing there won't be enough resources to recover from the pandemic, never mind handle another. Unless the sick and elderly are allowed to die."

"Made to die," said Armand. By lethal injection. Capital punishment for men and women whose crime wasn't killing, but taking too long to die.

Through the door to his study he could see the open files he'd been working on when the Roberges arrived.

They contained the mounting evidence he was quietly and privately collecting against those responsible for abandoning the elderly and frail in care homes during the pandemic.

It was Sunday afternoon. The next morning Armand Gamache had an appointment with the Premier of Québec. To show him the files. And to let him know, quietly, confidentially, that if there was any move to adopt mandatory euthanasia, or anything vaguely smelling of eugenics, those files would go public.

It was, he knew, blackmail. But he and his conscience could live with that.

That was tomorrow. Today he could sit quietly and comfortably in his living room, talking to friends.

"Will you charge Abigail with the murders?" asked Colette.

"We'll try."

Her eyes fell on the framed family photographs on the bookshelf behind Armand. "I can't believe he didn't shoot." Her gaze drifted over to Jean-Paul, carefully placing one book on top of another. "It was love, I suppose, that stopped him."

"*Oui.*"

Jean-Guy couldn't be the father he wanted to be for his children if he'd pulled that trigger.

Clara walked right by the mess on the easel and over to a canvas leaning against the wall.

Haniya watched her host and wondered if she should say something about Clara's whipped cream mustache, but decided not to.

Once a finalist for the Nobel Peace Prize . . .

Clara lifted the paint-stained sheet, and there was silence.

"It's wonderful," muttered Gabri.

"It's brilliant," said Olivier.

When Colette and Jean-Paul left, Armand went across to Clara's.

The others were in the living room, but he found Haniya in the studio. Staring at the painting.

She had her coat on and her Louis Vuitton suitcases were by the door.

Armand and Haniya stood side by side in silence, staring at Clara's painting.

Then, still looking at it, he asked, "Are you sure you want to leave?"

She turned and, for the first time, she saw not the deep lines down his face, or the scar at his temple, but the kindness in his eyes.

Then she turned back to the painting. "Sudan is my home. I think you understand that, Monsieur Gamache. It's where I belong."

"You and your machete?"

"Are you judging me?"

"*Non.* I'm asking."

Armand heard Haniya Daoud, the Hero of the Sudan, sigh.

"Sudan's awful. There's poverty, unspeakable violence. Women, girls aren't safe. But there's unimaginable courage too. And beauty." She smiled as she stared at the painting in front of her. "My village was rebuilt. I have a small home there. It isn't far from the White Nile."

She told him about the scents in summer. About the rain hitting the water. About the sound of the breeze through the savannah. All the little things that add up to home. To belonging.

"When I'm home, I walk there every day. I sit on the shore and pray."

"What for?"

She turned to him. "Probably the same thing you pray for. The same thing we all do."

She walked past him, out of the studio.

Reine-Marie was in the mudroom, putting on her boots and coat.

"I'll drive you to Montréal," she said.

"That's all right. I've called a taxi."

"There're taxis?" asked Myrna.

"Yes. I'm not sure what language the guy was speaking, but I'm pretty sure he said he'd meet me here."

They looked at Billy Williams, who grinned and put up his hand. Then he dropped it and took Myrna's.

"I think we can probably cancel the taxi," said Reine-Marie, and saw Billy nod.

"We're coming too," said Clara, and Myrna nodded.

"Why?" asked Haniya.

Clara turned to her, surprised. "Because that's what friends do."

Haniya's last glimpse of Three Pines was of two elderly people standing on the village green, one with a single finger raised, waving goodbye.

Jean-Guy had asked Armand to look after Honoré while he took Idola and Annie into their kitchen.

They sat by the woodstove.

"There's something I need to tell you," he said to Annie. "About how I once felt about Idola. About our decision."

Armand sat on the bench, with Fred at his feet. They watched Honoré play with some of the other village children as Henri danced around them.

Armand thought about what Clara had painted. It looked like a land-scape. At least that's what a casual observer would see. But if they were not quite so casual? They'd see it was actually a topographical map. One orienteers might use.

And if they paused a little bit longer? If they stopped trying to see it with their eyes, then they'd see what it really was. What really mattered.

They'd see the roads and rivers, hills and vast fields, the stone walls and forests and meadows come together. To form an image. Of a young woman whose face was scored. But not scarred. The deep lines were the route home.

"Papa, Papa," cried Honoré, though his words were indistinct.

Armand shot to his feet and ran to his grandson.

As he got closer, he saw that all the children, every one of them, had their tongues frozen to the goalpost.

A few minutes later, as he and Gabri knelt and poured warm water over their tender tongues, he wondered why they'd do such a thing. But Annie and Daniel had done it. And so had he, when he was their age. He suspected his father and mother probably had too, when they were children.

Some things were just inexplicable.

"Hold on," whispered Armand. "It'll be all right."

Haniya put her feet up on the footstool of her business class seat and gazed out the window.

As the miles piled up, as she got ever closer to Sudan, to home, she felt herself relax. Her body might not be altogether safe there, but it was where her spirit belonged.

Bringing out the small package Reine-Marie had pressed into her hand at the Montréal airport, Haniya unwrapped it.

Then she looked at the card. It was actually a worn and yellowed piece of paper. It still had Scotch tape on it, where it had been attached to the windowpane.

On one side it was signed by everyone, with cheerful messages. On the other was a rainbow and the words, in bright pink crayon.

Haniya Daoud clutched the card and the tiny framed photograph it came with, and looked out the plane window at the acres and acres of snow. At the landscape covered in millions and millions of works of art.

Ça va bien aller.

She thought maybe it was true.

ACKNOWLEDGMENTS

—

I started writing *The Madness of Crowds* at the end of March 2020, as I sat at home in quarantine. I'd made it across the Canadian border, and into my home, just as the border closed.

A day earlier I'd had dinner with a friend in New York City. Next thing I knew, I was racing to get home to a two-week quarantine that turned into a three-month lockdown. Then, then, then . . .

We all know what happened. No need to repeat it here. You lived exactly the same thing, whether your home is in Crete or São Paulo, Birmingham or Saskatoon. It was the first global shared experience.

People wrote to ask if I'd put the pandemic into the next Gamache book. How would it affect Three Pines? I wrote back to say that I thought the last thing anyone would want to read about, and relive, was the coronavirus pandemic. And I meant it.

But halfway through the first draft I realized I needed to talk about it. But how?

And so I decided to set *The Madness of Crowds* post-pandemic. As the world returned to "normal." But the bruising remained. The sorrow, the tragedies, but also the oddly rich blessings.

I wanted, as I suspect you did too, to believe that we would emerge. That families, friends, strangers could get together again, unafraid. Unmasked. That we could embrace, and kiss, hold hands and have meals together.

And so that's how the pandemic is handled in this book, as you probably know by now. And you'll also know that the experience, the theme of a contagion, reverberates throughout the book.

How crowds of decent people can be infected by a certain madness. How extraordinary delusions become popular.

And that brings me to the title. It's taken from a book, which is real and is also in Gamache's library, called *Extraordinary Popular Delusions and the Madness of Crowds*. It was first published in 1841 by Charles Mackay. It's a series of nonfiction essays looking at why sane people believe the nuttiest things. Things that, in normal times, they'd easily dismiss. Like Tulipmania. The South Sea Bubble. Like stories of hauntings. Witches.

What happens to tip people over into madness?

I'd first come across the book as a teenager when my mother, who'd gone back to work in her late forties and qualified as an investment dealer in Toronto, began reading it. It was suggested reading, and probably still is, for stockbrokers since so much of what they deal with is "smoke and mirrors." Perception rather than reality. And how perception can shape and actually become reality. A self-fulfilling prophecy.

That's what is visited on the village of Three Pines.

In order to write this book I needed help.

As always, the first person I want to thank is Lise Desrosiers, my great friend and assistant. Thank you to Linda Lyall (Linda in Scotland), who answers many of your letters (though I read them all) and manages much of the internet presence.

Thank you to Jennifer Enderlin and her son, Nick, for helping me to at least begin to understand about having a child who is so much more than their Down syndrome.

Thank you to Danny and Lucy and Ben McAuley, who run Brome Lake Books in my village of Knowlton, Québec, and who are great friends.

Thank you to Rocky and Steve Gottlieb. To Sally and Cynthia and Sarah. To Kirk and Walter. Brendan and Oscar. To Hardye and Don, Bonnie and Kap, Sukie, Patsy, Tom, Hillary, for your presence, virtual and otherwise. To Dorie Greenspan for the Gamache lemon cookies and your support as we both finished our books, and commiserated.

Her new book, out in October, is called *Baking with Dorie*. To Chelsea and Marc, for the Zooms with family. To Will Schwalbe, for your friendship and cheery messages, from one writer to another. From one friend to another. Thank you, Tom Corradine, for keeping me from becoming a complete blob—bastard.

To so many people who make life livable. And, of course, to the frontline workers locally and beyond, who really did make life livable.

To my brother Doug, who sheltered in place with me. We actually built a screen porch while in lockdown!

And when it came to the actual writing, thank you to Allida Black for her guidance. To TJ Rogers, who has, for more than a decade, defended and served survivors of torture and who helped me to understand what Haniya Daoud might have experienced. To Sam Wijay. To Dr. David Rosenblatt and Dr. Mary Hague-Yearl (who isn't entirely fictional) for help with the remarkable Osler Library at McGill, and the stain that was Ewen Cameron.

Thank you, Tyler Vigen, who really does have a site called Spurious Correlations and allowed me to use it and his name. And my friend, the gifted writer and thinker Andrew Solomon. At one stage I considered calling this book *Far from the Tree*—which was a nod to his own brilliant book. I wrote and asked how he'd feel about that, and he could not have been more generous.

Thank you to Kelley Ragland, my U.S. editor with Minotaur Books. To Paul Hochman and Sarah Melnyk and, of course, the man who leads them all, Andy Martin, the publisher. To Don Weisberg, who heads up Macmillan U.S. and is both smart and wise, and a fine man. To John Sargent, one of the great publishers of our generation.

Thank you to Louise Loiselle of Flammarion Québec, Jo Dickinson of Hodder UK, and all the publishers worldwide who work so hard to get these books into people's hands.

A huge, heartfelt thank-you to my amazing agent, David Gernert, and his wonderful team at The Gernert Company. And to the legendary Mike Rudell, who passed away and is missed every day.

Speaking of that, each day when I sit at the dining table in front of the laptop, I close my eyes and ask for help and guidance. For courage. I thank my own Michael, for never really leaving me. For always being here and helping me along the way. I thank my good friend Betsy. And I thank Hope Dellon—my longtime editor and friend.

I feel their presence every day. Guiding me along as I navigate life. Helping me as I write.

All this to say, if you didn't like the book, it's their fault.